Splinter on the Tide

Splinter on the Tide

PHILLIP PAROTTI

CASEMATE

Philadelphia & Oxford

Published in the United States of America and Great Britain in 2021 by
CASEMATE PUBLISHERS
1950 Lawrence Road, Havertown, PA 19083, USA
and
The Old Music Hall, 106–108 Cowley Road, Oxford OX4 1JE, UK

Paperback Edition: ISBN 978-1-61200-958-2
Digital Edition: ISBN 978-1-61200-959-9

A CIP record for this book is available from the British Library

Printed and bound in the United States of America by Integrated Books International

Typeset by Versatile PreMedia Services (P) Ltd

For a complete list of Casemate titles, please contact:

CASEMATE PUBLISHERS (US)
Telephone (610) 853-9131
Fax (610) 853-9146
Email: casemate@casematepublishers.com
www.casematepublishers.com

CASEMATE PUBLISHERS (UK)
Telephone (01865) 241249
Email: casemate-uk@casematepublishers.co.uk
www.casematepublishers.co.uk

For my family

1

The last thing Ash Miller had anticipated when he activated his commission in the Naval Reserve was that the very ship to which he'd been assigned would be blown up by his own Navy. Nevertheless, on December 12, 1941, in the sea just south of Key West, he was. He'd been riding the old four-piper destroyer to which he was assigned, the U.S.S. *Herman K. Parker*. Only 55 minutes before, after taking on fuel, stores, and ammunition, the ship had commenced a rapid transit toward the Panama Canal in order to pass through and join what remained of the Pacific Fleet at Pearl Harbor. By that time, Ash had already spent a year on active duty as an ensign. The *Parker*'s captain, he imagined, might still have considered him an amateur and green, but his brother officers, regulars all, seemed to have accepted him, particularly after he had shown himself to be quietly competent in his role as assistant navigator and as the deck officer who oversaw the crews manning the ship's depth charges. Three times, before the United States declared war, he had participated in lend-lease convoys, herding as many as 40 cargo-laden ships toward rendezvous with Royal Navy corvettes waiting along the chop line in the mid-Atlantic. Each time, after learning the fate of the *Reuben James* (DD-245), he knew that he risked being torpedoed and sunk by a German U-boat. But what he did not foresee was being blown up by an American mine.

Prior to the moment of impact, no one aboard the *Parker* knew that a minefield existed anywhere in their vicinity. As a Naval Board of Inquiry subsequently determined, a destroyer minelayer had indeed laid a field two days before so as to protect the northern approaches to Key West. Both the field and its exact location had been communicated to the appropriate shore authorities, but because of a breakdown in secure communications equipment, knowledge of the field had not yet been disseminated to the fleet. Even so, the field should have been anchored miles to the north of the track laid out by the *Parker's* navigator. Owing to unknown causes, one of those mines had apparently broken loose from its anchor and drifted south. Hence the impact, the explosion, and the sinking of the *Herman K. Parker*. But at the time, everyone believed that the ship had been attacked by a U-boat.

In thinking back, Ash knew that he had been fortunate. Thirty minutes before the *Parker* collided with the mine, after a cup of coffee and a late afternoon doughnut in the wardroom, Ash had climbed to the bridge and relieved the Junior Officer of the Watch. At the moment of impact, he happened to be standing on the port wing taking a bearing on a rusted fishing trawler that seemed to be scuttling toward Key West so as to reach port before nightfall. When the *Parker* struck the mine on the starboard beam and the center of the vessel suddenly heaved up like a breaching whale, Ash had been catapulted straight over the side and out into the sea, still holding his binoculars.

Ash could never quite remember how he entered the water but thought he might have doubled up into a cannon ball so as to avoid the impact of a belly flop. At the time, he felt sure that the ship had been torpedoed, so in the instant that he surfaced, he burst into motion in order to swim away from the sinking ship, arms pummeling the waves and legs kicking hard. In his haste, he did not see the ship break up, but he did hear the boilers explode, and when he turned, finally, and looked back, he saw nothing but a sea of floating heads to mark the men who had escaped and the *Parker's* high stern plunging from sight.

Without a life jacket, Ash did the only thing he could. Swiftly discarding his shoes, he removed his khaki trousers, knotted the legs at their ends, stretched them behind his neck, and slung them forward over his head, filling each leg with air, and then, holding the waist beneath him in the water, he kicked himself up over the crotch so as to use the inflated legs as water wings. Then, amid periodic movements to restore the inflation of the trouser legs, he set himself to wait in hopes that sharks wouldn't find him before help came.

And again Ash knew that he had been fortunate. He hadn't been in the water more than an hour before the trawler he'd been watching in the moment before the explosion closed the distance, spotted him, plucked him from the sea, and went on picking up survivors until she was crammed to the gunwales with 72 of the *Parker's* crew and nine of her officers. Four officers, including the captain, and 38 men—including, Ash assumed, the entire engineering section—had gone down with the ship. The others—despite their burns, gashes, scrapes, and saltwater-soaked lungs—some of them having swallowed some of the oil itself, still lived. Blissfully, after conducting a thorough search, the trawler made Key West before midnight, depositing the remains of the ship's company at the Key West Naval Station where emergency personnel stood waiting to receive them.

The days that followed swam together in a blur. Ash remembered interrogations, written reports, forms to be filled out, interviews with senior officers, the first night in the hospital under observation, trips to the exchange in order to be fitted for new uniforms, and six funerals, all of them conducted with appropriate military honors. More than anything, he remembered the palpable sense of fury that it had happened at all.

One month later, after the Board of Inquiry had settled responsibility for the disaster, after a thorough medical examination at Key West, and after the Navy had kitted him out in a fresh set of uniforms, Ash received orders to report to Atlantic Fleet Headquarters, Norfolk. Reluctantly, he said goodbye to the few remaining friends with whom he had served aboard the *Parker*. As things turned out, and much to Ash's later surprise, they passed from his life, one and all, as though they had never been.

2

When Ash reached Norfolk, he found the streets windy, wet, and cold beneath a dense January fog off the Chesapeake. The train he had taken, an express, had been packed, so from Miami to Jacksonville, Ash sat on his bag or stood beside it near one of the car's windows. When a number of passengers finally departed in Jacksonville, Ash found an empty seat and slept through much of the night as the train traversed the Carolinas. Waking about an hour out of Norfolk, Ash managed a dry shave in the car's washroom, and then, because someone slumped into his seat the moment he left it, he once more stood until the train reached the station where a paper cup of lukewarm coffee completed his morning ablutions. Discarding the cup into the trash and turning up the collar of his bridge coat against the damp, Ash walked outside and hailed a taxi.

From the U.S. Naval Station's main gate where the taxi deposited him, Ash bent into the wind and made his way toward the building which, according to the gate sentry, housed the Atlantic fleet's personnel offices. It didn't. Instead, the structure functioned as a land-based administrative headquarters where an obliging yeoman nevertheless stamped his orders and redirected him: "Personnel, Sir? That's across the way. Third deck."

Arriving on the third deck of the building indicated, Ash found not an office but a loft, a long, wide loft not unlike the floor of a warehouse where more than two hundred yeomen and a few junior officers seemed to be absorbed intensely while typing at high speed. There, after yet another yeoman examined his orders, he was told, "You are to see Lieutenant Commander Sims, Sir, all the way down the center aisle, second door to your right." No one so much as glanced at Ash as he walked down the aisle and entered a passageway, and when he found the door marked "LCDR Sims," he knocked once, hesitated for an obligatory two seconds, and entered.

"Ensign Miller, reporting from Key West, Sir," Ash announced, coming to attention.

"Relax and take a seat," said the man behind the desk without looking up. "You can smoke if you like. I'll be with you in a minute."

Ash sat down, removed a pipe from the pocket of his bridge coat, tamped some tobacco into the bowl, and lit it with his Zippo. The man in front of him, bent over a set of papers upon which he swiftly wrote, showed a closely cropped head of iron-gray hair. His blouse, hanging from a nearby coat tree, displayed ribbons from the First World War and well-aged gold stripes denoting Sims' rank. Ash considered and wondered if Sims, too, might be a reservist but dismissed the thought when the man put down his pen and looked up, projecting a weathered expression from a lean face, a pair of penetrating gray eyes underscoring the effect.

"Just get in?" Sims asked, extending his hand to give Ash's a firm shake.

"Yes, Sir," Ash replied.

"Pity about the *Parker*," Sims said. "I convoyed with her in 1918. She was a new ship then, just off the ways, and fast." He shook his head. "Sad business."

"Yes," Ash said. "Very."

"And what about you?" Sims asked. "Medical report says you're fit. Are you?"

"Yes, Sir," Ash said. "No complaints. I was lucky."

"Good," Sims said. "Then let's get down to business." And with that, he lifted a file from the corner of his desk and flipped it open. "Background checks first, right?"

"Yes, Sir," Ash said.

"Born 1915," Sims began, "on a small farm near Makanda, Illinois, Scottish heritage. High school, Carbondale. Graduated from the University of Illinois in Champaign-Urbana in 1936 with a double major in English and Journalism. Right?"

"Right," Ash replied.

"What language did you study?"

"German, Sir."

"Skip the 'Sir.' Just stick to the facts. Fluent?"

"No," Ash said, "but I can get by."

Sims made a note. "What did you do after graduation? Be concrete."

"The depression made things difficult," Ash said. "The only job I could find was with the Herrin *Bugle*, so I went down to Herrin and to the *Bugle* as a general dogsbody. I typed, I proofread, I ran errands, I wrote obits, I covered sports at Herrin High School, and I acted as a reporter for minor local news stories. The editor covered the major events. I also wrote and sold short stories to the pulps. After a year and a half, I quit because I wasn't making enough to cover my rent and my meals. A diet of beans, egg sandwiches, and hamburger gets old, fast."

"And?"

"That's when I went to New York and signed as a deck hand onto the S.S. *Winston James*, a freighter. Hard work, but better food and good pay. Finally, I was able to bank some money. We made three trips between New York and Brest carrying general stores, and then we returned to Charleston, took on a cargo of cotton, and delivered to Wilhelmshaven. I left the ship there. I'd saved some money by that time. I'd read a number of things about Nazi Germany, but I wanted to see what was going on for myself."

"And did you?"

"Yes."

"Give me your impression."

Ash sat back in his chair, took a puff from his pipe to gather his thoughts, and continued. "I found Germany to be a clean country and efficient—more so than France. But the Germans were overbearing, impatient, and arrogant to a fault. I caught one of those goosestep military parades in Berlin and thought it typified the whole German attitude. I saw a Pole beaten badly by some Brownshirts in Bremen for nothing more than refusing to give way to them on the sidewalk, and another time, from my hotel window above the street, I saw a Jew beaten half to death in Regensburg for what I thought was no reason at all. That did it for me. I didn't like the Germany I was seeing; I didn't think it had much in common with the country of Bach and Goethe, so I got out, made my way up to Rotterdam, signed onto another freighter, and came home. I spent only about a month traveling in Germany, but I wouldn't care to go back. France turned out to be a far more congenial place."

"Improve your German while you were there?"

"Some," Ash said.

"And what did you do when you came back?"

"I went to Chicago," Ash continued, "got on as a proofreader for the Chicago *Daily Dispatch*, found a recruiting office, enlisted, applied for a commission, and began doing weekend training at Great Lakes."

"And in October of 1940, you asked for orders to active duty?" Sims said, once more making a mark on a page.

"Right. I can't claim to be prescient, Commander, but with regard to Nazi Germany, things have turned out more or less the way I anticipated."

"Yes," Sims said, "so you applied for orders early with the result that you reported to the *Parker* on December 6, 1940 and remained aboard until the ship's sinking."

"Yes, Sir," Ash said.

"Run down your duties for me," Sims said, adding pointedly, "and I want an accurate self-appraisal."

"When I reported aboard," Ash began, "the captain appointed me assistant to the navigator. Lieutenant Stephen Thomas was both executive officer and navigator aboard the *Parker*, and he gave excellent instruction. From the beginning, he set me to amending charts and to piloting whenever we went to sea, and then he handed me a sextant and started me shooting the stars with him, morning and evening, and we shot sun lines at noon. Within a month, I could find the right stars to shoot, and within two months, I'd mastered the computations for celestial navigation, so by late spring of '41, I was doing most of the navigating unsupervised, and the captain and our various officers of the deck seemed to trust my work."

"What about battle stations?"

"I did a week's familiarization with depth charges at a school in Charleston last February," Ash said. "After that, I supervised the torpedo ratings manning *Parker*'s depth-charge racks. I know how to store the charges, change and set the detonators, and time an attack."

"Good," Sims said, making yet another note in the file. "What about watch standing?"

"I qualified as Officer of the Deck for Independent Steaming in September," Ash said. "Between September and the end of November, in company with five other escorts, we screened three convoys to the mid-Atlantic chop line, so I gained plenty of experience working maneuvering boards and handling the ship. After we returned from the last trip, the captain signed a letter qualifying me as an Officer of the Deck for Fleet Steaming, but I'm doubtful that the letter survived our sinking."

"The original didn't," Sims said, "but I have an endorsed copy here. What about collateral duties?"

"Alcohol and narcotics custodian," Ash said, "public relations, in the sense that I wrote news releases about the ship and the crew for hometown newspapers, and the publication of a mimeographed newspaper for the ship's company when we were at sea."

"So," Sims said, leaning back against his chair and once more fixing Ash with a penetrating gaze, "tell me, Mr. Miller, how would you rate your first year on active duty in the Navy?"

The question may have been unexpected, but Ash didn't hesitate.

"Excellent," Ash said. "I wouldn't have thought that I could learn so much, so fast. I had the good fortune to serve aboard a fine ship with a well-qualified crew and a congenial wardroom. I'm doubtful that any of my seniors found me to be brilliant, but I'm hopeful that I didn't prove to be a disappointment.

Personally, I found sea duty more than agreeable and would like to continue with it. Now that we're in this war, I'd like to see it through."

For a moment more, Sims said nothing, his gray eyes continuing to plumb the depths of Ash's face, but then, once more, he sat upright in his chair.

"It's good that you've found sea duty agreeable," he said, "because you are about to see a great deal more of it. Ever hear of subchasers, Mr. Miller?"

"I've heard of them," Ash said, "but I've never seen one. My impression is that they were small but used extensively during the First World War and pretty much disappeared after the war ended. I gather that they rolled a lot and weren't as fast as destroyers."

"You're right on all counts," Sims said. "I had command of one myself in 1918—part of the Otranto Barrage running out of Corfu to try to bottle up the Austrians in the Adriatic. After the war, mine was sold to France. Last I heard it was still in service, as a patrol vessel running out of Toulon."

Ash had never heard of the Otranto Barrage but figured it had to be a blockade of some type.

"Now listen up," said Sims, "and I'll give you the statistics, because the United States Navy is about to order between five hundred and a thousand new subchasers for whatever may be required of them—and all of them, Mr. Miller, are going to be staffed by reserve officers and crews that are largely made up from reserve sailors. At the moment, the Navy has neither the officers nor the sailors to man the ships that are already on the drawing boards, so within the next year, you are going to see the start of the most massive build-up of ships, equipment, and personnel that this country has ever experienced. Even as we speak, Lieutenant Commander E. F. McDaniel, a highly competent Naval Academy graduate, is headed for Miami. There he expects to begin training thousands of reserve officers and sailors for duty aboard subchasers and other small craft. But the school is not yet up and running, so for the time being, the Navy is going to have to use what it has. Nazi U-boats are already sinking ships not far off the coast, some of them close enough so that people on the beach can see them go down. I've seen one myself, a tanker on fire off Virginia Beach, and it wasn't pretty. Thirty-two men killed on that one, and not an escort vessel anywhere in sight. So, once more we've been caught with our pants down, and we're in a pinch. For convoy duty alone, we need those subchasers now, all of them, but we aren't going to get them for six months to a year. In the meantime, a lot of merchant sailors are going to die. Take my meaning?"

"Yes," Ash said.

Sims put his elbows on his desk and leaned toward Ash as he spoke. "The fact that Allied merchant vessels are being sunk right off our Atlantic beaches is something top secret, Mr. Miller. Not a word about that hard fact is to leak out to civilians. Our nation's leaders are adamant about doing everything they can to keep from throwing the American people into a panic. But have no doubts about it, the war is right on our doorstep, and it is deadly. So, mum's the word, and that command is absolute. Understood?"

"Yes, Sir," Ash said.

"Lend-lease is all very good," Sims continued, "but before fast destroyers can escort the really big convoys to England, food has to be raised, raw materials have to be gathered, guns, tanks, and planes have to be manufactured, and mountains of supplies have to be collected and made ready to ship. And what that means is that the merchant marine is going to keep single ships and small convoys steaming constantly up and down the Atlantic and Pacific coasts, bringing in and moving ore, foodstuffs, oil, and God only knows what else from every corner of the world. Hitler will no doubt deploy his U-boats everywhere in the Atlantic from Tierra del Fuego to the Gulf and the Caribbean and straight on north to the tip of Greenland. And what that means, Mr. Miller, is that strapped as we are for effective escort vessels—the big destroyers doing the job in the mid-Atlantic and on the routes to England—we're going to rely on rapidly built subchasers for coastal convoy duty. Thus far, we haven't even organized a full-fledged convoy system along the coast. Still with me?"

"I am," Ash said.

"Right," Sims said. "So here's the scoop. Way back in 1917, a friend of Mr. Roosevelt's—and possibly at Mr. Roosevelt's urging when he was Assistant Secretary of the Navy—a naval architect named Albert Loring Swasey presented the Navy with a design for an effective antisubmarine warfare vessel. On the basis of that design, at least 440 SC-1 class subchasers were constructed, and the designs for the new chasers the Navy is about to build are only slightly changed. In a nutshell, the ships are to be about 110 feet long, nearly 18 feet in the beam and built with a draft of only about 6 and a half feet. Displacement will be near a hundred tons, hundreds of tons less than a standard destroyer. The ships will run on diesel, which is a major change from the First World War types that ran on gasoline. For ease in handling, they will be twin-screwed with twin rudders and have a top speed of between 17 and 18 knots. For the time being, they will be armed with a First World War vintage 3-inch 23-caliber gun mount forward and three new Oerlikon 20mm mounts amidships with the possibility of mounting a .50-caliber machine gun aft between the depth-charge racks. Forward of the 3-inch gun mount, the chaser will carry Mark 20 mousetraps with eight 7.2-inch contact projectiles which, if dropped on a submerged U-boat, will blow the rascal to smithereens. On the fantail, the chaser will carry release chocks for depth charges and two K-guns for projecting charges to greater distance. Detection will be either by direct sight if a U-boat is on the surface or by sonar should it be submerged. My chaser carried two officers and 24 men, so the ship was undermanned. What the Navy is planning for the new design is a complement of three officers and 27 men to upgrade the vessel's efficiency."

Sims had rattled off the spiel so fast that Ash felt he'd barely had time to comprehend it.

"I don't want to sound impertinent, Commander," Ash ventured, "but I'm guessing that you have something in mind for me regarding subchasers."

"Good guess," Sims said, without breaking his tone. "After speaking with your former executive officer last week and on the basis of your records as we have them and the substance of the interview we are presently conducting, the United States Navy with my recommendation would like to offer you command of one of the first new subchasers to come off the ways. According to Lieutenant Thomas, you are a competent navigator, and you have a strong year of seagoing experience already behind you; you've also qualified as a Fleet Officer of the Deck, and in my estimation, you have the circumspect maturity to handle the job. You have a choice, of course: either you take command of the subchaser I have in mind for you, or I can send you straight back to sea without prejudice as a division officer on another destroyer. What say you, Mr. Miller?"

Suddenly, Ash felt like he'd been kicked in the solar plexus. The only other time in his life when he'd felt a similar reaction had been mere months before, after the captain of the *Parker* had signed his letter qualifying him as an OOD for Independent Steaming and then left to go down for supper, leaving Ash with total responsibility for the ship and the men. In reality, the captain had been only a sound-powered telephone call away and a few steps from the bridge, but in the moment, the responsibility had seemed crushing and had nearly driven Ash to his knees. But he had risen to it, accepted it, and done the job.

"I'd like to take the command," Ash said evenly. "I'll give it my best."

"Good," Sims said, "that's what I thought you'd say. As I'm sure you must realize, this is going to be a citizen's war, an amateur's war, and that makes it our war, Mr. Miller. The regulars, the professionals, are enormously competent, but there simply aren't enough of them to meet the nation's needs, not even if every Naval Academy graduate since the turn of the century could be called back into service. So if we are to fight back against these bastards and defeat them, the whole thing depends on us, the volunteer reserves, and on how well we rise to meet the challenge. Once we've done our job and won, then we can go home and leave peacetime duty to the regulars—but not now and not for a long time to come."

Ash agreed with a mere nod of his head.

"Right," Sims said, opening a drawer and drawing out a thick manila envelope which he handed across his desk to Ash. "You've got a set of orders in there, another set of documents regarding your command, and a train ticket which will get you from here up to Portland, Maine, by nightfall tomorrow. I couldn't find a sleeper for you, but you've got a reserved seat, so you'll have to catch what sleep you can sitting up. You'll be met in Portland and taken up to Yarmouth, to Anson's Boatyard on the Royal River. The place is small, but it does sound work, and that's where your chaser is being built. You, your officers, and your crew when they arrive will be billeted in The Jarvis House—a small, family-run hotel for summer visitors about two blocks up from the boatyard. I don't think you'll find any visitors there at the moment, but keep an iron grip on your crew because I don't want to hear of any untoward incidents from them while they are there, and like I've told you: security has to be absolute. Got that?"

"Yes, Sir," Ash said.

"Your crew will begin reaching you quickly," Sims continued, "so put them straight to work. Stores, equipment, charts, publications, and everything but ammunition will be coming up rapidly from Portland, so you are going to have to be on your toes, both with regard to the crew and with storage and readiness. When the time comes, and it will come quick, you are to commission without ceremony and go to sea because you will be needed for convoy duty as swiftly as you get underway. That means your people are going to have to coalesce on the job without any time to workup, so it will be your responsibility among others to weld them into an efficient crew. Drill them, Mr. Miller; drill them until they think there's no tomorrow, and then drill them some more."

Ash knew at once that he faced a grind, a grind the likes of which he had never faced before, but he was up for the challenge. He steeled himself to do what had to be done.

"Heretofore," Sims said, "subchasers, even though they are commissioned ships in the United States Navy, have avoided carrying names. Instead, they have been identified by numbers only: SC-143, SC-221, SC-506, and so forth. Yours, Mr. Miller, is going to fall into a different category and will be called Chaser 3 for reasons that I am now going to explain. Near the end of the First World War, an updated design and one very much like the design which will govern all of the new chasers that the Navy is to build was put into motion for three prototypes. Your particular chaser, Chaser 3, was in fact 80 percent completed in 1918, and at the time, she was assigned a number which was then canceled and retired when the war ended. So your ship, enlarged and reconfigured for better, larger engines, has been sitting in a boathouse for more than 20 years, waiting in case she was ever to be needed again—and now she is. Chaser 1 is being completed at a yard on Maryland's eastern shore; Chaser 2 is only about 60 percent ready at a yard on Long Island. Rather than resurrect retired numbers, and because all three vessels are really in a class of their own, someone in the Navy Department in Washington came up with the Chaser appellation, and that's the name she'll go by."

Ash smiled. "If the Navy can live with it, so can I," Ash said, trying on a joke. "It seems apt."

For the first time since Ash had entered the cubicle, Lieutenant Commander Sims showed him a smile. "Exactly," he said. "Now, let me tell you what I think you will find the most difficult part of your job, at least in the beginning. With regard to crew and because the recruit depots are only beginning to get up to speed, I've been able to purloin some experienced talent from the regular line, a couple of them with hash marks, but your unrated people will come to you straight from boot camp. Your officers are another matter, and there's the rub; both will come to you straight from the midshipman training program aboard the *Prairie State*, the midshipman's school docked in New York and built atop the hull of the old U.S.S. *Illinois* (BB-7). Those two will be as green as grass when they arrive, so it will be up to you to bring them up to speed as rapidly and efficiently as you can. Until you do, you are going to have to stand around the clock watches with them, which means you will be getting precious little sleep. But here's a hint that might be useful: if it turns out that your bosun is capable, you might train him up to be one of your OODs; that would free you up to supervise watches and still get a few hours' sleep from time to time. I did that on the Barrage, and it worked well."

"Thanks for the suggestion," Ash said. "I hadn't imagined the Navy would tolerate an enlisted OOD."

"On tugs and small craft, it's done all the time," Sims said, "so no worries on the Navy's account. Simply use your best judgment and go on from there."

"Yes, Sir," Ash said. "I will."

"One final thing," Sims said, rising to his feet as an indication that the interview was about to end. "Your train doesn't depart until 1530 this afternoon, so once you leave here, get over to the Navy Exchange, buy some new shoulder boards and collar devices, and have the tailor re-stripe your uniforms. In order to give you a leg up on this job and some visible seniority over the two ensigns and crew you'll have coming aboard, the Navy is advancing you early to the rank of lieutenant (junior grade). Good luck, Mr. Miller, and good hunting. If you can find one of Hitler's damn U-boats, sink it for me."

At 1530 that afternoon, wearing new shoulder boards on his overcoat and fresh stripes on his blues, Ash boarded a train for Maine, stowed his bag on the luggage rack, and settled himself in his reserved seat. Three hours later, as he passed through Washington, D.C., he glanced out the window and saw that it had begun to snow.

3

Later the following afternoon, beneath a lightly falling snow, the naval rating who met Ash at the Portland station drove him to Yarmouth and then straight to Anson's Boatyard where he arrived just before dusk. To Ash's surprise, he found Chaser 3 already in the water and tied up inside a secure but well-lit boat house where several of Anson's shipwrights, their weathered faces showing their years, were making last-minute adjustments to a variety of fittings, touching up the paint work here and there after the rigors of the launch, and thoroughly cleaning the ship before the crew began to arrive in order to put her into commission.

"Built her in 1918," Anson said with a gleam in his eye. "In my prime then. Thought she was my best work ever. Still do. Laid her up topside on one of the ways in hopes that they'd want her one day, and now they do. Want to look her over, Lieutenant? Want a tour?"

"Yes," Ash said, sensing the old man's enthusiasm.

Starting at the jackstaff and the bullnose through which Ash expected to pass his anchor chain, the old man led Ash back between the two mousetrap racks and down into the forward berthing compartment.

"Tight space," Anson said, "only about 18 by 10 feet, but we've rigged it to sleep 18 men with the remainder bunking back aft. Access to the head is through that hatch forward."

Glancing forward between the fold-up bunks on either side of the space, Ash sensed an immediate morale problem. Clearly, his men were going to have to get along with each other because they would be living their lives cramped together like sardines in a can. Harmony, he realized, would be an absolute necessity that he would have to encourage.

"The pop-gun's new as the day it was made," Anson said, leading Ash up out of the berthing compartment and onto the main deck, "but it's also old.

Never been fired. Been hidden away in some depot since the last war, I suspect. Mounted it for you only yesterday, but it's still covered with cosmoline, inside and out. Left the cleanup and maintenance for your gunners 'cause we don't do weapons here."

"Right," Ash said, knowing that the same would hold true for the Oerlikons and whatever small arms the ship carried.

From the main deck, Anson then took Ash up onto the flying bridge to show him the location of the Pelorus, the signal lamp, and the various voice pipes before the two descended into the pilot house for a look at the helm, engine controls, and the chart room at the rear.

"Can't be sure," Anson said, "but I guessed that you'd have shavetails coming aboard as junior officers. Pretty much means that you're going to be up here day and night 'til you get 'em trained, so we rigged you a couple of eye hooks in the chart room where you can sling a hammock when you need your sleep."

"Mr. Anson," Ash said, "you're a prince."

"Made you a hammock too," Anson smiled. "A strong one. It's in the stowaway under the chart table."

"I can't thank you enough," Ash said.

From the pilot house, the two men descended into the ship's wardroom and officer berthing compartment. The wardroom table seemed to be a fold-down affair with three metal chairs capable of being hooked down to the deck so as not to slide when the ship rolled. Ash's single berth, a narrow one, stood to starboard; a double bunk for the juniors stood to port with a tiny head immediately forward.

"What's forward between the wardroom and the crew's compartment?" Ash asked.

"Didn't take you in there," Anson said, "'cause I've still got men working in those spaces. Sonar, radio room, and a tiny ship's office. They're compact, but adequate."

Ash made a mental note to have a look at them later.

Remounting the ladder to the pilot house, the two men once more exited onto the main deck, looked over the flag bag arrangements and the three Oerlikons that were grouped port, starboard, and aft like the points of a triangle, and then descended into the engine room to the big GM diesels.

"They're both in, they seem to be in pristine condition, and they're ready to go," Anson said, "but like the guns, we've left it to your people to do final inspections and bring them up to full operation."

"Good enough," Ash said. "My hope is that I'll have whatever engineering chief they're assigning me up here within the next few days. I intend to put him straight to work."

From the engine room, the two men dropped down into the after berthing compartment, which would also function as the ship's mess deck, examined the galley which stood immediately forward of the space, and looked over the range that had been installed.

"No refrigerator?" Ask asked.

"No refrigerator," Anson said with a shake of his head. "BUSHIPS won't spring for them on these vessels, so prepare yourself. All of you are going to be eating one meal after another out of cans and what you beg, borrow, or steal fresh from the big boys. If you can find a little reefer to glom onto, we've installed a fitting, but it would have to be a small one—something that would fit into an apartment ashore somewhere."

"I'll have to see what we can do," Ash said.

"Another thing that you might find inconvenient," Anson said, "is that the wardroom's food, in order for you to eat it hot, has to be packed in a container and carried up to you."

"I imagined that," Ash said, making one of his first decisions, "so to ease the strain on the cook, my officers and I will eat with the crew. One officer has to inspect the mess every day anyway, so we'll kill all the birds with the same stone, and that may remind the men that we're all in this together."

"Wise choice," the old man said. "I have yet to see a sailor anywhere who cottons to officers who want to think they're elite yachtsmen."

Following an examination of the depth-charge arrangements and a descent into the lazarette to look at the tiller and estimate what might be used as spare stowage space, both men climbed up onto the main deck and walked back across the brow and into Anson's small office.

"Well," the old man said, looking Ash right in the eye, "what do you think?"

"I think you've done a fine job," Ash said. "I think she's first-rate. I'm going to be proud to command her."

The old man smiled. "That's all I wanted to hear," Anson said. "She'll give you good service, Mr. Miller. She'll roll, you know, but she's eminently seaworthy, so you'll live through it, and I'm going to leave some empty paint buckets aboard to use as barf buckets. With a new crew, you'll need 'em 'til your men get their sea legs. Once your stores begin to arrive and you get 'em stowed, I think we can commission her within three weeks, and then you can take her to sea. Sound workable?"

"That sounds fine," Ash said.

"It's snowing again," Anson said, "and it's well after dark. I'm about to go home. Can I give you a ride up to The Jarvis House?"

"I'd be grateful," Ash said, glancing at the snow swirling against the window.

ᑕ

The Jarvis House—a three-storey red brick structure on a leafless tree-lined street leading up from the river—showed itself, by means of its high, oversized arched windows and ornate cornice, to have been something probably dreamed up by a 19th-century architect with a Victorian attitude. Inside, Ash found the ceilings high, the furniture antique, and the atmosphere quiet. Mrs. Jarvis, a woman who Ash imagined to be in her mid-fifties, greeted him cheerfully, helped him register, and then handed him a foot-square sealed box. "This arrived for you not ten minutes ago by special messenger, from the Naval authorities in Portland," she said. "Would you like me to have it taken up to your room, along with your bag? The dining room will close in about 30 minutes, so if you haven't yet had your evening meal, you might want to step in and order while things are still in motion."

"Thank you," Ash said, "I think I will."

The dining room, as Ash had expected, seemed bereft of seasonal visitors: no late-fall leaf viewers or early winter sports enthusiasts. Instead, beside a table flanking one of the room's high, arched windows, he saw what he imagined to be a husband and wife stopping for a night in transit to somewhere. Ten feet away, three men who looked to Ash like day laborers tucked heartily into steaks, while near the rear of the room, Ash spotted what appeared to be a salesman with a sample case on the floor beside him and, at another table, a man who could have been a book keeper or a clerk of some type. With their dinners finished, and their plates taken away, both men seemed to be giving their attention to papers of various sorts. When Ash walked into the room carrying his overcoat and his hat, his sleeves showing his new gold braid, all of the diners looked up briefly, examined him from head to toe, and returned their attention to their plates.

Selecting a table on the opposite side of the room from the married couple, Ash folded his coat over the back of one chair, placed his hat on the seat, and sat down in the other. Seconds later, before Ash could read beyond a menu entry for the evening's special, Catalonian rabbit stew, the click of a pair of high heels signaled the approach of another diner. This time, when the curious diners looked up, none of them, Ash included, averted their eyes with anything that could be confused with speed. She was stunning. Carrying a book to a table beside a flower arrangement, the girl, with her lovely head of dark auburn hair, was slim, well proportioned, smartly dressed, and very attractive. In that moment, Ash knew that he was in trouble. Returning his attention to the menu as best as he could, he decided on the Catalonian stew, savoring its rich flavors and forgetting momentarily the beautiful woman across the room absorbed in her book. Later, following the completion of his meal, he congratulated himself for having made an excellent choice. Then, he stood up from the table, took up his hat and coat, and left the room, giving the girl one last surreptitious glance on his way out.

Immediately, Ash crossed the lobby, rang the bell at the desk, and asked Mrs. Jarvis if he might have a word.

"Now," Mrs. Jarvis said, when she'd shown Ash to a seat in her office, "what can I do for you Mr. Miller?"

"Mrs. Jarvis," Ash began with some hesitation, "I'm not quite sure how to approach this subject, but perhaps it would be best for me to say simply that I foresee a possible problem."

Helen Jarvis was not new to the world, so, for a matter of seconds, she studied Ash's face without altering her expression.

"The problem of which I think you speak," Mrs. Jarvis said carefully, "is twenty-five years old, unattached, and sitting in the dining room from which you have just come. Am I right?"

"Yes," Ash said. "Understand, please, that I don't ask for myself, Mrs. Jarvis, or at least not directly, but I have 27 sailors arriving here in the next ten days, along with two junior ensigns, and at the moment, I don't know a thing about any of them. I intend to exercise a firm hand, but whether one or another of those men qualifies as a 'hard lot' is still to be determined. My interest, I assure you, is to curtail trouble before it develops, so if the lady is a permanent resident, I thought it best to consult with you. I wouldn't like her to be … inconvenienced in any way."

Helen Jarvis smiled. "I think you're acting the part of a gentleman, Mr. Miller, and I appreciate it," she said. "The *Miss* in question is one of our school teachers here; sixth grade, if I'm not mistaken, and she is indeed a permanent resident, but Harold and I have already taken that into consideration, so we are way ahead of you. While you, your officers, and your crew are billeted with us, we have arranged for the lady in question to reside uptown at The Eiseley Hotel, and with a very patriotic gesture, The Eiseley has agreed to cover the difference between their much higher rate and ours in order to accommodate her and the United States Navy."

Ash felt a sense of relief. "Mrs. Jarvis, if you don't mind, please convey my respects to the young lady and my regrets for turning her out."

"Why not say so yourself?" Helen Jarvis offered. "If you would like to meet her, I will be happy to make the introductions."

Ash raised his hand. "I'd like to, Mrs. Jarvis," he smiled, "she's a most attractive young lady, but at the moment, that is a door that I don't dare open. The last thing I can afford is a distraction, and the Miss across the way looks like a distraction for the ages."

Helen Jarvis laughed. "I take your point, Mr. Miller. I do take your point," she said. "We'll leave it alone, and I will convey your respects."

Closing Mrs. Jarvis' door behind him, Ash mounted the stairs, went straight to his room, hung up his overcoat and blouse, and gathered his bearings. The room was clean and modestly furnished with both a desk chair and an easy chair, the easy chair promising a degree of comfort for whatever time he spent in residence—if, that is, he spent any time in the room at all. Settling himself in the chair, Ash unsealed the box which the Portland Naval authorities had forwarded, and from it, he immediately lifted 29 personnel records. What Ash wanted most at that moment, particularly after two days spent on the train, was nothing more than a good night's sleep. Instead, with a sigh, he picked up the telephone and called the desk.

"Mrs. Jarvis," he said, speaking into the phone. "Might the kitchen be able to supply me with a full pot of coffee before it closes?"

4

Between 2000 hours and 0100 the following morning, Ash combed through the service records of the men he knew he was about to command, learned what he could about their backgrounds, training, and behavior, made notes, and willed himself to anticipate their arrival. And then, finally, he allowed himself five hours of sleep, rose, took an early, hasty breakfast in the dining room, and headed for Anson's Boatyard. Outside, though the sky was overcast and the air cold, the snow had ceased to fall, and while he wouldn't have called the day pleasant, at least it dawned without wind.

Ash found Anson and his people already at work by the time he arrived. Mr. Anson immediately left what he was doing, took Ash inside the carpentry warehouse, unlocked the door into a storeroom, and handed Ash the key.

"Ain't big," Anson said, "but we've cleaned it out so you can use it as an office while we finish the work. Stove there heats with wood; plenty of it out back, scraps and such, and a pile of oak firewood that you can git goin'. Them sheets of plywood folded up against the wall can be lowered flat so as to give you a couple of desks. Place is secure. Locked tight as a tick at night, and we got two night watchmen who keep a sharp eye on things inside the yard's fence. Anything else you need, jus' let me know."

And with that, the old man was out the door and gone before Ash could thank him properly.

Ash hadn't been in what he'd begun to think of as the "Ship's Office, Chaser 3," for more than 20 minutes and barely had time to fire up the stove, before a fully loaded Navy stake truck careened into the yard at far too dangerous a speed, slid to a stop at the foot of the incline, and disgorged its passengers—a surly looking petty officer with a beer belly and two equally surly-looking seamen. All three of them wore filthy dungarees, their pea coats hanging open, and had cigarettes dangling from their mouths. Through the window from inside the office, he could see the two seamen slouch instantly against the sides of the truck, thrust their hands in their pockets, and begin spitting and snickering, while the petty officer swaggered slowly up the incline toward Mr. Anson and then, after first scratching his ass, shouted at him from a distance, "Hey old man, where's yousc hooligan Navy swabs want this crap delivered?"

That did it for Ash. Even before Mr. Anson could respond, Ash was out the door and striding forward with an angry expression on his face.

"You three," he barked, "ditch those butts right now, button those pea coats, and get up here *fast*!"

Ash had struck like a bolt with thunder, and from what he could see on the men's faces, their attitudes registered an instant shift from shock to fear.

"Line up," Ash snapped, "arm's distance between each man. *Atten-tion*! Hand salute!" When the arms came up, Ash returned the salute and gave a sharp order for "Parade rest!" Then, he showed the petty officer an iron jaw. "Don't you ever call anyone 'old man' again while you are wearing that uniform. The gentleman you have just so insolently insulted is the owner of this boatyard. By the time he was 21, he'd already achieved more than you might be likely to achieve in your lifetime, so you will address him always as Mr. Anson or Sir, and if I hear a word different, I will have you on report. Now, I want to see a movement order for these stores, an inventory, and a bill of lading, and then Mr. Anson will show you where to unload."

The petty officer didn't hesitate. He lugged his guts to the truck on the run and returned as fast.

With the appropriate papers in his hands, Ash dismissed the trio and then followed Mr. Anson to yet another storage area adjacent to the boathouse where Chaser 3 was tied up. There, under Ash's close supervision, he checked off the inventory for each item delivered, while the trio, now working like well-trained boy scouts, unloaded and stacked the consignment with dispatch.

"I apologize for those three," Ash said to Anson as they watched the truck depart. "They're the worst I've seen since I first joined up."

Mr. Anson grinned. "You'll be lucky if you don't see far worse before this thing is over," he said. "It takes all kinds, you know, but if these old eyes don't deceive me, here comes a sailor of a different stripe."

"Looks like the first of them," Ash said, "and that one looks like he might be my boatswain's mate."

"Agreed," Anson said. "Straight as a stick and with just the right swagger. I'll leave you to it, Mr. Miller, and I hope it goes well."

And it did go well. Spotting Ash from near the boatyard's gate, the man came forward directly, set his sea bag on the snow beside him, came to attention, and threw Ash a smart salute.

"Samarango, Boatswain's Mate 1/c, reporting for duty aboard Chaser 3, Sir," he said in a voice that carried a slight New England accent.

After returning the man's salute, Ash said, "Glad to have you aboard, Samarango. You're the first man to report. Come inside; we have an office of sorts in here, and before you look at the ship, we need to have a talk."

By Ash's estimation, Alvaro Samarango spread about 180 pounds over a 6-foot, well-proportioned frame, his face accented by a full but well-trimmed mustache over a firm jaw.

"According to your service record," Ash said, "this is your eighth year in the Navy, and you come from Fall River, Massachusetts. I'm told that there's a large Portuguese colony in Fall River and that they send out a considerable fishing fleet. Ring any bells?"

Samarango smiled. "Yes Sir," he said, "my father owns a boat. Before I joined up, I fished with him for three years, and then I thought I'd try for something more."

Ash nodded. "Good experience, your work with the fishing?"

"We went for Atlantic cod, off Greenland," Samarango said. "My father's got a good boat and a fair business, but for me, the Navy has been an improvement. I ain't partial to cod, Sir."

"Your record also says that you split your first five years riding two destroyers and your last three on a fleet tug, the *Aztec*. How many officers did she carry?"

"We were supposed to have five, Sir, but we only had four, including the captain."

"Stand any watches on the bridge?"

"Yes, Sir," Samarango said, "the captain had me standing JOOD watches in the same section as the exec, and the exec pretty much turned things over to me whenever he was navigating or busy with paperwork."

"That's fine," Ash said. "I'll soon have two ensigns coming aboard, fresh from *Prairie State*, the midshipman's school. They'll be green when they arrive, so I intend to put you on as JOOD with one of them until I get him trained, and then, if things work out and you come up to the mark, I'll want to qualify you and give you your own watch, to spread the watch standing into three full sections. With the ensigns, you're going to have to be a diplomat. These will be intelligent men, but they won't yet have a lick of experience. Do your job right, and we'll all thank you. Do it wrong, and our lives will become difficult. Understand?"

"Yes, Sir," Samarango said. "I'll travel with care."

"Good man," Ash said. "See that you do. Now, for the rest of it, you'll be the senior rating above deck, so I'm assigning you to the forward berthing compartment where you can keep an eye on the other 17 men who will be berthing up there. The space is going to be cramped, so I'm looking to you to keep the peace. We have a chief machinist mate coming aboard, Chief Stobb. The chief and the snipes will berth aft around the mess deck along with the cook and the mess cook. The chief will run the engine room and act as master at arms, and I'll expect you to support him in that capacity as assistant MAA. Any questions about my general drift?"

"No, Sir," Samarango said.

"All right then," Ash concluded. "Go introduce yourself to Mr. Anson; he's the man who built Chaser 3, the man who owns the boatyard. You'll probably have questions that you want to ask him. Then, go take a look at the ship. She's in the boat house, tied up to the pier. I expect more men to come in shortly, so leave your sea bag here. When you've looked things over, come back, and I'll give you an inventory for what we received from Portland right before you arrived, and you can begin checking stores. After the work day ends, march whoever we've collected up to The Jarvis House, see them fed, and get them bedded down. No liberty tonight, not until we have a full crew aboard and I can look them over and lay down some rules."

By the time Ash had finished with Samarango and dismissed him, he found that he had five more men waiting outside the office door.

"I'll see Chief Stobb first," Ash said to them, "and then each of you in turn according to seniority, second class petty officers first, third class petty officers next."

Chief Stobb looked to Ash like a gnarled version of Barry Fitzgerald, the actor he'd seen in a showing of *The Dawn Patrol* aboard the *Parker* before she'd been sunk. Lean, slightly stooped, and wearing Navy issue glasses, Stobb looked like a good wind might blow him right off the chaser's deck the first time they went to sea. But the iron grip with which Stobb shook Ash's hand belied his appearance, and the two hash marks sewn on his sleeve told Ash that Lieutenant Commander Sims had done more than right by both Ash and Chaser 3. Sims, bless him, seemed to be sending him experienced leaders and men who had already been to sea.

"Had a look at the ship yet?" Ash asked.

"Oh yes," Chief Stobb said. "I'd say that the Navy has done just right by us, Captain. That's a good plant they've given us. Just like the one on the coastal minesweeper I jus' came from. My guess is that I'll be able to give you 17 knots whenever you want it—18 in a pinch. And unless I miss my bet, I think it should be easy enough to train up the boot ratings the Bureau of Naval Personnel is sure to be sending us."

"That's good to hear," Ash said. "By my count, you'll be getting at least five, one of whom will have had at least six months on a yard tug in Charleston. The others will probably come to us straight from San Diego or Great Lakes."

"That's what I imagined," said the chief. "Fresh chickens, all of them. But don't worry, Captain; I know what to do with them, and as soon as they're here, I'll begin putting that plant in order. Where would you like us to bunk?"

"Aft," Ash said, "along with the cook and his mess assistant. As senior aboard, you're the designated chief master at arms, so come straight to me whenever you detect a problem. Samarango, the first class bosun, will act as your assistant; I've assigned him to bunk forward so that he can keep an eye on the fo'c'sle. We'll leave him to ramrod things above decks, but you're the chief engineer, so the plant is your sole responsibility. I'll rely on you to keep us running."

"Can do," Stobb said.

"Well, Chief," Ash said, "I guess we'd best get on with it, so trot over to where Samarango is checking in stores and see if there's anything in the mix that falls under your supervision. I think you may have two or three crates of damage control equipment in this load, so let me know if you find anything out of order."

"Right," said the chief, rising to his feet. "Pleasure to be aboard, Sir."

"Pleasure to have you," Ash said, seeing the man out.

Bell, the second class quartermaster, the next man to report, couldn't have stood much more than 5 feet 4 inches in height and said that he'd been born and raised in Willis, Texas, a village north of Houston. Bell had five years of experience as a quartermaster, three on a cruiser, and two on a fleet oiler, and despite the man's pronounced redneck accent, Ash realized that he knew his business.

"I noticed a consignment of Atlantic coast charts in the delivery we had this morning," Ash said. "Bring that crate in here, do an inventory, and find the chart that covers this part of the coast down to Portland. Our first trips will be in and out of the Royal River here and down to Portland where we'll degauss and make our compass adjustments."

"Yes, Sir," Bell said.

"And one more thing," Ash said. "My officers will be coming to us straight from the training ship in New York. They will have learned a lot in their navigation classes, but in order to turn them into first class navigators, you and I are going to have to work as a team, so give them all the help you can."

Ash could see at once that he'd presented his quartermaster with a whole new idea. Previously, he imagined, every officer with whom the quartermaster had worked had already been skilled with navigation. Immediately, Ash seized on an idea that had sprung into his mind fully formed.

"In my experience," he said, "Texans have always made excellent teachers, so I will be looking to you, Bell, to keep up the tradition."

The whole proposition constituted nothing more than pure bluff on Ash's part, but it worked to perfection; calling on the Texan's pride had clearly made a believer out of Bell and even caused him to inflate his chest a little.

"Right," Ash said, "that's all for now. If our sonarman is out there, send him in."

Raul Gomez, also a second class petty officer, was a Mexican-American who had spent five years on destroyers steaming out of San Diego and Pearl Harbor. At the time of the Japanese attack, Gomez had been lucky; he'd been on leave in the States, visiting his family. His ship, the *Downes*, had been bombed and disabled in dry dock, and no one knew when she might return to service. Commander Sims, having somehow stumbled onto the man's availability, had pulled a string and sent him to Ash.

"I'll bet you weren't having weather like this when you left El Paso," Ash ventured.

The creases in the man's Yaqui face curved into a smile, "No, Sir, Captain," he said. "It's about 80 degrees, the day I caught the train."

"Know how to handle an attack on a sub?" Ash asked.

"Yes, Sir."

"Think you can detect the difference between a bed of kelp, a whale, and a U-boat?"

"Think so," Gomez said, showing Ash a serious expression beneath his mop of coal black hair. "Done it before."

"Good," Ash said, "because you've got one of the most important jobs on the ship. We'll have some seamen coming in here from boot camp soon. Look them over, identify the most likely candidates, and let me know. And then, once I hand down the order, you can begin training them up as strikers for sonarmen because we'll need three of you standing watch on the repeater. We get a contact, I sound the alarm, then you get down there fast and take over the search. And that's the way it will stay until your new recruits know their stuff."

Once Ash felt certain that he and Gomez had reached an understanding, he dismissed the man and called in Teague, the third class gunner's mate who had been waiting outside, sitting on his sea bag.

Teague looked to Ash like he had come straight to Maine from the midst of a Nebraska cornfield. Redheaded and freckled, and with a broad set of teeth beneath pronounced high cheek bones, the man first struck Ash as a stand in for Edgar Bergen's ventriloquist's dummy, Mortimer Snerd, but when Ash looked the man over, noticed his tailored blues, and saw the firm expression on his face, he knew that his snap impression had been mistaken.

"What's been your schooling?" Ash asked.

"Four months' gunnery school at Great Lakes," Teague said.

"Know how to take down and maintain the Oerlikons?"

"Yes, Sir," Teague said, "and I've fired 'em too."

"What about the Mark 14 3"/23 caliber gun? Any experience with one of those antiques?"

"No, Sir," Teague said, "but I'm all checked out on the 3"/50, so I can't imagine that there'll be all that much difference."

"Good enough," Ash said. "So, let me give you what little I know about it. Apparently, on the gun we've got, a well-trained crew ought to be able to put out between eight and nine rounds a minute. The drawback is that the gun only has a range of about 8,800 yards. A German U-boat carries a 4-inch gun which means that it is fully capable of blasting us out of the water before we can get close enough to engage it. That means that once we establish a gun crew, you're going to have to drill them to perfection in order for us to be anything like effective. And the same goes for the men on the Oerlikons. Our 3-inch might not have enough penetrating power to sink a U-boat, but if we ever do get in close enough to a U-boat for you to cut loose on it, your first concern has to be to damage their gun so that it won't shoot or kill our gun crew before they can open up on us."

"Right, Sir, I think that's what I anticipated," Teague said.

"All right," Ash said, "see Mr. Anson, and if he gives you the go ahead, you can start taking down your guns and getting the cosmoline out of them. Any more men left outside when you came in?"

"Steward showed up just as I was coming in, Sir."

"As you leave," Ash said, "send him in."

Lajames Watts was the only designated striker, SDSN, that Ash had ever seen among the Navy's stewards and the only Black sailor to be assigned to Chaser 3. According to his records, Watts had passed through a Navy culinary school in 1935 and emerged as a full-fledged baker, but owing to the fact that the steward's rate was "closed," filled to its quota's capacity with rated petty officers, he would have to wait until one retired or died before he could ever be promoted to SD 3/c.

"You're from Georgia?" Ash asked.

"Yes, Suh, 'lanta," Watts said.

"What were your last two billets?"

"Cook for Rear Admiral Harkness, in Seattle, 'fore he retire Suh. Then I'se wardroom cook on da *Holland*. She a sub tender, Puget Sound."

"Think you can keep this crew happy, without a reefer, without much in the way of fresh meat or vegetables?"

"I think I knows a trick or two'll keep 'em tame," Watts grinned.

"Good man," Ash said. "Think a giant like yourself can make do in a small galley?"

Watts chuckled. "I'se generally makes do wheresever I goes," Watts said.

Looking the man over, taking in what looked to Ash like Watts' rock hard body, his thick hands, and his more than 6-foot frame, Ash knew that he'd found one more reason to thank Commander Sims for his attention to the ship. If, Ash thought, any one of these people coming aboard turned out to be prejudiced, the man would do well to keep his mouth firmly shut; if he didn't, Watts looked capable of pounding him straight down to the keel.

"Find Mr. Anson," Ash said. "When he gives you the go ahead, you can start cleaning up your galley and moving galley equipment aboard. Once we go to sea, a mess cook will be designated to assist you, and the officers will take their meals on the mess deck with the crew so that you won't have to pack food and take it up to the wardroom. That's all for the moment, so you can go out and start work as soon as Mr. Anson is ready for you."

Outside, Ash found no more petty officers waiting for an interview, but in the early afternoon, after Chief Stobb and Samarango had marched the other petty officers up to The Jarvis House for lunch and brought them back, a bus arrived at the gate and disgorged two more petty officers—Hill, a yeoman 3/c, and Polaski, a radioman 3/c—and 18 firemen and seamen, including Glick, the designated seaman who was to function as Ash's signalman. By Ash's count, his crew had arrived. All that remained wanting were two ensigns.

5

At dusk, walking beside Chief Stobb and following the enlisted contingent as Samarango marched them smartly up the street toward The Jarvis House, Ash looked ahead and spotted his two ensigns standing in the snow at the entrance to the hotel. Samarango, halting the crew in the shadow of the portico, threw the officers a sharp salute which both returned, and then he immediately began marching the men straight inside by files and into the dining room for their evening meal.

"Ensign Solomon, United States Naval Reserve, reporting for duty aboard Chaser 3, Sir," said the taller of the two men, announcing himself with reserved decorum as he quickly saluted Ash.

"Ensign Hampton, United States Naval Reserve, reporting for duty aboard Chaser 3, Sir," said the shorter man, also raising his hand in salute, his words breaking with slightly more verve.

"Welcome aboard," Ash said, returning both salutes before shaking each man's hand. "Have you registered yet?"

"Not yet," Solomon said.

"We were about to," Hampton said, "but then we saw you coming up the hill."

"Go in and register," Ash said, "stow your bags and then come down to the dining room, and we'll have dinner."

Fifteen minutes later, seated at a table for four directly across the dining room from where the remainder of the crew were thrusting their forks into heaped servings of a New England boiled dinner, Ash studied the faces of the two men sitting across from him. Wide set, beneath thick black hair that had been closely cropped, Jules Solomon's dark eyes looked thoughtful but determined above a long jaw and full cheeks that could become heavily and darkly bearded if the man ever failed to shave. Although Solomon's spine rested with apparent comfort against the back of his chair, Ash sensed that the man seemed wary, almost apprehensive. William Hampton III looked back at Ash from a longer, more angular face, his light blue eyes and thin lips projecting an expression that struck Ash as being half ironic but, nevertheless, curiously naïve. For the time being, Ash decided that he would take the implied irony for a pose and the masked naivete for the fact.

"Let's begin with you, Mr. Solomon," Ash said evenly. "I know that you list your hometown as Brooklyn, that you graduated from Rutgers in 1940 with a degree in mechanical engineering, and that after you graduated but before you reported to *Prairie State*, you supervised maintenance and repair at one of New York City's electrical generating plants. I think your past experience will be helpful with your duties aboard, but more about those in a few minutes. What I would like to hear from you, if you don't mind, is something more personal; whatever you'd care to tell us. I like to know the men with whom I will be going to sea."

Solomon furrowed his brow, clearly grappling with what he would say. Then, after a brief pause, with what Ash believed to be an engineer's practicality, Jules Solomon took a deep breath, leaned forward, and spoke directly.

"My father, Captain Miller, is a Ukrainian Jew who got out of Kiev before the Bolsheviks could take control," Solomon said, showing no further hesitation. "He came to the States in 1918, took out naturalization papers, and settled in Brooklyn. A year later, he met and married my mother, and they started a bakery which is now a first-rate and growing business. I started work there when I was six, and when she was old enough, so did my sister. She's now at NYU studying fashion design. I worked at the bakery until I graduated from Rutgers—it paid for my education. I wouldn't say we're a particularly religious family, but neither do we deny our heritage. The neighborhood in which I grew up seemed to be about evenly split between Jews and Italians. My father and mother both speak Yiddish as well as English, but our parents wanted us to grow up only speaking English. The irony is that in a pinch, I can also get by in Italian, or the dialect which passed for Italian in our neighborhood."

Ensign Solomon, Ash sensed, had said as much as he intended to say.

"Thank you," Ash said. "Now, if you don't mind me asking, what was it that attracted you to the Navy, and *why* before Pearl Harbor?"

Solomon sat up straight in his chair, and when he spoke, his voice took on a harder edge.

"Our family is not political, Captain, but we do read the papers, and the reports coming out of Germany angered us. And then, when Hitler and Mussolini showed us what they were about in Spain, my father and I detected a menace that we both believe has to be stopped. The servicemen I'd seen most often in Brooklyn all came from the Navy Yard. A number of them buy from us, yard birds and sailors alike, and not a few officers, so I'd gotten to know some, and I asked questions. A commander that I'd met finally put me in touch with the right recruiting office, and that's when I signed my papers. Pearl Harbor, I regret to say, came as a complete shock. Hamp and I were already going through our course on *Prairie State*, but prior to what we began hearing there, our family's attention had been so focused on things east that I don't think we were very much aware of what had been going on with Japan."

Ash nodded. "I agree with you about 'the menace,'" Ash said. "Not to wax philosophical, but it has always seemed to me that when evil raises its head, good men have to stamp on it, and now we've got to stamp on it in two directions. I worked my way to Europe on a freighter in '38 and spent a month traveling around Germany after I left the ship. I didn't like what the Germans showed me, turned around, came straight home, and signed up for the reserves. I'm guessing that we think alike on the subject. As a result of already being at sea last year, Japanese intentions were less of a mystery; on my last ship, we'd been expecting something, but Pearl Harbor, when the blow struck, shocked us all."

Solomon looked relieved and, for the first time since sitting down, seemed to relax in the light of Ash's approval.

"It is none of my business," Ash said, "but it would be helpful to know if you are facing any personal entanglements, such as an engagement, an impending wedding, or a marriage. Girlfriends don't count."

"No, Sir," Solomon said. "Nothing of the sort."

"One final question," Ash said. "What name do you prefer to go by?"

"Solly," the man said. "I've been called Solly for most of my life."

"Solly, it is," Ash said. "And now, Mr. Hampton, or Hamp, if you're the man Solly referred to a minute ago, let me hear from you. Is it to be William, Bill, Hamp, or something else altogether?"

"My contemporaries aboard the *Prairie State* seem to have christened me 'Hamp,' Sir, so between the three of us, unless you object, I think I'll stick with Hamp."

"Hamp, it is," Ash said. "From your record, I see that you were born in Westchester, did your schooling at Andover, spent three years at Lafyette, and left to enter midshipman's school aboard *Prairie State*. Those are the facts as I have them. I'll let you take it from there."

"I'm afraid," Hampton said, "that I had no other choice than to be born with the taste of a silver spoon in my mouth. I don't consider it my fault; I had no control over the circumstance. Back around 1900, my grandfather dabbled in some mining stocks and struck pay dirt with copper near Santa Rita, New Mexico. The stock prospered, and so did my grandfather, and not long after that he started buying banks, and then he opened a factory to manufacture rope and line during the First World War, and that also prospered. And after that, he bought other companies which manufactured paint, chemicals, and soap, and then he died, and my father took over his companies, banks, and mining interests. But all the while, my grandmother—I love her, you understand, but the woman is hard as nails and twice as unforgiving—well, my grandmother continues to exercise a controlling interest in everything, and my father, bless him, has no way to get out from under her thumb. The man is an excellent manager and well supported by my mother, but as the major shareholder, Grandmother Hampton calls all the shots. By the time I came out of Andover, she started calling the shots for me too, and did until, at the end of my junior year—when I found that I'd had about all of banking, finance, and accounting that I could take—I shook the traces and bolted, the Navy having offered me a worthwhile avenue of escape, a chance to prove myself to myself, and a more than respectable means of avoiding the family business. My grandmother, ensconced in her thirty gilded rooms at The Glade, instructed our banks to cut me off without a cent the moment she received the news that I had joined up. So, until my father can slip me something or my grandmother relents, I will be forced to live on an ensign's pay and avoid keeping company with the swirl of idle debutantes who, while comely, had become increasingly obnoxious to me, my grandmother having apparently found half a dozen that she meant to put in my way as suitable candidates for marriage following my expected graduation from Lafayette. Lafayette is a fine college; I had a good time there and did reasonably well, but it was Grandmother's choice rather than mine. I wanted to apply to the Naval Academy but was beaten down without mercy. A war at that time seemed unlikely, at least to my grandmother, so I was told that the most patriotic path I could take would be to devote myself to commerce and promote our companies. Eventually, I developed other ideas, so here I am."

While Hamp had been speaking, their waiter had brought bread to the table, and lifting the basket, Ash saw to it that the two ensigns helped themselves before taking a piece for himself.

Loquacious as Hamp's recitation might have been, even—Ash thought—as it bordered on the facetious, he nevertheless sensed that it contained the truth, or the essentials of the truth, that Master William Hampton III, Ensign William Hampton, had mustered the fortitude to free himself from a form of domination that he didn't like, declare his independence, and strike out on his own.

Solly, unable to contain himself as Hamp spoke, did not laugh outright, but the broad grin that he failed to contain while listening to Hamp spoke volumes about his sense of humor.

31

"I congratulate you, Mr. Hampton," Ash said, "for being more than forthright. Political considerations, then, played no part in your decision?"

"I regret to say so," Hamp said, "but no, not until I learned what my grandmother had been up to. I was having too good a time at Lafayette."

"I'm afraid that you have me at a disadvantage," Ash said.

"Two weeks before I signed on the dotted line," Hamp said, "my father informed me that my grandmother had been shipping chemicals—lubricants, if I am not mistaken—to Germany since January of '38. American neutrality, as far as my grandmother was concerned, seemed to be nothing more than a convenient ploy for making money. As a result, I have to live with the fact that my family seems more or less to have helped grease the wheels so that Hitler could roll into Poland and France, and for me, that became the tipping point."

For Ash, Hamp's straightforward admission suddenly pulled back a curtain to reveal a nasty but not unknown fact about the war. Other American companies had done exactly the same thing, disregarding the morality of their actions while rushing full speed ahead to supply Hitler with whatever he needed and reaping huge profits which they then, generously, passed on to their stockholders. During the Battle of Britain, even as Goering pounded England day and night, a major American oil company had continued to ship Hitler as much gasoline as his fighters and bombers could absorb, not to mention whatever diesel went into fueling their U-boats. Ash knew that he despised the people who facilitated such arrangements, the war profiteers, but he also knew that they were a brand of lice who were ever-present, that a war was on, and that he could do absolutely nothing about changing a system which had been in place for centuries.

"It's not much to say," Ash said, "but I sympathize, and I think you made the right decision. And rest assured, Mr. Hampton, no matter how much your gut feeling might try to tell you something different, you are not responsible for your grandmother. Now, turning to that other subject and discounting the discarded or avoided debs, I take it that like Solly, you foresee no personal or emotional attachments that might interfere with your duties here."

"None, Sir," Hamp said.

"Good enough," Ash said, as the waiter set down a plate of the New England boiled dinner in front of him. "Let's eat, and while we do, I'll tell you what I have in mind for you."

Though Ash had never been a fan of corn beef, much to his surprise, as he tucked into the meal, his suspicions of the night before were proven correct: The Jarvis House chef knew a thing or two.

"First things first," Ash said, showing both men a grim expression. "While the three of us sit here eating, Hitler's U-boats are sitting right out there, not 10 miles off the coast, hunting and torpedoing whatever they can find. How many of them are out there, we don't know, but they are sinking ships and killing merchant sailors right and left, and it is going to be our major concern to try to stop them. What I'm telling you is top secret, so you and the crew are not to breathe a word of it to anyone, anywhere, at any time, because Uncle Sam is dead set against throwing the civilian population into a panic. Absolute silence about that is to be the rule. Understand?"

Both men looked back at him with shock, their mouths agape. Then, snapping their jaws shut, they each firmly nodded their agreement.

"Solly," Ash then said, after swallowing his first few bites, "you are senior on the Navy List, so that makes you the executive officer of Chaser 3. That means that you are going to be responsible for administration, personnel, communications, and finally, with your engineering background, engineering. I think you have a more than qualified technician in Chief Stobb, so give the man his head, let him manage the plant and the crew in the hole; your job is to administer, supervise, and support, but I don't recommend getting your hands dirty unless something turns up that you know how to repair and they don't. That seems unlikely; Chief Stobb has considerable experience."

"Understood, Sir," Solly said. "Same arrangement as in the plant I managed ashore."

"Good," Ash said. "Hamp, as third officer, you will be responsible for supply, welfare, weaponry including guns, depth charges, and sonar, and with all of your financial background, the miserable job of being our mess treasurer. Not much to do as mess treasurer other than adjusting our monthly mess bills into the accounting for the crew's mess. To ease the cook's work, we will eat aft with the crew rather than in the wardroom. If one of you ever does bring a guest aboard, we could suspend that routine for a night, but I see no point in making a mess cook lug our food to us when we can easily take meals with the men."

When neither of the men made an attempt to protest, Ash continued.

"Both of you are commissioned officers now, but even so, I would imagine that both of you know yourselves to be green, so a word about handling the men. All three of us are responsible for maintaining good order and discipline aboard Chaser 3. What that means in practice is that professional, humane behavior is essential. I've seen new ensigns who try to throw their weight around with their enlisted people, and in almost every instance, that has led to nothing but trouble. We are extremely fortunate on this ship because the petty officers we've been sent are professional, regular navy ratings, one and all. I couldn't have imagined that when I received orders to this command; I expected to have an entire crew filled with untrained reservists. Our leading people are, much to my surprise, very well trained, so exercise your authority quietly, leave your petty officers to ramrod the seamen and firemen, and conduct yourselves with reason and good judgment. That doesn't mean that you have to put up with insolence or disrespect. I will not have that aboard. And if it does turn out that we have a bad egg, bring the man to mast, and I will deal with him. Take my meaning?"

Again, both men nodded their agreement.

"Good," he said, tucking into some more of the corn beef. "We received a consignment of stores this morning, so Chief Stobb and Samarango have been overseeing inventory and storage. In the morning, the three of us are going to have to get down to the yard and turn to with a vengeance. We've got an office of sorts down there, bales of reports to fill out, and stores to get aboard as long as Anson gives us the OK to go ahead with them, and we also have a watch bill to prepare. Hamp, as you may imagine, once Teague puts the guns in working order and forms the gun crews, we are going to have to drill those men and drill them again until they can man the mounts, load, and prepare to fire with split-second timing. When we will get a chance to fire at targets is anyone's guess, but for the time being, I want the drill to achieve perfection. And the same thing will hold true for the depth charges. Solly, when Anson's people clear out enough for you to start drilling the repair parties, give Chief Stobb the go ahead, and as far as I'm concerned, you can practice shoring up every bulkhead on the ship until the men can do it in their sleep."

Hamp and Solly paused mid-forkful and managed a "Yes, Sir" before returning to their dinner.

"Finally," Ash said, "even as you lecture the men and command them to silence about the U-boat threat along this immediate coast—and don't hesitate to remind them that a prison sentence will go with breaking that rule—you'll also need to lecture them about water. We don't have evaporators on this ship, so we can't make fresh water; we are limited to what we can carry in the tanks. When we are lucky enough to tie up alongside a tender or a pier with shore facilities, the men can take freshwater showers and do their laundry, but the rest of the time, for laundry and bathing, saltwater will be the order of the day. The Navy issues a special soap for it. It won't be pleasant, and I'm doubtful that anyone will like it, but for better or worse that will be the way of it."

Across the room, the last members of the crew to finish their meals seemed to be rising from their chairs and heading for the door to turn in for the night.

"No liberty for the crew tonight," Ash said. "I'll lay down my rules in the morning, and then, after we put in a good work day and they take their evening meal, I'll turn them loose until 2300. I think there's a pub a couple of blocks up the street called The Jolly Roger. Solly, assign Chief Stobb and Samarango to act as shore patrol. What I'll hope for is that the crew will begin to bond. What I want to avoid is anyone getting out of hand and starting trouble with the locals. Got it?"

"Yes, Sir," Solly said. "Want me to go along, Sir, and keep an eye on things?"

"No," Ash said. "For the time being, it will be best for the three of us to keep our distance. Within three or four months, depending on how this bunch gels, we'll probably be drinking a beer or two with them, but not at the start."

Half an hour later, as he sank into the easy chair which graced his room and looked back on his day, Ash wondered if he had struck the right notes both with the petty officers he'd interviewed and the two ensigns who had just walked down the hall to their rooms. In the moment, Ash couldn't help feeling himself a bit of a sham. Here he was, really an ensign with a single year of seagoing experience behind him, wearing the stripes of the next higher rank while trying to sound, act, and think like John Paul Jones, Nelson, or even Dewey before he steamed into Manila Bay. Was he up to it, was he ready? He would never know until he had done it. He could only surmise that every day would throw him something novel and unexpected. The best he could do would be to try to catch it and run with it. And on that thought, he went to bed.

6

The following morning, after Chief Stobb had formed and mustered the crew, Ash himself took charge and marched them to the yard. There, immediately inside the gate, he halted the men and delivered what he hoped would sound to them like the Sermon on the Mount, starting with something of a welcome aboard, then detailing some rules about work and behavior in the yard, and ending with an announcement about liberty following completion of the work day. And then, with all the authoritative force that he could muster, Ash laid down the law about the need for security.

"Court martial and brig time are assured for anyone who breaks the rules," Ash said, "because it's a fact of life that loose lips sink ships. Now, with that said and with each of you having committed it to memory, Hill will prepare your liberty cards today, and you must be prepared to show your liberty card and your I.D. Card at all times. Liberty this evening will commence at the completion of the evening meal and conclude at 2300. After 2300, anyone absent will be declared A.W.O.L. Yarmouth has a movie house where, I'm told, a new Bogart movie, *The Maltese Falcon*, is showing, and I rather imagine that you may find a soda fountain ..." Ash allowed himself a slight smile and listened for the snickers before he continued, "... or a pub or two, depending on your interests, but see that you obey the drinking laws, conduct yourselves with decorum, and treat the locals courteously. Finally, if you see one of your shipmates going over the top or getting into difficulty, remember who we're defending in this war, and get him back to the ship. That's all. Dismiss."

As the men dispersed to a wide variety of tasks, Ash turned to Solly and Hamp.

"Check with Chief Stobb, Solly, and bring yourself up to date on what he's doing. Hamp, see Samarango first, introduce yourself, check out what he has underway, and then go introduce yourself to Gunner Teague and Gomez.

Once you've brought yourselves up to date on the work that those men are doing and had a good look around the ship, come on up to the office and report to me. I want to be informed about our progress. Then, we've got a mountain of paper work to start doing, and my guess is that we may go right on doing it until somewhere near midnight."

In the office, Bell showed Ash a chart of Casco Bay that he'd tacked down.

"Once we leave here," Bell said, "I reckon that we can be down there to Portland in about an hour, as long as we make turns for 12 knots."

Ash studied the chart. Casco Bay seemed immense and well protected. Small wonder that COMDESLANT had selected it as one of the collection points for convoys preparing to depart for England or for convoys returning.

"As soon as we get radio going," Ash said, "I want Polaski to comb the traffic for all messages showing the minefields the Navy's laid around the entrances. I've seen some trouble with mines in my time, and I don't want any more. You and Polaski find the messages; then, you and I will update this chart to show exactly where the mine belts have been laid. That way we can check each other."

"I'll tell Polaski right now, Sir," Bell said. "Maybe he can get us something sooner."

"Good, do it," Ash said, dismissing the man.

Ash looked out the window and saw what he knew at once to be a gray Navy staff car coming through the gate.

Not already, Ash thought to himself, and then, snatching up his gloves and his hat, he hurried out to meet whoever happened to be descending upon him.

The passenger in question, a full commander, turned out to be congenial. "I'm Commander Fromkern," the man said, returning Ash's salute, "Assistant Engineering Officer on the COMDESLANT staff. I've been sent up to see how you're coming along with Chaser 3."

"I arrived two days ago," Ash said. "The crew and my officers came in yesterday, and we've already received some stores which are being inventoried as we speak. My engineering officer is just now meeting his chief, and my gunnery officer is over meeting the bosun and our gunner. The guns are still packed in cosmoline, but I've given orders to put them into operating condition. Mr. Anson, the builder, tells me that we will be able to commission her in about three weeks, and I intend to hurry that along. Once my officers return, we plan to start working up a watch bill and preparing our required reports. My hope is that my yeoman will be able to find a typewriter somewhere in that first consignment of stores."

"Sounds to me like you have things well in hand," the commander said. "I've been given to understand that you were on the *Parker*."

"Yes, Sir, I was," Ash said. "I was one of the lucky ones."

"On good terms with your captain, were you?"

"I thought he was a good captain," Ash said, "but I was the most junior ensign aboard and a little out of his league."

"You might be interested to know that he wrote you a sterling fitness report for the last reporting period," Fromkern said. "I think that's one reason you were tapped for this job. I knew him, you see. He was a student of mine when I taught chemistry at the Naval Academy. Promising officer, your captain, and a sad loss for the Navy. Which reminds me, I've brought you a new tactical pub and a sheaf of messages, some of them regarding the minefields around Casco Bay. See that you plot them on your charts. The admiral doesn't want any more accidents, and once you take your ship to sea, instruct your lookouts to keep their eyes peeled for strays."

"Yes, Sir," Ash said. "My quartermaster and I were talking about that when you arrived. We'll be relieved to have the latest updates."

"Secure stowage," Fromkern said, "for the pub, the messages, and for the chart when it's marked up. Don't want anything secret getting into the wrong hands."

"Right, Sir," Ash said. "We've got a confidential locker in the wardroom; I'll secure the message traffic, the pub, and the chart myself."

"Good enough," said Commander Fromkern. "Now, if you don't mind, why don't you show me about your ship. I haven't been aboard a subchaser since 1918 when I commanded SC-135 on the Atlantic convoys."

❧

"Obviously," Fromkern said an hour later as he and Ash reemerged from the wardroom and into the warehouse where the chaser's office was located, "Olie Anson has built your ship with care. She's better built than the one I commanded. It's clear that she's been given special attention. '*Festina lente*,' I think the saying goes, Mr. Miller; you're probably familiar with it."

"I am," Ash said. "'Make haste slowly.' Renaissance men like Drake and Raleigh seemed to revere the idea."

"Thought you might know it," Fromkern said. "Well, I'd say that Mr. Anson has put the phrase into practice here, and the results show. Now, a couple of things before I go. Continue to make haste slowly, Mr. Miller. Get Chaser 3 into commission as swiftly as you can, but don't rush to the point where you leave things undone. It can be no secret that you are needed for convoy duty right now. The U-boats are playing hell with our unescorted ships along the coast, and we are so far short of escorts that we don't have half enough to go around. Only last night, the krauts sunk one more off the Long Island coast, a tanker riding empty on its way back from Liverpool and headed for the

New Jersey piers. No matter how you cut it, that's a ship lost and our capacity to deliver fuel to our allies diminished. There are no certainties, you will understand, but if Chaser 3 had been available as an escort, it's conceivable that you might have been able to fend off the attack. That's pure speculation on my part, but I'm sure you see what I mean. Nevertheless, with regard to commissioning your ship, the other expression you have to remember is 'haste makes waste'."

"I'll keep that firmly in mind," Ash said.

"So, steady as you go, and see that you prepare your crew. The majority of your stores will reach you this week. Once Mr. Anson gives you the go-ahead, put the ship into commission, read yourself in as captain, run your acceptance trials as quickly as you can, and get down to Casco Bay. Anson will supply you with enough fuel and water to make the trip and give you some to spare, but you will fuel, water, and take on comestibles at Portland. Your depth charges, ammunition, and pyrotechnics will be brought out to your anchorage by lighter. There will be a machine gun in that consignment, but I can't tell you whether it will be a .30-caliber or .50-caliber gun; both are in short supply, so you will have to take what you get. Do double check to make sure that the ammunition supplied is the right caliber. We had a case a week or two after Pearl Harbor where the depot sent out .30-caliber ammunition with a .50-caliber gun. The men on duty took it aboard without checking, which meant that the ship went to sea with a useless weapon."

Ash shook his head in disbelief. "I'll make certain to double check that myself," he said.

"Good man," Commander Fromkern said, showing Ash a broad smile. "And in so far as you can do it, I'd follow that policy about everything."

"You can be sure, Sir," Ash said.

"Well, then," Fromkern said, offering Ash his hand. "I think I'd better be on my way and leave you to it. Good hunting, Mr. Miller, and good luck. Speaking for myself as well as the admiral, we'll rest easier once you and a hundred other of these chasers put to sea and start doing the job."

Commander Fromkern might have said more, but in that instant, distress signals coming from a medium-sized trawler half a mile downriver arrested the attention of both men. Commander Fromkern needed only a glance in the direction of the trawler to read the signs before ordering Ash to seal the gates to the yard, allowing no one to enter or leave until further notice. Then, he fairly leapt for Anson's office and the nearest telephone.

Barking orders to Solly, Hamp, Samarango, and Chief Stobb, Ash himself saw the gates closed and chained. Swiftly making his way back to Anson's office, Ash, like the remainder of his men, watched with grim astonishment as the wounded trawler approached one of Anson's docks. The blackened hole through the port quarter of its stern showed clear evidence that a surfaced U-boat had attacked it somewhere nearby, the lines of machine-gun holes across the port side of the little ship's pilot house and cabin adding a dark and nasty testament to the hard fact.

Fromkern reappeared almost immediately, once more warning Ash to guard the gates until the Navy's response teams—medical, intelligence, and salvage—could race the 11 miles up from Portland. Then, once Ash had given the order, both he and Commander Fromkern hastened to the dock where the trawler, with Anson's shipwrights receiving her lines, was attempting to tie up. Even before Ash could register the blood on the trawler's decks, Chaser 3's entire crew—save for Samarango, Chief Stobb, Solly, and Hamp who remained on the gates—had run to the dock. In a matter of minutes, they boarded the trawler and helped remove one dead fisherman from the pilot house and two more wounded, one of them badly, from the cabin immediately beneath.

When the trawler's captain, a grizzled New Englander with the short stem of a pipe still clenched between his teeth, finally emerged from the pilot house, he told Commander Fromkern that he'd been attacked in the midst of a fog bank no more than 8 miles east of Bailey Island. According to what Ash heard, the trawler had been moving ahead slowly through a wall of dense fog, making for Portland, when the fog had suddenly lifted up to a distance of no more than a hundred yards. In the same instant that the captain had spotted the stationary U-boat stopped on the surface, a German machine gun located on the conning tower had cut loose on them, instantly killing the trawler's helmsman and wounding the two men in the lower cabin. Reacting as swiftly as he could, the ship's captain had then thrown the wheel hard to starboard in order to disappear back into the fog; seconds later, the lesser of the U-boat's two deck guns, probably a 40mm, had cut loose and holed the trawler's stern just as she was passing out of sight back into the fog bank. Fortunately for the trawler, the round thrown out had been a solid, so rather than bursting, it had slammed straight through the trawler's stern and out the starboard side while doing only minimal damage. Had the U-boat's 4-inch gun been used, the trawler's captain imagined that he would have been sunk, if not blown to pieces. The captain ended his account with something that stuck in Ash's mind. In the second or two that he'd glimpsed the Nazi sub, he'd seen that the sea green conning tower on the U-boat had been distinguished by a single image—not an obligatory hull number but the huge silhouette of an immense black seahorse painted upright on its side.

Chaser 3 did not carry a pharmacist's mate, so Ash's green recruits—some of them horrified by the sight of blood and retching but fresh from their boot camp first aid training—did what they could to treat the wounded. As far as Ash was concerned, whatever they did proved useful, because both men were still alive when the Navy's medical and intelligence teams finally reached the yard. The trawler's captain and his two uninjured fishermen were removed to a secure location for debriefing, while the medical people raced for the Portland Naval Hospital and a salvage crew went swiftly to work on the vessel to disguise and cover up the damage that had been done to it by the German rounds.

"Caution your officers and crew," Fromkern warned Ash before he departed. "Not a word about what's been seen and heard here is to go beyond the gates."

"Understood," Ash said, saluting his senior as the commander stepped into his car.

Throughout the remainder of that troubled day, after being twice cautioned, no one spoke of the incident, but that it had left everyone in the ship's company with a staggering impression, no one doubted. In place of doing a mental postmortem on the event, consulting often with Chief Stobb, Samarango, and Teague, Ash and his two junior officers distracted themselves by working furiously on drafts for Chaser 3's watch bill. Because they were unfamiliar with anything about the men beyond the technical qualifications of the rated petty officers, they could not be sure that they were assigning precisely the right men to the collateral jobs that went beyond what they'd be called upon to do during normal running. Gomez, for example, had tapped two of the new boot seamen, Lipesky and Pierre, for training underway on sonar. Ash felt confident that he would turn both into qualified sonar operators, but Ash also had to determine—if or when he sounded the alarm for General Quarters and sent the crew running to their battle stations—if Lipesky would serve best as a loader for the 3"/23, or if his muscular bulk would make him a strong candidate for one of Chief Stobb's damage control parties. Would Hill, the yeoman, busily typing to Ash's side in a cramped corner of the office, work well behind the engine order telegraph in the pilot house during GQ, or should Ash assign him to assist with placing the detonators into the depth charges? The three officers just couldn't be sure. The best they could hope for was to try to make educated guesses, fix assignments, and adjust them in the light of future experience and the horror on the trawler which they had just witnessed.

An hour before the men were to break for lunch and march off to The Jarvis House, a second consignment of stores arrived from Portland, this one containing the ship's bedding, signal flags, and a considerable inventory of tools for work on everything from engine maintenance to Chaser 3's rigging. Samarango and Stobb handled the entire consignment without bothering Ash about it, went through the inventory with meticulous care, and left the officers to their work. Later, in the middle of the afternoon, after seeing everything else stacked and stored in the warehouse, Chief Stobb turned up in the office with the completed inventories and two boxes which he quickly presented to Ash.

"We received one crate of standard medical supplies and stowed it with the rest of the gear," Chief Stobb said. "These were included, and I'm guessing they shouldn't have been. I would have expected this stuff to come by guarded delivery. That first box is an alcohol consignment, medical for the crew and two quarts of the technical stuff for cleaning sonar and radio equipment and for floating the compass. The second one contains the ship's supply of morphine. 'Cause we don't have a pharmacist's mate, Captain, I thought you'd best take charge of it."

"Right you are, Chief," Ash said. "I had that duty aboard my last ship, so I'm already familiar with the required reports. I'll lock both boxes in the wardroom safe."

"Hamp," Ash said, as Chief Stobb disappeared outdoors, "how much first aid did the *Prairie State* teach you?"

"Multiple hours on several days, Sir," the ensign replied.

"Good," Ash said. "Think you could stitch up a gash or close one with butterflies?"

"In a pinch," Hamp said, "if I have to."

"All right," Ash said. "I'm designating you the ship's physician. These guys are young, so let's hope that they're healthy, but if we do run into an emergency and I'm busy on the bridge, you'll have to handle it. And just for general purposes, why don't you keep a bottle of aspirin and a dose of castor oil handy; I'm guessing those will see us through the most of our problems. We'll have a medical book or two in the stores, so you'll need to read up on the basics, like how to stitch up deep cuts and treat superficial wounds."

"If you don't mind me asking, Sir, what about sea sickness?"

Ash laughed. "From what I understand about these chasers, it's going to be rampant, particularly during our first times out. Mr. Anson told me that he would leave some empty paint buckets for us. The short of it is that the men will have to work through it, because we have no other choice. If we have a chronic case, and the man ever spits up blood, he'll have to go ashore, and that will be permanent. I've known of such cases, but I've not yet seen one and hope I don't. Let me know at once if something like that turns up. I won't have a man's health ruined because his body betrays him."

"Nothing medical that we can do for a man like that?" Hamp asked.

"No," Ash said, "not in my experience."

In the evening, following supper, and after another warning about keeping their silence regarding the day's events, liberty commenced with a number of the men heading toward the movie house and whatever other pastimes

Yarmouth had to offer. By prearrangement and beneath a light snow falling crisply from the dark sky, Ash, Solly, and Hamp returned to the yard where the night watchman unlocked the warehouse for them so that they could return to work in their office. There they remained, as Ash had foreseen, struggling through the watch bill and a growing variety of reports until 2300, when they finally admitted exhaustion and went back to the hotel. There, Stobb reported the crew had turned in with no men absent and no troubles in town.

Ten days later, after having worked the same schedule non-stop for the duration, Ash realized that regardless of the complexity of what they'd been doing and in spite of his considerable earlier reservations, things were starting to take shape. Bit by bit, no matter how confused the first days had been, Ash, Solly, and Hamp were getting to know the men with whom they would serve. The immense paperwork that accompanied the commissioning of a ship had begun to sort itself out, the actual construction seemed to be moving ahead faster than either Mr. Anson or Ash had anticipated, and with Anson's full cooperation, the stacks of stores staged in the warehouse were diminishing at something like light speed as the crew carried them aboard in order to stow and equip the ship. By that time too, the Navy salvage crew had repaired the damage to the trawler so that it could be inconspicuously towed down to Portland. Ash had no idea how the Navy had silenced the trawler captain and the two uninjured fishermen; he never saw them again.

"Mr. Miller," Anson said to him on a Saturday morning. "I don't know quite how we done it, but if your people are ready, I'll turn the ship over to you next Thursday. We've still got work to do on the tillers, and I expect to complete work in the pilot house on Tuesday, but in all other respects, she's as ready as she'll ever be."

Ash couldn't help himself. For a moment, his face lit up like a beacon.

"Thought that might please you," Anson said. "Ain't quite the three weeks I promised when you got here, but I didn't think you'd mind."

"The Navy, Mr. Anson, will be overjoyed," Ash said, "and I can't thank you and your men enough for all of the hard work you've put in. She's a thing of beauty, and I'm more than pleased with the attention you've lavished on her. We'll plan for trials on Thursday, the minute we commission and I take command, and then if adjustments are required, I'll hope that we can complete them on Friday or over the weekend. Sound good to you?"

"Sounds fair enough," Anson said.

"Hill," Ash said to his yeoman the minute Anson left, "go find Teague and ask him to report to me at once."

Hill bolted for the door; five minutes later, Teague came into the office showing a daub of grease over the corner of his cheek and bleeding across one knuckle. Hill followed behind him.

"You all right, Gunner?" Ash asked. "Haven't injured yourself, have you?"

"I'm fine," Teague laughed. "Stumbled against the breech block on the 3-inch."

"Well," Ash said, "take care of yourself, Teague. Can't afford to have you injured, you know; you're essential aboard this ship."

"I'll take more care, Sir," the man said, showing Ash a broad grin. "Happy to report, Sir, all guns are operational. The 3-inch took some time, but that old rascal and the Oerlikons are in perfect working condition and ready to fire, long as the depot gives us something to shoot. I've been drilling the gun crews; they ain't up to speed yet, but they will be, and if you'll give me permission, Sir, I'd like to rope that chubby boot, Zwick, as a striker. He's done good work helping me put the guns into condition, and he seems to be sharp about the mechanics involved and shows an interest in taking them on. I think he might have a fine eye for distance too; I've made him pointer on the 3-inch, and every time I give him a target, he estimates the range the same as me."

"Fine," Ash said. "You've told me exactly what I wanted to know. Continue with the drills, tell Zwick that he can strike for gunner's mate, and when we get down to the anchorage and the lighter comes alongside, be double damn sure that the ammo they send us is the right stuff for our guns. Apparently, they've made a mistake or two in the past, and we don't want that happening to us. That means that you'll need to check everything from the 3-inch right down to the small arms. It won't do to try to load .38 rounds into the Thompson or our .45 sidearms. And we'll be getting a machine gun for the mount on the fantail as well, so that's going to have to be broken down and cleaned up before we can use it. Give some thought to stowage of the machine gun. Can't have it exposed at sea, but we'll want it somewhere close where we can mount it in a hurry if we need it. Got all that?"

Teague nodded.

"Good enough, Gunner. And if you see Chief Stobb and Samarango out there, ask them to come up here."

Chief Stobb and the bosun arrived together no more than a couple of minutes after Teague made his exit.

"Chief, Bosun," Ash said, acknowledging each man in turn, "Mr. Anson tells me that we can commission next Thursday, so you can pass the word. Dress blues for the commissioning evolution and then working uniform immediately thereafter, because I intend to take us out and go straight to trials. I'm thinking that we'll transit down to Portland for fuel, water, provisions, and ammunition on Monday. After that, my best guess is that we will start doing escort duty about as fast as COMDESLANT can hand us a set of orders. Warn the men that they'd better be ready. I'm going to expect seasickness once we put to sea for real, but if you haven't told them already, you might as well tell them now: they'll have to work through it, barf buckets in hand if they need them, because we have too few men to spare them from their watches. After they go off watch, for the first two or three days, I'll let them take to their beds. Once they're through the dry heaves, I'll look to the two of you to get them working regular."

Samarango and Chief Stobb both smiled. "For the new ones," Chief Stobb grinned, "the gentle lapping of the waves will come as a revelation."

"And let's not forget the calm serenity of the seas," Ash added. "Now, Chief, how about the repair parties? Are you confident that they can prevent us from sinking?"

"I've run them through every drill that I can dream up," Stobb said, "and several times. They've got the idea, Sir, and I think they can keep us afloat."

"Let's hope," Ash said. "What about your engine room crew?"

"They're as ready as I can make them sitting here tied up," Stobb said. "Soon as we get the diesels running and head out, I'll double the effort. Right now, they're eager, and I think they'll shape right up."

"Boats," Ash said, "what about the deck force?"

"Kaufmann, one of the boots from Great Lakes, ain't the brightest star in the sky," Samarango said, "but he's good with his hands—a hard worker and strong. The rest of them come up to the mark and will make good sailors. Pasoni spent a summer on a tuna boat out of San Francisco, so he's been to sea. I've worked them on line handling drills and rigging, but aside from talkin' to 'em about mooring and anchoring, I won't be able to give 'em any practice 'til we actually do it. I assigned that boy from Kentucky, Denison, to help in the galley as mess cook; he said he'd cooked some for a CCC camp in Oklahoma. With regard to Gomez, Polaski, and the other ratings, they're working up the men to stand watch in their spaces, and Glick, the signalman, seems to know his stuff. I've watched him practice with the light and on the key, and he's fast."

"All right," Ash said. "See to the spaces once we've finished moving the stores aboard. Make sure everything is tied down tight because you know how this thing is going to pitch and roll. Make whatever advanced preparations you can for going to sea because we are about to enter the lists."

Later, when Ash, Solly, and Hamp sat down to their evening meal, Ash showed each of the two men sitting across from him a deadly serious face. "I'll tell you both right now what we are going to do on Sunday," he said, charging his voice with as much gravitas as he could project.

45

Immediately, both men looked up from their plates, tense and expectant.

"All three of us are about to become seagoing officers," Ash continued, "so all three of us are going to take the afternoon off in order to prepare for sea by squandering our time in trivial, frivolous pursuits. The two of you might want to visit a museum or perhaps read poetry with a spinster somewhere. I'll leave it up to you, but whatever you do, be sure that you take the waters and refresh yourselves. As you do, be sure that you bear in mind that important naval rule: 'to hell with the women and children, make way for a naval officer.'"

Unable to keep a straight face, Solly broke out laughing.

"If by 'taking the waters,' you mean spending all afternoon in bed, napping and reading the papers," Hamp said, "I will be most grateful, Sir."

"Your gratitude will stand you in good stead," Ash said. "Make the most of it because I expect the Navy's going to begin pressing us hard, quick."

7

The following Sunday, after a light lunch at The Jarvis House and contrary to Hamp's claim that he planned to spend the afternoon in bed, Solly and Hamp followed a majority of the crew up the snow-packed street to see a new Errol Flynn movie entitled *They Died with Their Boots On* at the Yarmouth Rialto. Before lunch, Ash had overheard a few of their boot sailors talking animatedly about the flick. According to them, the film promised to be more entertaining than a traveling burlesque show. Skeptical, Ash went back up to his room, sat down in the easy chair, and reluctantly turned his attention to the chapters in Knight's *Modern Seamanship* that covered mooring and anchoring. After a fashion, he knew that he was about to be tested on both counts and didn't intend to be found wanting.

Two hours later, having reviewed and committed to memory the most pertinent facts, Ash finally stood up, put down the book, and reached for his blouse. The time had come, he reasoned, to take a break and go for a stroll, even if he had to hug the inside of his greatcoat in order to ward off the freezing weather.

Outside, although the day remained gray and overcast, the wind had died, and Yarmouth, even for a Sunday, seemed strangely silent, almost hushed, its citizens having retired either for afternoon naps or in order to glue themselves to their radios for whatever mid-afternoon entertainment the air waves provided. Setting himself a steady but moderate pace, Ash walked up the street and inland, past the Rialto, past shops and stores still showing a plethora of winter fashions, past The Eiseley Hotel to which the attractive "Miss" from The Jarvis had decamped, and on past a small library and a snow-covered semi-circular park. Looking ahead, his eye settled on a small ornate sign overhanging the sidewalk, the placard's blue and gold colors presented in the English style so as to announce "Queen Bee's Tea and

47

Coffee." When he had set out that afternoon, Ash had entertained the idea of drinking a couple of beers at The Jolly Roger, but the farther he walked, the more the frigid humidity rolling off the Royal River seemed to penetrate. It was Sunday after all; The Jolly Roger might not even be open, and drinking ice-cold beer on an ice-cold day quickly lost its attraction. Instead, by the time Ash spotted the Queen Bee's, what he most wanted took the form of a strong, hot cup of coffee. Ash opened the door and passed inside.

Much to Ash's surprise and delight, the interior of the Queen Bee's resembled that of the English pubs he had seen in photographs. Where he had half expected a white tiled floor and a soda fountain arrangement of wire tables and chairs, he found in their place dark wood paneling, a serving counter with an overhang where the cups and saucers seemed to be stored, small oak tables with cushioned chairs, a row of deep, wooden high-backed booths along the wall across from the counter, and a welcome fire burning in the grate at the room's end. As far as Ash could see, he was the only customer. Pleased that he could relax in peace, he proceeded to the counter where an elderly woman with a well-arranged blue-gray coiffure appeared from a back room.

"Coffee or tea?" the woman asked him in a voice that carried a strong English accent.

"Coffee, please," Ash said.

"House blend, or one of our specials?"

"I'll try the house blend, if you please," Ash said.

The woman smiled. "Had one of you Navy lads in last week," she said. "He liked it."

"I'm sure I will too," Ash said, thanking the woman as she handed him a mug embossed with twin photos of Roosevelt and Churchill.

"Are you English, by chance?" Ash asked.

"Born English, naturalized American," the woman said. "Came over in 1926, but it don't matter much now since we're all in this together. That Mr. Hitler's a bad piece of work. Trust you boys and the Royal Navy will cut him down to size."

"That is certainly the plan," Ash said, flashing the woman a smile. "Anywhere?" Ash continued, gesturing to the empty tables.

"Please yourself," the woman said, returning his smile and retiring from the counter.

Ash removed his overcoat and walked to the back of the room. He placed his coffee mug on a table, settled his hat and coat on an adjoining chair, and sat down facing the warmth from the fire. Only after he had comfortably seated himself and taken a first sip of his coffee did Ash happen to glance to his right. In that instant, Ash nearly tipped his coffee straight into his lap—sitting not 6 feet away from him, the auburn-headed Miss that he had first seen at The Jarvis House seemed to be looking straight at him from the booth nearest to the fireplace.

"I beg your pardon," Ash said, starting to rise. "I didn't mean to disturb you; I didn't realize that you were sitting there."

"Not at all," the woman said, a touch of amusement evident in her voice.

As Ash stood up and started to reach for his mug and his coat, the woman raised a hand to stop him.

"Please, Mr. Miller," she said, showing him a smile. "You haven't disturbed me at all. I've been sitting here reading Agatha Christie for lack of anything more profound, and you aren't in the least in the way. We seem to be the only ones in here today. Mrs. Jarvis gave me your message and told me your name. Why don't you join me? I'm Claire Morris."

Ash gathered his wits, then, coffee in hand, slid into the seat across from Claire. "Ashford Miller," he said, returning a smile. "And once again, I apologize for the way my ship and I have put you out of your lodgings. I hope the inconvenience hasn't been too great."

"The inconvenience, as you call it Mr. Miller, has been much more than comfortable. The Eiseley Hotel treats me like something of a queen, and I'm not used to that."

Ash pondered a response that approached something like "if a woman looks like a queen and has the lips, eyes, and hair of a queen, it is no surprise that she is apt to be treated like a queen," but stifled the impulse as being miles too forward. Instead, he merely said, "I'm glad to hear they're giving satisfaction."

"I think Mrs. Jarvis thought that I might be a threat of some kind to your sailors," she laughed.

"I rather think that Mrs. Jarvis and I worried that it might be the other way around," Ash said. "I seem to have a good crew, but before they all arrived, we had no way of knowing."

"Well," she said, "you can rest easy on that point because I have been living well, quite beyond my normal means, so the Navy has advanced a notch in my estimation."

"If so," Ash said, "I regret to tell you that the good times won't last much longer. We'll be putting to sea before long, so I suppose that you will be moving back."

"I suppose so," Claire said, "but I won't lament. Mrs. Jarvis is a dear, and the food at The Jarvis House has always been exceptional and a slight cut above what The Eiseley can offer. There are times at The Jarvis when I find it a strain not to overindulge."

Claire Morris had avoided overindulgence with about the same degree of attention as a *Vogue* model, Ash observed, but once again, he kept the thought to himself.

"The Catalonian stew I had on the day I arrived was excellent," Ash said, "and anyone who can make a New England boiled dinner palatable—that's what they served the night the crew arrived—qualifies as a master in my opinion."

"Just so, and I hope they'll give you lamb or pork loin at least once before you leave. We had them last month, and they melted in the mouth."

"We had the lamb two nights back," Ash said. "It was a treat."

Then Ash changed the subject. "Mrs. Jarvis told me that you teach school here—sixth grade, I believe she said. Do you find the work agreeable?"

Claire flashed Ash a broad smile. "Sixth graders, Mr. Miller, are right on the verge of becoming teenagers. The boys are so filled with energy that they are almost always a handful, and the girls are just discovering how to be saucy. It is sometimes a struggle, but most of them are quick learners, so I endure. I can't say that I am sold on teaching for life, but when I came out of Middlebury in '38, jobs were hard to find. This one came up, so I took it, and I have to admit that they've been very good to me. Our pay scales are better than a host of other schools around Portland, so I'm more than pleased when I hear about what some of my contemporaries are earning. What about you, Mr. Miller—are you career Navy or merely in for the duration?"

"To tell you the truth," Ash said, "I don't know. I'm a reserve officer, of course, but I activated my commission a year before we got into the war, and thus far, I find that I like the life. Before coming here, I was on a destroyer that had the misfortune to be sunk by a mine off the Florida coast. If that hadn't happened, I'd still be an ensign, but I've been given command of the ship that's being built down at the yard, so the Navy has advanced my rank, apparently in order to increase my chances of being effective. At the moment, owing to nothing more than necessity, I seem to be learning at high speed, but soon I will have to begin paying the bill. My hope is that I'll be up to it, that—if you don't mind me inflating the whole idea—I'll be able to rise to the challenge. Normally, I dislike that expression; 'rise to the challenge' seems revoltingly trite, but there it is."

"My father commanded a torpedo boat during the First World War," she said, "what the Navy is now calling a 'small destroyer.' He was regular navy for 25 years. He died in 1936, but we talked about his command once, and if you don't mind me saying so, before he went aboard and read himself in, he said that he felt exactly the way you seem to be feeling. My guess, Mr. Miller, is that a considerable degree of apprehension and self-doubt goes with the job. Isn't that the way you see it?"

"Yes, exactly," Ash said, "and I suspect that it's probably the same for every man who accepts a command. Nothing for it but to leap in and give it one's best, and hope for a corresponding return."

Claire nodded her agreement. "And before you joined the Navy," she said, "college, work, anything unusual?"

"Ha," Ash said, "I popped out of college in 1936 with degrees in English and journalism and didn't find jobs any easier to come by than they must have been around here, so I spent a year pounding the pavement as a cub reporter on the *Bugle* in Herrin, Illinois. I also wrote a few short stories for the pulps, but the take was so minimal that when I finally thought that I faced starvation, I gave up both jobs and signed on as a deck hand with the merchant marine. The food and the pay offered immense improvements. Made a trip to Germany, didn't like what I saw there, came home, and joined the reserves. And then, as soon as regulations would permit, I asked for orders to active duty because I sensed this thing coming."

"You've actually written stories, and published them?"

"For the pulps," Ash said. "A few detective stories and three or four westerns. Serious literature they were not. I have no pretensions about them. And the pay wasn't very good either. If a person sat in a room and turned them out one after another, he or she might make a poor living at it, but magazines like *Colliers* and *The Saturday Evening Post* eluded me. I did publish a couple of serious stories in reputable literary magazines, but neither of those paid me a penny, and I simply couldn't afford to keep it up. So, I decided to throw it over and go to sea. I might go back to writing someday, but I have no regrets. For the time being, I've had to put anything resembling serious writing—beyond the piles of paperwork that the Navy demands—on hold."

"My father used to grumble about the amount of paperwork he had to do," she grinned. "He said that if he generated anything less than a foot-high stack during a given year, he imagined the Navy would consider him a slacker."

"I can't be sure," Ash laughed, "but I think my officers and I have generated at least that much across the past three weeks."

"With more still to come?"

"With a lot more still to come," Ash said.

They talked on, Ash and Claire Morris, easily and without restraint for another hour, and then, glancing at a clock on the wall, both recognized that they needed to return to their hotels for the evening seating. Ash helped Claire into her coat, admiring the scent of her hair as he did so, and then walked beside her to the entrance of The Eiseley.

"Am I likely to see you again?" she said, turning and offering Ash her gloved hand at the hotel entrance.

"Probably not," Ash said, taking the hand held out to him and holding it for a lingering moment. "This has been the most pleasant afternoon I've spent in Yarmouth, but I won't be able to get away like this again. And I'll regret it," he said, giving her a look which he hoped conveyed his feelings.

"I'll regret it as well," she said. "If you ever come this way again, for an upkeep or something of the kind …"

"Yes," Ash said. "You can be sure."

Later that night, as Ash sat down to dinner with Solly and Hamp, he asked, "How was the shoot-em-up? Errol Flynn win the girl and triumph over the forces of evil?"

"No," Solly said.

"Not exactly," Hamp said. "That flick was about Custer."

"Oh," Ash said, "that explains it, I guess."

"And what about you, Sir, where did you disappear to this afternoon? We looked for you, but you weren't here when we came back. Thought you might like a beer up at the Roger."

"I," Ash said with restraint, "spent the afternoon taking tea with a spinster."

"We saw a spinster that I would certainly like to have taken tea with," Hamp said quickly. "She was just coming out of The Eiseley when Solly and I bought our tickets at the theater. Glorious redhead. A real dish!"

"Mind your manners, George," Ash quipped.

Immediately, both Solly and Hamp looked up, their mouths dropping slightly open.

"Well, you sly dog … *Sir*," Hamp exclaimed.

"I'm afraid I don't know what you're talking about," Ash said, bending over his plate with a smile.

8

At 0800 on the following Thursday morning, according to Ash's experience, Chaser 3 became the most strangely commissioned ship in the United States Navy. Contrary to tradition which required trials first, assumption of command next, and commissioning last, the certainty which COMDESLANT demonstrated about the ship's condition and readiness reversed nearly everything having to do with normal procedure. Seconds after the magic moment, in an act *assumed* to be occurring simultaneously with the vessel being placed on the Navy's list—with the crew in pea coats but wearing dress blues and standing to attention on the fantail of the little chaser, all of them having moved aboard the day before—Ash read himself in as their commanding officer and saw the ship's commissioning pennant run up. He then ordered them to prepare for final trials, as though real or normal or regulation trials had already taken place, which they most definitely had not. Curiously, after weeks of snow and heavy gray overcast, the evolution went forward beneath a clear sky, the sea gulls floating on nothing more than crisp, windless air. By 0930, the Special Sea and Anchor Detail was set and the big diesels were finally running. With Ash on the bridge to con the ship, Solly in the pilot house to keep a check on the helmsman, and Hamp on the foc'sle to watch and learn from Samarango's handling of the deck crew, Chaser 3 was underway, threading between the buoys on the Royal River and making good her course toward the upper reaches of Casco Bay. There, between Merepoint to the northeast and the mine belts laid near the tip of Chebague Island to the south, the ship was to conduct its so-called final trials.

The crew and the ship experienced glitches of course, any number of them. This boot stepped into the bite of a line and had to be jerked to safety before the bite closed and took off his foot at the ankle; that one misidentified a security light on the beach, mistaking a flood light on a lamppost for a lighthouse, and yet another had confused line 3 for line 4 when Ash had ordered the correct line to be taken in when he'd first gotten underway. Another of the green sailors, victim of a traditional prank, had actually gone down to the engine room and, to Chief Stobb's delight, asked him for a bucket of steam. Polaski in radio had reported a blown tube which was quickly replaced. Stobb had found three small oil leaks, all of them corrected by means of tightening pipe fittings, and when, finally, it came time to lower the sonar dome, Gomez hadn't been able to do it until he and a workman that Anson had placed aboard had discovered a loose connection in an electrical junction box. As Ash expected, adjustments were made, minor imperfections were dealt with, and final acceptance requirements were gradually checked off. Then, across a long afternoon, running up and down the bay at varying speeds, Ash, Mr. Anson, Chief Stobb, and Solly worked out the ship's power-to-speed ratios so that whatever speed the bridge ordered could be answered at once by the watch in the engine room.

They kept at it all day, testing the engines in every conceivable way, checking out standard and emergency steering, testing and proving sonar, sound-powered phone communication, signal lights, running lights, depth-charge release mechanisms, distributions systems for water and fuel, and even the portable anchor davit. Thrice, amid the shallower waters north of Cousin's Island, Ash anchored the ship, Samarango working to train his anchor detail, Hamp mastering some of the complexities as he watched the evolution proceed.

They came in at dusk, the boot seamen congratulating themselves on having become sea dogs on the basis of their first 12 hours in the bay. "Piece of cake," said Grubber, a fresh-faced kid who'd come to the ship straight from Great Lakes after growing up on an Iowa chicken farm. "Nothin' to it," said Meyer, another midwestern farm boy who'd trained up in San Diego. "That Chief Stobb don't know shit about bein' at sea. Them snipes never see it from down in that hole of theirs. Smooth as glass out there." The petty officers who overheard this talk rolled their eyes but didn't bother to say, "Just wait." Instead, with repressed grins, they went about their business with the kind of foreknowledge that Zeus must have enjoyed when he gave birth to Athena.

Ash, Solly, and Hamp, once the ship had tied up and secured its engines, descended into the wardroom, threw their hats onto their respective racks, bent their heads together over the fold-out table, and prepared the immediate message that would notify COMDESLANT's chief of staff and chief engineer that Chaser 3 had been tried and was ready to answer all bells.

"Things look better than expected?" Solly asked Ash, once their message had gone to radio.

"Yes," Ash said, after a slight hesitation. "I can't speak from experience, but I'm guessing that most ships do trials first, spend two, three, four weeks making adjustments, modifications, and repairs, do more trials, and then go into commission. Frankly, I've been stunned to see the way DESLANT handled us, but we can give Anson the most credit; he's done a first-class job all around. This ship's tight, clean, and ready, and she runs like a honey. The war, I think, accounts for the fact that the usual honors and ceremonies have been truncated and pressed forward."

"Think we might be given some time off over the weekend?" Hamp asked, showing Ash and Solly the smile of a tomcat. "I had a thought that the three of us might enjoy running up to The Eiseley and meeting a few of the locals while indulging ourselves with modest refreshment as a prelude to light entertainment."

"I think, Mr. Hampton," Ash said slowly, with an acid tone, "that our masters at COMDESLANT are going to stick out their commanding fingers, pinch ensigns by the ears, and snatch them straight down to the fueling facilities with something approaching the accelerated speed of light. And after that, I think we are going to witness any number of otherwise stalwart individuals start barfing up their breakfast as soon as we put to sea. I regret to disappoint you, but I would expect orders to arrive about as soon as our ammo is stowed and our tanks are topped off. The 'locals' are bound to feel deprived by your absence, but there's nothing for it. Let us hope that they find a means to console themselves."

"Oh," Hamp said, "you mean that COMDESLANT hasn't been extensively impressed by all of our hard work?"

"You can bet on it," Ash said.

"How will they notify us?" Solly asked. "Message or messenger?"

"Message," Ash said. "With radio up and operating, by message. I'll wait for it. You two go ahead and turn in because we'll probably pipe reveille at 0300 in order to get down to the foot of Casco Bay by sunrise. I won't put money on it, but I'm guessing they'll want us as soon as the net tenders are able to open the gates so that we can get up the channel."

"*That* early?" Hamp said.

"That early," Ash said.

Without hesitation or much more in the way of conversation, Solly and Hamp peeled off their uniforms and turned in for the night. Ash, leaving word with the radioman about where to find him, went up to the pilot house, bent over the chart table, and once more studied the location of the minefields guarding the conglomeration of ships he knew to be anchored in Casco Bay. Then, reassured about mine belt distributions, he turned to examining the locations of individual buoys and the anchorages, one of which he imagined that COMDESLANT would designate for his use. At 2215 that night, when the radioman found him and handed him the expected message, Ash was still in the pilot house measuring distances on the chart with a pair of dividers. The message when handed to him carried no frills:

Pending operational assignment, proceed Casco Bay. Moor, Buoy 16, 0715, for fuel, water, and ammunition. Report completion by signal light.

Ash read the message twice, ordered the deck watch to sound reveille at 0300, and turned in, thinking that it had been a long day and knowing in his bones that another would follow.

At 0300 on the dot, Samarango piped reveille for the crew. Half an hour later, after a hurried sweep-down, the crew went to breakfast.

"Joy 'em," Watts announced as he served out their mess trays "'cause these is the las' fresh egg y'all likely to gets. We'se goin' ta da powder kind right quick after today."

Ash set the Special Sea and Anchor Detail at 0415, and 15 minutes later, Solly climbed up to the bridge to tell him that Chaser 3 was ready for sea with all hands at their stations for leaving port.

The line handling that morning went off without a hitch. Pushed by a light breeze, the chaser gently drew away from the dock. Then, by backing her smartly on one engine while going ahead on the other, Ash quickly turned the ship in Anson's boat basin. Speaking with a steady tone into the voice tube, Ash ordered all engines ahead one third with turns for 3 knots and started down the river toward the bay. To Ash and the crew's surprise, an immediate cheer went up from the beach. Beneath a flood light attached to the boat house, the builder, Mr. Anson, had assembled his entire work force to witness Chaser 3's departure, and following a tradition that Ash imagined went all the way back to the Vikings, the collected shipwrights were saluting and cheering the fruit of their labors as she made her way to the sea.

"Run up the Bravo Zulu for 'Well done,'" Ash called to Glick, and within a matter of seconds, the signalman bent on the hoist and ran it up to the yardarm, once more eliciting a cheer from the men they were leaving behind. With the lookouts calling out the buoys, Ash took the chaser downriver and out into the bay.

Considering how calm the bay had been the previous day, Ash had imagined that it might stir up like hell. Fortunately, to his surprise—and to the relief of the petty officers who didn't like the thought of having to take on everything from provisions to ammunition with a green crew of seasick sailors—the morning sea continued to be utterly tranquil, with hardly the hump of a wave anywhere in sight. It was a wonder; there could be no doubt about it. An hour later, when they finally made the sea buoy that heralded their approach to the swept channel and sighted the net tender preparing to open the entrance to let them pass through, the dawn had just started to break, an Aurorean blush gracing the eastern sky. And then, without undue hesitation, Ash faced his first major trial of seamanship.

Owing to the lowly rank he'd held aboard the *Parker*, Ash had never been on the bridge when his captain had moored the destroyer. Instead, he had been stationed on the fantail of the ship, supervising line handlers. There he had gleaned what he could of the procedure by glancing up the sides of the ship, catching glimpses of the ship's boat crew as they put a man on the buoy, passed the line, and then hooked up finally by means of shackling one of their anchor chains to the buoy. Nevertheless, only days before, Ash had pored over the appropriate entries in Knight's *Modern Seamanship* until he thought that he knew them by heart. So, first finding and then approaching buoy 16, he ordered the ship's wherry into the water with one of Samarango's green seamen aboard to make the connection; then, with the boat crew rowing like they were in a race, Ash moved Chaser 3, to within 10 yards of the buoy and held her in position while the wherry sent the seaman scrambling up the side of the buoy and onto its top. With Samarango barking orders from the fo'c'sle and Ash holding the ship in position by means of light adjustments to the engines, the messenger was passed, a larger line with a hook was pulled over, and finally, the anchor chain, detached from the anchor, was pulled over by the seaman and shackled to the strong steel ring on the top of the buoy.

Ash felt a sudden wave of relief. From the start, he'd imagined that someone, somewhere, on one of the surrounding ships, some observer designated by COMDESLANT, had been watching and judging his every move, and his worst fear—that the ship would have to attempt the moor multiple times before she could finally hook up—drifted away in an instant.

"Mr. Solomon," Ash said, speaking firmly to the pilot house through the voice tube, "pass a 'Well Done' to the crew. I consider the moor to have been made in a manner smart, shipshape, and seamanlike."

"Aye, aye, Captain," Solly responded, registering precisely the kind of support that Ash expected. Strict attention to duty, no frills, no implied horseplay, merely an order given and a straight answer that it would be carried out. On top of the relief and satisfaction he felt for having made his first moor without trouble, Ash felt an additional boost to his morale in the belief that Solly was going to make a good exec.

With signal lights flashing back and forth between harbor control and Glick, not ten minutes passed before Ash received word that a yard oiler would soon be alongside to top off Chaser 3's tanks. From the bridge, Ash called down to Samarango to stand ready, and when he looked up, he could already see the oiler, a mile distant, coming out to them from the fueling piers located somewhere along the reaches of Portland's inner harbor.

They needed less than an hour to top off with fuel, the chief petty officer commanding the yard oiler descending from his tiny bridge onto the well deck in order to exchange words with Chief Stobb while the ship was alongside and the transfer was underway. After the oiler disengaged and pulled away, the chief came to the bridge to report "a full consignment of fuel taken on." Then, almost casually, he added grimly, "Don't know if there's anything in it Cap'n, but that chief on the oiler told me the krauts sank a freighter last night, 'bout 20 miles out, down off Portsmouth."

"That puts them right on our doorstep," Ash said. "If that's true, we ought to see some message traffic about it pretty quick."

And they did, not 20 minutes after Stobb passed the news to Ash and at about the same time a tug pushed a water tender up alongside, Solly and Stobb once more supervising as the tender filled their tanks with a fresh water supply.

The freighter—3,500 tons, relatively small, and riding independently and largely empty on its way down from Halifax en route to Baltimore—had gone down in less than seven minutes, taking five of the crew with her while 16 managed to scramble into the only lifeboat they'd had time to launch. By pure chance, they'd been found and towed in not four hours after the sinking by a minesweeper that came across them while headed for upkeep to a Rockland yard farther up the coast.

As soon as he'd read the message, Ash passed it to Solly and Hamp, and then he delegated Samarango and Chief Stobb to inform the crew.

"For better or worse," Ash said, "it's bound to grip their attention, tighten their resolve, and give them an additional motivation for remaining alert on watch." He was right.

Provisioning, also from a lighter, commenced as soon as the water tender drew away, Watts seeing to it that they took on as much fresh bread, as many potatoes and fresh vegetables as they had room for, and enough hamburger to serve the men spaghetti for supper. "Tomorrow'll be soon 'nough," he told Ash, "fo' me to 'gin serve 'em that can salmon, an' powder egg. They most won't like it at firs', Cap'n, but dey ain't seen what I can do with it yet. It'll go down good, my cookin'. Den dey like that spam better den t-bone steak."

"Watts," Ash said, "you've got an uphill climb ahead of you."

"You jus' watch me climb, Cap'n Sir. Dem boy think dey die and gone ta glory."

Ash grinned; he couldn't help himself.

With Chaser 3's galley spaces filled to overflowing, bags of fresh bread hanging from the overhead, and two crates of onions crammed into a sheltered corner of the lazarette, a tug removed the provisioning barge. Around 1300 that afternoon, after a sandwich and a cup of coffee, Solly came to Ash in the mess deck and reported that an ammunition barge equipped with a portable crane was approaching.

"Had a look through the binoculars, Captain," Solly said. "Looks to me like the ammo barge is carrying a chief warrant officer, a salty chief warrant by the looks of him."

"Solly," Ash said, "if you ever find a chief warrant officer that isn't salty, let me know. We could probably charge admission to see him. Those guys are usually 40-year-career men who would rather die in service than step a foot ashore."

As the barge drew abreast of them and threw over its heaving lines, Hamp joined them. Together, they returned the warrant officer's salute as the barge passed over its mooring lines, edged in against their fenders, and tied up.

The warrant officer, clad in a boiler suit and wearing a cap whose cover looked like it might have been snatched straight from a grease bucket, the cap device of which looked like it had been constructed of chipped barnacles and glued back together, seemed a bulky man but a short one. As he stood, hands on hips, looking the trio up and down, Ash imagined that he could detect a smile, not of derision but of mild disbelief on the man's face. How, the man seemed to be wondering, could the United States Navy send a trio of spring chickens like Ash, Solly, and Hamp out to command anything? To the chief, Ash thought, they must have looked like peach-cheeked midshipmen going for their first sail in a knockabout or a dingy.

"Chief," Ash said, "if you'd care to step aboard, I think we can offer you a decent cup of coffee."

"Thank you, Captain," the chief said, his fists still doubled against his hips, "but I'd better not. I've got a green boy on the crane this afternoon, and I don't want to risk him dropping one of them depth charges on your deck and blowing us all to hell."

"I take your point," Ash said. "Well, then, we're ready when you are. Mr. Hampton here and Gunner Teague will work with you on the inventory, and I'll want all three of you to double check the lot numbers on each item. I don't want a slip up, you'll understand; I don't want us going to sea with the wrong caliber ammunition for the right guns." Ash tried to sound jocular, knowing it wouldn't do to ruffle the warrant's feathers.

"Good idea," the man said. "And one more thing, Captain."

"Yes?" Ash said.

"I'll hope this Gunner Teague of yours is a dead shot because we've only got ten rounds for that 3"/23 caliber gun you're carrying. Foul up at the factory somewhere; they misdirected our consignment to Staten Island, so what we're giving you is sound and stable, but its World War I vintage, and it's the most we've got. Couple of minesweepers took near everything we had last week."

Ten rounds! Ash thought, a nasty burning sensation invading the interior of his stomach. Ten rounds! Ten rounds for Chaser 3's main battery while any U-boat they were likely to meet would be carrying well over two hundred rounds for its 4-inch deck gun! They'd be sitting ducks. It was the war, of course, but that didn't make it easy to swallow. Some twit sitting somewhere in Pennsylvania, or Indiana, or even the hills of Kentucky had screwed up monstrously through inattention, ignorance, or plain indifference, and screwed *them* in the process. It couldn't be helped; it had to be lived with and somehow overcome until whatever orders they were given took them into a port where an adequate supply of 3-inch could be taken on and stowed in the magazine.

"Nothing for it, Chief," Ash said, his jaw hardening as he said so. "I guess we'll have to fight, if fight we do, on a shoelace."

"I've brought you plenty extra for the 20mm," the chief said. "And I've found you a fairly new .50-caliber machine gun that'll need a good cleanup."

"Thanks," Ash said, "that's something." But was it, really? On the surface, beyond 2,000 yards, Ash knew that the Oerlikons would be ineffective, and the .50-caliber even less so. As anti-aircraft guns, Ash knew them to be much better, but the thought of the *Luftwaffe* attacking the ship anywhere along the Atlantic coast almost made Ash break into laughter. Well, they'd do what they'd do because it would be what they'd have to do, and then, they'd try to make the best of it.

"All right, Chief," Ash said, "let's get to it."

Carefully but with reasonable dispatch, the little crane began transferring depth charges onto Chaser 3's fantail, where Hamp and young Cornfeld, Teague's designated torpedoman, began removing the detonators from their cases, setting them on safety, and inserting them into the barrel-like, explosive casings of the depth charges. Forward, meanwhile, under Solly's watchful eye, gun ammunition, small arms ammunition, and pyrotechnics began coming over the side, where nervous sailors ramrodded by Teague and Samarango carried them gently to the ready boxes behind the guns or struck them below to their designated magazines. Throughout the evolution, the smoking lamp remained out, and from time to time, Ash could see that handling the ammunition made this or that sailor nervous. But by 1600, the job was complete, and the ship had returned to what would become its standard plan of the day with evening chow to go down at 1700.

As soon as the final ammunition inventory had been checked and double checked and the appropriate papers signed in triplicate, the warrant officer and his barge crane departed. At that point, standing on the main deck across from the pilot house, Ash called up to Glick, who looked down to him from the signal platform.

"By signal light to COMDESLANT: 'Chaser 3 *is ready for sea.*'"

Glick leapt to the ladder, climbed to the bridge, and sent the message by flashing light. Not 30 minutes later, as Ash sat in the wardroom, once more going over the inventory, Hamp dropped down to report what looked to him like a fairly well-appointed gig approaching from the direction of the inner harbor.

"I was on deck and saw her when she first started out," Hamp said, "and she's headed straight for us without a single deviation since she first appeared."

"That sounds like DESLANT sending us our orders by messenger," Ash said. "I'll come up."

Fifty yards out, the gig cut its speed, allowing the rooster tail behind it to subside while the bow hook emerged from the boat's well and scrambled forward to hail the ship. Then, after Hamp signaled the ship's permission to come alongside, the gig's coxswain whipped the small boat in so that an ensign had only to reach across the gunwales in order to hand Ash a sealed packet.

"Orders, by my guess," the ensign grinned, saluting Ash and wishing him luck, and in the next second, the boat's coxswain swung the boat away at full throttle, heading straight back toward the inner harbor.

Back in the wardroom, seated at the table with Solly on one side of him and Hamp on the other, Ash broke open the packet and began to read.

"Pipe reveille at 0400," Ash said after a few minutes of careful study, "with breakfast to go down at 0430, and I'll want the Special Sea and Anchor Detail set at 0530 so that we can be underway by 0600. We're assigned to be the single escort for an empty tanker and three freighters making for Hoboken. One of those freighters appears to be slow, so the convoy speed is set at 8 knots, and we'll run a zig-zag pattern all the way down. Just off the top of my head, and considering the fact that we'll have to clear around Cape Cod, I'm guessing that we'll have to go about 400 miles, which means something more than a two-day trip. Once we see the ships into Raritan Bay, we're released and ordered to proceed to the Coast Guard piers on Staten Island where a full consignment of 3-inch ammo is supposed to be waiting for us."

"Generous of them," Hamp said.

"Very," said Ash. "Let's just hope we don't run into a U-boat before we get there. Somewhere out there on the way down, Hamp, you can warn Teague that we'll test our guns, the Oerlikons and the .50-caliber; I won't waste any of the 3-inch until we have some rounds to spare."

Hamp indicated his agreement.

"Now," Ash said, "we haven't talked about the next subject yet, but this is the time, so pay me close attention. Once we pass the sea buoy tomorrow, I intend to set Condition III watches and start training the two of you and Samarango up to the point where you can be considered qualified Officers of the Deck for Fleet Steaming. Needless to say, you'll have a lot to learn, so for the time being, I'll swing a hammock in the pilot house and sleep there when I think that I can. The essential point for you to understand is this: I'm the man who's responsible for the ship and the lives of the crew. That's what it means to be in command, and I will expect both of you to understand that and act accordingly. I'll give you the con once we get out there in the morning, but if you spot a tin can in the water, a ship on the horizon, a whale, a log, or a U-boat—anything, day or night—and it doesn't matter if I'm asleep, sick, or even wounded, you are to report it to me at once. And that goes as well for anything like an engineering casualty, an equipment failure, or even a dust up between members of the crew that happens aboard. Even course and speed changes are to be reported to me. From here on out, the only thing that can relieve me of my responsibility for this ship and relieve you of your responsibility to me is if I am killed in action, at which point Solly will have to step up and assume command, and if Solly is killed, Hamp, you've got it. Am I making myself clear?"

Ash had sobered them; he'd meant to, and he could see from their eyes that his point had been made.

"All right," he said to Solly, "let's get Bell up to the chart room, pull out the charts, and lay out the track so that we can see where we'll be going, and then, you can pass the word to the crew."

And thus, they prepared for sea.

9

On February 22, 1942, alone and manned by a half-green crew, one thousand yards out ahead of three freighters and a tanker riding high, Chaser 3 sortied from Portland and went to war, Lieutenant (j.g.) Ashford Miller USNR, commanding.

On the bridge, muffled in foul-weather gear against the harsh winter cold, Ash ordered sonar's echo sounder to be lowered so that it could start pinging. Then, after coming around to the southeast while still under the shelter of Cushing Island, and with only the first faint traces of dawn beginning to break far out on the eastern horizon, Ash turned to Hamp, who had drawn the early morning watch.

"Go below and make a quick run through, stem to stern," Ash ordered. "This isn't going to be like yesterday. We've got a sea running out there, and we're going to meet it the minute we come out from under the lee of this island that's protecting us. Be quick, but make sure everything is secured, and warn Watts to stand by for rolling in the galley. I'm guessing that you've got about ten minutes, so go."

Hamp disappeared down the ladder onto the main deck. Seconds later, Ash watched him descend down the Booby hatch into the fo'c'sle. In the meantime, periodically shooting bearings on known lights and recognizable points of land, Ash mentally tracked his position, checking regularly with Bell, who was taking readings of his own from the compass in the pilot house and then plotting them on the chart to record the ship's progress.

"How long before we're out from under the lee?" Ash called down.

"I'd give us another couple of minutes, Cap'n," Bell replied.

Hamp climbed back onto the bridge as Ash shut the voice pipe.

"All secure, Sir," Hamp said, "except for those two crates of onions in the lazarette. Someone left the keeper bars sitting on the deck, so I reinstalled 'em."

Watts had served the crew scrambled eggs laced with fried spam and onions for breakfast that morning, and Ash imagined that Denison, the mess assistant who'd been sent to fetch the onions, had left the keeper bars off the storage racks in his haste to return to the galley. "Mention it to Watts?" Ash asked

"Yes, Sir; he said he'd take care of it."

"Whoa!" Ash laughed, suddenly reaching for a handrail as Chaser 3 took a hard snap roll to starboard. Equally surprised by the motion, Hamp only kept his footing by throwing an arm around the post that supported the signal light, but when the ship snapped back and fell into the trough, he'd prepared and set his feet for it, and he managed to stand, legs spread, without having to clutch the post. From below, both fore and aft, the two men could hear the crew's reaction, shouts of alarm mixed with the kinds of raucous laughter that usually accompanied a thrilling carnival ride. The consternation, Ash assumed, arose from the boots, the laughter from the petty officers. The ship rolled back to starboard once more, and Ash knew that the heavy roll, a roll that he estimated to be 30 degrees, would continue until they rounded Cape Elizabeth and turned south so as to start down the coast; that, he hoped, would give them a following sea. That they would continue to roll, Ash felt certain, but with the sea behind them, coming down from the northeast, their roll might be slightly reduced, offset by whatever yawing developed as the ship began to pitch. No matter how it developed, Ash knew that they weren't going to be comfortable.

With enough light to see by and after checking astern to make sure that the convoy was maintaining its spacing and distance, Ash once more turned to Hamp.

"Take a good look to port," he said. "I'd say that those waves hitting us from the northeast must measure about 8 to 12 feet. That's what a State 5 sea state looks like, and the number goes up or down from there. Have a good look and commit what you see to memory. And then Mr. Hampton, when you're ready, I'll give you the con, and in about 15 minutes, once we're a little farther out, we'll start to zig-zag, and you can practice giving orders to the helm and judging how well he turns."

"Captain," Hamp said, suddenly showing Ash a wan face and a strange expression, "shit, Sir, I think I'm going to be sick."

"Barf bucket's right beside you, tied to the rail. Just go right ahead, Hamp, whenever you feel like it. I don't feel so hot myself." And Ash didn't. It was the result of coming straight out into the trough after a more than hearty breakfast, and Ash knew that he couldn't do a single thing about it. He'd known from the start that chasers rolled and rolled heavily even in relatively moderate seas, and Chaser 3 was obviously going to be no different from the rest of her type in that regard. Fight it he must, and fight it he would, but considering the amount of time he would have to spend on the bridge, he counted himself lucky. Sleepless he might be, might have to be, but fresh air was often the best medicine for seasickness—fresh air, and the ability to look ahead with a clear eye and see what was coming.

Fifteen minutes later, Ash called down through the voice pipe and announced to the pilot house, "This is the captain speaking; Mr. Hampton has the con," and Hamp, after already having thrown up twice, stepped to the pipe, mustered as strong a voice as he could project, and announced, "This is Mr. Hampton, I have the con, steer course 165 magnetic and make turns for 8 knots," and heard the words repeated to him from below. After ordering Glick to raise the appropriate signal flags, Ash gave Hamp the order to commence their designated zig-zag pattern. Their zig-zag would prolong the voyage, but in so far as Ash was concerned, by hopefully confusing a U-boat commander's firing solutions, it might give them the best possible chance for avoiding a torpedo—unless, by some amazing stroke of luck, Gomez happened to stumble onto a sonar contact and give Ash the chance to hold down, damage, or even sink an attacking U-boat with depth charges. The possibility seemed unlikely, if not downright unthinkable. Ash knew that he was out there in Chaser 3 doing a job alone that, at a minimum, at least three or even four escorts might be hard pressed to accomplish. But at the moment, caught once more with its pants down, the United States Navy didn't have the escorts to send, so they sent what they had; it was the best they could do, and Ash intended to give it the best that was in him.

Before Solly came up to relieve for the 0800–1200 watch, Hamp had gone to the bucket twice more, but he remained game. His head nevertheless sometimes hanging, he encouraged the lookouts who were each as sick as he was, and tried to set an upbeat tone, while giving the helm the frequent changes of course that their zig-zag pattern demanded.

"And you, Solly," Ash asked as his executive officer climbed onto the bridge, "how are you feeling this fine salty morning?"

"Not fine, Captain," Solly replied, his face pale. "I've upchucked a couple of times, but I'm starting to get a handle on it. Seems better up here than down below."

"What's it like down there?"

"Eggs, spam, and onions everywhere," Solly said. "Stinks like hell, Sir, and the decks are a mess. They're even throwing up on the bulkheads, some of the petty officers as well as the boots, but Samarango and Stobb, in between wiping a few faces down with wet towels, are also making them clean up their mess. We set a rule, each man cleans up for himself, no matter how sick he is, no matter what the sea state, and no waiting."

"Good man," Ash said. "They won't be happy, but it has to be done. As we knew from the start, they'll have to work through it. There's no other choice."

Prior to rounding Cape Elizabeth, noticing that the smallest of the freighters had already begun to have trouble keeping up, Ash cut the convoy's speed to 7 and a half knots and reorganized the ships into a tight box at 500-yard intervals; then, with the maneuver complete and after ordering their turn south, he resumed the formation's zig-zag. By that time, Solly had relieved Hamp, and with the turn, the ship's roll had blissfully reduced itself to a mere 20 degrees. Nevertheless, as the chaser began to yaw and pitch before a following sea, the boots in particular had reluctantly discovered yet another form of motion that they found no less discomforting than the roll.

Solly, Ash was pleased to notice, standing with his legs set apart and his feet planted firmly on the deck, quickly learned how to absorb the pitch and roll with the flexibility in his knees. While he might have thrown up his breakfast before coming on watch, he managed to hold the malaise in check, and his color actually began to improve once he became involved with his duties on the bridge. It wasn't that Hamp had been in any way deficient—he hadn't been—but Solly, Ash realized, showed signs of being a quick study, and Ash imagined that he would develop into an excellent watch stander.

At 1020 that morning, with the convoy adjusted to the zig-zag and plowing south at a steady speed, Ash ordered Solly to maneuver the ship out onto the formation's port beam. There, after notifying all four ships by means of a flag hoist that he intended to test his guns, Ash sounded the alarm for General Quarters and sent the men to their battle stations. It was not, in Ash's estimation, a very successful evolution. With two thirds of the crew seasick, they were slow—minutes too slow to suit the ship's needs—and Ash knew it and determined that he would correct it. Still, with all battle stations finally manned and ready, he went ahead with the gun shoot, expending ten rounds from each of the Oerlikons to prove Teague's competence in making them ready, and another ten or 15 rounds from the .50-caliber to make sure that it, too, could perform if needed. Throughout the exercise, which didn't last 20 minutes, here and there, this or that sailor still threw up, necessitating a quick wash down over the main deck. Meanwhile, below decks according to Hamp at least three more men had turned to with swabs and scrub buckets. And when, finally, the clean-up ended and the men had returned to their bunks, Ash once more sounded the alarm, brought the crew to General Quarters, and continued repeating the evolution until 1500 that afternoon when, finally, he thought the men had achieved a speed that battle would demand. And then Ash spoke to them over the ship's address system.

"This is the captain speaking," he announced. "It does not matter that you are sick; it does not matter that the sea is rough. If you are not fast enough going to General Quarters, the Germans will kill us." Ash paused to let the idea sink in and then said, "That is all."

Ash did not go down to the mess decks for lunch that day. Instead, around 1130, Denison brought a spam sandwich and a cup of coffee to the bridge, and on that combination, mustard slathered over the meat, Ash made his meal. Samarango then relieved Solly, and an hour later, after assuring himself that Samarango, enlisted boatswain's mate though he might be, knew exactly what he was doing without Ash having to watch his every move, Ash went down to the chart house, climbed into the hammock that he immediately slung, and managed to sleep for an hour before Bell woke him so that he could go back to the bridge and order the next General Quarters drill.

Around 1600 that afternoon, at about the same time that Hamp relieved Samarango as the junior officer of the deck and with the ship screening out ahead of the convoy, Pierre, the watch stander sitting before the sonar scope, reported a strong contact several hundred yards off the starboard bow. Immediately Ash ordered the quartermaster to examine the chart for sunken wrecks on the reported bearing, but before the man could report back to him, the contact broke up. This led Gomez, who had leapt into sonar, to classify the contact as a probable school of fish, and Ash was satisfied that Gomez had made the right call.

By that time, Ash's tiny convoy had steamed nearly 60 miles south of Portland and into a position several miles to the southeast of Portsmouth. No sooner had Hamp relieved and Samarango gone off the watch and the sonar contact broken up than the port lookout had shouted that he'd seen a man in the water, two, perhaps three hundred yards off the port bow. Immediately, Ash raised his binoculars to scan the distance, reasoning that it might be a survivor from the freighter which the Portland petty officer had reported sunk off Portsmouth on the previous day. With the entire watch intensely focused on scanning the waves, they indeed spotted the man, rising and falling as each succeeding swell passed beneath him, but when they changed course and drew alongside, they discovered at once that the man was not a survivor. He was stone dead, riding like an inert cork within the confines of his kapok life jacket, his right arm blown off below the elbow, his chest and abdomen perforated by steel splinters, one of which protruded from his boated body like a needle in a pincushion.

With grappling hooks, Samarango and three deckhands hoisted the corpse aboard, grotesque evidence of the immediate danger that all of them faced. By Ash's orders, Samarango encased the remains in canvas, sewed up the seam, and stowed the cadaver aft in the space between the depth-charge racks so that the body could make its final transit for delivery to the mortuary detail on Staten Island. Most of the crew, but not all, had filed past the corpse before

Samarango had wrapped it into canvas. In some cases, the sight had added revulsion to the sea sickness that most of them were already enduring. In others, it merely added anger and awe to what they had already seen on the trawler. In all cases, the effect had been sobering. The men were no longer safe and secure on inland American streets and farms and they knew it. They knew, too, that aside from the men with whom they served, they were utterly alone.

During the first of the evening dog watches, the 1600–1800, Ash ordered the formation onto a more southeasterly course, his intention being to clear Cape Cod during the night with 10 miles to spare. And then, while bracing himself against the rail, almost inadvertently his mind drifted from the corpse and back to Yarmouth, to the afternoon he'd spent with Claire Morris. *Quality time*, he thought; that's what the wardroom on the *Parker* used to call quality time—time spent with a nice-looking woman in a comfortable place with enough conversation to lend the moment spice. Ash wondered if he would ever get back to Yarmouth, if he would ever see Claire Morris again. Then, taking a grip on himself, he dismissed the idea. Such thoughts, he knew, could be distracting, and out there in the Atlantic with a spindrift blowing off the waves, distractions became dangers that could get a man killed. Suddenly, Ash found himself wondering if the dead seaman on the fantail had been distracted by something in the moment he'd been hit, but as Ash knew, the idea didn't bear thinking about.

At dusk, even though distant lighthouses on the beach allowed them to fix their position by careful piloting, Ash nevertheless ordered Bell to bring up his sextant; together, the two of them shot three stars, after which, leaving Hamp alone with the lookouts, they dropped down to the chart house to work out their calculations, both men doing the math jointly but on separate check sheets. Bell, Ash discovered, worked fast and accurately, a little faster than Ash, but when the job was complete, their calculations jibed. The fix was not pinpoint, but the tiny triangle that resulted was close enough to confirm Bell's piloting, and for Ash, that was what mattered.

"Well," Ash said with a slightly disappointed grimace, "it isn't perfect, but it'll have to do. Responsibility for the gap has to be mine. I'll need to rock the sextant with a sharper eye."

"This is already a lot better than the last navigator I worked with," Bell said flatly. "His triangles were half an inch on a side, Captain."

"Thanks," Ash said, "but I'll try to do better in the morning. Who's the bearing taker up here tonight?"

"Rollo," Bell said. "He's the boot from Kenosha, Cap'n, the kid with the red hair. I gave him some training on the beach, before we commissioned, and I went over the chart with him this afternoon. He's sick like the rest of 'em, but if he can keep his stomach down, he ought to be fine. He's a sharp kid, only about 19, but he understands how to time the period of the lighthouses so's to identify 'em correctly. I think he'll do fine and make us a good striker. Rest of the time, of course, Samarango will have him on the deck force."

"Good enough," Ash said. "I'll check on him and let you know how he does when you come up to shoot morning stars."

To Ash, the lights on the beach, lighthouses as well as business and street lighting both, seemed criminal. Everything, he knew, from the tip of Maine to the last Florida key should have been blacked out totally. Instead, so as not to induce panic among the coastal communities, the United States of America remained fully lit, the bright glow ashore throwing any ship at sea into perfect silhouette for whatever U-boat that might be stalking it. It was another of those things over which Ash had absolutely no control, and he regretted it. With the Nazis virtually at their throats, with ships burning and men dying right at their front doors, the Americans on the beach were sitting in perfect comfort, probably with their feet propped up, drinking tea, coffee, or something stronger, listening to their favorite radio programs, living fat, dumb, and happy, in perfect ignorance of the snakes that were waiting to strike them. Would they panic if they knew the truth? Would they turn tail and run if they could see the dead body that Ash was bringing in? Ash didn't think so, but the decision to inform them of the danger, he knew, had never been his to make.

During the night, the sea settled to something Ash judged to be approaching a State 4. Gradually, their roll subsided slightly to a more comfortable 15 degrees, and the ship seemed to pitch less. Solly stood the second dog watch followed by Samarango for the evening watch, and then Hamp once more came up to stand the deck for the mid-watch before Solly came back again for the 0400–0800, and thus, the ship fell into a pattern.

It was the early watch that Ash had always disliked the most because it was the watch that most tested his ability to stay awake. During those last dark hours of the morning, his system, for whatever reason, most wanted to shut down and sleep. That first morning at sea proved to be no different, so with Solly on the deck and Hamp already turned in, Ash took himself in hand. He'd been on the bridge for most of the preceding 24 hours, long enough to grow fatigued and know it.

"You've read and signed my night orders," Ash said to Solly, "so carry them out, keep a sharp eye, and call me at once should anything develop. I'm going to sack out until Bell wakes me to shoot stars." And with that, he went down to the chart house, climbed into his hammock, and managed to sleep for more than an hour before Bell woke him for morning stars.

The star fix Ash and Bell shot that morning turned out to be far more precise than the one Ash had shot the night before.

"Good one," Bell said. "Looks to me, Cap'n, like Nathaniel Bowditch would have been proud to have shot this one."

Ash laughed. "Don't I wish," he said. "How do you come to know about Bowditch?"

"Quartermaster's school," Bell said. "One of our instructors knew all about him. That chief had pretty much memorized *The American Practical Navigator*. According to him, Bowditch once had nothin' more than a two-minute break in the clouds to shoot a fix going into Boston or New York—I can't remember for sure—and he not only shot three stars that quick but worked out a perfect three-point fix in a matter of minutes. To hear that chief tell it, he'd pulled off about the greatest feat of navigation anyone had ever seen."

Ash knew that Bell's story about Nathaniel Bowditch might or might not have been a myth, but there could be no question about Bowditch's competence. The man had been a legend for more than half a century.

"I think," Ash said, "that if we can navigate with this degree of success, I'll be perfectly willing to leave the glory to the man. I'm going to stay happy if we can merely keep from running aground."

This time it was Bell's turn to laugh.

During the night, the small freighter on the after, inland corner of their square formation had fallen behind to the point where she was out of position and behind by more than half a mile. Ash had already sent up a flag hoist in order to urge her to rejoin, but by the beginning of the morning watch, the freighter had not responded. Ash waited until Samarango had relieved Solly, and then, having expended his patience with the merchant ship, he turned and spoke the order.

"Boats, come around, crank on turns, and let's go herd this oblivious sheep back into the fold."

Immediately, Samarango called for left full rudder and 12 knots, and within less time than Ash had imagined, they'd reversed course and started to pitch as they scudded north into an oncoming sea.

"She's more maneuverable than I thought she'd be," Samarango said to Ash without taking his eyes from the waves now breaking over the bow and throwing green water down the sides.

"She is," Ash said, "and far more maneuverable than a destroyer. That's bound to make life easier for us."

Minutes later, once more reversing course and taking off turns, Samarango slid in alongside the lagging merchantman's beam where Ash lifted his megaphone and asked to speak to the captain of the vessel. The captain of the freighter, a tall, thin man wearing steel-rimmed glasses and an old derby, was none too swift in coming to the wing of his bridge. When he arrived, finally, and looked down at Ash with a tight-lipped expression that clearly conveyed his contempt for Chaser 3, Ash anticipated a stubborn, uncooperative response.

"Good morning, Captain," Ash called up to the man. "You need to put on turns and rejoin, or I won't be able to give you my best protection."

The captain of the *Orion Light*, for that was the ship's name, looked down at Ash and smirked. "Oy, sonny," the man shouted back in what sounded to Ash like a Newcastle accent, "ol the pertection tha' puppy o your can give ain't worth spit."

"*Oy*," Ash called back, mocking the man's tone but without heat, "you put on turns and catch up with the convoy, Captain, or this puppy is going to leave you to steam independently. There's a U-boat in the area; it sank a freighter about your size two nights back, and we picked up the corpse on our fantail from that vessel yesterday. That ship went down in seven minutes and took five men with her. You think about it, Captain, and make your choice." And with that, Ash turned to Samarango. "Twelve knots, Boats, and take us straight back up abeam of the rest of the convoy."

Looking astern a few minutes later after Chaser 3 slid into position and resumed her zig-zag on the beam of an empty oiler, Ash saw two or three puffs of black smoke emerge from the stack of the lagging freighter. Within an hour, the merchantman was back in position, and that was where she remained for the rest of the transit.

Later in the morning, after he had seen to a thorough scrub down below decks, checked the spaces to make certain that nothing had broken loose and gone adrift, and finished the paperwork that Ash had asked him to complete, Solly climbed to the bridge.

"Radio patched a shore station into the mess decks while the crew was eating breakfast," he said. "I guess this battle for the Bataan peninsula in the Philippines is becoming fierce, and it doesn't look like we can do much for them other than offer encouragement."

"First Pearl, then Wake, now Bataan," Ash said, shaking his head. "It doesn't look good."

"No," Solly said, "it doesn't."

"Anything else in the news?"

"Not much. I think Gable issued a statement about Carole Lombard. I gather he's pretty broken up."

"I don't know who wouldn't be," Ash said. "I saw her in *My Man Godfrey*, and she was stunning. I'd guess she was one of the most beautiful women in Hollywood. How long had they been married?"

71

"I think she was married to William Powell first," Solly said. "She'd only been married to Gable for a couple of years."

"Pity," Ash said.

"Tragic."

"Change of subject," Ash said. "How did breakfast go down with the crew?

"Watts fed 'em oatmeal. Watts said it would stick to their ribs and settle their stomachs, but only about half the crew showed up. The rest of them are still sick, still throwing up, and sticking to their bunks except when they have to go on watch."

"My guess," Ash said, "is that they'll begin coming out of it about the time we make the Lower Bay and start up into The Narrows. I expect a few more to be sick the next time we sortie, but after that, I think most of them will find their sea legs. What about you?"

"I won't say that I'm in the pink," Solly joked, "but I've got it under control."

"And Hamp?"

"I think he tossed his supper last night, but he's doing fine this morning. Said his last watch cured him. He's down in the wardroom at the moment, clutching the table with one hand and writing out an expenditure report for the ammo we test fired yesterday."

Throughout the remainder of that day, save for the sighting of some floating garbage in the water, a pair of porpoises, and an empty oil drum which Teague sank by means of five rounds from the .50-caliber, the lookouts spotted nothing of consequence. Sonar remained equally tranquil so that the biggest problem Gomez faced came with keeping his watch standers awake and alert. In radio, the only messages that Polaski had to handle came as weather alerts for seas so distant that Ash barely gave them a thought. Nevertheless, it remained cold on the bridge, the bite coming off the beach west of Nantucket clawing at Ash's face with such force that he put his pipe into his pocket and pulled his woolen scarf up over the bridge of his nose.

During the afternoon, with Hamp on the bridge and once more feeling fit, Ash went to the chart room, pulled off his heavy weather gear, threw himself into his hammock, and slept for three hours straight, Hamp only waking him once to report a fishing trawler crossing port to starboard, 5 miles distant, heading apparently for New London. At 1530, as directed, Hamp had sent the messenger to wake Ash, and after once more tugging on his foul weather gear, feeling only slightly more rested than before he'd gone down, Ash climbed back onto the bridge.

"Can't say for sure, Captain," Hamp said, "but it looks to me like the sea is calming down to something between States 3 and 4. We're still rolling but only about 12 degrees either side of center line."

"The boys below will be thrilled," Ash said.

"I'm thrilled, no question about it," Hamp laughed. "Didn't like being sick. Think I'll skip it from now on."

"Wise of you," Ash said. "Very wise. Anything else going on?"

"Nothing. We've had nothing but quiet up here since you turned in, nothing but this frigid wind that's been blowing over us the whole time. I can't for the life of me see how we can have fierce wind and a calmer sea at the same time."

"I'd guess it might have something to do with the Gulf Stream," Ash said. "That wind feels like it's coming down straight from Canada, but the currents might be coming up from Florida, and that might account for the difference."

"Another question, if you don't mind, Sir."

"Shoot," Ash said.

"Does this convoy have such a thing as a commodore riding one of those merchant ships? And I thought too that they were supposed to be putting Navy gun crews on merchants, but not a one of these carries a gun of any kind."

"At the moment," Ash said, "I doubt that the Navy has enough guns to go around. From what Mr. Anson told me, I think we were lucky to get the old 3"/23 that they've given us. I'm guessing that the last one built probably came out of the factory in 1918. In time, ships like the ones we're herding will probably get at least one gun each for self-defense and a crew to serve it, but I'll bet the crews are only starting to train now and will probably only emerge from their schools about the same time as guns for them begin to emerge from whatever new factories are building them. And in answer to your other question, for better or worse, for a convoy this small, I'm about as close to a commodore as the Navy can find. For those 30, 40, and 50 ship convoys going to England, the Navy pulls retired commanders and captains off the shelf, puts them aboard one of the merchantmen, and gives them some degree of control over the formation, but a screen commander apparently controls the escorts."

"How long do you think it will take us to catch up with our needs?" Hamp asked.

"If I had to guess," Ash said, "I'd say a year. We've got a huge industrial plant in this country, but it will take more than a snap of the fingers for the powers that be to bring us up to speed."

They talked on for a few more minutes, and then the watch relieved.

Solly, when he relieved for the first dog watch, reported that the crew's general health seemed to be showing improvement, something he deduced from the fact that more than a few were actually complaining about being hungry.

"Growing boys," Ash said. "They've been running on empty now for more than 24 hours, and they need to be filled up. As the saying goes, I'd say that they are nearly out of the woods. What is Watts serving tonight?"

"Sausage stew," Solly said. "The sausages are canned, and so are the vegetables that he's putting in with them. I checked before I came up. Believe it or not, I'm hungry myself."

At 1730, for the first time, Ash went down and took his evening meal with the crew on the mess decks. The men, the petty officers, and those boots who were able to find a seat at the table for the first sitting conversed quietly in Ash's presence. His proximity was a new thing to them. Once or twice, in response to questions that he put to them, they answered forthrightly, but none of them asked Ash a question, which was pretty much what Ash had expected. With regard to the sausage stew—something which blended the canned sausages, sauerkraut, carrots, potatoes, and cauliflower—Ash found it restaurant quality. Watts, he realized, was going to prove a treasure. As he glanced around him, he could see that the men at the table had adopted the same opinion.

Ash didn't linger, and when he rose finally, motioning the sailors at the table to keep their seats and continue eating, he made a point of stepping to the galley entrance and speaking to Watts.

"Excellent stew, Watts. I'll look forward to having it again when the time comes."

"Sho now, Suh?" Watts said, glancing up from the range with a broad smile.

"Sure," Ash said, and then, stepping smartly, he climbed back on deck and made his way to the bridge.

Around 0630 the next morning, after timing their arrival to coincide with sunrise and after a trying voyage that had, of necessity, served as their genuine shakedown, Ash signaled the ships in his convoy to arrange themselves in a line astern of the oiler and led them past Breezy Point into Raritan Bay. There, with the job safely concluded, he released the convoy, leaving them to pursue their individual ways. The captains of the oiler and the two large freighters sent signals to thank him; the *Orion Light*, as Ash expected, passed him without dropping so much as a word. Finally, with all chicks secure in the coop and with radio silence no longer necessary, Ash communicated with Harbor Control, received permission to enter port, proceeded into the Lower Bay, passed through The Narrows, and made his landing at the Coast Guard piers on Staten Island. Much to his relief, he found his full consignment of 3"/23 ammunition waiting for him, under guard, on the pier and a Navy mortuary detail waiting to take off the grisly cargo that Chaser 3 had carried in from the sea.

10

With Chaser 3 tied up to the pier and stable, the crew recovered from their seasickness. Although the men remained fatigued from their ordeal, they nevertheless struck the 3-inch ammunition below and into the magazine efficiently and without mishap, completing the job in a little over an hour. Hamp and Solly then descended to the wardroom to prepare the required inventories and radio messages that would report what they had taken aboard, and Ash, knowing the condition of his men, gave Samarango and Chief Stobb the word that after a thorough clean up, those men not needed to stand the In Port watch, could turn in and sleep if they wished. After dismissing both petty officers, Ash glanced up the bay toward the glistening towers of Manhattan and spotted a motor whale boat half a mile distant, aimed straight for the slip, coming from the general direction of the Brooklyn Navy Yard. That is when he anticipated that he was about to receive another set of orders. Minutes later, he did.

"Here's the scoop," he said to Solly and Hamp, 30 minutes later, after he had taken the packet to the chart room and studied it thoroughly. "We're in port for the remainder of today and tomorrow, and we go out again the day after, at sunrise, as escort for an ore carrier, a grain ship, an oiler carrying aviation gasoline, and some kind of refrigerator ship headed for Central America, all of them American bottoms. We're to pick up a fifth ship coming out of Wilmington near the entrance to Delaware Bay, another freighter, and deliver all five into the Chesapeake. Half the crew can go on liberty today; half can go tomorrow, and because I intend to stay aboard and catch up on my sleep, you two can take both days off. Enjoy yourselves, but don't wear yourselves out, because we are once more the lone escort for this run, and we'll have to be sharp. Solly, this ought to give you a chance to visit your family, and Hamp, you're free to do whatever you do on your own."

"Hamp's coming with me," Solly said. "I alerted the folks that we might be coming. My mother has promised to feed him a complete Jewish dinner."

"It'll be a new experience for me," Hamp said. "Might even convert me; my Anglican forefathers will feel no loss."

"Sounds like the two of you are well covered," Ash said, "and Solly, my regards to your family. I'll look for the both of you to be back here by 2300 tomorrow night."

Ash turned the liberty party loose at 1000 that morning whereupon most of them headed straight for the Staten Island ferry and the attractions, if not the flesh pots, of Manhattan. Solly and Ash, muffled in their overcoats, departed not long after. After first checking in the galley to insure that Watts had ordered stores as needed to replenish what the crew had consumed, Ash then went down to his bunk and slept for ten hours straight. When he got up, he went ashore to shower and shave in the officer's quarters at the Coast Guard station. Then, he walked out onto Staten Island, found himself a cafe, ate a steak, a baked potato, and a piece of Dutch apple pie, and returned to the ship where he slept through the night, waking after reveille had been piped and the ship had been washed down. In the chart room, not long after, Ash found the appropriate charts for the trip down to Norfolk, picked up a set of dividers, and began laying out the track for the following day, marking in the point of their intended rendezvous with the ship from Wilmington, while, at the same time, studying all of the lights and buoys that he could expect to help with his piloting on the transit.

An hour before lunch, having committed to memory what he thought he needed to know in advance, Ash climbed up to the bridge, picked up his binoculars, and began reacquainting himself with what he could see of the New York harbor. From where Chaser 3 had tied up, Ash was unable to see the Navy Yard because Brooklyn Heights interposed itself across his line of vision. Twice he saw destroyers coming out of the East River and, not far behind them, a cruiser; he guessed that they were on their way, escorts and big boy, to join in the battle for the Atlantic. Scanning south, he received a sudden jolt when he saw a fleet tug, her deck gun blackened and knocked asunder, the forward bulkhead of her superstructure equally blackened and considerably splintered, towing a freighter that looked to be down at the bow, the ship's prow much mangled, twisted or ruptured steel plates, girders, and rails upthrust in all directions. Clearly, the ship had been attacked by a U-boat on the surface, and the tug, coming to the rescue, had also been damaged, both vessels attesting to the destructive power of the U-boat's 4-inch deck gun.

As the pair struggled up The Narrows, Ash found the sight sobering, even downright chilling—but not without hope. Fixed to the top of the tug's mast, he could also see a broom, an indication that by near-miraculous chance, the tug, with its single 3"/50, had actually hit and sunk the U-boat. How, Ash wondered, had she done it? And how, after her own gun and fo'c'sle had been blown to smithereens? Studying the tug more closely, he saw that beneath her beak, the big tug's reinforced bow had crumpled inward by a good 3 feet, and that is when Ash deduced that the tug had rammed the U-boat. When he knew, he also sought and found the supporting evidence—eight men standing on the fantail, bare headed and wrapped in blankets, German sailors, prisoners, guarded by a single American sailor armed with a Thompson gun. It would be something to tell Solly and Hamp when they returned and something to remember. The remainder of the German crew, Ash assumed, must have gone down with their boat. Would Chaser 3, Ash wondered, hold together well enough to sink a U-boat by ramming? He didn't think so. He thought the impact might shatter her. On the other hand, if the chaser could ride up on a half-submerged U-boat and tilt her enough to flood her in some uneven way, it might be enough to take her down while the chaser still remained intact to slip off. The possibility presented a problem that Ash did not know how to solve; considering speed, battle damage, wave height, the angle of collision, and half a dozen other factors, he knew that there were simply too many variables to contemplate or follow to a logical outcome.

Through his binoculars, Ash continued to watch the ships until they moved into the Upper Bay south of Governor's Island. There, the fleet tug turned over its tow to a pair of civilian tugs, which immediately began pushing the crippled freighter up the Hudson while the gray tug turned up the East River toward the Brooklyn Navy Yard. Her crew, Ash thought, could expect to enjoy a well-earned leave period while the vessel remained dry-docked for repairs.

Starting in the early afternoon on the same day, a convoy must have arrived in Raritan Bay. Not long after Ash had been down for his lunch and returned to the chart house, one ship after another began entering The Narrows, three oilers riding high and empty, 12 freighters also riding high, also apparently empty, seven more riding lower and probably bringing in cargo of some kind from England, and a lone cattle boat that even Ash could smell from a distance. And in their wake, Ash had a good look at the one Canadian and five American destroyers that had served as the convoy's escorts after it had crossed the mid-Atlantic chop line while steaming west.

Ash slept again for part of the afternoon, rose around 1600 to write a letter, and then went to the mess decks for the first sitting, once more placed at the head of the table, with Samarango and Chief Stobb seated to either side of him.

"See that convoy come in this afternoon, Cap'n?" Stobb asked as soon as Watts began serving.

"Yes," Ash said. "Did you see the fleet tug and its tow that came in just before?"

"I think that tug must have rammed a U-boat," Samarango ventured. "Looks to me like she was carryin' prisoners back aft."

"Right," Ash said, "that was my guess as well. So, what about it, Chief, do you think Chaser 3 could ram and survive? I'm not being flippant; I'm wondering about the strength of our construction."

"Hard to say, Cap'n," Chief Stobb said, chewing on the thought. "Maybe if we slid up on top of her and wrecked her stability somehow. But if we hit straight on, and hard, we might just as easy shatter our bow."

"That was my guess too," Ash said.

Then the subject of Benny Goodman came up, the three men exchanging words about their favorite recordings, and then Samarango mentioned Jack Teagarden and his version of "St. James Infirmary," something he'd heard Teagarden play live somewhere. For the remainder of the meal, the three men talked back and forth about the little they thought they knew regarding the evolution of New Orleans jazz, with here and there a remark about Louis Armstrong or Jelly Roll Morton, and once, from Hill, the yeoman who was sitting farther down the table, they heard a remark about Bix Beiderbecke. The other men, content to bend over the tasty salmon patties that Watts had fried for them, listened, occasionally nodded their heads in agreement with what they gleaned, but remained mostly silent, either cowed by the seniority at the head of the table or quieted by a disposition to silence while they ate. And then, the meal finished, the men dispersed, Ash returning to the wardroom, the others either going on watch or back to their bunks, leaving the mess table clear for the second sitting.

Later, after walking through the spaces and inspecting the ship from the bow to the lazarette, and after appointing Chief Stobb as Command Duty Officer for the evening, Ash stepped ashore, took a bus up McClean Avenue, found himself a well-lit business district of sorts, and began to walk. The weather remained cold and bitterly so, but Ash needed the exercise and knew it. Earlier that day, barely awake in his bunk, his leg had suddenly cramped, the Charlie-horse causing him to leap from his rack in order to stamp it free. He imagined his two days and nights on the bridge to be the root cause, a condition necessitating a change, and so he walked, and after 30 minutes moving inland up McClean and another 30 coming back, he found himself a drug store that remained open, sat down on a stool at the soda fountain, and treated himself to a hot fudge sundae before he returned to the ship.

Well before the Cinderella hour which, for the crew, Ash had set at 2200, the men were back, relatively sober, excited and talkative about the adventures they'd had in New York. Two thirds of the section on liberty that day had never been there before, and from what Ash could hear coming up from the forward Booby hatch, Manhattan had met them with open arms, the cab drivers had given them free rides, and the women had swooned over them all the way up from the Bowery to the Bronx.

"I suspect some slight exaggeration," Ash said to Stobb, who had come forward along the deck to report that all hands were present on the ship and accounted for.

"And each lie bigger than the one before," Chief Stobb said, meeting Ash's grin.

"Just so, Chief, just so. Let me know when one of them finally reveals that he's been seduced by Joan Bennett or Greta Garbo, and we'll see that the news is posted on the bulletin board outside the ship's office."

"You can bet on it," laughed the chief.

By the time Solly and Hamp returned at 2300, a light snow had started to fall, and both came down into officer's quarters blowing on their hands, regardless of the gray gloves that each had been wearing.

"Cold coming back on the ferry?" Ash asked.

"Perishing," Hamp said, "but well worth the trip. Solly's mother cooks like an angel, and you wouldn't believe what they produce in their bakery. Their coffee cake is the best I've ever put in my mouth, and the turnovers are to die for."

Solly smiled. "Brought you some," he said, producing a box.

"Thanks," Ash said. "I gather from the size of the box that you have more than one in there."

"Half a dozen," Solly said, setting the box on the table. "Thought we might share them out in the morning. Interesting day? Get some rest?"

Ash answered in the affirmative, and then, as the two of them removed their overcoats and prepared to turn in, Ash told them about the damaged tug and its tow and about the convoy that had arrived during the afternoon.

"I suspect the tug captain and his crew are in for a gong," Solly ventured.

"That would be my guess," Ash said, "and well deserved. If they really did sink a U-boat out there, I'd imagine that the C.O. will be advanced to a bigger ship, possibly while his tug is still in dry dock. A success like that is bound to breed promotion."

"Reserves ever command those things—fleet tugs, I mean?" Hamp asked. "Not that I'm expecting ever to command one, you understand; I'm just curious. Not trying to get ahead of myself."

"Ha," Solly laughed. "I'll have to remember to tell that to my sister next time I see her. She'll dissolve with laughter."

Ash looked up quizzically. "I detect a story here somewhere."

"Now, now," Hamp leapt to say, "won't do to bother our captain with idle gossip and gross exaggerations."

"You should have heard what I've been listening to as it came straight up out of the Booby hatch," Ash said.

"Something out of the Booby hatch is about right," Solly laughed, and this time a good bit harder. "We hadn't been home for ten minutes before Master Hampton over here takes one look at my sister when she comes into the house, helps her off with her coat, and asks her for a date the next time we put in here. Honest to God, I thought Chana was going to faint dead away!"

"According to the crew," Ash laughed, "every woman up and down Fifth Avenue has been fainting dead away at the mere sight of them. Hamp, you seem to have gone them one better and to be upholding what is rapidly becoming a Chaser 3 tradition."

Hamp, and not without actually blushing, suddenly became serious. "Chana is a lovely girl," he protested, "and smart as they come, and a perfect lady, and all I did was ask her if she might like to see a movie with me when we next put in here, and she said that she would think about it and probably accept. And I guarantee, Solly, that I will treat her with every consideration."

By this time, both Solly and Ash were laughing so hard that they could barely keep from doubling over.

"So, right out of the gate?" Ash asked.

"Right out of the gate," Solly replied.

"Not one to let the grass grow under his feet, our Mr. Hampton?" Ash teased.

"Not so much as a single blade," Solly said. But then, seeing Hamp squirm in embarrassment, Solly put a hand out and clapped him on the shoulder. "For what it's worth, Hamp, and for all the attention that Chana is liable to pay me, which is just about zilch, you have my permission and my good wishes to go out with my sister any time she accepts the invitation. I don't doubt for a minute that you will behave like a gentleman."

"The same goes for me," Ash said, stifling the urge to roar. "And if she is as pretty a girl and as much of a lady as you say, you can thank your lucky stars that we got in here, no matter how sick you were on the way down from Portland."

"You know," Hamp said, recovering himself, "Solly almost bilged me completely by telling her about that. And he went into unnecessary detail about what I looked like bent over a barf bucket."

"Well, I hope you responded in kind," Ash said.

"Oh yes," Hamp said, recovering his color, "I was very descriptive."

"And Chana?"

"Chana," Hamp grinned, "was enormously amused and regretted not seeing Solly sick for herself. She said it would have served him right for having lorded it over her while they were growing up. She suggested that I keep a record. However, Mrs. Solomon seemed less enthused, so we let the matter drop with a word or two about the needs of the Navy, and that's when Mr. Solomon broke out laughing and said 'I told you so.'"

"I have no idea when we might get in here again," Ash said, "but I'll keep my fingers crossed for the both of you. You, Solly, for a shot at one of your mother's home cooked meals, and you, Master Hampton, for the chance to squire the lovely Chana to the movie of your choice."

"Ha," Solly once more broke out laughing, "what our Master Hampton does not yet realize is that just about any venue the two of them frequent will be Chana's choice, or I can't tell a hawk from a handsaw. My sister, Hamp, has a mind of her own and a will of iron, so even as you give her every consideration, I'll be hugely surprised if she doesn't get the better of you. Not to worry, though; you'll probably look just fine with a ring through your nose."

11

The following morning, Chaser 3 cleared The Narrows before sunrise, picked up the ships of her convoy in Raritan Bay, and proceeded into the deep Atlantic without hindrance. Once out into open water, with a State 3 sea running from almost dead astern, Ash swiftly organized the convoy into another box formation and began turning down the coast. Above the Jersey shore, the sky remained gray, overcast, dismal, but the freezing temperatures of the preceding days had risen by several degrees. As Ash expected, the little ship once more began to yaw, not greatly but enough to make at least three of the crew seasick, so before the 0800–1200 watch relieved, Samarango had overseen two scrub downs forward and one on the fantail aft. Ash had brought the ship out that morning, but as soon as the last sea buoy had been passed and the convoy formed, he rapidly gave Hamp the deck and set their zig-zag according to pre-selected plan in the governing Navy tactical manual. Momentarily, Ash wondered if Hamp appeared to be about to join the few suffering from *mal de mer*, but when Ash thought to mention Chana, Hamp seemed to take a grip on himself, perked up appreciably, and greeted Solly enthusiastically when the man came up to relieve.

"Not to make too much of it," Ash said, after Hamp had gone down, "but I think the lad was about to be sick until I mentioned your sister; that perked him up like a stalk of new grown corn."

Solly laughed. "They seem to have hit it off," he said. "I wouldn't have thought it, given Hamp's moneyed background and Chana's ideas about the distribution of wealth, but with regard to human relations, you never can tell."

"They're a muddle, no question." Then, changing the subject, he added, "I see a mast on the horizon … two masts, about four points off the port bow. Merchantmen, I'm guessing, making for the City. Given their angle off the bow, they ought to pass well to port. We're going to have to keep a close watch on things; I expect more traffic in this direction than we had coming down from Portland."

"Yes," Solly said, "stands to reason."

Their second convoy, freed from the plodding *Orion Light*, steamed at a steady 10 knots. Following the track that Ash had laid out for them, the ships set a course that kept them between 8 and 10 miles from the coast, close enough for Ash and Bell to pilot by sight, far enough out from the beach to avoid underwater obstacles, difficulties with the currents, and anything like excessive interference from fishing boats. Their progress, somewhat slowed by the necessary zig-zag, remained uniform at something approaching 8 knots made good so that by 1500, they were far enough down the New Jersey coast to be pitching through a higher sea several miles east of Barnegat Bay. That was where Chaser 3 ran into her first spot of trouble.

Looking back on that event, Ash could never quite explain it to himself. In fact, he found the moment almost existential, accidentally absurd, the inadvertent but timely intervention of pure chance. With Samarango on watch, Ash had caught a couple of hours' sleep in the hammock. Then, waking and turning out, he pulled his foul weather gear back on and climbed almost without thinking back to the bridge, glanced once at the compass to confirm the course the helmsman was steering, glanced again, astern, to assure himself that the spacing of the convoy was in order, and then glanced off the starboard bow a point or two in the direction of Barnegat Light. Suddenly, lifting his binoculars to examine something in the distance, his whole body went rigid. "*Shit!*" he called out. "*Mine in the water! Sound General Quarters! Left hard rudder! Glick, signal to convoy: 'Port turn to 090, Immediate, Execute!' Helmsman come left to 090!*"

With his eyes fixed on the mine, Chaser 3 responded as Ash hoped she would, and then, Ash stopped all engines, waiting, as the crew erupted from wherever they had been working and raced to their battle stations.

"Teague to the bridge!" Ash called below as the gun crews manned their weapons. "Lookouts, peel your eyes for mines!"

Suddenly, Ash knew that he had to keep track of more things than he'd ever before had to face in a single moment. Chaser 3 had to be kept in position so as not to lose sight of the mine as it rose to the top of one wave after another and disappeared into the troughs behind them, the convoy had to be maneuvered so as to keep it clear of danger, additional mines like the floater he'd discovered—if they existed—had to be sighted and kept in view, and the event had to be handled with dispatch so as not to delay the convoy or endanger it. As Teague raced up the ladder to the bridge, Ash ordered the convoy to slow its speed to 3 knots and to steam in a square pattern, 2 miles on a side, while he took action to eliminate the danger. Then, with Teague standing beside him, Ash did his best to put his gunner onto the mine.

"There," Ash said, "two points off the starboard quarter, about 70 yards out. See it?"

With a minimum of urgent coaching, Ash directed Teague's line of sight.

"Got it," the gunner's mate said after scanning the wave crests.

"That doesn't look like one of ours," Ash said, his voice steady, his pulse finally coming under control. "I think it's German, probably launched from the U-boat at some time in the last day or two. We can't leave it out here; we've got to blow it or sink it. What's your best recommendation?"

"I'll try to blow it with the 20mm, Cap'n," Teague said, "but it might just sink if I get it in the right spot. Hell of a concussion if she blows."

"Oh, don't I know," Ash said, "and a risk of damage to ourselves in the mix. Can you still do it if I open the range?"

"I'll try," Teague said. "I'll give it my best shot, Cap'n."

Ash opened the range by another 30 yards and then gave the order so that Teague could take the mine under fire with the aftermost Oerlikon.

When Ash gave the order, Teague, manning the 20mm himself with the help of his loader, sank the mine in less than a minute. It took him 24 rounds to do it, and miraculously none of them struck a contact detonator so as to explode the mine.

In the meantime, a sailor nicknamed "Skinny" Krupp, a tall, thin seaman apprentice serving as starboard lookout, had sighted a second mine another 200 yards out, only seeing it as it crested an immense swell where the spindrift flew away from it in an irregular way. Once he'd guided Ash onto it, Ash put on 3 knots and maneuvered Chaser 3 into a position downwind so as to give Teague the best possible chance for catching the mine as it floated up the face of each wave onto their crests.

This time, Teague struck a contact detonator with his third round, and the mine blew, throwing a geyser of sea water a hundred feet into the sky, shaking the ship like a leaf with the force of the concussion and showering them with sheets of downwind spray.

"Solly," Ash called down to the pilot house through the voice tube, "damage control reports to the bridge as soon as you and Chief Stobb can inspect the spaces. And send Polaski up here with some message blanks. I've got to message COMDESLANT and Naval Headquarters, Norfolk, about this so that they can promulgate an alert."

For 30 more minutes, making no more than 5 knots, Ash searched the area, looking for more mines. Finding none he quickly put the convoy back on course and resumed speed, working out ahead of the box, searching on either side of their zig-zag. In the meantime, after a thorough inspection of the ship, Solly returned to the bridge with Chief Stobb in tow, both men reporting no serious damage. A water connection had vibrated loose so as to spring a tiny leak and been immediately repaired, some of Watts' mess utensils had been shaken from their racks, and a fire extinguisher had broken its strap and crashed to the deck.

"But the hull remains intact?" Ash asked. "No leaks?"

"No leaks," Chief Stobb said. "Sounded the bilges myself. She's in good shape."

"I guess we can thank Anson for that," Ash said. "He built her strong."

"We had the same thought," Solly said.

"Nasty things, mines," Stobb remarked. "Damned lucky you saw 'em comin', Cap'n."

"Yes," Ash said. "Let's just hope our luck holds. Sighting one of those things tends to make the blood run cold."

"This has been a really interesting day," Hamp said to Ash as soon as he relieved for the first of the dog watches. "If you don't mind me asking, is that what it was like on your other ship, the *Parker*—the concussion, I mean?"

Ash tried to remember and couldn't. "To tell you the truth," he said, "I can't quite say because the first lift, or wave, or whatever launched me straight into the air. I was more or less in flight as the vibrations passed under me, and then, I hit the water after they'd moved out and beyond where the ship was going down."

Hamp didn't press the point, and Ash didn't offer to expand on it. It was done—the *Parker* was gone, sunk—and now, Chaser 3 was everything, had to be everything. His stomach still in knots, Ash went to the mess deck for his supper, knowing that his worries about the ship had been ratcheted up by one more notch. Intellectually, command was turning out just what he'd expected it would be, exactly what any reasonable human being could expect it to be, but experientially and emotionally, being the chaser's C.O. seemed to be thrusting him into the unexpected and the unknown at every turn.

Over supper, Ash, Solly, Chief Stobb, and Samarango, the four of them sitting at the head of the table, talked over the mine, and when Teague came down, he joined the conversation.

"If we'd had more of a sea running out there," Teague said, "I can't guarantee that I could have hit them rascals. Might have had to go to the 3-inch and blow 'em by proximity. That Oerlikon is great for anti-aircraft fire and for hittin' somethin' bigger like say a PT Boat or one of them U-boats, but takin' out that mine was like tryin' to shoot a flea off a dog's back."

"You think, then, that the 3-inch might do a better job?" Ash asked with a straight tone of inquiry.

"Cap'n," Teague said, "I'm jus' guessin', but now we done it once with the 20mm, I think the splinters from a 3-inch-shell burst might give us a faster result."

"I'll make a note," Ash said, "and if we ever come within range of another mine, we'll try it—if it's a floater, that is. I have no idea how we'd deal with anything more sophisticated like a magnetic mine or one of those delayed-action types that only pops to the surface after two or three ships have passed over it."

"They make mines like that?" Solly said, showing some astonishment.

"I'm afraid so," Ash replied. One glance down the table showed that he had shocked everyone. "But thus far, I haven't heard that any have shown up on this side of the pond," he continued, eliciting a collective sigh of relief. "We'll just have to keep the lookouts sharp and up to the mark; that will always give us our best chance for detection."

The word would get around below decks in a hurry, Ash knew, and if it prodded the lookouts to bump up their attention to duty, the revelation would have served its purpose.

At dusk, as Ash studied the distant horizon with a practiced eye, he spotted another small convoy coming north on a reciprocal bearing and maneuvered his own flock so as to pass it outboard. Within the hour, and even as Ash and Bell shot their stars beneath last light, nine vessels, all of them fully loaded, with a minesweeper and another fleet tug acting as escorts, passed to starboard, none of them showing lights, all of them making more than 12 knots according to Solly's calculations as he timed their passage.

Ash knew about radar. He'd heard about some of its capabilities, but in that moment, he came to understand what it might mean to a ship like Chaser 3. As things stood, with nothing more than the lookouts to rely on and in the midst of a pitch dark night, without anyone showing running lights as a means for judging another ship's position and speed, Ash and his lumbering chicks might have run smack into the other convoy, physically, with great destruction to both of them. Equipped with radar, Ash could have spotted them at a greater distance and maneuvered accordingly. Considering the scarcity of the new radar inventions and the size and importance of his ship to the Navy, Ash did not imagine that she would ever be given a set. He amused himself by wondering if feeding carrots to the lookouts would improve their night vision as current myths suggested.

Leaving Solly to man the deck, Ash slept through the last three hours of the 2000–2400 watch but got up for the mid-watch as Samarango came on, knowing that their approach to Atlantic City might add complications to the voyage. As Ash expected when he climbed to the bridge, the lights of Atlantic City, although still distant, nevertheless threw a glow from over the horizon. The lookouts, he knew, would be pleased; their ability to see oncoming ships in silhouette would be improved, but the same thing would hold true for any U-boats that might be on the hunt, so by means of flashing light, Ash signaled a course change to the convoy, took them farther out into the Atlantic and well over the horizon before once more turning south and continuing on their track toward Norfolk. He'd anticipated the move from the moment he'd read his orders at Staten Island. To avoid the glow from off the beach entirely, Ash would have had to make a detour of more distance than he could afford, so having slightly increased his chances to avoid being detected by a U-boat, something he imagined to range by between 10 and 15 percent, he continued running, striking a course that would eventually take him past Cape May and the mouth of Delaware Bay to the point where he anticipated meeting the ship, a freighter, which was supposed to be coming out to join him.

Ash slept again between 0100 and 0300, but at 0300, the radioman on watch, Grubber this time, woke him in the chart room.

"Message, Cap'n," Grubber said, all business and standing at attention. "Just received from COMDESLANT."

"Be easy, Grubber," Ash said, swinging out of the hammock and starting to read the message under the red lens on his flashlight. "No need for formality at this hour."

"Yes, Sir," Grubber said, sagging a little.

The message contained two lines. The first delivered a well done to the command: "BRAVO ZULU, sinking enemy mines." The second notified Ash to expect two ships coming out of Wilmington that morning, a collier being added to the mix.

At 0400, without an ounce of preparation or advanced notice, Ash's tiny convoy found itself suddenly surrounded by fog, fog so thick and dense that Ash could barely see the fo'c'sle from his own bridge. With the use of voice radio prohibited, visual signaling in order to slow the ships in the convoy was out of the question; the signal light couldn't have penetrated the fog, and, locked in darkness, not even the best signalman would have known where to direct the beam. Instead, Ash had to rely on the operations order governing the convoy and count on each ship under his care to continue to zig-zag in accordance with the precise times set in the pattern. If they did not, they risked the dissolution of the convoy as each of them drifted off in independent directions or, worse, collision. Realizing that he was virtually blind, suddenly facing the unknown, Ash woke the ship and brought them quickly to General Quarters in order to be prepared for any eventuality that might materialize in the midst of the fog. To Ash's shock, the eventuality that most worried him suddenly materialized not 200 yards distant. Breaking unexpectedly into an open hole in the fog and beneath the dawn's first dim shade of gray, Ash sighted a black shape, an apparent U-boat, running on the surface, charging its batteries beneath the cover of the mists. Instantly, machine-gun rounds slammed into Chaser 3, splintering the edge of the starboard gunnel, shattering a running light, and wounding one of Teague's loaders who crashed to the deck screaming beneath the ready magazine. Even before Ash could draw a breath, the U-boat began to disappear into yet another fog bank, the mere outline of its conning tower and its stern still exposed, giving Ash the second or two he needed to direct Teague onto the target, and Teague barely enough time to slam out a single 3-inch round from the main battery before the U-boat utterly disappeared from sight, the raging passage of Chaser 3's single shot no doubt forcing the Nazi captain instantly to submerge even as Ash himself once more rushed into the fog bank somewhere behind where the sub had gone down.

As one of Teague's gunners knelt to tend to the wounded man, sonar reported a hard contact to port. Within 20 seconds, owing to temperature gradients in the water or the ineptitude of the rating on the sonar repeater, the contact was gone—and gone finally before Ash could so much as order the fantail to drop a single depth charge on a legitimate target. From start to finish, the entire engagement had been a freak, a lightning flash, a never to be repeated gash in the cycle of time lasting less than a minute but long enough to leave Ash shaking with fury and shocked with wonder. Had Chaser 3 been equipped with radar, Ash believed that he could have executed an attack while avoiding collision with his convoy, but as things stood, he didn't dare deviate from his zig-zag pattern, owing to the danger of colliding with one or another of the ships he was trying to shepherd. The only advantage that he could see in the moment was that the U-boat, with its periscope masked by the fog, would be unable to execute an attack of its own, and if or when the convoy did emerge from the fog, Ash intended to station himself astern of them in order to dissuade the U-boat if it tried to stalk them from somewhere behind.

The wounded sailor—Wilkins, a seaman, removed by Hamp to the mess table for treatment—had not been struck by a German round. Instead, splinters from the damaged gunnel had been driven into his thigh, and those, not without pain, Hamp managed to extract before applying a burning antiseptic and a bandage that was both thick enough and strong enough to close the wounds. That they would remain painful and keep the man in his bunk for several days, Hamp said that he felt certain; that they would leave the man permanently damaged, Hamp strongly doubted.

In the event, and after an hour's steaming, Ash and the convoy emerged from the fog bank beneath a cold but fully breaking dawn with the U-boat nowhere in sight, Ash confident that if the German had indeed submerged and remained so in order to escape further attack that its underwater speed would never be enough to allow it to catch up with the convoy. That his convoy had avoided utter dissolution in the midst of the fog came as another surprise. Each of the ships had drifted—there could be no doubt—but by sticking to the zig-zag pattern, none of them had moved so far out of formation that they couldn't be easily gathered. So, within the hour following, all of them moved back into the formation that Ash had set for them and proceeded on their way, Ash feeling waves of relief over the almost unthinkable fact that they had escaped relatively unharmed without a single ship being either gunned or torpedoed. How Ash had stumbled onto the U-boat remained a mystery to him, but given the German's position and the events preceding its sudden appearance, Ash concluded that it was probably the same vessel which had laid the mines that Chaser 3 had destroyed on the previous day.

Chaser 3 and her little convoy made rendezvous with the new freighter and the collier south of Cape May later that morning, not long after the watch had been relieved, Ash directing both ships into positions on the convoy's right flank so that the box became a rectangle, with three ships across the front rank at 500-yard intervals and three across the rear rank behind them. Then, as before, with Chaser 3's sonar pinging, the convoy went on its way at 10 knots while zig-zagging, Ash maneuvering in a random circuit from one side to the other, with variable advances out in front of the ships and occasional periods where he dropped back behind the formation in case the U-boat might be found stalking them.

Three more times that day, they were met by small convoys headed north, two shepherded by a single escort each—a destroyer in the case of the first and a minesweeper in the case of the second. In every case, Ash flashed a warning about the possibility of meeting a U-boat ahead. The third convoy which consisted of only five ships had no escort whatsoever, but upon close examination, Ash did notice that the freighter leading the pack carried a 3"/23 mounted high up on its fo'c'sle, and through his binoculars, he could see two white-hatted sailors working around it. And then, around 1500 that afternoon, as the ship approached Ocean City, a single ocean liner passed them, her decks filled with passengers, many of them waving from a distance as the ship raced by.

Hamp, although he didn't have the watch at the time, happened to be on the bridge standing next to Ash, holding some papers that Ash needed to sign.

"Jeez," he said, "aren't they taking a hell of a chance steaming independently like that?"

"I can't be sure," Ash said, "because I didn't figure her speed, but I'd estimate it to be something in excess of 25 knots, give or take. At that speed, she can outrun any U-boat she's likely to meet. There's a risk, you're right, but unless she practically runs directly over a U-boat, it is much diminished. Give her another six months, and I'll bet she starts carrying troops somewhere rather than paying passengers. How's Wilkins?"

"He'll be fine, in so far as I can see," Hamp said. "Two of those splinters went in about an inch, and a small one less deep. I'll have him looked at as soon as we tie up somewhere, but I'm not too worried."

The remainder of their trip south proved uneventful save for the fact that Ash heard a gin rummy tournament had been started down on the mess deck. Participation was limited to off-duty men who were not needed elsewhere, the prize being a bucket of draft beer, if the winner happened to be of age, or a pre-paid movie ticket to the film of the winner's choice, if he turned out to be underage, distribution of the prize to be withheld until the ship next gave the men liberty. On the bridge watch, Glick as well as the lookouts dropped occasional hints designed to make Samarango, Hamp, or Solly reveal when that liberty might be expected, but they had no more of an idea when the ship would be in port long enough for time off than Ash did. Liberty for the crew, as with shore leave for the officers, would be determined by the pace of their operations and nothing else, and Ash had no way of knowing what to expect in that regard. They might have a night or two in Norfolk when they arrived, but then they might not, so Ash kept his silence. Better not to dangle plums in front of them that he could not deliver; better to let whatever orders they received speak for themselves so that everyone, officers and crew alike, would think themselves in the same boat, and on that matter, as with no other, leave the heat for COMDESLANT to take.

In the offing, while the convoy made a safe entrance into Hampton Roads, delivering its ships into the Chesapeake by 1100 hours the next morning, COMDESLANT did not allow them much of a breather. Alongside the naval piers, Chaser 3 took on fuel, topped off her water tanks, and received and stowed two crates of stores, along with a quantity of fresh bread. Without so much as allowing the crew time to go ashore for a freshwater shower, the chaser was turned right around again and sent north as the escort for three oilers riding low in the water, two refrigerator ships, a freighter loaded to the gills with Texas cotton, and an ammunition ship carrying the output from some depot or depots located to the south. The oilers and the freighter were destined for Delaware Bay and, probably, the ports of Wilmington or Philadelphia; the ammunition ship was to be turned over to yet another escort somewhere off Cape May and proceed on her way to join a massive convoy collecting in Casco Bay prior to a departure for Liverpool or Glasgow. In the event, Chaser 3's third convoy left Norfolk at 1600 that afternoon and reorganized from a line astern into a five-ship box 2 or 3 miles east of the Cape Charles lighthouse. Judging the ammunition ship, at that particular moment in the war, to be the most valuable of the five, Ash placed her at the center of the formation but opened the distance between the ammo carrier and the merchantmen on her flanks to a thousand yards in straw-grasping hopes that if a U-boat did succeed in stalking them, one or another of the flanking ships would absorb the torpedo. In doing so, Ash had taken a risk, he knew, because if an attacking U-boat did manage to hit the ammunition hull, the resulting enormity of the explosion might be enough to damage or sink them all. Still, he thought, better to lose a few bales of cotton or a shipload of oil than an entire cargo of hard-to-replace ammunition destined for men actually in the fight somewhere. It was the kind of decision that men sitting behind typewriters in the newspaper offices where he had worked would never be called upon to make. For men like Ash, riding seagoing splinters in the midst of the Atlantic, he rather imagined that it would be the kind of decision that they would always have to make because there would be no one else to shoulder the responsibility.

As the ships lumbered north into rising seas, Bell reported that the barometer had started to drop.

"Dropping quick?" Ash asked.

"Not quick, Cap'n," Bell replied, "but she's been going down slightly across the past three hours."

"Looks like we might be in for a bit of a nor'easter," Ash said.

"If you don't mind me sayin' so Cap'n, I'd just as soon not," Bell replied up the voice tube.

Ash laughed. "We'll keep an eye on it," he said.

"I hope you've got your rain slicker handy," Ash said to Hamp who was Officer of the Deck, "because it looks to me like we've got a gale coming. Get the word down to Samarango and Chief Stobb and have them pass the word to stand by for heavy weather."

The storm when it came proved to be far less than a full blown nor'easter, but that didn't matter much to the men riding Chaser 3, because within an hour, the winds had produced waves of at least 20 feet, all of them coming in from the north and northeast, their combined effect causing the ship to pitch like a mean horse with a burr thrust under its saddle. As the front passed, it brought a blinding rain, a rain that blew in cold and eliminated almost any chance Ash might have had for keeping visual track of the ships in the convoy. Huddled inside their slickers with heavy sou'wester rain hats tied beneath their chins, Ash, Hamp, and the lookouts endured, made their best efforts to keep the convoy in sight, and rode up and down the oncoming waves like men straddling the balance point of a vicious see-saw. All the while, Chaser 3 took green water over the bow, the waves crashing back over the 3-inch to pound the windows of the pilot house. Once more, more or less trapped in their bunks, men became sick; once more the barf buckets came out; and once more the swabs and the scrub buckets followed.

"You might have warned me about this," Hamp shouted to Ash over the screech of the wind. "I could have cut class and stayed in Brooklyn with the lovely Chana."

Ash was pleased to see that Hamp remained game.

"*What?*" Ash shouted back, "and miss this gentle lapping of the waves? You have to remember, my man, that a good woman is a good woman, but a good ship is a ride!"

An hour later, after passing through the front, the rain subsided. Somewhere above the dense cloud cover that hung low in the sky, Ash knew the moon to be waxing, and as a result, the lookouts and the watch were once more able to monitor the convoy. The freighter had slipped out of position, but her captain, alert to the lapse, put on turns and brought her back into place without Ash having to prod him, and for that, Ash was grateful. Even with the worst of the storm behind them, the seas, much to everyone's displeasure, did not moderate until the following morning, when the waves managed to drop down to what Ash estimated as a steady 10 feet. In heading into them, the ship continued to pitch until noon, when, not far from Cape May, Ash saw the body of the convoy plow away to port in order to enter Delaware Bay. Meanwhile, Ash exchanged the ammunition ship he'd been shepherding for three freighters, two oilers, and four colliers that an aging four-piper destroyer led out to him before taking over responsibility for the ammunition ship and heading north beside her.

Having been warned ahead of time by a message from COMDESLANT, Ash ordered the largest convoy he had yet tried to escort into a three-ship by three-ship box and started them south on a return transit to the mouth of the Chesapeake, all of them arriving safely and without incident save for miserable bouts of seasickness aboard Chaser 3, the sickness brought on rapidly by her incessant roll and the fierce yawing that accompanied a following sea.

This time, after fueling and topping off with water, Ash had been directed to take the ship alongside a destroyer tender for the night, the tender providing the men a plethora of fresh steaks, fresh vegetables, a gallon of ice cream, freshwater showers, overnight laundry for every man in the crew, and a showing of *The Great Dictator* with Charlie Chaplin for entertainment. Ash did not give the men liberty, and none went ashore. They had known before they tied up that reveille would be piped at 0400 the following morning so that they could take out a convoy of four freighters and one collier bound for Charleston.

12

The trip to Charleston differed from Chaser 3's previous voyages because for this voyage, a minesweeper—one commanded by a persnickety lieutenant—accompanied them, the lieutenant's seniority placing him in command of the convoy. As a result, while the minesweeper pressed out ahead, screening back and forth from port to starboard across the convoy's narrow front, the lieutenant's frequent flag hoists sent Chaser 3 racing down one side of the assembled ships and up the other—an evolution that became far less than pleasant in the rough waters east of Cape Hatteras and which Ash thought to have been ordered at two or three times the frequency necessary to protect the convoy. In fact, given the relative inactivity of the minesweeper, the whole exercise struck Ash as bordering on the officious. Regardless, Ash carried out his assignments promptly, made something of a pest out of himself on the lieutenant's behalf by nudging merchant captains who had slipped out of position by as little as 200 yards, and remained ever alert to the sweeper's flag hoists, which kept popping up like unwanted relatives at every skip and turn of the zig-zag.

The hoist that finally gave Ash and Solly—Solly standing as Officer of the Deck when it came in—a moment of relief accompanied with no little amusement had been designed by the lieutenant as an obvious rocket; only in this instance, much to Ash and Solly's well-concealed pleasure, it turned out to be a rocket which backfired. The rocket came by flashing light, Glick rattling it off, word by word, as the signal was flashed.

"From the sweep, Cap'n: *Equipment adrift on fo'c'sle; rectify.*"

Ash and Solly glanced down at the fo'c'sle, then at each other, and stifled their laughter.

"To the commodore by light," Ash said, "*In the event U-boat sighted, mousetraps elevated for immediate engagement.*"

94

"I don't think he knows what mousetraps are," Solly said quietly.

"Probably never seen them before," Ash said. "I'm guessing that a reply will be delayed until he finds someone aboard who can identify them for him."

The delay lasted five minutes, the reply limited itself to "*Good hunting.*"

By that time, everyone on the bridge and in the pilot house knew about their commodore's shortcomings, the watch section's laughter being universally shared.

Two or three hours later, the convoy sighted and then collected five more ships coming out of Pamlico Sound. One of them, a rusted hulk flying a Panamanian flag, appeared to be carrying pigs, the stench coming off the ship detectable even at a distance. This, too, seemed to lighten the load, the crew, each time they plowed past her, claiming that they were being forced to endure an ordeal that no sailor in the United States Navy should ever have to suffer.

"I suppose it does tweak the nose," Solly said, "but I think we're hearing a degree of exaggeration here that exceeds a multiplication by ten."

"Fits right in with the way they said that Joan Bennett and Garbo were supposed to have fainted dead away at the sight of them during our stay in New York," Ash said. "With seagoing sailors, a fisherman's lie seems to be the spice of life."

In the middle of the night, for the first time, south of Onslow Bay and not more than 15 miles east of Bald Head Island at the entrance to Wilmington, Gomez reported a solid sonar contact which he almost instantly classified as a possible submarine. Within seconds, Ash sounded the alarm for General Quarters and notified the commodore in the minesweeper. Then, as the minesweeper's captain ordered Chaser 3 to investigate and attack, he kicked up the convoy's speed in an effort to effect their escape.

By the time Solly reported all battle stations manned and ready, Ash had already turned toward the contact, taken the chaser up to 16 knots, and alerted Hamp to set two of their depth charges in the rolling racks for 50 feet and the two on the K-guns for an even 100, and then, with Gomez calling up ranges and bearings from sonar, Ash raced in to make his attack.

"Range 900, bearing 085," Gomez shouted up to the bridge from the sonar scope.

Ash steadied up on 085 and spoke to Hamp, who had raced to his station on the fantail in order to supervise the depth-charge crews. "Ready, Hamp?"

Hamp immediately replied that the detonators were set and that the crews were ready.

"Range 800, bearing 080," Gomez shouted. "He's swingin' left, Cap'n; I think he'll try to turn inside us!"

That the U-boat, if it was a U-boat, would try to avoid the attack by turning inside it, Ash knew, but he knew too that while the U-boat commander might be anticipating a destroyer, it seemed unlikely that he would be anticipating a subchaser that, in so far as Ash knew, had a turning circle so small as to be able to keep up with him.

"Range 600, bearing 065!"

Ash continued to meet the contact's turn, the little chaser heeling, pitching into each wave, speeding in, running quick and steady on the power of her big diesels. Meanwhile, Ash, Solly, who was back on watch, the lookouts, and Glick, all gripped the rails in order to keep from sliding across the wet deck, the mast leaning as they followed the slipping contact.

"Range 300, bearing 050! She's turning tighter, Cap'n!"

"Left hard rudder!" Ash called down the voice tube. "Depth charges, standby!"

Seconds later, as the turn tightened and the range closed to 100 yards, Ash dropped turns, steadying the ship at 12 knots in order to provide a more level platform for launching his depth charges. Then, steering 2 or 3 degrees ahead of where the contact was reported and breathing hard as Gomez shouted out that he'd lost contact because it disappeared into the sonar's ground return, Ash gave the order to fire, both K-guns blasting away with resounding KRUMPS even as Hamp reported both rolling charges away over the stern. Without hesitating, Ash put on turns and began to open the range in order to give the ship more distance from the concussions that would shortly follow and which would also give Gomez the best chance for regaining contact. Then, following an elapse of mere seconds, the two stern charges blew, sending up huge geysers in the ship's wake, lifting and pushing the stern with the their blast waves even as they showered her with spray. Not three seconds later, the charges from the K-guns exploded, port and starboard astern, lifting yet greater mushrooms from the sea while spreading their plumes of sea water in all directions.

"Anything, Gomez?" Ash called down to sonar, his voice tense, his throat tight.

"Nothin', Cap'n," Gomez reported after a few seconds' delay. "No contact."

"Keep at it," Ash called down, and then he turned to Solly. "If the sweeper is still within range, have Glick flash her this message: *Made depth charge attack. Lost contact. Commencing box search.*"

Glick managed to flash the sweeper in the last few minutes before she drew out of range and received their instant reply: *Prosecute 60 minutes; rejoin.*

Gomez regained contact only once across the following hour, and Ash made only one more attack. Then, with the possible U-boat having apparently gone deep beneath a thermal layer, Chaser 3 lost contact entirely, the German having slipped away and made his escape.

Disregarding his orders, Ash stuck with his attack for another half hour, executing a widening box search for the contact. When the search failed to turn up a single return echo, he reluctantly took the ship all the way up to 17 knots, turned south, and finally caught up with the convoy on the following morning after a long chase. If Gomez had put them onto a U-boat, Ash didn't believe that they had sunk it, but the job Chaser 3 had been sent to do had become a success when the convoy escaped without damage, and Ash knew that he ought to be content with seeing that job, the most important one, well done. The persnickety lieutenant had called Ash alongside when they'd rejoined the others, and then, speaking through the loudhailer, talked down to Ash as though he and the sweeper had been in the business of sinking a U-boat every time she went out. This, Ash was pleased to notice, miffed those members of the crew who happened to be on deck to hear the exchange, but Ash himself had kept his silence, his only reply being to say that he'd hope to do better with his next contact.

"I'll bet money that guy is a reservist," Solly said to Ash after they'd pulled away and taken up station behind the convoy. "If you don't mind me saying so, he sounds downright full of himself. I might be wrong, but I'd expect a regular to have a little better grasp of things."

"I'd say that pseudo-Guards mustache he's sporting gives the game away," Hamp said, permitting himself a laugh. "If that doesn't show us his colors, I can't imagine what might."

Ash smiled. "Takes all kinds," he said.

Outside Charleston, they turned over the pig ship and three freighters to a convoy of seven that steamed out to meet them, an armed Coast Guard cutter relieving them of their escort duties as the new convoy formed and sped on its way south. Chaser 3 then fell astern of the sweeper and followed her into port before being released to break away toward the fueling pier where she topped off with fuel and water late in the afternoon. From there, she had a short trip to the nearest destroyer tender, which once more provided fresh provisions and the kinds of services that Ash and the crew had come to appreciate.

Reveille the following morning went down at a congenial 0600, but by 0800, they were once more underway, leading out a single Navy sea plane tender that the appropriate fleet command had elected to move from Charleston to Jacksonville. The captain of the deep-draft vessel carried four stripes on his sleeve, but unlike the sweeper's C.O., his grasp of their transit while alert, seemed both firm and assured, the various orders he handed down to Ash coming to him by means of simple flag hoists or signals by flashing light that showed Ash an appreciation for the protection that Chaser 3 was trying to provide. As with all of their convoys, radio silence remained tight, their voice

97

radio unused, and when Ash finally delivered the ship, he received a warm thank you for his troubles.

Ash did not take his ship into Jacksonville for the night. Instead, pursuant to a COMDESLANT dispatch, as the sea plane tender disappeared down the channel into Jacksonville, Ash picked up a net tender that was being transferred and a deeply laden U.S. Navy oiler, both of them bound for Key West. With their zig-zag included, Ash estimated the trip to be well over 500 miles, the longest transit that they had yet undertaken. To Ash's surprise, it also turned out to be the most tranquil voyage that Chaser 3 had yet made. South of Jacksonville, as the early March hours began to stretch into days, the seas calmed down to a more than reasonable 3 to 4 feet, the skies brightened, and the air temperature rose swiftly, bringing with it an unwelcome humidity. South of Daytona Beach, Hamp, acting in his role as supply officer for the ship, finally saw to the issue of a special navy soap that was supposed to be effective for salt water. At that point the men began washing both their clothes and themselves in sea water dragged up in buckets from over the side, saving their dwindling supply of fresh water for drinking and for the galley. No one particularly liked it, but given the high humidity, the amount of sweat coming off their bodies, and the need for maintaining an acceptable level of personal hygiene, everyone washed with the soap and then, predictably, groused about it with grunts and chuckles.

The commanding officer of the net tender, Ash learned, turned out to be a reservist, a junior grade lieutenant like himself, who had formerly been third mate on a freighter out of Baltimore. The commanding officer of the oiler was a regular, a four-stripe veteran like the C.O. of the sea plane tender and, as such, the designated commodore for their transit. In one regard, however, he differed greatly from any previous senior that Ash had met—he appeared to have a galloping sense of humor, which became instantly recognizable in the flashing light messages that he sometimes sent: *Pop over and take a gander along the port quarter.*" "*Those three tars peeling potatoes on your fantail, do they come as standard subchaser equipment?*" "*1700. If we were in port, it would be happy hour. The Kaiser didn't drink, and think what that caused!*"

"This guy is downright loquacious," Solly laughed.

"He's one of a kind, that's for sure," Ash replied.

But when it came to actual operations, the oiler's captain seemed to know exactly what he was doing, taking them out at night so as to avoid being too much exposed against the lights from the beach, directing Ash to precisely those points where he could be expected to detect an impending U-boat attack, and causing him to drop back just far enough each night to interfere with any stalker coming up on them from behind.

"This guy needs to hire an agent," Hamp said after one of the oiler's more amusing dispensations. "He could make money doing stand-up routines in the officer's clubs."

Ash agreed, but at the same time, he realized that with four stripes on his sleeve and something in excess of 20 years of experience, the oiler's captain knew his stuff. Their transit to Key West, longer by a full day than anything they had yet put in, went off without a hitch.

Contrary to expectation, after fueling and taking on water and fresh provisions, Chaser 3 did not rush straight back out to sea. Instead, she was actually ordered to tie up alongside the quay and given two days in port to allow for upkeep and rest. The crew, when Ash informed them, reacted like they had died and gone to heaven. Polaski, winner of the gin rummy tournament, looked forward to collecting his bucket of beer, and the rest of his duty section looked forward to standing by to assist in the event that he couldn't finish it. Samarango, taking the duty section in hand, put them immediately to work washing down with fresh water, and then, with paint and brushes above deck and lubricants below, Samarango and Chief Stobb set the watch section to doing upkeep and maintenance with unexpected speed. Within an hour, after going ashore for freshwater showers and changing into the liberty uniform promulgated for Key West, the off-duty section hit the beach and headed straight into town, to, Hamp said, "disport themselves while soaking up the Hemingway atmosphere, or to soak themselves like Hemingway while disporting in the atmosphere." Ash, Solly, and Hamp, leaving Chief Stobb as Command Duty Officer, first showered ashore and then returned to the ship, but from there, once changed into the uniform of the day, they made for the club and their first drink in weeks.

Inside the club, Ash, Hamp, and Solly went straight to the bar, Solly and Hamp calling for bourbon on the rocks even before they could reach the rail and belly up. The enlisted bar tender, an individual with slicked back hair and a sly smile who obviously took himself for an accomplished professional, lifted a bottle, flipped it once through a mid-air somersault, caught it deftly, and poured the drinks before either Solly or Hamp could get out their wallets. Then, he turned to Ash.

"An' what's yours?" he said, looking Ash up and down, the mere hint of a smirk showing in his eye.

Ash could not determine whether it was his low rank, his off the rack uniform, or the bartender's obvious dislike of officers in general that led to the man's attempt to belittle him, but it didn't matter. For more than a week, Ash had anticipated a good slug of Scotch, and he meant to have one.

"Scotch on the rocks," he said, offering the bartender a straightforward response.

"Afraid not," the bartender snapped back. "Last of it's gone. An' the convoys ain't bringin' more over. So it'll have to be somethin' else, Loot." This time, the smirk ran from ear to ear.

Before Ash could say another word, he felt another man step up to the bar beside him, turned, and found himself standing beside a full-blown rear admiral, the first admiral of any stripe that Ash had ever approached to within a thousand yards.

Immediately, the bartender changed his expression, snapped his skinny frame to attention, left Ash, stepped sideways, and said in sycophantic tones, "Evening Admiral. Your usual?"

"Right you are, Slope," the admiral said with a smile, "my usual."

Instantly but without the previous flourish, the bartender named Slope set a glass on the bar, withdrew a bottle of single malt Glen Garioch from beneath the counter, and began to pour the admiral's drink. As he did so, the admiral happened to glance in Ash's direction.

"Evening, Sir," Ash said, straightening up as a mark of respect.

"Good evening," the admiral said jovially. "Just in, are you, off that new subchaser that's tied up at the quay?"

"Yes, Sir," Ash said.

"Captain, are you?"

"Yes, Sir," Ash said again.

"Nice ship," the admiral said. "Commanded one myself once, just after the first war. Rolls a bit, a subchaser, but you'll never find anything that maneuvers better, and unless I miss my bet, your crew will bond like iron. First command?"

"Yes, Sir," Ash said.

"Congratulations," said the admiral. "Say, looks like you don't have a drink yet because I thrust in here ahead of you. What'll you have, Captain? Just say the word, and Slope here will take care of you."

Ash turned to the bartender. "I think I'll have what the admiral is having," he said carefully, looking the man named Slope right in the eye.

"Make it straight from my bottle," the admiral said, "and put it on my tab. It's going to be a long war, but right at the moment, we've got plenty of Scotch to go around, and I see no reason why those of us who like it shouldn't enjoy it."

Slope, never once raising his head, went about pouring Ash's drink like he was all business.

"Right you are, Sir," Ash said, relishing his first sip. "And thank you."

"Not at all," laughed the admiral. "Seagoing officers get little enough time off, and when they do, they need their juice."

Ash intended to introduce his officers to the admiral, but Solly and Hamp, perhaps intimidated by so much gold on the man's sleeve or simply reluctant to intrude, had edged away down to the far end of the bar so as to be out of reach.

They talked on then, Ash and the admiral, for several minutes, the admiral pleasantly inquiring into such things as Ash's origins, how he had gained his commission, and his former service aboard the *Parker*, and then, when the two men finished their drinks, the admiral excused himself and left to join a dinner party that he was apparently hosting in the dining room.

Rejoining his two juniors, Ash gave them a smile.

"Things seem to be looking up," he said to them, ignoring Slope as the bartender poured him a second Glen Garioch on the rocks.

Solly grinned. "You seem to be keeping heady company," he said. "We imagined that you'd deserted us."

"Wish you'd stuck around," Ash said. "Thoroughly nice man, the admiral. He's the base commander here. I would have liked for you to have met him. No desertion intended, but suppose I treat you both to a steak as a reward for services performed."

"Would those services include the two of us being sick over the barf buckets?" Hamp laughed.

"Something like," Ash said, as the three men carried their drinks into the dining room.

The club gave them good steaks, slathered with mushrooms, and the three men ate heartily, topping off the feast with pieces of coconut cream pie that had been piled high with genuine whipped cream. Then, glasses of brandy in hand and treating themselves to cigars, they sank back into their chairs.

"Ever think you'd be living like this?" Solly asked.

"After a fashion," Hamp said, "and surrounded by money from a girl of her choice—I think it's what my grandmother always intended for me. The comfort is agreeable, but being bred like a beast is something I'm happy to avoid."

"Never imagined anything like this," Ash said. "Working for the paper in Herrin, I was lucky to be able to afford a burger and chips for a once a day meal."

"Looks like you've found a home in the Navy," Solly said.

"Possibly," Ash said.

"Indubitably," Hamp said. "And what about you, Solly? Finding it agreeable, are you?"

"What I'm finding it," Solly said, "is an experience that I never imagined. This is a lot different from Brooklyn, I can tell you, and even with the rolling and pitching, I'm finding that going to sea isn't all that bad. The captain isn't getting much sleep, and I can imagine that that is one hell of a strain, Sir, but for the two of us, beyond the normal stresses of watch standing, it hasn't yet forced us to our limits, and that's probably a good thing. About what's coming, who can know?"

"Yes," Ash said, "who can know?" And then, "Well, I suppose you could say that we've put a dent in Florida's beef supply, and I think we've killed off these cigars, so ready to go back to the ship and turn in, are we?"

An hour later, all three were sleeping soundly for the first time in a week.

13

During the weeks that followed, as March slowly gave way to April and then to May, Chaser 3 became, in Ash, Solly and Hamp's collective opinion, a work horse fated to pull plows down furrows that never ended. Three times in ten days, they made runs between Key West and Tampa, shepherding coastal vessels that had been released by other escorts for them to pick up outside the mine fields and take north. Two runs back and forth from Key West to Havana followed, neither offering the crew a night's liberty, and then they escorted several freighters to the mouth of the Mississippi, leaving them outside the delta to make their own way up the river to New Orleans. Off Grand Isle, they next caught up with three oceangoing tugs towing empty fuel barges, took them to Galveston, and turned straight around in order to conduct two more tugs pulling three barges each back to Mobile Bay. From Mobile, they returned to Key West for a night's liberty before joining an old destroyer and the first chaser that they had seen aside from themselves in order to screen two oilers and 13 freighters headed for San Juan en route to more distant ports in Brazil.

The Caribbean heat by that time had become excruciating, or at least Ash found it that way. As a result, the crew, in order to take the sun, fight heat rash, and cool themselves to a limited extent, were permitted to go shirtless and wear shorts of a sort, cutoffs fashioned from worn out dungarees. At sea, shaving was also suspended, and while the three officers managed to retain a semblance of regularity by laundering their wash khakis at intervals, the crew rapidly began to look like a collection of pirates.

Running independently out of San Juan, Chaser 3 twice escorted high-riding oilers down to Caracas before screening others, all of them newly loaded with Venezuelan oil, back to San Juan, where they were picked up by destroyers and joined with much larger convoys destined for New York and

Casco Bay. Curiously, Ash thought, throughout the entire period, they never saw so much as a hint of a U-boat, a single piece of wreckage, or the slightest indication that a war was in progress. And then, moving north toward Nassau in company with two rusted bottoms flying Liberian flags, a Venezuelan oiler, and a tramp freighter out of British Guiana, things changed.

Chaser 3 happened to be out in front of the four ships that morning, moving from port to starboard across the head of the little boxed convoy, her sonar pinging away, and pitching slightly into an oncoming sea, the result of heavy gales which had preceded them in the days before. Hamp happened to be standing the watch, and as Ash watched him, he saw Hamp's eyes suddenly widen, and in the next second, he quickly jerked up his binoculars.

"Man in the water!" Hamp barked. "Three points off the port bow, about 500 yards. Looks like he's in a life jacket, just now floating over a crest!"

"Got him," shouted a sailor named Benson who was standing as port lookout.

"Don't take your eyes off of him," Ash snapped. "Man in the water's the easiest thing in the world to lose. Hold him, you two, and I'll take the con."

With Hamp coaching his line of sight, Ash finally picked up the floater just as the man once more slid over the crest of a swell and disappeared into the trough before rising after a nerve-wracking interval up the face of the next wave and coming back into sight.

Giving orders for Samarango to muster enough men to pull the floater aboard, Ash took off turns and maneuvered Chaser 3 so as to bring the man along the starboard side where they could throw him a line. Two minutes later, Ash watched from the bridge as the floater's head bobbed down the side where Samarango threw him the bitter end of a mooring line. The man in the water, having been exposed for Ash didn't know how long, seemed slow to take the line and slower still to make it fast around himself beneath his arms. Finally, after a few minutes' delay, he managed to tie a bowline across his chest, and Samarango's rescue party, by this time also working under Solly's supervision, managed to hoist him aboard, dripping like a half-drowned rat, and throw a blanket around him.

"Hamp," Ash said, "you're the designated medical authority aboard, so go back there and see what kind of condition this guy is in. When you know something, let me know, and when you get back there, send Solly up here to take the watch."

After dispatching Hamp, Ash called down to the pilot house, put on turns, and set Chaser 3 back on course to resume her escort duties. In the meantime, the convoy had come up so that he was now out on their starboard beam. Given the convoy's 10-knot cruising speed, Ash lost nothing for having stopped to pick the man up and knew that he would be back out ahead of his charges in no more than a quarter hour.

Seconds later, Solly climbed up to the bridge.

"I think you'd better take the watch while Hamp is seeing to this guy," Ash said. "How's he look? Any injuries that you could see?"

"I think you'd better go back there," Solly said, showing Ash a straight face. "From the looks of the swastika on his life jacket and the way his hair is cut all the way up both sides of his head, I'd say we've got ourselves a German prisoner. I'm guessing that he must have been out on deck and been washed overboard from a U-boat last night or the night before."

It was the last thing Ash had expected.

"Did you try to speak with him?" Ash asked. "Did he say anything?"

"What little German I know," Solly said, "is technical stuff, to go with the engineering I studied. I can't make heads or tails of anything else. I asked Polaski, but he says that he only knows Polish. I think you're the only one aboard who has a smattering of German."

"All right," Ash said, turning the watch and the con over to Solly, "I'm on my way. Take us back out ahead of the box and resume the zig-zag."

Ash went to the fantail. By the time he got there, the German was sitting up.

"Nothing wrong with him that I can see, Captain," Hamp said, "save for exposure and exhaustion. Watts is bringing him some soup. This guy's tongue is swollen to hell from lack of water. That ought to go down, soon as we get some fluids into him."

"*Nennen?*" Ash began, asking the man his name.

Half rising before lack of strength caused him to sink back onto the deck, the man threw out one arm and tried to shout "*Heil Hitler!*" But his swollen tongue only allowed for a ridiculous sounding "*Ha Hiler*" before his dehydration compacted the sound. Nevertheless, it was enough for Ash. Placing both fists on his hips, he spoke to the man in firm, authoritative tones.

"Hitler," he said to him in German, "is *kaput* here. You are an Allied prisoner of war. Do not mention Hitler's name again, or one of these men is liable to remove your life jacket and toss you right back over the side as food for the sharks before I can stop him. We will give you water and food and treat you according to the rules of the Geneva Conventions until such time as we turn you over to higher authority, but if you make one false move, my men will have orders to shoot you and throw your body over the side. *Ya?*"

"*Ya*," the man finally snarled.

He was a burly man, the German, thick but not tall, not at all the Nordic type that so often appeared in Nazi propaganda, but rather a man with a swarthy face and dark brown hair who looked like he could be trouble once he recovered from the worst of his ordeal, and from what Ash could see, that might come in only a matter of hours.

"Boats," Ash said, turning to Samarango, "this man is to be treated humanely, but what have we got below in the way of restraints? Handcuffs, leg irons?"

"Set of handcuffs, Cap'n," Samarango said. "Want me to get 'em?"

"Yes," Ash said. "Let's get some of Watts' soup into this guy, and some water, and once you've done that, get him up to that stanchion beside the flag bag, and handcuff him to it. Not too tight, mind. No need to injure him, and let him keep the blanket. He'll be out of the weather there and out of the way, and in these seas, he'll be sheltered, and then you can issue Glick a .45, and Glick can keep an eye on him until we get into Nassau. And keep me informed about his condition. He's a lucky bastard to have survived, but I don't want him folding up on us if there's something wrong with him that we haven't spotted."

"Yes, Sir," Samarango said.

Two hours later, no more than 20 miles northwest of where they had picked up the German, Ash, Hamp and the lookout spotted a lifeboat in the water. The boat, when they reached it, turned out to be carrying the captain of a freighter named the *Vincent Lane* along with his chief engineer, his third mate, and 11 of the 22 sailors that had previously made up the crew. Two of the men were badly burned, and one of them had lost a hand. According to the captain, they'd been torpedoed two nights before but had had time to launch one of their two lifeboats. When Ash found them, they were starting to show the effects of being about to run out of water.

Chaser 3, without taking the men aboard, took the lifeboat in tow, waited for the convoy to come up, and with minimal difficulty, managed to see all of the survivors transferred onto the Venezuelan oiler. He did not tell them about the German sailor that he had picked up.

"I don't suppose that we'll ever know for sure," Ash said to Hamp, "but I'm guessing that the man we have handcuffed beside the flag bag was washed overboard from a U-boat that was stalking the *Vincent Lane*. That's why I didn't particularly want to bring them aboard. You never can tell, of course, but one of them or more might have tried to kill him, and then we'd have had a hell of a mess on our hands."

"They're far better off aboard the oiler," Hamp said, "particularly if the oiler has someone who knows how to treat burns. All we've got aboard is a can of petroleum jelly, and I can't imagine it would have been much help with the way those two men were burned."

"Probably not," Ash said.

In Nassau the following day, Ash saw the German turned over to a pair of British red caps who placed him in a paddy wagon and drove him away to be interrogated by the Royal Navy's intelligence section. Ash did not speak to the man as he walked ashore, and in so far as Ash knew, the German offered no one a word of thanks for his rescue. Ash simply felt relieved to be rid of him.

The ship didn't remain for long in Nassau. After taking on fuel, water, and some fresh bread, Ash once more headed out to sea, bound for Savannah in company with a refrigerator ship carrying perishable cargo up from Rio de Janeiro. Two hours later, north of Nassau, they came upon wreckage, a few splintered planks, an empty barrel, and two men, wearing life jackets, both dead, floating in the water, the sea birds already having pecked out their eyes. Nothing about the wreckage that the crew hauled aboard gave any indication of the ship to which the men had belonged. In the pocket of one of the dead men, however, Solly found a wallet, wrapped in oil cloth, from which he extracted a paper indicating that the holder had been appointed second mate of a Dutch freighter, the *Alkmaar*, three months before, which suggested to Ash that the ship had been in transit north from Dutch Guiana or one of the Dutch islands when the U-boat had caught up with her. The bodies, already bloated and swollen from their time in the water, rapidly began to give off the sweet, sticky odor that no man could avoid associating with death, so much so that within the hour, Ash called Samarango to the bridge.

"We can't have that for the next two days," Ash said, indicating the smell. "Sew them up in canvas, weight them, and we'll bury them at sea. I'll read the service; off duty men to muster on the fantail for it."

"With a single stitch through their noses to make sure that they're dead?" Samarango questioned. The man wasn't being facetious; he was reminding Ash of the traditions of the sea.

"Personally," Ash said, "I don't see the need, but this is the bosun's work, so I will leave it to you to do as you see fit."

"Understood," said Samarango.

Two hours later, with the off duty men assembled on Chaser 3's fantail around the depth-charge racks, Ash read the burial service, and in accordance with the traditions of the sea, the two men were committed to the deep.

The remainder of the voyage proved uneventful. Two days later, Ash released his charges north of Tybee Island from whence they proceeded up the Savannah River toward whatever shore facility beckoned them. Then, bringing Chaser 3 back outside the bay, Ash set a course for Charleston where he intended to refuel and replenish while awaiting his next assignment. Two weeks later, near the end of May, and after moving a variety of coastal freighters up and down the sea lanes, Ash finally received orders to escort two British, one American, and one Norwegian freighter from the mouth of the Chesapeake into New York.

"Have you informed Hamp yet?" Solly asked, showing Ash a sly smile.

"No," Ash said.

"I will expend my best effort," Solly ragged, "in attempting to moderate his euphoria."

"Yes," Ash said, "and a timely warning to your sister, if you can reach the phone booth before Hamp, might also seem wise."

"I anticipate the moment," Solly laughed.

But the voyage, which should have finished without incident, did not. With the onset of dusk on the evening before they were to make New York, Ash suddenly received a flashing light signal from the British freighter on the inshore side of the formation, a frantic missive reporting that one of their seamen had just fallen overboard. Immediately, Ash put on turns, reversed course down the inshore flank of the convoy's box, barely managed to locate the man who had at least remembered to flick on the tiny flash light clipped to his life jacket, and successfully recovered him. Then, as swiftly as Chaser 3 would respond, Ash once more reversed course and sped north to rejoin his little convoy which had continued its zig-zag at the reduced speed Ash had ordered.

With the sun showing its last yellow traces to the west over Atlantic City, Ash had enough light to come up alongside the British ship, wait for them to rig a boom, lower a bosun's chair, and hoist their dripping sailor back onto his own deck. But in the minutes that Ash was alongside, masked by the height of the freighter from the wide Atlantic to the east, things changed.

During the moments in which Chaser 3 effected the transfer, save for voice commands from the freighter's deck and Ash's own responses shouted up from below, the seas remained silent. Then all hell broke loose. Ash and everyone else aboard Chaser 3 heard the thundering flat crack of a not too distant gun and the resounding impact of the round on what Ash knew to be the American freighter on the forward, outboard corner of the convoy. Confirmation followed instantly as Ash sighted debris flying into the water forward, well out beyond the bow of the British ship to which he had come alongside. By that time, Ash had already sounded General Quarters and, in a flash, determined upon a course of action, swinging instantly away from the freighter, reversing course, putting on maximum turns, and electing to round the stern of the freighter even as Teague and his gun crew manned the 3-inch.

From the instant that Ash had heard that first round fired, he'd known that the convoy was being attacked by a U-boat on the surface. Why the German had surfaced for the attack, Ash could not understand. Ash reasoned that the U-boat commander could have remained submerged and fired off torpedoes at will. Perhaps the enemy boat had already expended its torpedo load, or the German was having trouble with his tubes or the compressed air system that sent the fish on their way? Ash didn't know, didn't care, and didn't take time to think about it further. Instead, he did the only thing he could think to do—he attacked, hoping to give himself a slight edge by coming around the stern of the freighter which had been masking his presence so as to start his attack from a direction that the U-boat might not have anticipated.

Calling on Chief Stobb for maximum turns and every extra ounce of speed, Ash swung his circle and brought Chaser 3 ripping out from behind the British freighter at an almost instantaneous 17 knots in the same moment that the German U-boat threw out a second round, this one blasting into the American ship's stern with enough of an impact to throw steel and debris in all directions.

The German's shooting was less than spectacular. At first, Ash imagined that the rise and fall of the swells might be giving the Nazi gunners fits, but then realized that approaching from outboard to the east but aiming west, the German gun layers had the sun directly in their eyes. That's when Ash decided that the U-boat had indeed expended its torpedoes or it would never have risked such a difficult and dangerous attack.

As Chaser 3 rounded the freighter's stern, Ash had his glasses up. It didn't take him three seconds to spot the U-boat some 4,000 yards out, its gun still pointed toward the American freighter, its white-shirted crew even then rushing to load yet another of its 4-inch shells. "Fire!" he ordered. Teague slammed out the first round. A distant splash followed, indicating that it had landed not 30 yards beyond the U-boat's bow, and over. Through his binoculars Ash could see that the German gun crew had dropped the round they were rushing to load. Clearly they'd been shaken.

Teague's gunners slammed out their second round within the space of a breath; with this one, Teague connected, the round striking the U-boat's stern gun, its anti-aircraft emplacement, unseating and displacing the gun while throwing burning debris in all directions including up over the U-boat's conning tower.

Like frightened mice menaced by a stooping hawk and probably on their captain's orders, the German gun crew, rather than contest the engagement, turned tail and ran. They disappeared instantly into submarine's hull even as the U-boat's skipper was already flooding her tanks and taking her down in an emergency dive, Teague's third round splashing not 20 yards ahead of her and throwing up a geyser that once more showered her conning tower. The last thing that Ash saw of her before that conning tower disappeared beneath the waves was the giant coal-black seahorse painted on its side.

While radio flashed out a coded message to alert COMDESLANT about the U-boat's presence, Ash did his best to anticipate the escape route that the U-boat would attempt. Indeed, Gomez swiftly picked up a solid sonar contact which indicated that the sub had turned away from the convoy, her sonar track showing her to be making for the mid-Atlantic. Three minutes later, racing ahead at full speed, Ash dropped a depth charge pattern at a point he thought to be directly ahead of the U-boat; then, still in contact and after pulling a tight turn, he dropped a second pattern, both without results. Solly rushed to the bridge with a DESLANT message ordering Ash to break off whatever attack he was making and stick with his convoy, the convoy of four already having opened the distance between themselves and the suspected contact by as much as 5 miles.

Frustrated and not a little exasperated, Ash broke off his attack and turned north. Minutes later, as two low-flying, sub-hunting Catalinas appeared overhead, calling for Ash to direct them to the supposed area in which the U-boat had headed, Ash knew why—the Catalinas would hold the U-boat down. While they did, the German would have no chance for stalking and catching up with the convoy, and if the Nazi did surface for any reason, the Catalinas, armed with depth charges, not to mention possible bombs, would make short work of him. But Ash did not believe that the U-boat would surface. In fact, unless the sub's skipper had to charge his batteries, Ash didn't believe he would again surface until he thought himself fully safe and well away from the area.

Within the hour, running at maximum speed, Ash managed to rejoin the convoy. Miraculously, only one man on the American freighter had been injured, and no one had been killed, but the U-boat's 4-inch gun had thoroughly wrecked the peak of her fo'c'sle, peeling back burned steel and twisting it into blackened and grotesque shapes as though it had been the skin of a rotten orange, and leaving the crown of the fantail in not much better shape, twisted stanchions and girders showing considerable blast damage where the round had impacted. Only later did Ash learn that the forward hold had been packed with a cargo of howitzer ammunition for the United States Army's field artillery. They'd been lucky, Ash realized. Had the U-boat's gunners thrown a round into that compartment, just forward of the freighter's superstructure, the explosion might have been enough to sink or damage the entire convoy. The revelation left Ash shaking. He decided he would spare the remainder of the crew from this knowledge, although it did perhaps explain to him why he'd been ordered to disengage and return his attentions to the convoy.

Throughout the night, Ash remained on the bridge, alone with his thoughts, Solly, Hamp, and Samarango, each in his turn, consulting with him only in the course of official business. Finally, around 0300, when Ash could feel his pulse quieten to a more normal pace, then—and only then—did he sling his hammock in the chart room and allow himself to sleep.

14

As before, Chaser 3 tied up, not inside the Navy yard but to the Coast Guard piers on Staten Island and this time in a nest of other chasers—newer ones which, only days before, had finished with the training course that had been established for their officers and crews at Pier 2 in Miami. Immediately and somewhat to their surprise, Ash, Solly, and Hamp found themselves surrounded by a virtual whirlwind of chaser captains and their junior officers, all of them fresh from the training school, all of them new to the job, none of them ever having been out before on genuine convoys save for their transit up from Miami. Their ships, Ash learned, had been built in boatyards up and down the Chesapeake from whence they had gone down to Florida for six weeks of shakedown training. What they wanted, the lot of them, was to feed off Chaser 3's "vastly more experienced" officers, none of the newcomers realizing that Ash had only qualified Solly and Hamp as Officers of the Deck for Fleet Steaming mere days before their arrival in New York.

It wasn't that the new men distrusted their training; they didn't. To hear them tell it, they had been worked half to death, each and every day, both in the classrooms at Pier 2 and out at sea aboard their chasers, starting with a lecture in front of a lifeboat that had been shot through with bullet holes and spattered everywhere with blood, their instructors pointing to it and declaring that the Nazis and the Japanese were nothing more than a pack of ruthless murderers and that it would be their job to put a stop to such monstrous behavior. No, Ash reasoned, it wasn't the rigor and the effectiveness of their training that these men doubted; it was themselves. What they were looking for, all of them, in one way or another, was an edge, something that could or might give them a leg up on the Germans, something that might allow them to prevail and survive. When Ash realized as much, he knew that he couldn't give them what they were seeking. Instead, patiently, Ash, Solly, and Hamp offered them what they had or thought they had: minimal combat experience, some knowledge gained in handling Chaser 3 during heavy weather, notes about keeping small convoys together in relatively disciplined formations, a few tips about navigating along the coast, and moderate notions about what did and did not work in handling his ship's administration and managing the crew.

"I'm afraid," Ash said at the end of what had seemed a rushed hour, "that the little we know, we've learned on the job. You guys seem to be way ahead of where we started, and my best guess is that you will pick things up fast. The truth of the matter seems to be that the unexpected is always out there waiting, always ahead over the next wave, and if any one of you knows how to prepare for that, you're already a better man than I am, but I won't try to speak for Solly or Hamp in that regard. The best advice I can give is for you to remain alert, tend to business, and react when the need arises. And there are times, I think, when any decision at all is better than none."

Whether or not anything that the three "vastly more experienced" officers had told them would make a mole hill of difference in the futures of the men to whom he had been speaking, Ash couldn't have imagined. He simply hoped that he hadn't led one or another of them down a blind path.

Later, after the various officers from the new chasers had returned to their ships and as Solly and Hamp prepared to go ashore, Polaski emerged from radio with a message he said that Ash needed to see.

Ash took the message board and began reading. Ten minutes later, as Solly and Hamp were about to climb the ladder up to the main deck, Ash stopped them before they could start.

"This is Friday," he said. "According to COMDESLANT, we don't go out again until Monday morning. I don't know what the two of you have planned, but why don't you get back here by 2200 on Sunday night. Seems we're in for a change. We'll be leading out 19 ships on Monday morning, heading for Casco Bay, and the people we just talked to will be going with us. That means five chasers for the screen, and I seem to be stuck with being both the commodore and escort commander for this one. What that means in a nutshell is that I'm going to spend this weekend reading up on communications and screen patterns. I've got an idea about sector screening, where I will send these birds patrolling sectors around the convoy rather than forcing them to hold fixed positions relative to whatever ship we select as the convoy's guide. That will reduce the need for pinpoint station keeping, reduce the strain on the watch keepers, and introduce a degree of random movement among the chasers which will create uncertainty for any U-boat that tries to make an attack. I'll toy around with some diagrams, see if it seems feasible, and get the word to the others by Sunday evening. I'll brief the two of you when you get back."

"You sure we can't be of some help?" Solly asked.

"No," Ash said, "this is something I've got to work out for myself before we try it. And besides, if we keep Hamp from meeting Chana, we risk upsetting the entire order of the universe."

Hamp, who had experienced a moment of near apoplectic frustration while Ash explained his intentions, fearing that necessity might keep them aboard, brightened visibly.

"The lovely Chana," he said proudly, "has promised to meet me outside the Brooklyn ferry with a coach and six whereupon she has offered to convey the two of us to a showing of *Sullivan's Travels*."

"That sounds like Chana," Solly rejoined. "Romantic comedy and all the folderol that goes with it. I warned you, Hamp, if you don't watch it, that sister of mine will lead you right down to the water's edge and into the drink."

"I can only hope," Hamp said. "Let's go, the coach and six will be taking up parking space, and we can't have the locals upset, now, can we?"

"The 'local,'" Solly said, "will probably be drinking a cup of coffee or powdering her nose while a party of Marines tries to chat her up for a date."

Hamp, as though stung by an electric shock, disappeared at once.

"Have fun," Solly said. "I can sure see that I'm going to," and with that he too climbed the ladder, leaving Ash laughing behind him.

Moments later, Ash also climbed up onto the main deck and found Chief Stobb.

"I'll be sticking around tonight," Ash said, "so if you'd like to go over, Chief, I'll take the command duty myself."

"Thanks, Cap'n," Chief Stobb said, "but if it's all the same to you, I think I'll stick around as well and catch up on some sleep. I've done New York a dozen times. If my wife was here, we would make a night of it, but with her in Buffalo with her mother and our girls in school, there's not much on the beach for an ole brown-bagger like me. I've reached the age where a good steak and a bottle of beer beats the night life altogether."

Ash laughed. "Fine," he said. "See Samarango, if you will, and tell him he's got my permission to go ashore if he wants to, and if you plan to stick around this weekend, I might go take in a movie tomorrow night. If or when we finally get a long upkeep, I'll try to let you off for a week or two so that you can make the trip up to Buffalo, depending upon where they bring us in for the work."

"I'd be much obliged," said Chief Stobb. "Tin cans is different, of course, but with this wooden hull, I'm guessin' that they'll want to scrape us down before long, particularly after we put in all that time in the warm water down south."

Ash felt that he had come up suddenly short. "You're probably right, Chief. I hate to say it, but I hadn't even given our bottom a thought. You reckon we've got barnacles and grass growing down there already?"

"I reckon we've got some, Sir," the chief said. "I'll put the wherry in the water and have a look myself. And it won't hurt to put an arm down there and have a feel. I 'spect we've picked up somethin', but what I don't know is what kind of intentions DESLANT might have for maintaining this kind of hull. Guess we'll find out soon enough."

"In COMDESLANT's own good time?"

"Exactly," said the chief.

"Amen," said Ash.

Throughout the remainder of the afternoon and into the night, working with the Navy's premier tactical publications and his own sense of what would and wouldn't work best with the ships that he suddenly found he had to direct, Ash struggled with new screening patterns that he was trying to invent. Laying out a circle, putting the 19 merchantmen at the center in a box with five ships across the front, two more ranks of five behind them, and a third rank of only four, he next divided the outer circle into 40-degree sectors as though slicing a pie. From the start, he intended to station the escorts he would be commanding at least 2,000 yards ahead of the main body. Then, giving them a patrol depth of at least 500 yards each in their particular slices of the pie, he would allow them to maneuver back and forth across their sectors at random speeds along the base course for whatever zig-zag he called. By arranging the pattern, Ash hoped to give the convoy frontal coverage and protection across at least 200 degrees running all the way back to the convoy's flanks.

The proverbial rat in the woodpile would strike at night. After considering the matter, Ash also devised an offensive move that might, he hoped, solve his problem. If, after night fell, he shifted the screen pattern to a four-ship front, extending each patrol sector by 10 degrees, he could dispatch one of the five chasers to the rear to patrol for U-boats running fast on the surface, so as to intercept their attempts to stalk and attack the convoy from behind. Standard bent-line screens—screens in which each escort had to maintain a fixed position—seemed to be losing a lot of ships in the mid-Atlantic. Ash had no idea what COMDESLANT might think of his plan, and he knew that in putting it into practice he'd be taking a risk. If something went wrong, it was entirely possible that he'd be inviting a court martial. If, on the other hand, the plan worked, it might strike someone at COMDESLANT as innovative. The important thing, as far as Ash was concerned, turned on the possibility that the chasers' random movements might disrupt and confuse potential U-boat attacks, while carrying the added advantage of releasing watch officers from having to pay constant attention to station keeping rather than scanning the darkened horizon for U-boats before the enemy could close and attack.

The following day, having prepared a smooth draft of his plan, replete with accompanying diagrams of the screen patterns he'd designed, Ash made his way to the Coast Guard's administrative center, ingratiated himself with a lieutenant in one of the offices, and finally popped the question.

"Sir," Ash said, "I'm the designated commodore for some escorts that I'm leading out in a few days. I wonder if I might borrow the use of America's most potent weapon in this war?"

"Say again?" said the Coast Guard lieutenant, looking at Ash quizzically.

"Your mimeograph machine," Ash said.

"Yeah, sure, go ahead," the lieutenant said, chuckling to himself. "Should I charge you for the paper, or should I expect the Navy to reimburse us through channels?"

"I already thought of that, Sir; I brought my own," Ash grinned.

"Have right at it," the officer said. "We aim to please."

An hour later, Ash returned to the nest, invited the four captains of his forthcoming command onto Chaser 3, and held a pre-sailing conference, handing each a copy of the mimeographed plan that he'd so recently run-off for them. Patiently and clearly, Ash explained both his diagrams and his intentions, the four new captains readily absorbing what he told them. Ash knew from the start, because the men were green, very green, that he was taking advantage of them in a professional way. None of them had ever seen anything like the plan Ash handed them, but as a result—and much to Ash's satisfaction—they never once questioned it and absorbed what he had to tell them with an adaptability that Ash found refreshing.

"As always, we sortie first," Ash said, "so we'll form the screen as soon as we are out beyond Raritan Bay, and then, as the ships we're to escort come out behind us, I'll organize them into a compact rectangle of sorts by means of flag hoist and we'll depart for Casco Bay. After we see them safely through the mine belts, I will release you to proceed into the bay independently, and thereafter, I suspect that you will receive new orders from COMDESLANT. Any questions?"

For another hour, Ash and the four men surrounding the wardroom table talked minor details, having to do with everything ranging from weather observations to the test firing of their guns. Then, the party broke up, each of the men returning to his own ship, and at long last, Ash went ashore, showered in the Coast Guard facilities, donned his khaki uniform, and went back onto the beach, heading for the ferry. For better or worse, he intended to take a few hours off, go over to Brooklyn, have a meal, and take in a movie.

In Brooklyn, Ash felt surprised to find as many uniformed servicemen on the streets as he had imagined to be walking around Manhattan. Sailors, Marines, and a plethora of Army uniforms seemed to turn up everywhere, and if he didn't have to salute three or four times in each block, he quickly imagined himself to be drifting from his course and in danger of becoming lost in tree-lined residential neighborhoods. Finally, without expending too much sweat or becoming uncomfortable on this warm day, he made his way down to Bensonhurst, "Little Italy" Solly called it. There he found a *trattoria* that looked appealing, went in, and ordered *risotto* for a starter, to be followed by a plate of veal *picatta*, both of which, when he had finished them and sat back thoroughly satisfied, he polished off with a *grappa* and an espresso. Tipping the old waiter who had served him double for his troubles, Ash then emerged onto the street, found himself an air conditioned theater, stood in line with a number of other servicemen, several of whom had dates, bought his ticket, and sat down for a late afternoon showing of the Leslie Howard comedy *"Pimpernel" Smith*. Much amused, rested, and feeling relaxed, Ash made his way back to the ferry and to the ship before sundown, Watts whipping him up a mushroom omelet for his supper. Following that, he settled down to read until, not long before 2200, Solly and Hamp piled down the ladder on their last-minute return to duty.

"So," Ash said, looking up, "did the coach and six meet expectations?"

"After I rescued the lovely Chana from a band of pirates—" Hamp began.

"That would be three sailors, none of them over the age of 18," Solly said swiftly.

"And conducted her to her coach—"

"Think 1935 yellow cab, with broken springs and a sour dwarf for a driver," Solly said.

"We motored to the ball and a night of pure enchantment," Hamp said.

"What he means," Solly said acidly, "is that the two of them went to the Orpheum where it was dark, where it smells, where there is gum on the deck, and where the ushers all sound like refugees from Flatbush."

"You exaggerate," Hamp said, straightening his tie with a look of pure satisfaction on his face.

"What he seems to have liked most," Solly said, "was the dark. I've been given to understand that they held hands. Neither one of them could tell me a thing about *Sullivan's Travels* when I came in. Frankly, I suspect foul play."

"Nonsense," Hamp said, "I behaved like a perfect gentleman, just like I said I would."

"Yes, I noticed," Solly said. "When I got back, I found that he'd gobbled down six of the turnovers that I'd left sitting out on the kitchen table for breakfast the following morning, my oh-too-greedy sister obviously fattening him up for the kill."

"I don't know what you're talking about," Hamp said quickly. "Your sister and I enjoyed a very amusing movie; I brought her home before 2200, and once we arrived back at the house, she offered me some light refreshment in the way of a cup of tea and a snack, and then we engaged in nothing more than some quiet conversation before you came in and we all retired for the night. And let's not forget that in exchange for the snack, I treated her to dinner last night."

"*Vichyssoise* and cold lobster salad?" Ash suggested with a smile.

"*Ha*," Solly said, speaking directly to Hamp, "It seems pretty clear that our captain wasn't born yesterday, even if you, my man, aren't yet so much as out of your swaddling garments." Then he turned back to Ash. "*Vichyssoise*, he should wish. That sister of mine dragged him all the way to Manhattan, as though we didn't have a plethora of great restaurants in Brooklyn, made him pay a cover charge to get them into *Le Joyeuse*, and then stuck him for a full-blown lobster and a bottle of *Pouilly Fuisse*, not to mention what she stuck him for as the evening wore on."

"The lovely Chana and I wished to dance," Hamp said. "'Thoroughly splendid' doesn't even begin to describe the evening. Personally, I would call it 'enchanting.'"

"Yes, you would," Solly teased, "just like any prince who'd been touched by a wand and turned into a toad." Once more, he turned to Ash. "I warned him—you heard me—but he paid me no attention, and now he's so broke that I even had to loan him the fare for the ferry in order to get him back here safely. How the two of them got home from Manhattan last night, without having to hitch a ride, is the big mystery of the evening."

"I had some mad money tucked in my shoe," Hamp said. "It came in handy. And the lovely Chana has already agreed to accompany me to the museum the next time we are in."

"What museum would that be?" Solly asked. "Tiffany's?"

"All right," Ash laughed. "It seems clear to me that the two of you have recharged your batteries, so pull off your blouses, sit down here, and let me start filling you in on what I have in store for tomorrow."

"Perhaps," Hamp said, "Solly ought to say a word or two about this person named Keren who Chana seems to know."

"Perhaps not," Solly said quickly. "I visited her parents, that's all—old friends of the family. Keren just happened to come in from work while we were having coffee. I've known her since she was a kid."

Hamp turned to Ash, smiled, and raised an eyebrow.

15

Chaser 3, the screening ships Ash had under his command, and the 19 vessels in their convoy emerged from Raritan Bay by 0800 the following morning, formed into a compact body with a heavy Greek refrigerator ship serving as formation guide, and started northeast up the coast at 12 knots, zig-zagging in accordance with one of the Navy's many standard plans. Immediately, upon execution of the appropriate flag hoist, Ash started the escorts patrolling their prescribed sectors, and then Ash took Samarango in hand, instructing him about the new method of station keeping, something the bosun had never practiced before.

"You see how it's done, then?" Ash asked after giving his watch stander an hour's close supervision.

"Yes, Sir," Samarango said. "Beats the hell out of having to shoot a bearing to the guide and read his range with a stadimeter every five minutes ... if you don't mind me saying, Captain. This is the kind of station keeping that I could almost stand to marry."

"Enjoy it while you can," Ash said. "COMDESLANT might shoot me a rocket for having tried it."

They moved on then, the plot showing that they advanced slightly under 12 miles each hour owing to the zig-zag, but aside from a few fishermen looking for a catch and a destroyer coming down from Cape Cod with four empty oilers in convoy, they didn't sight so much as a single vessel the entire day. And to everyone's surprise, the seas remained utterly tranquil beneath a windless sky throughout a long morning and a longer afternoon. The sun finally set, glowing red and throwing a sheen over the water, at about 2015 that evening. As soon as Ash had shot evening stars, he reoriented his screen by means of flashing light, sending the most senior of the new chasers back behind the convoy where, he hoped, it might be able to intercept any U-boats that tried to sneak up and intrude on the convoy from astern. And before midnight, south of Nantucket—no more than 10 miles off the beach—to everyone's surprise, if not shock, one did.

As the action developed and as Ash later deduced, the U-boat's skipper had made a mistake. Making good speed on the surface, coming up on the convoy's port side from astern, the Nazi commander had apparently assumed that the convoy would not be as well protected as it turned out to be and that, on the inland side, it would be even less well protected than it would be to starboard where it might have expected an attack from the middle of the Atlantic. The U-boat commander also failed to imagine that the escort would have enough ships to patrol across the convoy's rear. As a result, an alert lookout standing watch in the chaser's crow's nest had managed to spot the U-boat's conning tower silhouetted against the glow coming off the distant shores of Nantucket, whereupon he had instantly sounded the alarm. The chaser's commander had then gone straight to General Quarters and attacked, the first indication Ash received that something was amiss coming with the distant, delayed sound of the new chaser's equally new 3"/50 going off, followed a few minutes later by the equally muffled sounds of depth charges being dropped, Ash catching the far away sounds of the depth charges even as sonar reported hearing them to the bridge.

Acting swiftly, Ash ordered all of the escorts to General Quarters, reoriented the screen to encompass only three ships, put on turns, and went tearing back down the convoy's starboard side in order to join in the hunt. By the time he reached the attacking chaser, the U-boat commander had not only long since submerged, but he had also escaped, the chaser leading the attack having lost contact without regaining it fully 15 minutes before when he'd dropped his depth charges. The chaser's captain believed that the frag ammunition he'd fired at the U-boat might have done some damage, but given the obscurity of the night, he couldn't be certain. Together, the two ships then spent another half hour boxing the contact area in a fruitless search. Banking on his belief that the U-boat's skipper wouldn't try the same ploy again, Ash sent a BRAVO ZULU to his subordinate for having attacked and forced the U-boat down while also flashing him an order to fall in astern as the two sped back to rejoin the convoy.

Allowing for variables, Ash found in the action a modest vindication of his tactics. Had he arranged his escorts in a standard bent-line screen, forward of the convoy, he felt certain that the U-boat would have gotten in among them and made a killing, perhaps sinking one or more of their ships. He'd been lucky, of course, and he knew it. The U-boat commander didn't appear to have been very experienced. He hadn't had time to scout the convoy owing to the brief period they'd been underway. Ash imagined that the German might have stumbled onto them, sighting them from somewhere south of Block Island, and made his approach astern without any foreknowledge about the size of the escort, and as a result, he'd overplayed his hand. Nevertheless, the man had also been smart enough to fold a bad hand, once he knew that he'd been dealt one, and in the offing, he'd managed to escape, probably using the same tactics that had defeated Ash in his own previous engagements.

Even as Ash once more dispatched the accompanying chaser to patrol astern of the convoy and moved Chaser 3 up to rejoin the screen, he also reoriented their patrol sectors, throwing the starboard sectors further down their flank. If the offending U-boat tried to resurface and come up outboard for another attack, Ash intended to be prepared. Ash didn't think the man would risk it, now that the convoy had been alerted, but with a hated enemy like a committed Nazi, one could never be certain, and it was his job to see that the German stayed away. At the same time, calling Polaski up to the bridge, Ash got out a message, alerting COMDESLANT that a U-boat had been sighted and attacked so as to warn whatever other ships happened to be at sea about a lurking danger in the area.

By the time Hamp relieved the watch at midnight, Ash felt certain that all of his watch standers had mastered the intricacies of the sector patrolling. Content with the fact that he had once more brought Samarango up to speed, Ash left Hamp on watch and descended to the wardroom only to find the lights still on and Solly still awake.

"I've roughed out an after-action report," Solly said, as Ash came down. "All you need to do is make whatever corrections or additions you think necessary. Otherwise, it should be ready. I think you ought to include the spare copy of that operations plan you handed around. If you ask me, sightin' that sub and making the attack proves your tactics."

Ash sat down and read the report. "This is good work, Solly. Thanks," Ash said.

"My contribution's clerical," Solly said, looking at Ash with a straight face. "The good work is all yours, Boss. I'd think DESLANT owes you a pat on the back."

"The irregularity of what I've tried could just as easily get me relieved and bring down a court martial," Ash said. "A week or two from now, you may find that you've suddenly been elevated to command."

"I think they'll show better sense," Solly said. "I'm banking on the idea that they'll appreciate initiative."

"Possibly," Ash said, "possibly not. The Navy likes to follow the rules, and the rules seem to involve time-honored bent-line screens. On the other hand, an escort of five subchasers with a lieutenant, junior grade as its commodore seems like a whole new thing, so if I escape the rocket for this sector business, that might be the only explanation."

"Well," Solly said, "I'll keep the faith and hope for something better. I think you deserve it, but I won't belabor the point. I've got to get some sleep. I go on watch in another three hours."

"Right," Ash said, "I'm going to try to catch a few *zzzzzs* myself."

Not long before dusk the following day, Ash saw his charges steam through the minefields into Casco Bay, released the other four chasers to proceed independently, and finally entered himself as the net tenders worked to close the channel behind him. Chaser 3 then anchored without going into Portland, took on fuel and water from a tender, and went straight back out the following morning, leading two Norwegian merchantmen and a seagoing Dutch tug towing barges, all three bound for New York. Once arrived, Chaser 3 replenished from yet another tender in Raritan Bay and turned straight around, once more bound for Casco Bay as independent escort for two coastal freighters carrying stores to the Portland Navy facilities and an ammunition ship, loaded to the gills, bound for the massive convoy forming in the bay and ultimately headed for Halifax. Moving through waters that again seemed blessed with early summer tranquility, the voyage proved uneventful. Once into Casco Bay and anchored while replenishing, Ash received notice by flashing light that he was required to appear at COMDESLANT Headquarters and that he could expect a boat within 15 minutes.

Ash had heard of an entertainment called "a uniform race" which upperclassmen often used when running Plebes at Annapolis. The trick seemed to involve sending a Plebe racing down one of Bancroft Hall's long passageways to his room where, in mere minutes, he had to change from service dress blue into service dress white and return to whatever upperclassman happened to be hazing him, before being sent once more to shift from the new uniform into some other combination of official naval dress. Aside from the apparent humor it afforded to the upperclassmen, the objective seemed to relate to how much the Plebe's weight could be reduced, in a matter of minutes, by pure sweat. Failure to enter into the spirit of the exercise could result in worse punishment—multitudes of pushups or even extended periods of adopting a sitting position, without a chair for support, while holding out a rifle at arm's length.

"Christ!" Ash exclaimed to a much-amused Hamp who lolled in his bunk while Ash raced to change from dirty, working khakis into fresh service dress. "If this is what those Canoe U. Plebes have to put up with, screw it! I feel suddenly fortunate to have escaped their ordeal."

"It appears to me," Hamp said, "that there is much to be said for being a reservist. Don't forget your shoulder boards."

Ash didn't, and as he stepped up onto the main deck, he did so just in time to find the boat's bow hook making up to Chaser 3's sea painter so that Ash could board it.

"I would guess," Ash said, as he turned over temporary command to Solly and prepared to leap over into the DESLANT boat, "that the rocket is just about to burst."

"If you are incarcerated," Solly said, "Hamp and I will muster a boarding party and come to the rescue."

"Laugh it up," Ash said, saluting as he left the ship, "I may need substantial relief before the cock crows."

☙

Inside the COMDESLANT Headquarters building, a yeoman checked Ash's I.D. Card and name against a typed list and then looked up.

"Commander Gibbons, Sir, Room 229, second deck. He's an assistant to the chief of staff for operations. You're down for an appointment at 2200 hours."

Ash took a look around. Uniformed people seemed to be coming and going everywhere.

"You set a watch at night in this place?" Ash questioned, "Or is something special on?"

The yeoman laughed. "Three watch sections, Sir," he said. "We run 24 hours a day, seven days a week, and to hear our masters tell it, *every* minute is special."

Ash found his way to Room 229, where a WAVE petty officer directed him to a chair across from her desk.

"He's got someone with him," she said, all business. "He'll be with you in a minute."

Ash waited. Fifteen minutes later, a lieutenant commander, looking red in the face and running with perspiration, emerged from the inner office, threw the WAVE a disgruntled look, and made straight for the outer door. That the man had received a rocket, Ash had no doubt.

"You can go in now, Sir," she said to Ash. "Knock once and go straight through the door."

Ash did as he was told, braced up inside, announced himself, and looked straight ahead.

"Take a seat," said the man behind the desk.

Without relaxing fully, Ash sat down in the straight-backed wooden chair, and looked up at the man behind the desk. Commander Gibbons didn't strike Ash as being the sort of gray-headed retread that Ash had come to expect among the staff officers to whom he had been introduced. Instead, it seemed instantly apparent to Ash that he was sitting in the presence of a comer—a sharp, relatively young commander who was on the rise and destined for better things. In place of salt and pepper hair, Gibbons sported a mop of dark brown hair, thick and curly over a pair of dark brown eyes with nothing close to crow's feet at the corners, and to Ash's surprise, he seemed to be showing Ash a hint of a smile across exceptionally straight teeth.

"I've read the after-action report you submitted regarding your next-to-last escort duty," the commander began. "You've obviously done something irregular, Mr. Miller. If this scheme you tried had failed and you'd had some ships sunk on the way up here, I think you'd have wound up in a peck of trouble. What made you do it?"

Ash hesitated. It wasn't quite the question he'd anticipated.

"As far as I know, Sir," Ash said, speaking tentatively, "our bent-line screens don't seem to be all that highly effective in the mid-Atlantic. Most of the work I've done so far has been as an independent escort, or at the most, with a two- or three-ship escort, and I have never yet been appointed leader of one of those. All of a sudden, I found myself designated to lead four other subchasers up here with the largest convoy I've ever gone out with, and I wanted to give us the best edge that I could devise, with perhaps some offensive capability added to the mix."

"Are you aware that the Navy has already been studying something along the lines of what you tried? Sector patrols of various types?"

"No, Sir," Ash said.

"You just thought this up on your own? And put it into practice on your own responsibility?"

Suddenly, Ash realized that he'd started to sweat. It wasn't that the office was hot; in fact, the place felt air conditioned. It was that Commander Gibbons' eyes were boring into him like a pair of high-speed drills.

"I knew that I was taking a risk, Sir, without consulting any higher authority, but at the time, it seemed our best chance for bringing all the ships through. I take full responsibility."

"All right, Mr. Miller, you can rest easy. For what my opinion is worth, I think you developed an intelligent plan and carried it out well. The Navy appreciates innovations that work, so your report with the admiral's comments appended has already been forward to the Navy Department in D.C., and the admiral is putting a letter of commendation in your file. Don't expect to be promoted to senior rank next week, but do accept our congratulations for a job well done. I don't know that you will hear from the Navy Department, but you might. In the meantime, carry on with the work that you are doing, and we wish you every success. Now, ever seen the plot?"

Ash didn't know what the man was talking about.

"No, Sir," Ash said.

Commander Gibbons stood up, extended his hand toward Ash who had risen with him, shook it, and said, "Tell Reese out there to take you down to the basement so you can have a look at the plot. Shows every ship we have at sea, shows where the convoys are, what escorts are with them, and where we've sighted U-boats. I think you'll find it interesting, if not instructive."

Petty Officer Reese took Ash to the basement, and there, Ash experienced a revelation. The plot turned out to be a massive map of the Atlantic. Colored counters—counters pushed around the horizontal board by sailors and WAVEs armed with long sticks not unlike pool cues—showed the location of every ship in the Atlantic, Navy and merchant alike, with specially colored counters to show where U-boats had been sighted or made a recent attack.

"What you see in this room, stays in this room," Reece said, with a knowing eye. "This is all top secret, so you may not talk about it when you leave here. The officers on the ledge above us are the routers; they assign escorts and send out orders which reroute the convoys at sea to avoid any U-boats that have been sighted. The Nazis are starting to collect U-boats into squadrons or packs and stretching them across wide distances, so it is getting harder to pass convoys through them without being detected. For what it's worth, this is something like a nerve center or central brain for fighting the naval war. I've been told, although I have no way of knowing, that the Brits have laid out something similar, both for the Royal Navy and for the R.A.F. There is a similar set-up down in New York, at the headquarters of the Eastern Sea Frontier. Seen enough?"

"Thank you," Ash said, following the WAVE back out.

Back aboard Chaser 3, Solly and Hamp were all ears.

"I'm afraid that you're stuck with me," Ash said. "I'm not to be shot at dawn after all."

"What, not promoted to admiral?" Hamp quipped.

"'Fraid not," Ash said.

"But it did go better than you'd expected?" Solly said.

"Really," Ash said, "they were very good about it. Seems we stumbled onto something the Navy is already looking into. DESLANT forwarded our after-action report to Washington, as a sort of commentary or confirmation of what they've already been studying."

"All's well that ends well," Hamp said.

"Yes," Ash said.

"Yes, *but* …" Solly chimed.

"We have orders?" Ash said.

"Right you are," Solly continued. "They want us through the minefields by 0700. We're picking up two empty tankers, two freighters, and a cable carrier, all of them coming down from Halifax, all of them bound for Boston."

"Are we the only escort?"

"We're the only escort," Solly said.

"You have to wonder," Hamp said. "Where are all of the rest of these chasers that they're supposed to be building? And what about the slightly larger PCs, and the destroyer escorts that are supposed to be coming off the ways?"

"I think we'll begin seeing a lot more chasers by the end of the summer," Ash said. "The PCs will probably begin showing up in the fall, but the DEs are going to take longer. Steel construction, even with the yards working full tilt, still can't be done in a day."

❧

The following afternoon, 40 miles south of Casco Bay, Ash sighted thick black smoke on the horizon and knew at once that a ship had been torpedoed there. Putting on turns and redirecting the little convoy he was escorting closer to the beach so as to lessen the chance for an attack from inshore, Ash made for the conflagration by pushing his herd all the way up to an unheard of speed of 14 knots.

The sea when Ash arrived was virtually on fire. Whatever tanker had been sunk—a small coastal oiler he later discovered—had been carrying crude oil north toward the mouth of the St. Lawrence, the ship steaming independently, the owners apparently thinking that they could snatch a profit by sending out something so small that a U-boat would ignore her. They were wrong, and the five or six men that Ash found dead and horrifically burned in the water, skeletal almost with their skin eaten away by the fire, showed the owners' mistake. Three men who had somehow been able to swim away before the fire could consume them were nevertheless covered with oil, black from head to foot, and one of them badly burned. The other two, having swallowed not a little of the oil, were choking to the point of already coughing up blood, and Ash didn't imagine that they would live; indeed, one of the men died before they reached Boston while the burned man had passed into delirium. The men already dead and burned beyond recognition, Ash left in the water, refusing to risk the ship by going into floating oil that might reignite at any minute. The sea, he reasoned, would either float them ashore where qualified morticians could be called, or swallow them, along with the sickening scent they were emitting, into the last refuge of a seaman's grave.

Four hours later, with two dead men on the fantail and another barely alive, Chaser 3 tied up alongside a pier at the Boston Navy Yard, offloaded her passengers into waiting ambulances, and settled down so as to begin refueling and taking on water beneath a flood of pier lights.

"What an awful way to die," Hill, the yeoman, said to Ash, as he handed him the typed report of their pick up for Ash to sign.

"Yes," Ash said, "awful."

"But if you stop to think about it," Hill said, "I don't suppose there is a good way."

"No," Ash said, looking out across the black waters of the bay, "I don't suppose there is."

16

May and then June offered Chaser 3 no break from the unrelenting pace of operations as she ran escort duties to and from Casco Bay, Boston, New York, and Cape May. As a rule, Ash considered himself lucky if he managed to tie up alongside the Coast Guard piers at Staten Island or to one of the piers in the Boston Navy Yard by 2100 on a summer night. Fuel, water, and stores would then be hastily taken aboard so that the crew could snatch a few hours' sleep before rising, usually by 0400 in order to make the last sea buoy and be back out in the Atlantic herding yet another collection of merchantmen toward a gathering convoy in transit to a more distant war. Twice during that time, once on a May morning and later during a sweltering June afternoon, the lookouts had spotted wreckage, debris, and, in the June sighting, a single dead seaman floating over the swells. The May incident had taken place about 12 miles south of Fire Island, almost within shouting distance of New York; the dead seaman, his hand still gripping the tiller of an empty lifeboat, they retrieved from the waters east of Cape Cod. In so far as Hamp could determine after examining the man where Samarango had laid him out on the fantail, the seaman had died from loss of blood, the result of a shell splinter that had pierced his right side just beneath his rib cage. Because they were putting into Boston that night, Ash kept the body on board and turned it over to a Navy mortuary detail the minute the ship tied up to her berth.

June finally gave way to the steaming humidity of July, and on the morning of July 2, 1942, Chaser 3, in company with a fleet tug, a Coast Guard cutter of considerable size, and two oceangoing minesweepers, emerged from the mine belts protecting Casco Bay and led out a convoy of 22 merchantmen, all of them bound for Raritan Bay and the sheltering piers beneath the shadowing towers of Manhattan. During the day, steaming at 10 knots, the convoy had made steady progress, Solly following Hamp for the afternoon watch,

Samarango following Solly to stand the first dog, Hamp coming on again for the second, with Samarango taking the evening watch until Solly once more relieved to stand the mid. Throughout that time, Chaser 3—taking her orders from the captain of the Coast Guard cutter who was, in this instance, the senior man afloat—had remained on the flank of the bent-line screen, guarding the port side of the convoy. Watts, having taken on a generous quantity of fresh ground beef that morning, served the crew large portions of his famous meatloaf for supper that evening. Later, Ash, having consumed every ounce of his own share and having every confidence in his watch standers, for once took himself to his bunk, read a few chapters of Trollope, and turned in, sleeping soundly and without a care in the world until he was almost thrown from his bunk by a not-too-distant explosion and a wave of concussion that caused Chaser 3's every plank to vibrate like a harp string right down to the keel. Leaping into his sea boots, Ash dashed up onto the bridge. Solly had already sounded the alarm for General Quarters, the crew were exploding from their bunks, and Gomez shouted up from sonar that he had a firm contact, two points abaft the port beam, range 1,600 yards.

Ash didn't wait. Taking the con, he put on hard rudder, swung the ship to port, cranked up turns for 17 knots, and raced toward the contact. Behind him, as he could see when he glanced back, a massively burning freighter, her holds still exploding, was going down by the bow, men who seemed no larger than ants in silhouette against the fires leaping into the sea from the doomed freighter's stern. With a U-boat to think about, he didn't linger over what he'd seen; instead, with a speed that surprised him, he focused all of his attention on the Nazi sub he believed himself to be preparing to depth charge.

It had come, the attack, as Ash had expected it would—when everyone had least anticipated it, on a warm night, on a calm sea, with the watches running like clockwork—and there hadn't been a single echo from the sonar to warn them, not, that is, until the ship had already been struck and was going down.

"Captain," Gomez shouted up the voice tube, "she ain't turnin'. She's runnin' straight toward the convoy. She's tryin' to get in there, inside the convoy!"

Ash continued to come around, trying to head off the submerged U-boat. If she got inside of him, she might torpedo one, two, or even three ships in quick succession and then maneuver so as to bring her stern tubes to bear, and that he absolutely had to prevent. Inside a range of 100 yards, Ash suddenly gave an order to swing the ship even more to port so as to unmask his starboard K-gun. Seconds ticked by, and then, when the time was right, Ash shouted "Fire!" his voice booming across the ship and heard the roaring KRUPPS as the K-gun fired. Instantly, Ash shouted "Right rudder!" down the voice tube, turning toward a point directly ahead of the U-boat's path in the hope that he would cross the sub's course and roll his ashcans straight down onto her bow.

Hamp, reacting to Ash's order, rolled four at the same time, and within seconds the sea erupted in Chaser 3's wake. As Ash threw the rudder hard to port, trying once more to cross the U-boat's apparent path, Gomez sent up word that he had lost contact amid the explosions. Within moments, having turned a full 180 degrees, Ash dropped another pattern off the stern. Then, as the charges exploded behind him, he opened the range in an attempt to aid Gomez as the man tried to regain contact with the U-boat.

"Anything?" Ash shouted down to sonar.

"No contact!" Gomez shouted back. Then, after perhaps 30 seconds, Gomez reported hearing something on passive mode that gave Ash a pause. "Somethin's going on down there, Cap'n, but I can't tell what. Got a crackin' sound, and then a bubble sound, an' then nothin'. Could be a sub breakin'up, but probably not"

"Stay on it, Sonar," Ash called back.

In the meantime, with the convoy warned and with Ash reporting a firm contact as he ran in for his attack, the senior officer in the Coast Guard cutter sent him a clear, unmistakable order: *"Prosecute contact until 0700. If no positive results, rejoin following search."*

"Think we got him?" Solly asked hopefully.

"No," Ash said, "but I think he's down there, probably lurking near the bottom and gone silent. I'd expect to hear plenty of sounds if he'd broken up, and we didn't. Gomez heard something, but that could have been nothing more than some German sailor banging on a pipe to close a leak. What we've got to try to do is pick the son-of-a-bitch up again so we can plaster him with another pattern and keep on plastering him until we do get him."

Taking the speed down to 8 knots, Ash began to box the area, widening the box by a thousand yards with each circuit. Down below in sonar, Gomez stayed on the scope, refusing to accept relief. Ash remained on the bridge, Ash, Solly, and the lookouts straining their eyes by the light of the stars to scan the horizon in the event that the sub tried to come up and run away from them on the surface. Hour after hour, the search continued with no results. When the sun finally did come up, showing them an empty sea without a trace of debris or oil as evidence of the U-boat's sinking, Ash reluctantly headed south, only catching up with the retreating convoy near the entrance to Raritan Bay the following night.

"Sorry the bastard got away," Teague said to Ash as they tied up to the Staten Island pier that evening. "My boys were ready, Cap'n; we wanted to take a shot at him."

"So did I," Ash said, showing his gunner a smile, "so did I. Hang in there, Teague. I'm going to do my best to get you a good clean shot at one of these coffins just as soon as I can force one to the surface."

"Not to worry," said the gunner. "You can count on us, Cap'n. That popgun is just itchin' to fire, an' when it does, we ain't gonna disappoint you."

"That's the ticket," Ash said. "We've just got to keep the faith, the both of us."

Later, down in the wardroom, as the three of them prepared to turn in, Ash looked at Solly and then at Hamp, and said, "I'd bet money that if we'd stayed out there for another 12 hours we'd have forced that U-boat to the surface in order to replenish his air. I don't think for a minute that we've sunk him, but we damn well might have done him some damage, and that might just have been enough so that he couldn't have stayed down throughout another night. No use crying over spilled milk, but I sure hated to walk away from this one."

Before either Solly or Hamp could reply, a skinny kid named Michelson, wearing his shirt open and a pair of dungaree cut offs, came sliding down the ladder, running in a message from radio where he'd been standing watch.

"Good news, Captain!" the kid said, thrusting out the message board, grinning from ear to ear. "Straight from COMDESLANT!"

"Michelson," Ash said, looking the kid up and down before taking the message board from him, "if we get a surprise visit from anyone senior to me, you are liable to be in a peck of trouble over that outfit you're wearing. I have no objections to it when we're out at sea, but for in-port watches, you probably ought to get into whites or at least a full set of dungarees."

"Yes, Sir," Michelson said, swallowing the correction but still smiling.

"Now," Ash said, taking the board, flipping it open, and starting to read, "let's see what this good news you're bringing me is all about."

Suddenly, Michelson seemed so excited that Ash wondered if the man might not be about to twitch.

Then Ash smiled, turned to be sure that Solly and Hamp were listening, and began to read: "*0800, 5 July 1942 Proceed Portland; offload ammunition. 0800 6 July 1942 Proceed Anson Boatyard, Yarmouth for upkeep. 0800 22 July 1942, Proceed Portland Navy Yard for equipment modification.*"

"Not a word about this until I announce the news to the crew in the morning," Ash said to Michelson, after he'd signed off on the message, and the radioman was about to depart.

"Yes, Sir," Michelson said, showing Ash a suddenly straight face.

Watching the man disappear back up the ladder, Ash imagined that the word would be all over the ship in less than five minutes.

"I guess," Solly said, seeing the man go, "that life's a wonder after all."

"I'd guess," Hamp volunteered, "that the ravishing tea-sipping spinster of Yarmouth is in for a surprise."

"Now, now," Ash said, "let's not go putting a cart before a horse. Solly, see Stobb and Samarango and work out a leave schedule so that each man can take a week's leave if he wants it. Stobb's family is up in Buffalo, so I want him to be able to get up there for a few days, which means that you will have to oversee the engine room in his absence. I'll need a fully working crew aboard to move the maintenance forward, but we ought to be able to handle what needs to be dealt with according to a reasonable rotation. My guess is that we'll once more be moved into The Jarvis House for the two weeks we're in Yarmouth so that Anson's people can get at the interior, and if that turns out to be the case, I want all personal gear to go in their sea bags so that they don't leave anything lying around. But for now, let's get some sleep so that we can shag out of here early in the morning and get up to Portland so the men can have a good liberty the night we arrive."

Yarmouth, on the morning after they had taken off their depth charges and ammunition—as far as Ash could see while threading the channel—hadn't changed much during their absence, but Anson's Boatyard was another matter entirely. Slightly beyond the dock where Chaser 3 tied up, everyone with eyes could see that two spanking new chasers were under construction and nearing completion. Not many yards up the beach from where the ships were on the ways, small Quonset huts had been erected to serve as temporary offices for the pre-commissioning crews, an ensign or two, as well as a few sailors coming and going from their entrances. And finally, on the gate, Ash spotted a sentry box as well as a gate guard and a sentry, both of them armed.

Mr. Anson met Ash as he tied up.

"How'd she run, Cap'n?" he asked, shaking Ash's hand and greeting him with a smile.

"Couldn't ask for a better ship," Ash said. "You built her well. She runs like a dream."

"Glad to hear it," Anson said, his smile broadening. "Any leaks?"

"A small one," Ash said. "Vibrations from an exploding freighter shook some caulking loose in the lazarette a couple of nights back. My damage control people patched it, but I'll let you put your seal of approval on it."

"Not to worry," Anson said rapidly. "We're gonna scrape your bottom, rework the hull seams, paint, and give her a thorough going over. We have a couple of technicians coming from the factory to help overhaul your diesels, and we're going to repack all of your bearings and give the pumps a thorough upgrade, check fuel and water lines, replace electrical lines where necessary, and unless I miss my bet, she'll be better than new when you take her out of here in a couple of weeks."

"What's the plan for the crew?" Ash asked. "I've been guessing that you'll want them off the ship, save for those working with you."

"Right," Anson said. "Sending some on leave, are you?"

"About half each week, in rotation," Ash said.

"Good. The rest of them can bunk up at The Jarvis House, along with the people from these chasers we're building. Plenty of room, and good food, as you know. Best, I think, if their personal effects go with them. I've good men here, but temptation is a nasty thing."

"I'll see it gets done," Ash said. "When do we start?"

"Now," Anson said. "Quick as you move 'em to The Jarvis, we'll start. An' I've cleared your old office so that you and your officers can have a place to work."

"Thanks," Ash said. "It'll seem like old home week."

Anson laughed, and half an hour later, Samarango marched the crew off the ship and straight out the gate, heading for The Jarvis House.

Inside the hotel, as the men going on leave stowed their sea bags in a secure storeroom and took their leave papers from Hill who carried them in a stack, the other men picked up their keys at the desk from Mrs. Jarvis and dispersed to their rooms. Finally, Ash, too, approached the desk where Mrs. Jarvis greeted him pleasantly.

"Captain Miller," she said, smiling. "Glad to have you back. Things seem to be popping here these days, but I've saved you a good room where I hope you'll be comfortable."

"It's good to see you, Mrs. Jarvis," Ash said, "and thank you." And then, after he'd signed the register and received his key, Ash looked up and said, "I'm guessing, Mrs. Jarvis, that Miss Morris has once more decamped to The Eiseley."

"That's right," his hostess said, her smile broadening. "Would you like her phone extension? She left it for you with, I think, the expression, 'in the event he ever returns.'"

Ash allowed himself the hint of a smile. "I'd be grateful, Mrs. Jarvis."

"I see that you have acquired wisdom during your absence," Mrs. Jarvis said with a laugh. "I think it is a wise man who knows a good thing when he finally takes the time to see it."

"I will hope to take my place among the sages," Ash said, returning Mrs. Jarvis' good wishes.

"One thing," the woman said. "Claire Morris works during the day, at the public library. School teacher, you know. Has to have something to tide her over during the summer. I mention it because she doesn't leave the library

133

until five o'clock in the afternoon, so if you want to see her beforehand, you're going to have to walk over. It's uptown a few blocks, on the right."

"Thank you," Ash said. "Good to know."

"Isn't it," said Mrs. Jarvis. "You might want to take out a card. Reading is such good fun."

Ash laughed, climbed the stairs, found his room, and stowed his gear. Then he returned to the yard where Solly and Hamp were bent over their fold-down plywood desk arrangements, sorting through work orders and making out work assignments for the enlisted men that would be remaining in Yarmouth.

"Ha," Hamp said, looking up from work he was doing, "take tea with the spinster yet?"

"Work first, refreshment later," Ash said.

"Hear, hear," Solly laughed. "I hope we are setting you a good example."

"Nonsense," Hamp said. "We are just biding our time. The whole purpose of this in-port hiatus will become manifest on Friday night when the lovely Chana and a person of interest arrive here by train from the City. Rooms have been booked for them at The Eiseley to relieve them of having to fend off advances from the inferior elements."

"Spoken like a true WASP," Ash laughed. "And who might the 'person of interest' be? Some bathing beauty from Atlantic City, no doubt."

"One of the lovely Chana's running mates, to chaperone her, I'm sure," Hamp said. "I have assumed an elderly *dueña*, hirsute and vastly overweight, a retired governess possibly or even a female stoker from a Russian freighter just down from Murmansk."

"Eat your heart out," Solly said, slightly fuming. "I intend to tell my manipulative sister that she looks like a toad alongside a swan."

"You will have understood" Hamp said to Ash, "that the lovely Keren has agreed to join in this little lamentation of swans that we have invited for the weekend."

"So it would seem," Ash said. "I commend you both."

"Perhaps you and the spinster might join us for tea," Hamp continued, "if not for sport and recreation."

"If this lad thinks he has enough money saved up to permit my sister even a moment of her preferred recreations," Solly said, "he is a sadly mistaken. Chana, I can almost guarantee, will be looking forward to more lobster followed by expensive desserts. I intend to see that she is limited to plates of scrambled eggs and occasional burgers washed down by refreshing glasses of water or, at the most, coffee. Otherwise the two of us will need to visit loan sharks with very negative results."

"Don't look to me," Ash said. "I'm as poor as a church mouse. Perhaps Hamp ought to put through a call to his grandmother at … where did you say, 'The Glade'?"

"That, you will never live to see," Hamp said.

The three of them then turned to work, Ash going aboard to where Mr. Anson had drawn the ship up onto the beach in order to make a last inspection before Anson's work crews turned to their tasks, Solly and Hamp continuing with the papers that held their attention. At noon, all three went up to The Jarvis House, where Samarango had seen to the watch section's sitting before taking them down to the yard to begin with their own arduous chores. Following the lunch, Ash saw Solly and Hamp head back, and only then did he turn uptown, looking for the public library.

Ash found what he was looking for soon enough in an unimposing building located in the midst of a small park. He stopped on the steps, brushed a mote of dust from the front of his khaki service dress, and went in, the transformation of the light from outside to inside momentarily blinding him until his eyes adjusted. Then, glancing to one side, he spotted her, Claire Morris, sitting behind the reference desk, her auburn hair radiating a rich copper color even beneath the artificial lighting. Without hesitating, Ash stepped forward. Claire looked up, saw him, and flashed him a sudden, lovely smile that Ash quickly absorbed right down to his toes.

"You're back," she whispered, holding out her hand. "So good to see you."

"It's good to see you too," Ash whispered, taking her hand and feeling its warmth. "You're working, I know, and I don't want to interfere, but I wondered if we might arrange for a drink later, after supper? I have to eat with the crew at The Jarvis House where the Navy is footing the bill."

"The Eiseley has a cozy little bar," she said at once. "Much quieter there than at The Jolly Roger, and far less crowded. Would that do? Say eight o'clock."

"Perfect," Ash said. "I'll look forward to it."

"So will I," she said, once more showing him a pair of bright eyes. "I'm glad you're back. I can imagine that you need a breather."

"It's good to be ashore. We're plumb exhausted, all of us." He did not add that Claire Morris promised to be the exact breather that he needed, the best possible breather of all.

17

The Eiseley's bar—a comfortable lounge hung with long velvet curtains to muffle the sound and fitted out with a few well-cushioned booths and darkly painted tables and chairs—did provide an attractive place for a drink and some quiet conversation. When Ash walked into the room a few minutes before eight, he found the only customers to be a pair of ensigns, seated in a corner, talking over glasses of beer, while an elderly couple sat at a table, cradling what looked to be cups of coffee. Ash, greeting the bartender's nod and indicating that he was waiting for someone, seated himself in a booth in view of the entrance. A few minutes later, Claire appeared at the door, spotted him at once, and came toward him. She had swapped the plain cotton skirt and blouse that she had been wearing in the library for something slim, black, and fetching. Ash, when he stood to greet her, felt slightly breathless upon seeing her.

"Just continue to look entirely natural," she whispered, suddenly putting a hand on his shoulder while reaching up to give him a buss on the cheek. "That's for the two ensigns back there, to keep them at a distance. They're nice boys, I'm sure, but they've each been into the library twice this week to ask me for a date, and I'm afraid that they're both a little young for my taste. So, if you won't mind me using you in this way, I'm hoping that the sight of us together might finally blunt their interest."

"The poor lambs," Ash grinned, as the two of them sat down across from one another.

Immediately, the bartender came over.

"What will you have?" Ash asked.

"A brandy, I think," Claire said.

"Have you, by any chance, a Calvados?" Ash asked the bartender.

"I do," said the bartender, indicating that he was impressed. "Not much call for it around here, but I've a good bottle which I will be delighted to open."

"I'll have one," Ash smiled.

"What is Calvados?" Claire asked at once.

"Apple brandy, from Normandy," Ash said. "I'd never heard of it until I got to France, and then I learned to like it in a hurry."

"I'll have the same," Claire said, speaking to the bartender.

"You didn't have to change," Ash said, after the bartender departed to pour their drinks. "I thought you looked lovely this afternoon, and I'm sure you've had a long day."

"A girl likes to put her best foot forward," Claire said.

"And a fetching foot it is," Ash said. "I rather regret that I can't respond in kind, but I'm afraid it's going to be khaki or navy blues for the duration."

"Nothing better," Claire said, looking him right in the eye. "I've thought about you a good deal while you've been gone," she went on, "enough so that I don't want to beat about the bush, fritter away the time, or waste a moment if you think we can make something of this—of us. Do you?"

Even in his wildest imagination, Ash had not anticipated anything so unexpected and abrupt.

"Yes," he said, after studying her face for a moment and finding it sincere, "I've been thinking about you since the moment that we met."

"I'm glad," she said, suddenly taking his hand and squeezing it as Ash squeezed back.

The bartender returned, set the two Calvados in front of them, and then discreetly retreated.

"Let's drink to it," Ash said, lifting his glass.

"Let's," Claire said flooding him with a warm smile.

It was done, the agreement between them sealed with a *clink*.

"*Oh*," she said, taking a sip, "this is lovely."

"I assume you're talking about the brandy," Ash quipped.

"Only tangentially," she said, "but it, too, reaches perfection."

"I suspect," Ash said, "that there have to be ground rules."

"That's generous," she said, "but some are necessary. I have to go on living here. For what it amounts to, I have a position to maintain, jobs to hold down, and I can't have people talking, or worse yet, submitting complaints to the schoolboard. You do understand that?"

"I do," Ash said.

"Aside from drinks like this and occasional meals, this hotel and The Jarvis House have to be off limits," she continued.

"Same for me," Ash said.

"Aside from walks, or meals, or coffee, or movies, nothing public around Yarmouth then."

"Also agreed," Ash said.

"I have a friend," she went on, "who owns a cabin—a sort of vacation beach house—up on the Kennebec River south of Bath. It's not far, and there's a bus that runs up to Bath. She's offered the place to me for the weekend, so if you think you can get away …? "

"I can get away," Ash said without hesitation.

"I'll pick you up at the bus station in Bath at ten o'clock on Friday evening," she said. "My friend's also lending me her car."

"It's a date," Ash said.

They talked on, nursing one Calvados and then another, until ten o'clock. Claire declined a third, saying that she had to be at work the following morning and needed her sleep. Ash then walked with her toward the elevator, but as they passed two closed doors in the hallway, Claire reached for one of the handles and said, "You need to see this room; it's a beauty."

As she quickly opened the door and stepped through, Ash followed her, and then, Claire turned, closed the door behind him, put her arms around Ash, and kissed him long and passionately.

"That's an appetizer," she said, "for what I hope will seem like a feast this weekend."

"What a delicious promise," Ash said.

"Here," she said, taking a tissue from her purse, "let me clean you up before I send you back to your people."

"I'm doubtful that any of them will be sober enough to notice," Ash said. "My guess is that most of them will come weaving down from The Jolly Roger much later tonight. This is their first liberty in weeks, if not months."

"Still," Claire said.

"Yes," Ash said.

When Ash finally returned to The Jarvis House half an hour later, Hamp and Solly were still sitting in the lobby, reading *The New York Times*.

"There's a hell of a battle on at a place called El Alamein in Egypt," Solly said.

"Paper say anything about Guadalcanal?" Ash asked concealing any hint of the weekend he planned with Claire.

"Yes," Solly said, "the Marines are having a hell of a fight around Henderson Field, and from what I can glean from the paper, there have been some naval battles out in Iron Bottom Sound that don't bear thinking about, but the details are awfully sketchy."

"And the Germans have taken Sebastopol," Hamp added. "What's that at the corner of your mouth, Boss? Looks like blood."

"Catsup," Ash said, instinctively reaching to wipe the incriminating evidence away. "I just treated myself to a burger."

"I'll hope the spinster enjoyed it," Hamp said. "Was that before or after the tea-sipping?"

"About tea-sipping," Ash added, "I'm sure that Chana will know best."

"Oh, don't I hope," Hamp said.

"Try to restrain yourself," Solly jibed. "These effusions of yours are becoming revolting."

"I can only suppose," Hamp said, "that the person of interest settles for a hearty handshake after a date. Pity, Solly, you seem to be missing out on so much."

"Clearly," Ash said, "this lad needs a good night's sleep with a good laxative as a bed partner. He's obviously loaded with beans."

"Ain't that the truth," Solly laughed. "Big day tomorrow, let's go up."

And they did.

Ash registered more than mild surprise over the amount of trash Chaser 3 had acquired across her bottom during their months in southern seas, but he found himself equally gratified by the energy which Anson's workmen applied in scraping her down, removing barnacles, and sanding her smooth. Elsewhere aboard, the work went forward with the same degree of attention, the factory technicians, Solly, and the snipes tearing into the engine overhauls with gusto, efficiency, and genuine concern. In the little office inside Anson's warehouse, Ash worked with Hamp to bring the required paperwork under control and to sift through the bales of official Navy correspondence and publications that arrived for him to filter. One, an intelligence document marked *Secret*, gave Ash a surprise because it anticipated that the Nazi admiral, Dönitz—commander of Hitler's U-boat fleet—seemed to be gradually withdrawing his marauders from the Atlantic coast to concentrate them in packs for mid-Atlantic attacks on the major convoys. The reason given was that America's coastal convoys were becoming nigh on impenetrable. Ash let out a grunt of disbelief when he read that; he had seen no evidence of the numerous escorts that the message seemed to imply. From Ash's point of view, the available escorts had been stretched thin, or even thinner, since the day he had first taken Chaser 3 to sea, and with regard to sinking allied merchantmen along the coast, the Germans seemed as proficient and ubiquitous as ever.

In the evenings, after taking his dinner at The Jarvis House, Ash allowed himself to bask in the aura that Claire seemed to radiate every time he went to pick her up. One night, as the two of them topped off their dinner with an espresso and a piece of pie at Queen Bee's Tea and Coffee, the English woman who owned the place joined them for an hour's banter before other customers arrived. Another night, the two of them went to see *That Hamilton Woman* with Vivien Leigh and Laurence Olivier.

"Handsome devil, Olivier," Ash said.

"Beautiful woman, Leigh," Claire said.

"And apparently," Ash said, "a sight more beautiful than the real Lady Hamilton, if the accounts I've read prove anything. I think she was supposed to have been a little more than plump and rather homely."

"The illusion almost always improves upon the reality," Claire said, "when switching from life to film, I mean."

Another night, while the air remained still and the cicadas put up a clatter, the two of them walked, well up Main and all the way out to Yarmouth Junction and back, twice crossing the river over a picturesque little bridge, talking and simply enjoying being together without, momentarily, anything to distract them. Then, on Thursday evening, the two of them once more sat over Calvados in The Eiseley's lounge, Claire again setting Ash mildly afire with the help of her little black dress.

"Tomorrow night, then, at the station in Bath?" she said, after once more kissing him inside the ballroom.

"I'll be there," Ash said.

On Friday afternoon, and because he already knew the way, Ash guided Solly and Hamp to the station, whereupon Solly turned to Ash and said with a broad grin, "We'd best counsel the lad, here, not to behave like a schoolboy in heat, don't you think?"

"Christ," Hamp snapped back, "and this, from the guy who just spent over an hour picking the dust from his uniform with a pair of tweezers!"

"Anticipation," Ash said augustly, "is the enemy of calm. Take an example from me—a sound military bearing and quiet self-assurance is what these arriving beauties of yours will be looking for, so I'll expect you both to rise to the occasion and uphold the honor of the service."

"And that's how you've been conducting yourself with all of this tea-sipping that you've been doing?" Hamp said.

"You can count on it," Ash said.

The train arrived, and the two girls, carrying their bags, were the first to step lightly from the coach. Immediately, Hamp and Solly stepped forward to relieve the girls of their luggage, and then introductions were made, Ash enjoying the music of the girls' *Nu Yark* accents. Chana, a trim creature with light brown hair, was not the toad of Solly's imagination; in fact, she was as lovely as Hamp had advertised, equipped with a perky personality, and, like Hamp, something of a tease. The "person of interest," the girl named Keren, came with much darker hair, an inch or two more height than her friend, and a more restrained manner of speech. But in the minutes they spent together, Ash noticed that the girl seemed also to possess a wry sense of irony that he thought might suit Solly perfectly.

"I'm surprised, Captain," Chana said with a smile, "to find that you are actually flesh and blood. We were given to understand you to be a man of granite."

"Only when dealing with ensigns," Ash said. "The rest of the time, I am as tame as a lamb."

"And when might we meet the tea-sipping spinster who apparently has the lamb in tow?" Keren asked, showing Ash a sly smile.

"Sunday night?" Ash said, without skipping a beat. "Over drinks at The Eiseley?"

"At last," Hamp said.

"Sounds good," Solly said.

"Sure," both girls said at once.

Ash saw them all into a cab, and then, making his way to the appropriate station, Ash boarded an early bus for Bath.

In Bath, Ash stowed his bag in a station locker, walked out onto the street, found himself a coffee shop, and nursed a cup of so-so coffee for an hour while he waited for the clock to click off the minutes. Then, at 2145, he returned to the bus station, retrieved his bag, and once more stepped out to the street to wait for Claire, who pulled to the curb at precisely 2200 in a black 1935 Ford coupe.

"Want a ride, sailor?" Claire called through the open window.

"Don't mind if I do," Ash replied.

They weren't 20 minutes driving down to the cabin, a two-bedroom bungalow really, and once they arrived, Ash could see that Claire had been there earlier; both a bottle of hard to obtain Scotch and a bottle of Calvados were already arranged on the kitchen counter.

"You came up early," Ash said.

"I wanted to buy groceries and a few other little things," Claire said, "so that we don't have to go out, unless, of course, you want to. Like a drink?"

"What about you?" Ash said.

"I'll take a Scotch," Claire said.

"I'll join you," Ash said. "Where under the sun did you find it?"

"There's a place in Bath that still apparently gets some down from Canada," Claire said. "How the Canadians are getting it is anyone's guess."

"Perhaps some of those enterprising officers running corvettes guarding the convoys between Halifax and Glasgow are bringing it back with them in cases," Ash laughed.

"You may be right," Claire said, "because from what I know, it has virtually disappeared everywhere else."

After Ash poured their drinks, they sat down, the two of them, on the sofa and looked at each other.

"Here's to us," Claire said, raising her glass.

"You're on," Ash said, clicking his glass against Claire's and taking a sip. "Which reminds me, Solly and Hamp seem to have lured their own young lovelies up from Brooklyn for the weekend. I met them at the station before I came up. Nice girls, really, the both of them, and they're anxious, the four of them, to meet the 'tea-sipping spinster' with whom I'm supposed to be keeping company. I suggested The Eiseley's lounge on Sunday night for drinks. Think we might be able to oblige? I'd think that little black number you've used on me would just about make their eyes pop out."

"Oh, you sly rascal," Claire said. "But of course. I'd love to meet them. We elderly spinsters have to do our best to encourage budding romance among the young."

"Actually," Ash laughed, "those romances seem to be moving pretty well under their own steam. Hamp came back utterly besotted from his very first introduction to Chana, and while Solly is considerably more circumspect, I gather that whatever he has going with Keren—the woman Hamp likes to refer to as the 'person of interest'—seems to be something of long standing."

"Your boys, then, have not been slow off the mark."

"Not at all," Ash said. "Chana is Jewish, of course, so if Hamp is as serious about her as he seems to be, I would imagine that the WASP grandmother up in Newport or wherever—the one who tried to put Hamp under her thumb and who controls all the money in her family—will just about blow a gasket when she hears about it, and that ought to make Hamp as happy as a clam. As far as I can see, he is utterly without prejudice, something I admire about him, and with Solly as an example, I'd imagine that his family couldn't be better people if they worked at it."

"What about the religious complications?"

"I don't think Hamp has a religious bone in his body," Ash said. "I don't think it would matter, and from what I can tell, Solly and his family only go to synagogue once or twice a year, if that often."

"Which raises a question—what about you?" Claire said.

"Protestant. I was raised to believe in the Almighty," Ash said after a moment, "but I don't wear it on my sleeve. You?"

"Lapsed Catholic," Claire said. "I still believe that children should be given religious training, but I've learned to make my own decisions. From what you're telling me, we seem to move along the same lines."

"So we're on then, for Sunday night?" Ash said.

"Oh yes," she smiled. "I look forward to meeting all of them. It will be a treat."

About the time they'd finished half of their drinks, Claire rose, told Ash that she had something to see to in the next room, and disappeared for a few minutes, leaving Ash to savor his Scotch. Then, not ten minutes later, Claire suddenly reappeared wearing nothing but a tight black slip that seemed to cling to her like a silk glove.

"The shops in Yarmouth offer nothing that approaches Hollywood splendor," she said, "and I didn't imagine that you'd appreciate summer flannel, so I'm afraid that this is the best that I could find. I hope I don't disappoint."

Ash felt like he'd been hit with a hammer. Claire Morris seemed to him more beautiful, more seductive, and more alluring than anything he had ever imagined.

"You don't disappoint," he said. "You look ravishing."

"Then let's adjourn to the bedroom," she said. "I think I'd like to try to besot you in the wildest possible way."

"I'm totally at your disposal," Ash said, stepping forward and enfolding her in his arms.

Later, lying side by side with her soft breasts pressed to his chest, she put her head up against Ash's ear and whispered. "I love you. That was better than I could have imagined."

Ash pressed her to him. "I love you too," he said. "And regarding something you said earlier, the reality of you, my dear, outstrips the illusion by more than I can measure."

18

Late on Sunday afternoon, Claire drove Ash back to the bus station in Bath.

"I hope you enjoyed the weekend," Claire said as they drove into town.

"Nothing ever finer," Ash said, "and I mean that, love."

"It was utter bliss," Claire said, "and now that you've seen what I have to offer, I hope you're so thoroughly besotted that you will want to do exactly the same thing next weekend as well."

"You can count on it," Ash said, as Claire slid to the curb in front of the Bath bus station. "See you at The Eiseley, then, in about two hours."

"Perfect," Claire said, giving him a kiss. "And see that you don't sit down next to the prettiest girl on the bus and try to chat her up on the way down to Yarmouth, my love."

"Couldn't possibly," Ash said. "I'm much too exhausted."

When Ash reached The Eiseley that evening, he found Solly, Hamp, and their girls already parked around a comfortable circular table in a corner where the bartender had just delivered their drinks.

"Ah," Hamp said, "our master arrives. *Siéntese, Jefe.* What'll you have?"

"I think I'll wait for Claire," Ash said, pulling out a chair and sitting down. "I hope you've had a delightful weekend, the four of you."

"You see," Chana said, giving Hamp a dig, "how a gentleman behaves. He *waits* for a lady and is obviously attentive to her every need."

"I must observe," Hamp said, "that he's setting a dangerous and thoroughly unnecessary precedent. If he were to persist in that kind of behavior, a woman could start expecting it, and that would be an ordeal for any man to endure. I must undertake to instruct him and give him guidance."

But before he could say another word, Claire arrived wearing her little black number and instantly produced the effect that Ash had imagined that she would, all four of the others staring wide-eyed and rising to greet her as Ash made the introductions.

"What we are dying to know," Keren said as the party resumed their seats, "is what kind of tea the two of you sipped this weekend."

"Orange pico, with a slight hint of peppermint," Claire said smoothly, everyone at the table dissolving into laughter. "And you?"

"Oh," Keren said, "we were very sedate. These two limited us to sips of Earl Grey at that place called the Queen Bee's."

"We wanted somewhere with plenty of light," Chana said, "So that this one and my intrepid brother over there would behave with decorum and keep their hands to themselves."

"I defy you to say that we didn't behave with perfect manners," Solly protested.

"Keep your shirt on," Chana said. "I simply want your Commanding Officer to know that we kept you in line."

"Remind me to hire you as 'welfare mistress' for Chaser 3," Ash joked. "And then, once you've put these two through their paces, I'll let you start on the crew, because there's no telling what they've been up to."

"Hill and Polaski seem to have taken up with a couple of local girls," Solly said.

"We met them at the movies," Keren explained.

"Where Michelson, Teller, and that kid named Zwick provided witty commentary," Hamp added.

"Nothing untoward, I trust," Claire said.

"All in good fun," Solly said. "In fact, that Michelson is something clever. He had us all laughing."

"I suspect," Ash said, "that after word gets around about having seen the two of you with Chana and Keren, your stock will improve immensely with the crew. You may even be asked to sign autographs."

Hamp beamed. Solly turned slightly red.

"Oh, stop," both girls said at once.

"Orange pico, anyone?" Claire said, flashing a radiant smile.

They talked on, the six of them, over two successive drinks, and then, while Ash and Claire said goodnight, Solly and Hamp collected the girls' luggage, called a cab, and took them to the station where they were catching the night train for New York.

"You've the makings of a happy ship," Claire said, once more kissing Ash good night inside the ball room.

"Yes," Ash said, "and for my money, you're the best thing about it. What say I treat you to supper tomorrow night?"

"You're on," Claire said.

Throughout the week, at Anson's Boatyard the work went forward unimpeded. Within days, Anson's crew had scraped down the hull, sanded, re-caulked seams, painted, and signed off on the papers for hull maintenance. Meanwhile, in the engine room, the factory technicians, working with Solly and the snipes on board, had made good progress overhauling the engines, while Chief Stobb and two other firemen began tearing down and overhauling their pumps. In the midst of all of this, on Wednesday afternoon, yet another Navy staff car came through the gate, passed straight by the two Quonset huts where the other chasers were building, and drew up in front of the warehouse where Ash kept his office. When it finally stopped, Commander Fromkern stepped out. Ash snatched up his hat and immediately hurried out to greet him.

"Making good progress, are they?" Fromkern said, after Ash had saluted him and the two had shaken hands.

"Yes, Sir," Ash said. "Hull's back in shape. The tech reps you sent and my engineers are getting the plant in condition without any trouble. I think everything will be completed on time or a day or two before."

"Been able to give your people some leave?"

"Yes, Sir," Ash said. "One section went last week; the others are away right now."

"Good," Fromkern said. "They get rusty, you know, if the op-schedule doesn't give them some time for themselves. What about you and your two officers?"

"Ah … we've spent some quality time with friends, Sir. I think you could say that we've been well satisfied."

"Excellent," the commander said, showing Ash a grin. "Glad to know that the environment satisfies. Now, about this equipment modification that you're scheduled for down in Portland. I've wrangled you a radar and a very good third-class petty officer to maintain it. I think it will take us about three or four days to install it. We'll have to reinforce your mast a trifle and make some other adjustments, but once you get it on, I'm guessing that it is going to make your life one hell of a lot easier—for navigation, for station keeping, particularly at night, and for hunting U-boats."

"I'm stunned," Ash said, nearly euphoric. "I never imagined we'd get a radar on something this small."

"Production's finally getting up to speed," Fromkern said. "I'm not going to say that these sets are perfect, but they're the most effective things we have for finding U-boats and bringing the krauts to heel. We're starting to equip aircraft with radar as well, and a combination of air search, working in conjunction with our escorts, is making a swift difference, particularly along the coast."

"I saw an intelligence report that said that the Nazis are drawing back into the mid-Atlantic," Ash said.

"That's partially true," Fromkern said, "but not entirely. Krauts sank a tanker not three nights back, no more than 12 miles south of Cape May. Ship went down within three minutes, taking all hands. Escorts didn't even get a contact. So it's still hostile out there, and dangerously so. That's why we're trying to put radar on as many of the escorts as we can, as fast as the sets can come out of the factory."

So, Ash reasoned, conditions were changing, but it also seemed clear that they weren't changing fast enough.

"There's one other thing that we're working up as well," the commander continued. "Got the idea from the British, but we're putting together some small task units that we're starting to call Hunter-Killer groups: a few destroyers, destroyer escorts, and corvettes, working with jeep carriers—merchant hulls with much smaller than usual flight decks but with some effective aircraft. We've got one or two of them roaming around in the mid-Atlantic along the chop line, all of them with the primary responsibility for finding and sinking U-boats while breaking up their Wolf Packs. Thus far, when the weather is right for flying, it looks like they're an effective deterrent, and if we get enough of them out there, they might even become deadly. You won't be joining them, of course. A chaser simply isn't fast enough to keep up with them."

After looking at Ash's paperwork regarding the upkeep and speaking for a few minutes with Olie Anson, Commander Fromkern returned to Ash, shook hands once more, and wished him God speed. Then, as quickly as he'd arrived, the man was gone, his staff car whipping through the gate trailing a thin cloud of dust in its wake.

⌇

"You've a smile on your face," Claire said as the two sat over coffee in the Queen Bee's that evening. "Particularly good day?"

"Yes," Ash said. "Can't tell you much about it, but our survival chances have been improved. And anything that offers a better guarantee that I'll be able to get back here with you when the war allows looks like a good thing to me."

"Take hold of as many things like that as you can," Claire said. "I don't suppose the Navy would consider stationing you in Yarmouth, would they?"

"No," Ash said, "although the mere idea sounds thoroughly delightful."

"What do you suppose they actually intend for you?" Claire asked.

"I'd only be guessing," Ash said.

"Go right ahead and guess, love."

"Well," Ash said, "I've been in command of Chaser 3 for about six months now. From what I've heard about other ships our size, I'm guessing that they'll leave me on board for another 12 months at the least and then move Solly up to command as my relief. Hamp, of course, will then move up as the X.O., and they'll draw a third officer from the schools somewhere."

"And you, where will you be assigned?"

"My assumption," Ash said, "is that I will either be sent down to Miami as an instructor or be assigned as a department head or as the exec on a destroyer escort of some kind. The yards are beginning to turn them out one after another, and that's probably where experienced chaser captains are going to go. I won't have enough seniority to command one of those ships; lieutenant commanders will probably get them, but if I'm promoted to lieutenant between now and then, a hitch as an X.O. may be in the cards."

"And whether you stay in the Atlantic or go out to the Pacific is strictly a matter of chance?"

"Yes," Ash said. "And for us, that stinks, I know, but there it is."

"I'll keep my fingers crossed," Claire said, looking up with a reassuring smile. "There's a war on, you know, so we'll have to take what comes."

"You're a trooper," Ash grinned.

"You bet," Claire said, "and oh my, but do I ever intend to show you some trooping this weekend."

"Should I bring combat boots?"

"Stock up on energy pills, if you can find some," Claire said. "You'll be shipping out next week, but before you go, I intend to give you the best weekend of your life."

On Friday night, coming in on the evening train, Chana and Keren returned from New York to enliven Hamp and Solly's weekend, but Ash was not there to greet them. Instead, he had already taken the bus to Bath, where Claire once more picked him up at the station and drove him down to her friend's bungalow. There, without hesitation or inhibitions, the two of them spent the vast majority of their weekend in bed, shamelessly making love, unable to get enough of each other. The following Sunday evening, when the two finally joined Hamp, Solly, and their girls at The Eiseley, both, regardless of the fact that they looked as placid as doves, showed signs of exhaustion around their eyes.

"Oh, dear," Keren said to Claire as she sat down beside her, "you do look like you need a drink. Long swim, was it, miles and miles up and down the coast?"

"Oh yes," Claire mused, "but the water was wonderful. Ask for Calvados, won't you Ash, perhaps a double."

"Pick up a few seashells?" Hamp said to Ash. "Comb the beach for driftwood? See any porpoises during your swim?"

"Claire and I took tea in Bath," Ash said. "Pleasant walks, counting light posts, a little gin rummy, some contemplative viewing of the sunsets, and so forth. Lovely weekend. Very restful."

"Be careful you don't fall off to sleep in your chair," Chana said. "Those sunsets look like they've exhausted you."

"Hamp," Solly said, "Chana looks like she needs another drink. I think her tongue's about to become unstrung."

"Never you mind," Keren said, patting Solly on the knee. "Chana's merely being polite."

"And what, if I may ask," Ash said, "did the four of you get up to this weekend?"

"Bird watching," Hamp said. "Chana wanted to count sapsuckers."

"Pleasant walks," Solly said. "Keren wanted to bathe in fall colors and collect a few mementos for her memory book."

"Have you ever heard such a pair of asses in your life?" Keren said, pinching Solly's arm.

"Insipid to the point of nausea," Claire laughed, taking Ash's arm and squeezing it. "Like hearing something from Fauntleroy's *Etiquette Book for Little Boys.*"

"Officers and gentlemen," Ash said, "officers and gentlemen, and the three of you wouldn't have us any other way."

On the following Wednesday morning, Ash once more backed away from Anson's dock and took Chaser 3 down the channel into the upper reaches of Casco Bay, made Portland with minimal effort, tied up alongside an assigned pier, and working closely with Solly and Hamp, welcomed the yard's chief engineering officer aboard to complete the necessary paperwork for their modifications. Then, before anyone had a right to expect it, a crane came down alongside on the pier while a welder went up the mast to begin detaching the crow's nest from its fittings. At the same time, a radar repeater and a necessary antenna were delivered to the ship and left crated on the pier, sitting under canvas, while materials were assembled for reinforcing the mast, the engineering officer telling Ash that he intended to finish the installation by Saturday afternoon, so that Chaser 3 could once more put to sea.

Not ten minutes after the crew secured from quarters the next morning, Samarango reported that a radarman 3/c had reported aboard, and Ash asked to see him.

"So," Ash said, "your name's Moroni and you come from Herrin, Illinois, by way of Great Lakes and the radar school. Part of Herrin's Lombard community, were you? Know the Calcaterras, the Oldonis, the Brancas, by any chance?"

"Yes, Sir," Moroni said, a surprised smile spreading across his face. "You know the place?"

"I spent a year in Herrin working for the paper," Ash said. "Know the place well. Good folks. They'll expect you to be a credit to them."

"Yes, Sir," Moroni said.

"The question I have," Ash said, "is how well do you know this radar we're getting?"

"The SF-1, Cap'n? I know it, Sir. Trained up on it at the school. I can operate it, and I can repair it. Range on a good day is about 16 miles, nautical. Ground return's sometimes a problem, but I know a trick or two to reduce it. Good little system when she's workin' right."

"We'll look to you to see that she does just that," Ash said. "Where are you bunking? We've got cramped quarters here."

"Bosun got me a place up forward, Sir. Said that a petty officer rates a bunk, so one of the seaman's slinging a hammock. I feel kinda bad about it, puttin' a man outa his bunk, but the bosun says that's the system."

"And so it is," Ash said. "Glad to have you aboard, Moroni. Give us your best and perhaps you'll spot a kraut that we can sink."

"Yes, Sir," Moroni said.

☙

On Friday afternoon, with Moroni and the shipyard's technical people making final adjustments to the newly installed SF-1 radar, Ash took a room for the night at one of the better downtown hotels and then went to the bus station to collect Claire.

"I've missed you," he said, as she took his arm. "It's pretty obvious to me that I'm not going to like being away from you."

"It's a little piece of hell that the war has forced on us," Claire said, "but I don't suppose we're alone in our predicament."

"No," Ash said, "I don't suppose we are. I guess there must be a few million others in the same boat, a boat far more crowded than Chaser 3. Any special requests about where you'd like to dine? Lobster, or perhaps something French? I hear there's a good place over on Federal Street. One of the chiefs at the yard says that the chef's from Bordeaux."

"Sounds delicious," Claire said, giving his arm a squeeze, "and then, I'll take you straight to our room and give you a lovely dessert."

"Pumpkin pie?" Ash said, "With whipped cream?"

"I'll let it be a surprise," Claire said.

Their dinner, a fine cut of beef rolled and baked in a pastry shell and accompanied with a souffle, couldn't have been better. But it was the dessert—something that they lingered over until well into the wee hours of the morning—that satisfied them most, and then, to the discomfort of both, the feast ended, Ash rising and pulling on his uniform as he prepared to return to his ship.

"I won't make a scene," Claire said, standing in front of him as she reached up to kiss him goodbye. "I love you, Ash. Come back to me. I'll be waiting."

"I love you too," Ash said. "Look after yourself for me, and I will be back to love you more at the first opportunity."

And so, leaving Claire standing in her robe, Ash returned to Chaser 3, backed into the channel, and took his ship to sea.

19

On the morning that Chaser 3 left Portland, she picked up a convoy of eight merchant bottoms in Casco Bay and escorted them all the way down to Cape May, in company with a new destroyer escort commanded, as Ash had imagined, by a regular lieutenant commander who knew his business and made good use of the chaser, particularly at night when he stationed her on the convoy's flank to guard against stalkers. The first thing that Ash noticed, almost from the outset, was that Commander Fromkern had been right; with the SF-1 operating at peak efficiency, life on the bridge suddenly became several times easier than it had been. To keep in practice, Ash and Bell still shot the stars morning and evening in company with a sun line at noon, but with the radar working, they really didn't have to; Ash could glance at the radar scope, shoot rapid ranges and bearings to three recognizable points of land, as long as they were not too far from the coast, and have his navigational fixes plotted within seconds. At the same time, with all of them showing up as blips on the screen, he could keep track of the precise position of every ship in the convoy and, based upon the size of the blip it produced and its movements, the destroyer escort with which he was operating. Radar, he decided, was a magnificent invention, a seaman's dream come true.

Dropping off one convoy at the mouth of the Delaware, Ash and the DE picked up another, which they then took down to Norfolk before turning around, after a brief replenishment, and guarding yet another back to Cape May. As the days turned into nights and the nights into days, August dissolved into September and September into October as Chaser 3, working with this or that DE or this or that combination of subchasers, moved international merchantmen up and down the coast between half a dozen different ports, never once making New York, never once making Casco Bay. Twice during that time, Ash saw ships torpedoed. The first, a freighter carrying both stores and grain, went down slowly, Ash guiding Chaser 3 in close enough alongside to take off the entire crew without a single injury or death. The second—a smaller freighter that nevertheless seemed to be carrying ammunition of some kind in its forward hold—blew itself to smithereens so quickly that the only survivors appeared to be the two lascars that had been blown clear when the ship exploded, and only because they were standing on the fantail at the time. In each instance, it had been the attending DE that had led the hunt for the offending U-boat, while Ash had been relegated to shepherding the remaining ships in the convoy to safety.

On another night, south of Charleston—a calm night with a mere hint of a mist hanging in the air—Ash received the fright of his life when, glancing casually to port, he gasped to see the phosphorescent wakes of three torpedoes racing towards him at such high speed that he knew he didn't have a prayer of avoiding them; then, to his chagrin, he watched, astounded, as three glistening porpoises rose straight up out of the sea, flipped backwards, and disappeared into the deep. For half an hour more, the same chase continued, the playful creatures obviously homing on the sound of Chaser 3's sonar. In each instance, Ash nevertheless felt like he'd been slugged in the gut, never knowing for sure whether he was seeing one more approach of the teasing porpoises or real death-dealing torpedoes from a lurking U-boat. It was unnerving, that experience, and unsettled his stomach for hours, one of the mysteries of the sea.

Finally, in early November, Chaser 3 went into port for three days' upkeep, in Key West. As far as Ash was concerned, Key West was better than nothing, each of the watch sections enjoying two full days of well-deserved liberty in a place that supplied them with adequate quantities of beer, entertainments that proved lively, and the warm freedom to go ashore without having to wear pea coats. In fact, throughout their stay, the men shifted back from blues to whites, the Caribbean heat and humidity remaining high throughout their time there. But for Ash, Solly, and Hamp, about the best that they could hope for turned out to be a couple of drinks each night at the club followed by a well-cooked steak. Key West, tiny paradise that it might have been, remained much too distant for Claire, Chana, or Keren even to dream of trying to reach.

"Romance by letter, scented or otherwise, can only make the heart grow fonder," Ash quipped, as he reread one of Claire's letters for the third or fourth time.

"Somehow," Hamp said, "I find that exchanging Chana in the flesh for the pleasure of her prose style is much less compelling than I could wish."

"Florid, is she?" Ash asked.

Solly broke into unexpected laughter. "More like illiterate, I'll bet," he said.

"Nonsense," Hamp said, "I hang on her every word. Jane Austen should have been so smooth."

"You're kidding," Solly laughed.

"Not at all," Hamp said. "There's a world of feeling in three little words. She writes 'I miss you' right here at the start. That's music to the ear."

"That kind of prose is called purple," Solly said. "I had no idea that Chana could be so loquacious."

"And Keren," Hamp said, "has she sent you endearments?"

"She writes that her cat is shedding," Solly said, "and wonders if she should take the beast to the vet's."

"Very passionate," Hamp said.

At that point, after a knock, they were interrupted by Samarango.

"Cap'n," the bosun said, showing Ash a serious face, "it's Teague. He's got a personal problem and requests an interview."

Ash folded Claire's letter back into its envelope and returned it to his locker.

"I'll meet him in the chart room," Ash said. "That'll afford him some privacy."

Five minutes later, Samarango brought Teague to the chart room.

"I understand that you have a problem," Ash said. "Lay it out for me, and I'll see if I can help."

Teague, in so far as Ash could read the man, didn't look so much distressed as angry.

"It's like this, Cap'n," he said. "Don't know if you knew it or not, but I'm married. Been married for two years. Had a place in Omaha, the two of us, 'fore the war started, but I signed up early, January of '41. My wife didn't like it then, and appears she don't like it now. The bank and my mother has both wrote. My wife's gone. Cleaned out our bank account and must have faked a power of attorney 'cause she's sold the house, and she didn't have no right to do that, not without my signature. I didn't leave her no power of attorney."

Not all romances, Ash realized, ran the smooth course that his and Claire's seemed to be running.

"You've got leave on the books," Ash said, "nearly a year of it built up. Do you want me to give you emergency leave?"

"No, Sir," Teague said, drawing himself up. "I got a job to do here, and there ain't no one else can do it, so I ain't goin' on leave. This war's more important than that gal, no matter how much dirt she's done me. But I got somethin' else in mind."

"Spill it," Ash said.

"I hear tell that Navy intelligence has an investigative branch," Teague said.

"To tell you the truth," Ash said, "I don't know for sure, but I'll look into it for you, and I'll do it today. Why don't you put the facts down on paper for me, and if ONI looks into things like this, I'll pass along anything you give me. Is that what you'd like?"

"Yes, Sir," Teague said. "I'd be much obliged. It's one thing if that girl wants to walk out on me, but sellin' our house out from under me, that's a crime in my book, and I mean to see that I get my share back from her. She can take her share, an' good riddance, but I got equity in that place, and I sure as hell deserve my part back from her."

"Understood," Ash said.

Later that afternoon, after finding his way into the right ONI office, Ash presented what he had to a lieutenant commander manning an investigative desk, and to Ash's surprise, the lieutenant commander accepted the assignment with ease.

"We'll get onto it," he told Ash. "We work with the FBI on cases like this, and we have more of them in a year than people would imagine. Girls like that usually wait until their man is at sea, and then quick as a snake strikes, they clean him out and blow the scene. Most of them don't go very far, so we've had considerable luck in tracking them down and seeing a degree of justice done. Sometimes, even here on the beach, it's an uglier world than it looks."

On the night after Ash had spoken with the naval investigator, Chaser 3 experienced its first run in with the Shore Patrol. Around 2300, a Shore Patrol van drew up and stopped on the pier. As Ash watched, two husky sailors wearing SP brassards, night sticks, and leggings, threw open the rear doors and pulled Rollo from the interior, whereupon, with each man grasping one of Rollo's arms, they escorted him to the brow and brought him straight down onto the quarterdeck in order to turn him over to Ash.

"Fightin' at the EM club," the senior of the two said, after he had saluted Ash and handed over some attending paperwork. "This one's got a black eye, but he broke the other one's nose."

"All right," Ash said. "If he can stand, I'll take it from here, and thanks for bringing him back."

Rollo sagged a little as they let him go, the senior shore patrolman giving Ash a grin and a twist of his head as though to say, "Lucky you," before the SPs retreated up the brow and disappeared into their van.

By that time, Samarango had come on deck to take charge of his inebriated seaman.

"What do you have to say for yourself, Rollo?" Ash asked, as Samarango took hold of the man's arm in order to keep him on his feet.

"Somabitch said chaser sailors is splinters in the fleet's ass," Rollo said, beer fumes issuing from his mouth like the waves off a gas jet, "so's I hauls off an' hit 'em, Cap'n, an' he goes down, an' then his buddy hits me. Big guy. Stinkin' drunk, and me mindin' my own business an' all."

Samarango, Ash noticed, actually rolled his eyes.

"Right," Ash said, trying not to laugh while lending a hard edge to his tone. "Two weeks' restriction to the ship as an extra duty man. Can't have you giving the ship a bad name, Rollo, so save your fighting for the krauts, and in future, set a better limit on the amount of beer you drink. That's all. Dismissed. Chief Master at Arms, take this man to his bunk and see that he turns in."

Later, at about the time liberty expired, Grubber, Krupp, and two of Chief Stobb's snipes, Teller and Armstead, came back weaving and singing down the pier. As Ash watched in disbelief, Teller missed the brow entirely and fell straight into the slip, only to come up sputtering and spitting as the deck watch threw him a line and rushed to haul him on board.

"Teller, you silly ass!" Chief Stobb barked when he came up to retrieve the man. "Don't you even think about goin' down into the compartment until I've hosed you down good with fresh water. An get that damn uniform off soon as you get to the fantail. You stink like hell!"

"What's it like up there tonight?" Hamp asked, as Ash returned to the wardroom and prepared to turn in.

"Lively," Ash said. "Rollo popped some sailor on the beach and came back with a black eye. Teller just walked off the brow and straight into the slip. Chief Stobb is back aft hosing him off. There's no telling how much crap and garbage is in that water, but from the looks of him, he came up covered with about half of it."

"Hmm," Solly said, "sounds like the boys back aft are going to smell him all night. That ought to sober them up in a hurry."

"If they don't lynch him first," Ash said.

"Very profitable, this liberty," Hamp said. "They seem to be rapidly developing into real seagoing Jack Tars after all."

"Yes," Ash said, turning off his reading light as he slid into his sack, "they do."

❧

On November 9, just in time to leave port on the tail end of a hurricane which passed south toward Honduras, Chaser 3 once more took to the sea, pitching and rolling beyond anything the men had seen for weeks. Almost immediately, three of Ash's supposed Jack Tars became seasick, but after tossing their cookies, none of them gave so much as a thought to seeking relief in their bunks and went about their routines with a resolution born of the fact that they were resigned to their fates.

The convoy they picked up—16 vessels gathered from various stretches of the Caribbean—was bound for Charleston with an escort of three chasers overseen by a DE which carried the escort commander. With the outer bands of the hurricane still strong enough to strike them on the starboard quarter as they worked north, the pitching, rolling escorts still yawed uncertainly in the oncoming seas.

"Geeze," Solly said to Ash on the bridge, "if this doesn't feel like being trapped inside a cocktail shaker, I don't know what would."

"Ain't that the truth," Ash said, dodging a sheet of spray that suddenly whipped back over the plunging bow and up against the bridge screens, "but we're lucky to have advanced this far north. Key West is probably getting plastered with rain by now. That, at least, we escaped."

Around midnight, finally, the convoy outran the storm's orbit, the wind, what little remained of it, coming from dead ahead. As a result, the yawing ended, but with a strong sea running, Chaser 3 continued both to pitch and roll, the sea only beginning to moderate two days later as the untroubled convoy approached Charleston.

Much to the crew's displeasure, Chaser 3 did not go all the way in that night, did not tie up to a pier, and did not grant liberty. Instead, replenished by a yard oiler in the outer harbor and without being able to take on fresh provisions, she no more than topped off with water and fuel before COMDESLANT sent her straight back out to sea where, in company with yet another DE, a corvette, and five subchasers, she joined in escort for a 40-ship convoy headed for San Juan and destined, ultimately, for parts east.

"Holy shit, Sir!" Polaski exclaimed, rushing up to the bridge and thrusting a message board into Ash's hands. "We've landed in North Africa, Sir! Big invasion! Morocco, Algeria, it appears we're getting at Rommel from the ass end!"

Ash took the board, flipped on his flashlight with the red lens, and began to read.

"He's not kidding," Ash said to Hamp who was standing as Officer of the Deck. "According to this, we apparently hit the beach on 8 November, so it's starting at last. I'm guessing that's where this batch is headed—North Africa—with destroyers and DEs to take them on from San Juan."

"I've got a friend who's a platoon commander in the Big Red One," Hamp said. "I wonder if he's over there. Anything about the units involved?"

"No," Ash said, "and I don't suppose they'll say. Security and all."

"By the way," Hamp said, changing the subject, "it's more than 1,300 miles down to San Juan. We gonna run on one tank, all that way? We'll be cutting it kind of thin if we do."

"Not to worry," Ash said. "According to the op-order the DE commander has put out for us, we're going to do an underway replenishment halfway down. We've never had to do one before, but this time, we do."

"Tricky, is it?"

"Yes and no," Ash said. "I imagine we'll go up inside the convoy to do it. The oiler will be on a set course with a set speed; probably 12 knots, and every other ship will conform to her. First ship will move up alongside while the second will take a lifeguard position about 500 yards behind her. A bolo heaving line will come over from the oiler to us; we'll then pull across a messenger line with heavier lines to follow, and finally a steel cable which will be attached to our tripod by a pelican hook. Then the hoses for fuel and water will slide down the cable so that we can make them up to our fittings. They'll probably pass us a distance line as well with a sound-powered phone line attached. There are flags on the distance line so that we'll know how many feet we are from the oiler at all times, and the real trick is to con the ship so as to remain about 40 feet from the oiler throughout the evolution. I won't say that it isn't tense, because the OOD has got to remain sharp and alert every minute so as to give minor corrections to the lee helm for speed and to the helmsman in order to hold a relatively steady position throughout. As long as the seas cooperate, it isn't too bad. If we have rough weather, it becomes a hell of mess, in terms of difficulty."

"And once the tanks are topped off?"

"The lines are sent back, one after another, and then we break away and return to our station in the screen."

"You'll be the one keeping us aligned with the oiler?" Hamp asked.

"Going alongside," Ash said, "but I'll want you and Solly up here on the bridge with me in case either of you ever has to do it in future. I intend to give both of you the con at one point or another, so that you can have a go at it and see what's involved. Chief Stobb and Samarango are perfectly capable of handling the lines, the hookups, and the replenishment proper."

"Something to look forward to, then?" Hamp grinned.

"Yes, like killing a rattler, or something like that," Ash laughed.

The route selected for their transit to San Juan took them outboard of the Bahamas along the western edge of the Sargasso Sea. Regardless of conditions farther to the north where, Ash imagined, ice would already be forming on the decks of the convoys bound for Iceland, their transit ran through much warmer waters, and for once, the sea also remained relatively calm, the waves seldom cresting at heights of more than 6 feet. To Ash's way of thinking, the sea seemed almost gentle, and on the morning of their third day out, the DE's skipper, relaying orders from the oiler where the convoy's commodore was stationed, put up a flag hoist calling for the screening escorts to refuel. Chaser 3 turned out to be the fourth chaser to go alongside.

"Chief," Ash said to Stobb in the minutes before he prepared to move up into lifeguard position. "Watch them like a hawk. I don't want one of our people to hook the diesel line up to our water tanks by mistake. That's happened to others, more than once, and I sure as hell don't want it happening to us."

Chief Stobb laughed. "No, Sir," he said. "I'll handle it myself, Cap'n. Right as rain, all the way."

"Samarango have everything ready on his end?"

"Yes, Sir," Chief Stobb said. "Been rigged and ready for the last hour."

"All right," Ash said. "Let's get to it. I expect a flag hoist any minute now."

The flag hoist came, and when it did, Ash put on turns, reversed course, whipped around behind the convoy, and came up smartly into the lifeguard position inside the convoy and 500 yards astern of the oiler, all lookouts gluing their eyes to the chaser alongside the oiler in case a man fell overboard. Twenty minutes later, as the refueling chaser sent back the lines and broke away, Ash once more put on turns, ran up alongside, and slipped into position to take on fuel.

Immediately, as everyone took cover to avoid being struck, a bosun on the oiler swung the lead-weighted bolo and then heaved it over. As soon as it landed on the chaser's deck, Samarango and his deck crew seized it and began to pull the messenger across. Thereafter, the lines came over without a hitch, Samarango seeing to their hookup with the efficiency of a thoroughgoing professional while on the bridge, Solly and Hamp watched Ash con the ship so as to keep her in a steady position alongside. The fuel and water lines then slid down the cable on which they rode over from the oiler, the flexible tackle that controlled them on the oiler giving and taking, releasing and retracting tension so as to conform to the minimal rolling and pitching of the two ships. As Ash looked back and forth between the oiler and his own deck where the connections were being made, he saw to his satisfaction that Chief Stobb had stepped forward and secured the correct hoses. A word to the oiler over the sound-powered phones started the big ship pumping, and once that evolution began, Ash turned the con over to Solly for five minutes' practice and then to Hamp. With their tanks topped off, the connections were broken, the hoses retrieved, the lines sent back, and the final pelican hook tripped so that the connecting cable snapped back through the air to the oiler's side. Chaser 3—topped off, fueled, and free—put on turns and broke away, proceeding up through the convoy to rejoin the screen.

"Well done, all hands," Ash announced by means of his megaphone. He then reset the normal watch sections. When Samarango came up for the afternoon watch as OOD, Ash waited until the watch had been relieved and settled into normalcy, and then moved up beside his bosun and started a private conversation with the man.

"When do you take your exam for Chief?" Ash asked.

"In January," Samarango replied.

"I have no doubt that you'll pass it," Ash said, "and I'll see to your promotion as soon as the Navy will allow it. But there's this as well. You've been doing the job of an officer up here since we first started out, and I'd be more than pleased to recommend you for Officer's Candidate School if you'd like to give it a try."

Samarango hesitated. "I don't have the education, Cap'n. I think they want at least two years of college, an' I ain't even got that."

"What they want right now," Ash said, "are experienced line officers. You've got the experience they're looking for, and I think they're making provisions for people like yourself to do the college after the war—if you intend to stay in, that is. I'd hate like hell to lose you, but North Africa or no North Africa, this is going to be a long war, and OCS would be a good career move. Give it some thought. No rush. And when you make a decision, come and see me."

"Thank you, Cap'n," the man said. "I'll think about it."

"Do," Ash said. "I think you've got the right stuff for it, and I think it would open some doors for you."

Things went well for the remainder of that afternoon until, during the first dog watch, a 5,000-ton freighter loaded with foodstuffs hauled out of the convoy and stopped dead in the water owing to a breakdown. Seconds later, by means of flashing light, the skipper of the DE signaled Ash to detach and guard the freighter while she made repairs. Hamp, having the deck, pulled away from the screen immediately, reversed course, crossed behind the convoy, and began to circle the freighter with the radar rotating and the sonar pinging to provide the big ship the best protection he could give her.

"Pisser, this," Hamp said, as Ash came to the bridge to join him.

"Sitting ducks, the both of us," Ash said.

20

Whatever troubled the big ship turned out to be something that kept her stationary for more than four hours, so that when the two ships finally got underway around 2100 that night, Ash estimated that the convoy might be as far as 40 miles ahead of them. The captain of the freighter, an American out of Baltimore, seemed as anxious to rejoin the convoy as Ash, so when he told Ash that he thought he could make 16 knots, the two of them, zig-zagging only mildly, took off lickety-split to catch up.

Ash remained on the bridge until around 0100 that morning, but with both sonar and radar operating effectively in relatively calm seas, he once more slung his hammock in the chart house and turned in, leaving Hamp on watch, confident that Hamp would call him if anything turned up. Ash reasoned that by making up about 4 nautical miles on the convoy for each hour they were underway, they would rejoin sometime late the following morning.

Ash managed to sleep through the mid-watch and for about an hour into the early morning 0400–0800, but at 0515, Solly called into the chart room, woke him firmly, and summoned him to the bridge.

"Radar's picked up something funny," Solly said. "I've got Moroni up here on the scope, and I think you'd better have a look. Might not be anything, but then again ..."

Ash went straight to the radar.

"Where's the convoy?" he said.

"Still out of range," Moroni replied. "I'm guessin' they mus' be up there, 20 miles or more."

"What have you got then?" Ash said, rubbing the sleep from his eyes and trying to concentrate on the radar.

"There," Moroni said, pointing to a spot on the scope. "It comes and goes, Cap'n. 'Bout 12,000 yards. See, there it is again."

Ash looked. Twice, the sweep on the scope went around, turning up nothing, and then, on its third circuit, Ash saw a blip, a small one—a blip almost so insignificant that he might have questioned its existence.

"When did you pick this up?" Ash asked.

"Krupp picked it up first, Sir, and that's when he called me up here. That was 'bout 15 minutes ago. We wasn't seein' it much at first. Now, it's showin' up more."

Ash studied the scope.

"Anything on sonar?" Ash said.

"Nothing," Solly said. "I just got Gomez up. Pierre's on watch in there at the moment."

"Pierre knows his stuff well enough," Ash said, "but you did the right thing. Get 'em up, Solly. Sound General Quarters. I don't know what we've got up there, but if that's a U-boat stalking the convoy, I want to be ready. And get Teague up here; I want to talk to him as soon as he's up."

Five minutes later, following a flurry of running legs and flashing elbows, Chaser 3's battle stations were manned and ready. In the meantime, Ash had taken the ship up to 18 knots, Chief Stobb promising that he would give Ash everything the plant had while assuring him that both engines were running like well-tuned clocks. By that time, Gomez was on the scope in sonar and reporting nothing, and that's when Ash told him to shift his mode from active to passive.

"If this radar contact turns out to be a U-boat," Ash told Gomez, "I don't want him to hear us pinging on his listening device; I'm guessing he'll be in passive and listening for the convoy's screw beats up ahead of him. If we can catch him on the surface and get up close enough to shoot at him, I'll want you to switch back on the minute we open fire. Got that?"

"Yes, Sir," Gomez called back. "Soon as we fire."

"Right," Ash said. "And in the meantime, you listen for screw beats and let me know if you pick up any."

Then Ash turned to Teague. "All right Gunner," he said. "That shot at a U-boat that we've wanted … well, we might be about to get it. No nonsense now, no wishful thinking. How close do I have to get you before, given these seas, you think you can hit it? We'll be coming at it from behind, and whether this thing will have a 40mm back there or not, I don't know. If it does and we can see it, go for the gun first, and if you get in a good round, I'm guessing that it will hit the conning tower as well. If the damn thing turns and tries to shoot it out with us, go for the 4-inch forward of the conning tower. That's the worst danger we face. My guess is that she'll submerge pretty quickly as soon as we begin shooting at her. My hope is that you'll have time to get off three or four rounds and do her some damage before she goes down. So, what's your best range for opening fire?"

Teague looked at the seas, what he could see of them in the dark, and then at Ash.

"If you can get me in to 8,000 yards, I think I can hit her, Captain."

"Then that's what we'll try for," Ash said. "Check your rounds, and wipe 'em down. Don't want any dirt or salt fouling things up in the breech."

"Right," Teague said. "Loaders are doing it now."

"And if I turn broadside to 'em," Ash said, "order the Oerlikons to open up. They'll be out of range, but it might confuse the krauts and make them think we're bigger than we are."

"Yes, Sir," Teague said.

"Radar," Ash called, "give me a range."

"Ten thousand," Moroni called back, "and closing. Firmer contact, each sweep."

"Polaski," Ash called down to radio, "coded message to the DE: *Possible U-boat on surface astern of convoy. Estimate bearing from convoy guide, 310, range 18,000 yards. Closing for attack.* Get that straight off, and let me know as soon as the DE acknowledges."

Along the eastern horizon, Ash could see the first morning stars and knew that dawn was imminent. Soon, if not already, the U-boat would be putting on turns of her own, moving up fast on the surface, seeking to attack the convoy from behind as soon as she had enough of a sun to see precisely what she was attacking in order to calculate her torpedo solutions.

"Chief," Ash called down to the engine room. "Can you give me any more out of them?"

"Maybe another knot, Cap'n, if we go balls to the wall."

"Do it," Ash called back. "This is the time for it."

"Load and stand by," Ash called down to Teague.

Slowly, too slowly for Ash, a gray light began to creep across the horizon, the dark night fading away gradually to a pre-dawn haze. On the bridge, Ash and the lookouts strained their eyes to the limit, scanning ahead, searching for the contact.

"Good solid contact, 8,300 yards," Moroni shouted up.

Still they couldn't see it. Then, suddenly, they did—a raised U-boat's conning tower, greenish gray against the haze, blending with it but steadily emerging, dead ahead of them on what was obviously the same course that Chaser 3 had been steering. Ash could not see a stern gun, but given the distance, that didn't mean that the U-boat didn't have one.

"She's dead ahead," Ash shouted down to his gunner. "I can't see a stern gun, but we're down to 8,000, so as soon as you've got her in sight, you can open fire at will."

It wasn't what Ash had expected. Rather than leaping with excitement, everyone had gone instantly silent, still, almost cold with a freezing intensity that Ash could never have foreseen. As more seconds ticked by, the atmosphere only hardened.

"Sonar, stand by," Ash called down through the voice tube.

"Got her!" Teague sang out, quickly making an adjustment to the gun's elevation. Half a second later, without waiting for further orders, Teague pressed the firing key.

Instantly, Chaser 3's 3"/23 slammed out a round, a wave of smoke and cordite fumes sweeping back over the bridge even as Ash and the lookouts searched ahead to spot the fall of shot. Teague broke the breech to eject the spent casing, while the loader stepped forward to ram home another round. And then Ash saw the splash.

"Range perfect. Train right!" he called down, but Teague had seen the same splash and already adjusted. The adjustment had been spot on because, with what Ash instantly recognized as miraculous shooting, the second round exploded against the U-boat's conning tower, blowing something or someone, Ash thought, instantly over the side.

"Geez! Did you see that!" a lookout sang out. "We blew one of them bastards overboard! Holy Christ, Almighty!"

"Quiet on the bridge!" Ash barked as the sound of their third round going out drowned his command.

Teague's third round missed entirely, going long, but by that time the U-boat was already submerging, going down so swiftly that Teague's last round, another dead shot, caught only the upper lip of the conning tower just as the sub was going under, exploding a shower of spray and tearing away what Ash imagined as pieces of inconsequential steel as the boat disappeared beneath the waves.

"Sonar contact, bearing 125, range 6,500!" Gomez shouted from below.

"Stay on it," Ash called back. "Ready depth charges?"

Hamp reported the racks and K-guns ready as Ash tore ahead for his attack.

"Radar contact," Moroni reported, "bearing 130, range 13,000 yards."

That would be one of the escorts, coming back to assist, Ash imagined, thinking ahead to a two-ship search.

"Sonar contact, bearing 105, range 5,800 yards," Gomez called up. "He's turning tight, Captain. Very tight."

And suddenly, Ash knew why.

"Watch for a periscope," Ash shouted to the lookouts. "Teague, you see a periscope in the water, plaster it with frag, and keep pouring it out until I tell you to stop. That son-of-a-bitch is going to try to torpedo us!"

The increasing light helped. The lookouts picked up the periscope as soon as it broke the surface, the sunlight glistening off its forward lens, and Teague instantly began throwing out one round after another of fragmentation ammunition, the kinds of rounds usually used for air defense. It didn't matter whether he hit the periscope or not as long as he kept the sea boiling with a constant upheaval around it, making it hard or impossible for the U-boat's commander to see the chaser and calculate his shot. Nevertheless, the German fired a spread of two torpedoes, and Ash—alerted to their screw beats by sonar and with the aid of a hard rudder to starboard—avoided both. Then, with the sub once more submerged and going deep, Ash turned, ran for where he imagined the sub's bow to be pointed, and launched his attack, rolling off eight charges set for between 100 and 150 feet. Almost immediately, he believed that he had achieved a success when Gomez reported hearing an underwater explosion and what sounded to him like the U-boat's hull cracking under pressure from the exploding depth charges. Suddenly all contact was lost and they heard nothing, so that when the DE which had come back at high speed arrived, the two ships could find nothing to attack and began to conduct a box search.

Thirty minutes later, while the freighter Ash had been guarding proceeded on its way to rejoin the convoy, on the north side of the box, about where Ash assumed that Teague had first struck the U-boat, the DE picked up the mangled body of an *Oberleutnant* in Hitler's *Kriegsmarine*, the man apparently blown overboard by the blast. An hour's search turned up nothing else—not a single bit of debris, not a spot of oil, not even a torn bit of clothing—to mark the result of Ash's attack, so with the sub disappeared and no sonar contact to prosecute, the DE signaled Ash by flashing light to break off the search, join him immediately, and return to the convoy.

"You think he went deep?" Solly asked when he came up to take the watch.

"No," Ash said. "I think we spotted a U-boat and sank the same. I don't think this one got away, Solly, but we don't have a shred of evidence to prove it and never will. If they credit us with so much as a possible, I'm guessing that we'll have to rest content."

"Hard life if you don't weaken?"

"No question about it," Ash said.

❧

Two nights later, the convoy made San Juan, and against all of Ash's expectations, Chaser 3 went in and tied up to a pier at the foot of Old San Juan within sight of Moro Castle.

"How long are we here for?" Hamp asked.

"COMDESLANT's giving us two days," Ash said. "Solly, split the crew. One section on liberty tonight; the other goes over tomorrow. Old San Juan's supposed to be good liberty, but give them your speech before they go. I don't want any of them raising a ruckus, and with regard to this sub we think we've just sunk, tell them to keep it under their hats. No crowing about it. Loose lips and all that merely cause trouble. But give Teague and the gun crew liberty on both nights. It isn't much of a reward, I know, but it's about the best that I can do for them. They did some fine shooting out there, and they ought to have something to show for it."

To Ash's surprise, the commanding officer of the DE showed up not long after Ash had turned his liberty section loose on the town. With Solly and Hamp gone over to arrange for both fuel and stores, Ash took the man down to the wardroom and, for once, had Watts bring them up a pot of coffee.

The DE's captain, a Naval Academy regular named Blake from the Class of 1933, struck Ash as a well-adjusted individual, very competent at sea from what Ash had seen, and both personable and courteous in conversation. The man smoked a pipe, sat comfortably in a chair across the table from Ash, and seemed to enjoy the coffee that Watts brought up to them.

"I commend you for a good job on the way down here," Lieutenant Commander Blake said to Ash, after the two had made some small talk. "Now that we've got a moment, I'd like to hear chapter and verse on your engagement with that U-boat. It will all be in your official report, I know, but I have to submit one as well, and I'd just as soon know the details before we both start writing things up."

Ash laid out the facts as well as he could remember them.

"I know we hit him on the conning tower, twice," Ash said, finally. "The dead man you recovered is the evidence. The U-boat fired two torpedoes at us, but we managed to avoid those by means of a sharp turn to starboard, and I made my depth charge attack immediately afterward. My sonarman claims that he heard both an explosion, well after the depth charges had gone off, and breaking up sounds, but we didn't find a single piece of evidence to prove that we sank anything. I think we sank a U-boat, but I don't think DESLANT will credit it."

"Probably not," the commander said, "but for what it's worth, Ash, I think you got him, and I intend to say so in my report. How long you in for?"

"We go out again day after tomorrow," Ash said, "but I don't know yet who we'll be with."

"Well, enjoy your time in port," Blake said, standing up and offering Ash his hand. "Looks like the corvette and I will be joining a screen going east. I'm guessing North Africa. You're aware of the invasion by now?"

"Yes, Sir," Ash said.

"I haven't had advance notice," Blake said, "but I have to suppose that you'll be here a little longer than two days. I'm betting that you'll wait here for some empties coming back from the invasion and then see them through to the States."

"Thank you, Sir, and good hunting," Ash said.

21

For the two days that Chaser 3 remained in port, San Juan acted like a tonic for the crew. Faces that had grown sallow brightened, liberty men who trudged ashore like old men from the sea returned with a spring in their step, and on the beach, Ash noticed, the unmarried men who made up most of the crew seemed to have found enough female company to keep them occupied for the entire time they remained ashore. But even as Ash considered this change in his crew, he knew that at bottom, something else entirely had come into play. After months at sea, his band of one-time novices had truly bonded. They were no longer so many individual sailors from diverse backgrounds; serving together, they had welded themselves into a family. After their battles with the U-boats, they were veterans, full-fledged, and no doubt about it. Regardless of whatever any of them had imagined when they'd signed their papers and enlisted, they had now, finally, met an enemy that they could see and put something of a dent in his war machine. Beyond the one dead German naval officer, whether the dent was large or small, Ash couldn't say, but forever after, no one would be able to charge them with having sat out the war on the sidelines.

From time to time across those two days in port, Ash found himself also reflecting on the action just completed. Had they really sunk the U-boat? Ash thought they had, and in thinking so, he wondered how many Germans had gone down with it. When such thoughts occurred, he found that whether he liked it or not, he had to pause and consider his responsibility for killing 35, 40, possibly 45 men in a particularly horrible way. Had he not done so, he knew absolutely that the German skipper would have been only too pleased to have killed him, sunk Chaser 3, and put paid to every man aboard before charging straight ahead to sink and kill more amid the convoy. So, Ash knew very well that what he had done had been necessary; nevertheless, he couldn't stop himself from thinking of the men in the boat. Germans or not, Nazis or not, they were men, with lives and families, and if they'd gone down to the deep six, he was the man who had snuffed them out and put them there. It wasn't a pleasant thought, that one, but to restore the balance of his own mind, Ash reflected on the corpses he'd seen at sea, the men he'd found burned, the men he'd seen leaping from the stern of the sinking freighter, the men who'd never had the chance to escape from the ships the U-boats had sunk. Killing Germans was in no way a course of action in which he would ever take pleasure, but if it were the only way to get rid of Hitler and his crazed regime, Ash knew that he would do it, and keep doing it, and live with it until the job was finished.

On the day Chaser 3 was supposed to have returned to sea, COMDESLANT extended their period in port for an additional two days, the crew whooping with unrestrained joy when Ash passed the word. Then, finally, with hangovers aplenty and exhaustion showing on every face, they made their exit from San Juan, picked up two empty tankers on their way out, and escorted them to Caracas, where they anchored in the bay while the tankers took on their loads of oil. After that, all three ships turned right around and headed back to San Juan where yet another convoy was collecting before steaming for North Africa. All told, the trip used up a week, and by the time they returned to Puerto Rico, the first empty ships were returning from Morocco, riding high, anxious to get back to the States before loading up with new supplies and returning to the war.

"What have you got there?" Ash said to Solly, as he dropped down into the wardroom after securing the sea and anchor detail. Until the following morning when they were to start for the States as escort for the 20 returning ships, they were anchored out, 500 yards off the piers of Old San Juan, riding comfortably in the tranquil bay.

"*New York Times*," Solly said. "The bum boat that tried to sell us fresh vegetables also brought the paper; it's only three days old."

"What's the war news?" Ash asked.

"My guess," Solly said, "is that the naval battles around Guadalcanal are still fierce, but it looks to me like we've got 'em beat on the island. Eighth Army's recaptured Tobruk. But the biggest thing here is from Russia. Looks to me like the Russians have surrounded the German Sixth Army at Stalingrad. If that's true, it's huge. An entire German army, surrounded? Hitler must be shitting a brick!"

"I hope it's the size of a cinder block," Ash said. "How many men is that?"

"Well," Solly said, "far as I know, two or more divisions make up a corps, and two or more corps make up an army, or at least, I think—that's the way we do it, so I'm guessing—but I'd say that the Ruskies have put above 200,000 Germans in the bag."

Ash shook his head with something near disbelief. "Hard as this thing is for everyone," Ash said, "if you stop to consider mere numbers, the Russians seem to be carrying most of the load at the moment. They must have a couple of million men deployed along their front, all the way down from Leningrad to the Black Sea. Stalin keeps pushing for a second front; I wonder if he'll be satisfied with the fact that we're having a go at Rommel? I can't imagine that he will even notice what we're doing in the Pacific."

"I know he's got a knife at his throat," Solly said, "but it's a little much to expect us to invade Europe after we've only been in this thing for 11 months. I'm sure no expert, but if the Russians succeed in annihilating an entire German army, I'll bet we'll remember it as some kind of turning point in the war. Don't you think?"

"Could be," Ash said. "I wonder where they're getting the troops for an effort like that? According to Goebbels, the krauts captured over a million men on their initial thrust into Russia and almost took Moscow into the bargain."

"No telling what the Russians have had parked in Siberia," Solly said, "and with the Japs leaving them alone, and the Russians leaving the Japs alone, I'll bet Stalin's been running more trains from east to west than the Trans-Siberian Railway can handle."

"Genghis Khan revisited?" Ash said.

"Genghis Khan revisiting, and with tanks," Solly said.

They went out again the following morning, bound for Charleston by way of Grand Turk and Nassau so that the chasers could refuel, the high-riding tankers they were escorting already running empty after having discharged their loads in Oran. All told, steaming at 10 knots, the voyage took six days, and when Chaser 3 dropped off the convoy in Charleston, November had given way to December, and the weather had started to turn bitter. Replenishing in the outer harbor, Ash then picked up a convoy of nine, all of them bound for Cape May.

The transit from Charleston to Cape May turned out to be rough, a State 5 sea buffeting the chaser all the way, the ship pitching and rolling like a twig caught in a rapid, the men becoming variously sick around every bulkhead and stanchion. Wrapped in thick winter clothing and heavy foul weather gear, the deck watches found themselves sprayed continuously from the bow, the salt stinging their eyes, the wind burning their cheeks, the taste of sea water always on their lips. In the midst of the voyage southeast of Ocean City,

Gomez picked up a solid sonar contact which forced Ash to peel away from his charges and rush to the attack, Chaser 3 expending three depth-charge patterns before the contact broke up with no results, not even so much as a dead fish.

"Well?" Ash said to Gomez as he maneuvered to rejoin his convoy.

"Dunno, Cap'n. Could have been a school of shrimp, a bed of kelp. Might even have been a whale. After the fact, I don't think it was a sub. I was on it strong, and then, suddenly, it wasn't there, and it ain't the set; this rascal's workin' perfectly."

"I'm guessing kelp," Ash said. "Good thing the Navy's not charging me for the depth charges expended. I'd have gone broke by now."

Gomez laughed. "All in a day's work?"

"Unfortunately," Ash said.

They did tie up at Cape May for the night, making up to a pier at the Coast Guard Station where they took on fuel, water, and a supply of fresh baked bread. Watts, having run over and conned the Coast Guard out of a supply of fresh sirloin, managed to feed them steaks late in the evening, and upon those the crew slept like logs until 0400 when Samarango piped reveille so that they could make their exit in time to pick up a convoy coming down from Wilmington.

Given the North African venture, Ash had fully expected to guide the convoy south, but when the DESLANT message reached him around midnight, he was surprised to find that he would be guiding an empty troopship and four fully loaded freighters up to Raritan Bay.

"That's news," Hamp said, rising straight up in his bunk. "Think we'll get a night off, or two?"

"Chana and Keren seem to be in for a treat," Ash said. "We get up there on the 13th and don't go out again until the morning of the 16th, but let's have no phone calls to alert them; this info is marked *Secret*, so you and Solly will have to bide your time until we get there and hope that your birds haven't already flown off with a couple Marines. I understand that Marines are very popular in Brooklyn right now. Free drinks and all that, particularly after Guadalcanal."

"I thought the naval battles were the really big thing out there," Solly said, lying in his bunk.

"Oh, they are—or were," Ash said, "according to all of the intelligence reports that have come my way, but don't expect the civilians to know about those because they aren't being publicized. Too many ships sunk, too many sailors dead. The Marines had a hell of a fight of their own along with plenty of press to prove it, so that's what the folks are going to know."

"Sounds like we're being short changed," Hamp said.

"Sounds like business as usual," Ash laughed. "Imagine the press trying to make a story out of our little bout with the U-boat, or for that matter, imagine a war correspondent lasting more than three minutes on this wood chip as we brought her up from Charleston. We'd be lucky if he didn't throw himself overboard in an attempt to escape."

"Mundane is mundane," Solly said, turning on his side.

"We also serve who only pitch and roll?" Hamp said.

"Clearly," Ash said, "you've almost learned enough to command."

"Will you be taking tea with the spinster while we're in?" Hamp said to Ash.

"I don't see how," Ash said. "She's teaching, and given the distance, I don't see how she could get down in time for more than a handshake before she'd have to go back."

"Pity," Solly said, "we'll be thinking about you as we savor the fruits of our labors."

"Pity," Hamp said, "so near, and yet, so far."

"Careful," Ash said, "or I might find the two of you some watch duties that you'll need to perform. Overseeing the operation of Pump No. 3, counting the links in our anchor chain, itemizing the pages in our registered pubs, that sort of thing. Important work and such."

"You're a prince," Solly laughed.

"But if you are staying aboard," Hamp said, "I'm told that watching Pump No. 3 can be really absorbing, and idle hands can't be good for anyone."

Dispatching the empty troop transport into The Narrows on the 13th, Chaser 3 made up to the Coast Guard piers on Staten Island, and Ash sent the crew on port and starboard liberty. With Ash's permission, Hamp and Solly went over as soon as the brow had cleared, Ash telling them that they could take shore leave for the full time that the ship remained in port, but urging them to be back by the Cinderella hour on December 15.

With Solly and Hamp gone, Ash went over onto the beach, found the telephone exchange on the Coast Guard station, and, armed with a fist full of change, put through a call to The Jarvis House. Mrs. Jarvis, registering what sounded to Ash like genuine pleasure, put him straight through to Claire.

"Ash!" Claire exclaimed upon hearing his voice. "Oh, love, I miss you so much. Where are you?"

"Staten Island," Ash said, "and I miss you just as much, but it's too far to come. You have to teach tomorrow, the trains are packed for the holidays, and you'd no more than get here before we'd be gone and you'd have to turn around and go right back. I'm sorry as hell because I miss you more than I can say, but there it is."

Claire protested but admitted that he was right and damned the war that was keeping them apart.

"Any hope at all of getting back up here?" she asked.

"Honestly," Ash said, "I have no idea. We hardly know where we'll be sent from one day to the next. We've barely had six days in port since we left Yarmouth, and our putting into New York like this came as a total surprise. I'd expected us to be sent straight back south with convoys bound for North Africa."

They talked on, the two of them, until Ash finally said, "I'm on my last nickel, love. I've got to say goodbye." After Claire blew him a kiss over the line, and Ash said "I love you," the operator finally cut them off.

On the night of December 15, minutes before the coach turned back into a pumpkin, Solly and Hamp returned from Brooklyn, both of them herding the last of the ship's inebriated liberty party down the pier and onto the brow without the loss of a single man into the slip. Michelson, Grubber, and Krupp, each a little more under the weather than their fellows, were helped or dropped down the ladders into their compartments, but otherwise, Ash thought the crew would be ready in the morning

"Girls treat you to a big night on the town?" Ash asked as he followed Solly and Hamp down to the wardroom where they started throwing off their coats.

"We took the girls to the Met," Hamp said. "Solly should have warned me. They seem to do a lot of singing at these operas, and all the time, I thought we were going to a girly show, but the girls seemed to like it, particularly the soprano who died a tragic death."

"Very cultured, isn't he?" Solly said. "Wanted to know if that left the tenor free to date other girls afterward. I thought Chana was going to slap him."

"Chana should have," Ash said. "The poor soprano."

"What about the poor tenor?" Hamp asked. "Left without a main squeeze, and all that?"

"Why don't you ask him about the *haute cuisine* he suggested for after the opera?" Solly said.

"What are you talking about?" Hamp protested. "The hot dogs that Puerto Rican was selling looked really good."

"But you dined elsewhere?" Ash said.

"Chana knew of a place," Hamp said.

"I'll bet," Ash said.

"Cost us a couple of arms and a leg," Solly said. "Waiters in tuxedos, an obtrusive *sommelier*, the whole nine yards. I could have choked her."

"Nonsense," Hamp said. "It was perfectly enchanting, the whole evening, even if we did miss out on the hotdogs."

"Keren, bless her," Solly said, "has offered to cook us dinner at her house the next time we are in, and if she does, that might just give us a chance to become solvent once more."

"He's exaggerating," Hamp said. "The girls ordered salads."

"Piled high with gold leaf, or something close," Solly said. "This guy must think his grandmother's still footing the bills, and Chana has no shame about cleaning us both out. I'll be lucky if I can afford so much as a candy bar before March."

☙

On the following morning, 40 minutes after the COMDESLANT dispatch came through, Ash backed away from the pier, headed into The Narrows, and picked up a convoy bound for Portland, this one including the fully loaded troopship that he had brought up from the south only days before. Expecting that Chaser 3 would be once more heading south, Ash felt stunned, even astonished, at what promised a possible night in port and a chance to see Claire.

"Things seem to be looking up for you," Hamp said. "Patience is obviously a virtue."

"Possibly," Ash said. "We'll have to see if COMDESLANT can now deliver something more substantial than a quick run up and back."

"Perhaps the tea-sipping spinster knows someone," Hamp said.

"Perhaps the fleet is still sending as many convoys to England as it is sending south," Solly said, speaking practically.

"That appears to be the case," said Ash. "My spinster, Mr. Hampton, has a great deal of pull with me, but I don't think she knows a soul at DESLANT, and considering the wolves that man their desks, I hope that they never catch sight of her."

"Protective, isn't he?" Hamp said to Solly as they moved out ahead of the convoy and took station in the screen.

"And wisely so," Solly said.

Half an hour later when Polaski came to the bridge, grinning from ear to ear, in order to bring Ash a message, things looked up even more.

"Well, will wonders never cease," Ash said. "Just listen to this. *From: COMDESLANT To: CO, CHASER 3. Proceed Portland Navy Yard. Upon arrival 2100 19 December 1942, moor port side Pier 4. Proceed COMDESLANT Operations Office. Offload ammunition and pyrotechnics. 0600 20 December 1942, proceed Anson's Boatyard, Yarmouth for eight (8) days' upkeep. 0600 29 December 1942, proceed Portland for convoy assignment.*

Two nights later, when released from convoy escort in Casco Bay, Ash took Chaser 3 into Portland, tied up alongside Pier 4, and left Solly and Hamp to see to offloading depth charges and ammunition. Muffled in his overcoat and wearing rather than carrying his gray gloves, he stepped ashore to find snow on the pier, some ice, and a cold wind blowing down from Canada. Without stopping to tarry along the way, Ash made for COMDESLANT Headquarters.

On the second deck, after checking in first at reception where he was cleared to proceed, Ash once more made his way to Commander Gibbons' office where he again found Petty Officer Reese at her desk.

"I take it that you never go home?" Ash said, by way of greeting.

Petty Officer Reese smiled. "That's just about right," she said, "but the commander is about to be promoted to captain, so he'll also be getting a new ship soon, a spanking new light cruiser. I imagine that my whole routine may change here. New man at the desk; new routine in the office."

"I'll hope it goes well for both of you," Ash said.

Five minutes later, when Petty Officer Reese gave him the nod, Ash knocked once on the door and walked into Gibbons' office where, as before, he announced himself and stood at attention.

"This won't take long," the commander said, standing and walking around from behind his desk where he greeted Ash with a smile and a handshake. "You don't know what this visit is all about, do you?"

"No, Sir," Ash said, stiffening slightly.

"Well, Lieutenant Miller, if you will stand at attention for one more moment, I am going to award you a commendation medal. Normally, we do this sort of thing formally, with a ceremony at a parade of some kind, but there's a war on, you're about to go up to Yarmouth for upkeep, and you happen to be in port here at just the right moment. Reese," he called out, "send in the photographer."

Immediately, the door opened, and a squat Navy photographer's mate stepped through and held up his camera to take a photograph. Commander Gibbons then turned, opened a case on his desk, removed the commendation medal from it, and pinned it to Ash's breast as the flashbulb went off.

"Congratulations, Captain Miller. A citation will follow in due time, but the United States Navy is proud of you, proud of your ship, and proud of your accomplishment."

Ash felt lost, and as soon as the photographer left, he made his feelings known.

"Commander," he said, "I don't want to seem ungrateful—and I don't like to think that I'm looking a gift horse in the mouth—but this has to be a mistake. I haven't done anything that merits this medal. I thought these things were supposed to be for courage under fire."

"Apparently you don't yet realize that is just what you've shown when you've taken on the U-boats with which you've done battle," Commander Gibbons said. "In the first place, you attacked rather than calling for help."

Ash thought he had called for help just as soon as he could.

"In the second place, if that bastard on the way to San Juan had turned on you, he could have blown you out of the water and into match sticks with that 4-inch gun on his bow, but you got him first, scared him under, and then, not to make too much of it, Captain, you dodged two torpedoes and went in for an attack. While we don't know that you sunk him, there seems a strong probability that you did. The Commander of the Eastern Sea Frontier seems to think that was downright intrepid of you and believes that you acted in the best traditions of the service, under fire, and regardless of what you might think, I agree with him. Congratulations, Captain, on a job well done."

Ash, tongue-tied, finally stammered out a thank you and found himself dismissed with yet another of the commander's handshakes.

Outside, standing under the overhang at the building's entrance, Ash watched the snow come down and tried to fit what had just happened to him into some kind of context. He didn't feel in the least valorous—never had—and didn't think he ever would. Instead, he felt numb. At the time, when he'd first seen that blip on the scope, things had developed so fast that he hadn't had time to think about them—what he'd done, he'd done because it was the only thing he'd been able to think to do. Movies that Ash had seen, radio dramatizations that he had listened to, and books he had read had all presented similar moments, but moments in which their protagonists had struggled with decisions and, then, overcoming one set of odds or another, gone into action on the strength of hard-earned convictions. Ash knew he didn't fit this profile. He had simply done what he'd been trained to do without thinking very much about it, and it had turned out all right. Try as he might, he couldn't find courage in it anywhere. Add the fact that he might have killed 40 or more men with what he'd done, and it all seemed a muddle as he stood there in the night, mystified by what had just happened to him, silent, with snow stinging his face. Earlier that evening, he'd imagined that he might step over to the club for a drink before returning to the ship. Instead, bending into the wind, he walked back down the pier, boarded the ship, and went straight to bed without mentioning the medal to anyone.

22

Olie Anson met Ash with a sheaf of work orders the minute Chaser 3 tied up at the yard.

"Soon as I get your signatures on these," Anson said, "we'll get started. You won't be in long enough for us to scrape her down, what with Christmas to contend with and our work on them chasers building on the ways, but we'll have a go at fittings, interior bulkheads, caulking an' such, and we got you a small reefer to install. Won't hold much, but at least it'll keep eggs and burger meat cold for a week. You wanna send a bunch of your people on leave, it's OK by me. We don't need many of 'em for this work, and they'd be best off outta the way. Whydoncha check with me each mornin', an' then you can be free yourself?"

"You're on," Ash said. "I've had these guys pretty much cooped up since we left here this summer, so I think they'll be chompin' at the bit to get somewhere, anywhere, for Christmas."

Ash ordered Hill to type up leave papers for the majority of the crew. Learning that Gomez wouldn't be trying to make the trip to El Paso for the holidays, Ash then signed the crew's leave papers as soon as Hill could bring them to him, assigned Gomez and three seamen who were also staying aboard to establish a rotating deck watch in case any visitors showed up, and presented Solly and Hamp with leave papers of their own.

"I understand that New York is a very festive place at Christmas time," Ash said. "No need for Keren and Chana to thank me or send money, or anything of that sort. Give them my sympathy for dumping the two of you on them for Christmas, if not my love, and I'll see you back here the night before we're to get underway."

"Called the spinster yet?" Hamp quizzed.

"Want us to alert her so that she can brew up the tea?" Solly said.

"I shall make my presence known, all in good time," Ash said. "I think a phone call might be wise. I shouldn't like to show up on her doorstep unannounced, without giving her time to pour the drinks and roll out the red carpet and so forth. And I'd advise the two of you to do the same. I shouldn't like to hear that you have had to fight whatever Marines happen to be hovering around your girls' front doors."

"I can't speak for Solly, of course, but personally," Hamp said, "I expect to be greeted by trumpets, if not harps and choirs of angels, harkening from on high."

"More like a band of little gypsies, hired to pick your pockets," Solly said. "You have yet to understand my sister's mildly crooked ways."

"Not a problem," Hamp said. "I've been saving up."

They were away then, rushing—if not actually running—up the road in the direction of The Jarvis House and a taxi that might carry them on to the train station. After Ash had watched them go, he made his way to the office in the warehouse and dialed The Jarvis House.

"I hate to drop in on you without warning," Ash said, the moment Claire came onto the line, "but we're here, for eight days, Christmas included. Are you free?"

Claire shrieked, and then she quietly said, "I'll meet you halfway, love," and hung up the telephone before Ash could say a word in response.

Minutes later, halfway up the street, under a gray sky from which a light snow was already falling, and in front of more than one startled onlooker, Claire ran straight into his arms, planting a kiss on Ash that warmed him right through to his insides.

"I take it the rules have changed?" Ash said, when she finally released him so that he could hold her at arm's length and take in her face.

"You bet they have," Claire said, "and I don't care who knows it. This war's been putting me through hell, Ash. From one letter to the next, I don't know where you are, how you are, what you are doing, or if you're even alive. Three girls I know around here have already lost their men—one in North Africa and two on Guadalcanal. It's reached the point where I have trouble sleeping at night, not knowing whether you're safe, or wounded, or killed, so if anyone around here, *anyone*, intends to try on something prudish with me, I intend to tell them to stick it straight up their collective noses, if I don't turn around and slap them straight off."

Ash laughed and gave her a hug. "I love you," he said. "You're the best thing I've laid eyes on since we left here in August, and you look magnificent. Sure you didn't know I was coming?"

"No one breathed a word," Claire said. "I'll bet Olie Anson knew, but what Olie Anson knows, he keeps to himself. I could choke him."

"Don't do that," Ash said. "He's just taken nearly our whole upkeep right out of my hands for the time we're in, and that leaves us free to … to do whatever it is that you might like to do while we're here."

"I have some definite ideas about that," Claire grinned.

"I'm glad," Ash said. "What say we go up and see if we can't cajole Mrs. Jarvis into renting us adjoining rooms?"

"No need," Claire said, as the two turned and began to walk up the street toward The Jarvis House. "Mrs. Jarvis, love, is a wise and sympathetic soul, and I think she likes you. Two weeks ago, without me saying a word to her, she came to me and asked if you would be coming for the holidays. I told her no, I didn't think so, but she made me an offer, in the event you did come, that I couldn't refuse. It seems she owns an apartment which she rents out up in South Freeport, that's about ten minutes on the bus, and at the moment, it's empty and fully furnished. I think she's just had it painted. She doesn't intend to advertise for a renter until January, so before I even knew you were here, she'd asked me to go up and stay there for the next few weeks, just so the place wouldn't be empty, until she finally puts it up for rent. Possibly, love, she knew you were coming. Possibly, the Navy said something to her, about billeting, in advance. I don't know, but what she did say was that if you happened to show up by some miraculous chance, she would have no objections as long as we were reasonably discreet."

"I suspect that somewhere in her resume, she is marked down as your Fairy Godmother," Ash said.

"Oh, it gets even better, love. She's waived the rent. She says that as long as we keep the heat on, keep the pipes from freezing, and look after the place, we'll be doing her a favor."

"Probably so, with winter setting in," Ash said, "but I intend to pay her rent regardless."

"Then we'll go halves," Claire said.

"No," Ash said, "we won't. I still have one or two old-fashioned ideas, so on this one, I'm not going to budge. Her bargain is with you, and I think that's fine, but if I weren't moving in, I'd be up at the hotel, and the Navy would be paying her rent, so without quibbling, I want to make it up to her. Otherwise, she's taking a loss on me."

"All right," Claire said, giving way, "then let's go on up to the hotel. It will take me about 20 minutes to pack a bag, and then we'll catch the bus. And once we get up there, if you don't mind, I'm going to cook you the best meal you've ever eaten."

"Something like a culinary audition?" Ash teased.

"Absolutely," Claire said. "Perhaps I failed to mention that I spent a year at the Boston Cooking School before I decided to switch to elementary education."

Ash didn't know what to say; she'd caught him completely off guard. "No," he said finally, "I don't remember a word about the Boston Cooking School. So, what other little secrets might you be hiding away?"

"I intend to reveal them one at a time," Claire said, giving his arm a squeeze, "and with feeling."

The apartment Mrs. Jarvis lent them was small but compact, located directly above a shop that sold kitchenware, candles, and gifts to South Freeport customers. The cooking utensils that Claire found in the drawers did not turn out to be extensive, but she nevertheless pronounced them adequate to her needs. Before he could even take off his overcoat, she told Ash that she was going out to shop for groceries, alone and uninhibited, while he, she suggested, shop for a Christmas tree: "Something small, love, about 2 or 3 feet, if you don't mind. And a box of tinsel, if one can be found. I think we can skip the lights and the balls and so forth. Rationing may have put paid to them anyway, and we needn't go to the expense. But a tinsel-covered tree would look nice."

Detecting a degree of both purpose and concentration in Claire's intentions, Ash made no objections, the two exiting the building by means of the interior staircase that led up to it from beside the shop below and going off to their tasks along separate paths.

South Freeport struck Ash as being not much more than a village—a pretty one, he had to admit, but small—a sort of coastal resort that no doubt swelled during the summer months, boaters and sports fishermen descending in droves. Two blocks from the apartment, with a light snow still falling, Ash stumbled onto a Boy Scout Christmas tree lot, walked for a few minutes amid the trees, found a small one that he liked—the smallest the lot had to offer—and made the transaction. And then he promptly returned with it to the apartment before going out again to search for tinsel. When the five and dime couldn't produce a package, Ash wandered into a long but narrow hardware store that struck him as a relic straight out of the previous century, and there, a gray-headed clerk who looked to Ash like he had been born in the same century as the store, finally emerged from a back room with a single box of shredded tin foil.

"Last one in stock, and ya lucky to get it," the elderly man said. "Gov'ment cut off production. Usin' the stuff for the war some ways. Nobody throwin' tin foil away no more. Everybody savin' it and turnin' it in for them scrap drives. Best ya do the same after Christmas. Where's ya servin?"

"At sea," Ash said, paying the man.

"Destroyer, like?"

"Subchaser," Ash said.

"Roll a mite?"

"Rolls a lot," Ash laughed. "We tend to think of ourselves as bronc riders and hope not to get thrown."

"Ha," said the old man. "My grandson's on one of them jeep carriers. I'll tell him what ya said."

"Do," Ash said, "it'll make him feel a whole lot better."

Claire came back only minutes after Ash had arrived and taken off his overcoat.

"I got the tinsel and the tree," Ash said. "Tinsel seems to be in short supply. Something having to do with the war."

"The war," Claire said, "seems to be leaving just about everything in short supply. You should have seen what I just went through to get butter—real butter I mean. You'd have thought that I'd asked the grocer for his mother's watch or her wedding rings."

"Shortages are apparently the new normal," Ash said. "So, my love, what have you got there?"

"Ever had Lobster Thermidor?" Claire asked, starting to unpack her grocery bags.

"No," Ash said, "but the swells in Herrin used to talk about having it at The Palmer House in Chicago. They seemed to approve of it."

"You're in for a treat," Claire said. "It's one of my specialties."

"Thus far," Ash said, "all of your specialties have been treats, and then some."

Drawing out two lobsters from her grocery bag, Claire placed them on the counter and then happened to look up, and when she did, she froze.

"What's the ribbon for, Ash? It's new. You didn't have it in August."

"Something undeserved," Ash said.

"I've seen that ribbon; my father had one," Claire said, coming around the counter to take a closer look. "That's a commendation of some sort, isn't it, Ash? Isn't it? Have you been in action, love?"

For several seconds, as Claire searched his face, Ash said nothing, and then, finally, he spoke.

"We depth-charged a U-boat," Ash said flatly. "We came up on it from behind, while it was stalking a convoy, and took a couple of shots at it with the gun, and when it submerged, we depth-charged it. We might have sunk it, but we can't be sure."

"Seems you've kept a few secrets of your own," Claire said, her eyes flashing.

"With what the ship does, I'll probably keep a few more," Ash said. "Sorry, but that's the way it has to be."

"I worry, Ash."

"I know you do, and that's one of the reasons I didn't say anything about it in my letters. It's just the sort of thing that Solly, Hamp, and I have to censor out of the crew's letters. Just one more thing that has to be chalked up to the war."

"We seem to be chalking up a hell of a lot to the war," Claire said.

"Yes we do," Ash said.

"Your absence has been the worst of it," Claire said, "but the fact that you've seen action out there and been in danger makes me sick to my stomach, Ash."

"Oh for heaven's sake," Ash said, "don't throw up; it could ruin the lobster!"

"Not funny, Ash. Not funny at all!" Claire protested, as Ash held her close.

"I know," Ash said, "but the funny part is all we've got."

The Lobster Thermidor, something Ash waited for patiently, wasn't funny either. It was delicious, so much so that Ash bent over the shell in which Claire had baked it with a degree of pleasure that he thought he could never have imagined.

"You weren't kidding about the cooking school," Ash said. "This is heaven. Why did you stop?"

"I never really stopped," Claire said, "but something took us down to a Boston elementary school one day, and whatever it was—hungry little minds, happy little faces, their innocence … well, it sort of converted me and made me want to teach. Once in a while when I've been short, after taxes for example, I've gone up to the Queen Bee's and done some pastry baking, and occasionally, to supplement my rent, I put in an evening with the chef at The Jarvis House. He's quite good without me, as you know, but it keeps me from losing my touch. Mrs. Jarvis would have me in there three nights a week if I let her, but beyond special events like banquets or club dinners, I try not to interfere, and really, she can't afford to pay me beyond what I'm already doing. That's why I hold down the library job in the summers."

"You are full of surprises," Ash said.

"And I hope I always will be," Claire said. "Just wait until you see the surprise I brought back from Portland for you."

The surprise turned out to be a form-fitting nightgown that Ash thought put Claire one up on the famous *Life* magazine photo of Rita Hayworth that the crew had plastered onto nearly every bulkhead in their berthing compartments. It was, they said, what they were fighting for, and Ash had never tried to deny it. Claire, when she came out, looked so stunning that she left Ash speechless.

"You give me a whole new reason for living," he said finally. And when he said it, he knew that he wasn't kidding.

Ash didn't spend more than an hour at the boatyard the following day. Arriving late in the morning, he could see at once that Anson had the work well in hand and rapidly underway, so after signing off on two additional work orders, checking with Gomez about the skeleton crew left aboard, and packing a bag to take back with him, Ash withdrew, caught the bus back to South Freeport, and spent the afternoon in bed with Claire after which the two of them dressed and went out for a stroll over the snow and a Portuguese meal in an eatery run by a retired fisherman and his wife.

"It certainly isn't the Ritz," Claire whispered, "but the food here is always good, particularly the shrimp, the way he blends the garlic, tomatoes, and olive oil around them."

"And do you make this too?" Ash asked.

"Yes, but not as well as they do here. I think he may use a dash of paprika, and I haven't tried that."

All too swiftly the days slipped by until suddenly it was Christmas Eve. Outside, new snow had fallen, the air had gone still, and the temperature had dropped crisply to several degrees below freezing. Claire had once more cooked for the evening, serving up a fish stew according to a Galician recipe that Ash had found delicious, and then, sitting on the couch to listen to the radio, Ash had opened a bottle of Mouton Cadet that Claire particularly liked, and the two of them had listened to Lionel Barrymore's rendering as Scrooge in a radio adaptation of *A Christmas Carol*. Later, they switched the dial to music. And that night, for the first time, Ash had heard Bing Crosby sing "White Christmas."

"Haven't you seen *Holiday Inn* yet?" Claire asked. "It's a wonderful movie. Irving Berlin songs, and both Crosby and Fred Astaire at their best."

"No," Ash said. "About the only flicks I've seen since the war started are the ones I've been to with you, in Yarmouth."

"Wonderful songs, wonderful dancing, delightful comedy," Claire said. "We ought to check the papers, find where it's showing, and go to see it in the next couple of days."

"Sounds fine," Ash said. "Can I give you that for Christmas? We haven't been out to shop, and I don't have a thing for you."

"Oh yes you do," Claire said, "and if it won't conflict with your intentions, I'd like to start exchanging gifts before the bells ring tonight."

On Christmas morning, clad in nothing more than their bath robes, Ash and Claire sat across from one another at the apartment's kitchen table, drinking coffee and making a feast out of the cinnamon rolls that Claire had baked. In the apartment's front room, behind their tinsel-laden Christmas tree, the radio continued to play a mixture of Christmas carols and sacred classical music in a pattern that seemed to change every 15 minutes. With the room warm enough to permit it, Claire's robe remained fetchingly open near the top, open enough so that even with her hair in disarray after the busy night they'd spent in bed, she still looked alluring and, Ash thought, incredibly beautiful.

"I hope this won't strike you as too abrupt," Ash said, as Claire looked up from her plate and lifted her coffee mug to her lips, "but this war we're in really does seem to have canceled the old rules. I want to marry you, Claire. Will you accept?"

"Yes," she said without hesitation, a flush of happiness spreading across her face. "When?"

Suddenly, Ash felt warm all over. "I suppose," he said, meeting her smile, "that it depends on what kind of wedding you want to have."

Claire put down her coffee mug. "A girl has her dreams, Ash, and since you last went away, I've had a long time to dream, so if you really want to know, here's what would please me the most." She paused and gave Ash a penetrating stare, her face all business. "You get up, go down to the ship in the morning, and check on the work, and then you come straight back here. By then, I'll have had time to comb my hair and get into something appropriate, and then we'll go straight out, find the Justice of the Peace, and have him marry us. No fru-fru, no invitations, no guests, no wedding presents, no traipsing off to Niagara Falls—just you and me right here because this is the best. You've already brought me more happiness than I've ever known, and I'd be happy to live with you in sin for the rest of our lives, so marriage is simply the icing on the cake. I want to have your baby, Ash, just as soon as we can make one."

Ash didn't know what to say. Claire had again stolen his breath away. He'd imagined that their marriage, if Claire accepted him, would have to be put off for months while the prospective bride did whatever prospective brides liked to do before getting married. He'd imagined having to make a journey somewhere to Claire's home, having to meet friends and family, having to endure all of the niceties that normally went with such occasions. But once more, Claire had surprised him and shown him in an instant how the rules had changed. Claire had tossed Mother's little etiquette book straight into the fire and seized the moment, challenging Ash as she did so.

184

"You surprise me every time," Ash grinned. "What, no engagement ring, no announcements by the town crier, no endless fittings for the wedding dress of the century?"

"Why would I need to do any of that if I've got you?" Claire said. "A pox on the whole of it!"

"I'll do my best to be back by ten o'clock," Ash said, "and I'll horsewhip the bus driver if he tries to dawdle."

"That's my man," Claire said.

"One thing," Ash said. "About having a family. I'd hate to interfere with your best laid plans, but perhaps we ought to give ourselves a year or two, to ourselves, the Navy permitting, and perhaps we ought to think a little about how I'm going to feed and clothe the lad—"

"Or lass," Claire cut in.

"Or lass," Ash confirmed, "which automatically means double the expense, I'm sure."

"Now stop that," Claire said, with a glint in her eye. "Little girls are quite practical to raise, and I sew."

"Lord," Ash said, "what will pop out next. Do you also work on cars?"

"You will be pleased to know that I can not only change a tire but also do a tune-up," Claire said.

"You are gold beyond my wildest dreams," Ash said, leaning across the table and giving her a kiss. "But that doesn't change the fact that I'd like to be able to support a family before we start one."

"We'll negotiate," Claire said.

"And I intend to hold you to that," Ash said.

&

They were married the following day at 11 am civilian time by a slightly bemused Justice of the Peace who'd stopped shoveling his sidewalk in order to accommodate them.

"Funny hour for a wedding," the J.P. had said, when he pronounced them man and wife. "Usually, I hold these things off until after lunch."

"We decided to seize the moment," Claire said.

"Lieutenant," the J.P.'s wife, their principal witness, said as the J.P. once more wrapped a scarf around his neck and prepared to return to his snow shovel, "I'd say ya got yourself a bargain here. A woman that knows her mind's worth a pound of salt in this world. I hope you're very happy, the both of you."

Taking the bus up to Bath for the afternoon, they actually did go to see *Holiday Inn*, Claire telling Ash that she thought it the perfect Christmas movie, a probable classic, and Ash agreeing with her. Then they took the bus down to Yarmouth and invited Mrs. Jarvis to dine with them while they sprang what they hoped would be their little surprise on her by announcing that they were married.

"My dear," Mrs. Jarvis said to Claire, "I don't want to disappoint you, but I marked the two of you out for one another the first time Captain Miller spoke to me about you. This war has done a lot of evil for an awful lot of people, but in a few instances, it has also done some good, and you two are the example. And Captain, I won't take a cent in rent on the apartment, and I'm adamant about that. Consider it my wedding present to the both of you."

☙

Ash and Claire made the best of the three remaining days they spent together. Regardless of her objections, Ash did push her into a South Freeport jewelry store where he made her select a ring, and over her additional objections, he called down to the paymaster in Portland and arranged both for a housing allowance and for a monthly allotment from his paycheck.

"Good with money, are you?" Ash asked.

"When you get back here again," Claire said, "you will find that I've built us a nest egg that will astonish you."

"No betting on the horses, now," Ash teased, "and no betting on the hockey games either."

"You can count on it," Claire said.

In bed and out of it, neither wasted the time that remained to them, but then, finally, at around 11 pm on the night of the 28th, Ash kissed Claire goodbye, helped her dry a few tears, and returned to the ship, leaving her in residence in the wartime home that they'd decided to keep.

By the time Ash got back, Solly and Hamp had already returned from New York, the crew was back on board, and Anson had pumped them enough fuel and water for their morning run down Casco Bay.

"Well," Hamp said, dropping his feet from the top of the wardroom table to the deck as Ash came down the ladder, "look what the cats have dragged in."

"If I find that you've both stowed away Chana and Keren somewhere aboard," Ash said, "the two of you are going to be in considerable trouble. Good week in New York, was it?"

"Excellent," Solly said. "Keren cooked, my mother cooked, and Chana burned something. We ate like kings on roasted turkey, a brilliant roast beef, and a shriveled piece of charcoal, glazed with coal black asparagus and egg hardened to the consistency of steel."

"He exaggerates," Hamp said. "Chana is really quite good in the kitchen."

186

"He's talking about necking," Solly said, "not about her cooking. I advised my mother to send her daughter out for a course somewhere."

"And what about you?" Hamp asked. "The spinster pour you some Pekoe tea? Sip, sip!"

"The spinster is no longer a spinster," Ash said. "She is now Mrs. Miller." The wardroom went silent.

"You're kidding?" Solly said. "Aren't you?"

"Holy shit!" Hamp exclaimed. "He's not!"

"We got married the day after Christmas," Ash said. "And nothing could be finer. You boys should try it sometime. Gives you a whole new perspective on life."

"Congratulations," Solly said, rising to his feet and shaking Ash's hand. "She's a wonderful girl, Claire, and she'll make you a wonderful wife. Well done, Ash. Well done!"

"Same here," Hamp said, turning serious for once. "Chana and Keren think the world of her, and so do I. You are a lucky, lucky man. What decided you?"

"We couldn't find a reason to wait," Ash said. "For better or worse—and in our case, for better—the old norms seem to have disappeared and a whole new set seems to have come into play. We took a good look at the facts on Christmas morning, and then we acted on them."

"Good decision," Solly said. "Very."

"I suspect that the male population of Yarmouth will go into mourning," Hamp said.

"Seems likely," Ash said, "that I have shown them no mercy."

The following morning and with a strong tide running, Chaser 3 backed from the pier and once more went to war.

23

The sailors on the ammunition lighter who restored Chaser 3's depth charges, gun ammunition, and pyrotechnics in Portland also brought out news that there had been heavy fighting in Tunisia and that the troops on Guadalcanal were pushing the beaten Japanese hard toward the western end of the island.

Teague, who came up to report their ammunition stowed, brought Ash the news.

"Guy on the lighter said that we might bag as many as ten or twenty thousand Japs out there on the Canal," he told Ash.

"Good," Ash said. "That'll even the score some."

They were away after the replenishment almost immediately, herding three empty freighters and a high riding tanker to New York. The uneventful trip took two days of rough running through high winter seas, but once they reached Raritan Bay, rather than rest, they were replenished by a tender and went out again at once, along with a PC and two other chasers, the four of them escorting two tankers and several well-loaded freighters toward a transfer to take place east of Cape May. In the midst of the transit, along the Delaware coast, the escort commander, the skipper of the PC, received a message that a tanker had gone aground off Fenwick Island shoal, broken up, and lost some of her crew overboard. A search appeared to be underway, and Ash was detached to participate, urgent warnings about safe navigation and shallow water coming through at the foot of the signal. The escort commander then ordered the two other chasers to proceed with the convoy while Ash headed toward Fenwick Island to join the search.

Arriving on station at the island and taking soundings with the lead line to avoid running aground himself, Ash joined a small Coast Guard cutter and two fishing boats that had been pressed into service. Together, the four of them combed the area out to a distance of 5 miles; finally, in the last

188

daylight hour, Ash sighted two men floating with the current in their life jackets. One of them, an American merchant sailor—covered with oil even after hours in the sea—was already dead from exposure. The other, a man who could barely speak, was nearly so. Ash transferred the men to the Coast Guard cutter, and when the search was discontinued, hastened south to rejoin the convoy, something he did not manage to do before reaching Cape May where the ships had already been handed over to three DEs assigned to take them on to Charleston.

For a single night, Chaser 3 tied up at Cape May, replenished, and got underway again at dawn, plowing back north in company with a fleet tug, a second chaser, and two empty troopships, both of them heading for piers on the Hudson. With the seas running high, Ash found the voyage arduous. Once more, men were sick; once more, the crew found themselves reduced to eating cold sandwiches, and once more, Samarango and Stobb fought a battle, not against the Germans but merely to keep the decks swabbed down and the stench below within tolerance.

"Solly in his bunk?" Ash asked as Hamp relieved Samarango on the deck.

"Yes," Hamp said, "and I'd be there too, in a heartbeat, if I didn't have to stand the deck. How come you're not in your hammock? Not indulging in a bout of masochism to make up for the absence of your wife, I hope?"

Ash ducked as a wave of spray came flying up from the bow. "My stomach feels like a churn at the moment," Ash said. "Facing the sea like this seems to be the only thing holding it in check. I can't help wondering what the troops are going to feel like once they board those troopships and take off for parts unknown. Those things look relatively steady up alongside what we're going through, but are they?"

"Met an officer off a troopship over Christmas," Hamp said. "They got bunks built six high in the berthing compartments, and from what he told me, the only safe spot is in the top bunk. Guy on the bottom gets barfed on by everyone above him. He said they're like sick dogs for the first three or four days going over, and that the interior of those things stinks to high heaven; the stench can make a man sick even when the ship is tied up fast to the pier. Once they get to England or wherever, the troops practically run off the ship in order to breath fresh air."

"No lack of that here," Ash said, as the two men ducked behind the wind screen, another sheet of spray flying up from the bow. "I suppose we ought to count ourselves lucky."

"What was it like on a destroyer?" Hamp asked.

"It could get bad," Ash said, "and once up off the tip of Long Island, it got very bad, but it was never like this. It never felt quite like plunging off a cliff and then being jerked straight up again."

Twenty miles south of Raritan Bay, in response to an urgent dispatch, Ash fell in alongside the fleet tug and turned east on a straight course of 090 magnetic. Somewhere out there, about a hundred miles distant, a freighter, the *Meldon Empire*, had struck a mine. Her crew had managed somehow to stop the flooding and seal off whatever compartments were already flooded, but her bearings had seized up, so she was dead in the water, taking a pounding from the sea, and unable to get underway. The tug, if they could reach her in time, would have to bring her in; otherwise, if the pounding continued, she would probably break up and go down, taking her crew of 43 merchant sailors with her. On the strength of their depth charges and the possibility that the U-boat which had dropped the mines might still lurk in the area, Chaser 3 had been assigned to go along with the tug to give her and the freighter what protection he could, and act as escort once the tug began to tow.

"That tug's got a 3"/50," Ash heard Teague say to one of the gun crew. "She's a mite better armed than we are, so I wonder what we're s'posed to do."

"It's the depth charges," Samarango told him. "That tug ain't got any, so if she's towin', we'll do the huntin'. That make sense?"

"You got it," Teague said.

At 16 knots, it took them nearly seven hours to work out far enough to find the *Meldon Empire*, and when they did they discovered her down at the bow with a 15-degree list. The good news, as Ash perceived it, was that she didn't appear to be on fire. The bad news came with the fact that she was leaking oil and would leave a trail that any U-boat in the area could follow all the way to New York.

As Ash began to circle the freighter and the tug—holding a distance from them of about a thousand yards, lookouts alerted, his radar searching and sonar pinging—he watched through binoculars as the tug's crew went swiftly to work, passing a messenger and finally their great towing hawser up through the freighter's bullhead as they took her in tow. Then, finally, after some delay, at a speed of no more than 5 knots, they started for New York.

"Solly," Ash said, when the watch relieved. "How are we on fuel?"

"I had Chief Stobb sound the tanks before I came up," Solly said. "We've got about 60 percent. Should be more than enough to make Raritan Bay with a good 10 or 20 percent to spare."

"No leaks anywhere?"

"No leaks," Solly said, "and the engines are running smooth, both of them."

"That's a comfort at least," Ash said, "but the more fuel we use up, the more this rascal's going to roll, and I'm not about to flood the tanks with salt water just to improve our stability. I hope the troops are ready for this; it's liable to be the worst ride they've ever had."

It *was* the worst ride they'd ever had, ever. With a State 5 sea and 12-foot waves coming straight against them from the beam whenever they weren't riding into it bow on or catching it from the stern, Chaser 3 began rolling nearly 35 degrees and sometimes 40, leaving the crew no alternative but to take to their bunks and strap themselves into them. On the bridge and on the gun mount which Ash knew he had to keep manned, the men lashed themselves to stanchions or rails and simply tried to hold on, and then, 50 miles from New York, while being tossed harder than poor Sancho Panza in his famous blanket, Gomez got a solid sonar contact 8,000 yards off the starboard beam, and Ash was forced to sound General Quarters and go over to the attack.

Oddly, even with the waves as high as they were running and with spray flying back like sleet into their faces, the port lookout actually caught a glimpse of a periscope before it disappeared, but the sighting made no difference. Before Ash could even close to within 2,000 yards of the U-boat, the German had rapidly worked out a firing solution and launched a torpedo. To Ash's consternation, the torpedo struck, blowing a massive hole in the *Meldon Empire*'s starboard side even as Ash signaled Hamp to begin rolling their first depth-charge pattern.

Gomez managed to hold the sonar contact long enough for Ash to shoot off a mousetrap array and drop four entire depth-charge patterns on the German, each one of them causing the sea to boil and shaking the ship like a leaf. But with sonar contact finally lost and no visible results to suggest that Chaser 3 had either sunk the sub or damaged her in any way, the tug captain—senior officer for their attempted rescue—called Ash back to help pick up the crew of the *Meldon Empire*. By that time the freighter's crew had also admitted defeat, their ship sinking out from under them with increasing speed, no matter how much effort they'd expended in trying to save her, and the fire that had ignited in the freighter's mid-section had exploded completely out of control.

Cursing the U-boat and his failure to sink her, Ash raced back to the *Meldon Empire*, nearly losing two of his own men on the way as the pounding waves swept up over the side and knocked them off their feet. Zwick managed to snatch a lifeline before he almost went over the side. Benson, loosed from the gun mount to which he had previously lashed himself, broke his wrist in the fall he took and was only saved from the sea by Teague, who had the presence of mind to reach out and grab the thick collar of the man's life jacket before he was swept away.

"Christ," Ash said to himself, "what next?"

What came next, for Ash, proved to be the short version of hell. By the time Chaser 3 returned to the freighter, those men who had not been killed when the torpedo exploded in the ship's engine room had abandoned ship.

Some of them were floating on rafts. Others wearing life jackets were riding up and down over the waves. Most of them were covered with oil, and many were injured, and the wind seemed to be blowing the choking smoke from the fire everywhere, making it hard to breathe and harder to see. The tug, already working ahead of Chaser 3, had started to pull the survivors aboard, but it was exceptionally hard going owing to the turbulent seas. Had the sea state been anything like it was in previous instances where Ash had recovered men who had gone overboard, he would have had an easy time of it, but with the seas running a good 13 feet and higher, Chaser 3 would move in to pick up a man only to find the man plunged into the trough, 12 feet below, as the ship towered above him. Then, before anyone could act to counter the motion, the chaser would plunge into the trough as the floating merchant sailor swiftly rode up the next wave until he seemed actually to be above them. Samarango and his men solved the problem as well as the sea allowed—throwing individuals lines with pre-tied bowlines and simply hauling them aboard—but not without buffeting them enough to knock the men nearly senseless by the time they were dragged on deck. For the men on the raft, he rigged a cargo net on the starboard side aft, so some of them could jump as the raft came up and the ship went down, and clinging to the side, those men eventually made the deck under their own power; injured men had to be secured with a bowline under their arms and dragged aboard. And all the time, as the *Meldon Empire* sank deeper and deeper into the blackening sea, Ash had to be alert to the moment when she would finally go down so that he would be able to break away and avoid the suction that she would produce.

They took 45 minutes to haul the survivors aboard, and the *Meldon Empire*—like the good ship Ash imagined that she'd been—cooperated, only going under about ten minutes after Ash finally pulled away. All told, he had picked up 17 men, the fleet tug having rescued 16 more, the remainder, a number Ash put at ten, having been killed in the engine room when the torpedo exploded.

The survivors, most of them in miserable shape, found refuge on the ship where they could, some on the mess decks, some in the forward crew's compartment, a few stowed on the deck in the wardroom. Once Chaser 3 and the tug got underway and began to zig-zag toward Long Island, Hamp opened an operating room of sorts on the mess table in the after crew's compartment and began tending to injuries as far as he was able, splinting three broken arms, one broken leg, and sewing up four gashes which, Solly later said, were good enough to find Hamp work as a tailor. About the men who had swallowed oil, Hamp could do nothing, their fellow survivors taking up their care as well as they could while Watts, even with the seas running high, lit off the range and managed to brew tea for all hands, the ship being British out of Liverpool and tea being the one thing that he could give them to try to brighten their spirits.

"I guess," Solly said to Ash when he came up to resume the watch, "that there are times when men can't win for losing. But for the life of me, I can't figure out what we're doing wrong. We should have had that bastard, and still he got away from us. I never wanted to hate, Ash, but after seeing what those men in the compartment look like I'm really beginning to hate those kraut-eating shits."

"I've hated them since the time I saw them in Germany," Ash said. "I never saw so many strutting, arrogant cocks anywhere. All I wanted to do was haul off and kick them in the balls, and for my money, this is the next best thing. I don't know if we got that one or not, but if it shook some of that overweening pride out of a few of them down there, scared them half to death, and damaged them enough to hold them down … well, that's something. Given what we've got to work with, I don't think we're doing anything wrong. They're just damned hard to sink, U-boats, so we'll just have to go on doing the best we can with what we've got."

Later that day, 30 miles north from where Ash estimated that he had made his attack, a Catalina out of Cape Cod sighted a U-boat on the surface, reported it damaged in some way, and dropped a depth-charge pattern on it. According to the report, the crew had been sighted abandoning ship, and later, while the Catalina had reported seeing men in the water, the U-boat had been nowhere in evidence. COMDESLANT had then dispatched a DE out of Boston to hunt for survivors.

"I'm guessing we got a piece of it," Ash said when he received the news. "I don't think we hit it with a mousetrap or we'd have heard or seen results. I'm guessing we damaged it with a depth charge and that it had to come up. I'd say that the position that the Catalina reported is too close to where we were for that not to have been the boat we attacked. I could be wrong, of course, but since Dönitz withdrew most of his boats to the mid-Atlantic, there aren't all that many along the coast anymore, so I think this one was ours, and good riddance. Pass the word around; tell the crew that I think we damaged one and that owing to their efforts the Catalina finally sent her down. That'll make the crew happy and give the *Meldon Empire* people a lift."

Half an hour later, Chief Stobb came to the bridge to see Ash.

"We're takin' some water in the lazarette, Cap'n," Stobb said, shifting a chaw of chewing tobacco from one side of his mouth to the other, something that Ash had never before seen him do and which Ash found slightly amusing in the midst of the turmoil that followed their engagement.

"How much?" Ash asked.

"Pumps can handle it, no trouble," Stobb said, "but them depth charges, them last ones, must have popped a seam or two. We'd best have it seen to, Cap'n. It ain't somethin' that we can do ourselves."

"All right," Ash said. "I'll get off a message."

Five hours later, as they entered Raritan Bay, the engineering staff at COMDESLANT had already sent them a message directing them to make the Brooklyn Navy Yard and tie up alongside one of the piers. With all lines over and doubled up by 2230 that night, Ash found himself slightly astonished to see three yardbirds come aboard with their carpenter's tools and go straight to work in the lazarette, the noise they made keeping the crew in the after berthing compartment awake until 0300 in the morning when the workmen disappeared, and at 0500 sharp, Polaski woke Ash with yet another message directing him to get underway in order to convoy two empty tankers south.

"Shit," Hamp said, rolling out and getting into his blues. "I thought we'd get at least one night in port. Keren will be faint with lament, and Chana will be like to throw herself from the top of the Empire State building."

"Hmm, possibly a small loss," Solly said.

"I think I'd neglect to mention that we were in," Ash laughed. "The mere thought that you two Lotharios have been within arm's reach, or at least within a taxi's reach, will ruin the both of those girls for a week."

24

So they moved south, escorting ships from New York to Cape May, from Cape May to Charleston, from Charleston to Jacksonville, from Jacksonville to Key West, and from Key West to New Orleans and Galveston, and without once putting in for a good night's liberty, the war continued. Gradually, January gave way to February, Ash, Solly, and Hamp surviving on the letters they received—the only things that could break the tedium of their transits—but even with Claire writing to Ash every day, the mail so often failed to catch up with them that Hamp declared himself on the point of despair.

"Patience," Solly said. "Once Chana drops that Marine sergeant she's probably been leading around and plundering, I'm sure she will write—if, that is, anyone has taught her to hold a pen by this time."

"I'm going to tell her that you said that," Hamp said.

"What you'll want to ask," Ash said, "is how her cooking course is coming along."

Solly broke out laughing. "Chana does not expect to cook, Ash. She expects to hire a cook, not to mention a lady's maid, with the vast sums that her husband will be expected to lavish on her. If Master Hampton here knows what's good for him, he will apply for a seat on the New York Stock Exchange, which is about the only thing that will ever satisfy my sister, unless, of course, he takes what he's learned about stitching up wounds and sets up as an expensive plastic surgeon after the war."

"Are you suggesting," Ash said, "that Chana will not commit to village life in Kansas or, perhaps, northern Michigan?"

"You've got to be kidding," Solly said. "Chana thinks the west coast is located on the outskirts of Newark. If anyone ever tries to move her 3 miles from Bloomingdale's, he'll have a fight on his hands."

"You two should go on stage," Hamp said. "If either of you had listened to Chana for five minutes you would have known that she is talking about 'the suburbs.'"

"Oh," Solly said, "you mean The Hamptons or, perhaps, Westchester, with a summer cottage in Newport."

"Exactly," Hamp laughed. "Chana is a girl who thinks ahead."

"Yes," Solly said, "and bringing home the bacon, as far as Chana is concerned, means driving home a Brinks armored truck filled with plenty of loot. Just remember, Hamp, as a good friend, I've tried to give you fair warning."

"And the 'person of interest,'" Hamp rejoined, "what dream has she?"

"Quiet apartment, tree-lined street, three children, greeting me at the door with pipe, slippers, and a good bourbon the minute I return from my labors," Solly said. "Practical girl, Keren. Intends to wait on me hand and foot."

"I'm going to remember all of this," Ash said. "It ought to make for peals of laughter about ten years from now."

Suddenly, Polaski appeared, leaping down the ladder into the wardroom. "Sorry, Sirs," he said with a smile. "Nothin' in the mail for youse officers when the tender handed the bag over to us, but they give me a Houston paper, if youse wants to see it."

"We do," Ash said, reaching for the paper which Polaski thrust toward him. "Want it back after we finish?"

"Yes, Sir," Polaski said, "so's the crew can see it."

"Right," Ash said, "we'll get it back to you."

"So," Solly said as soon as Ash began to read, "what's the scoop?"

"Stalingrad," Ash said, brightening. "The German Sixth Army has surrendered. The Ruskies are claiming to have bagged upwards of 250,000 prisoners!"

"Ha," Hamp laughed. "That ought to give the krauts a lift. I'll bet Hitler's wetting himself."

"Looks like we've got Rommel bottled up as well," Ash said, his smile spreading. "Patton's pounding him from the west while Monty's chopping him up from the south. That ought to about bag the whole of the Africa Corps. We'll probably have to go on rationing in order to feed the POWs."

"Can't happen too soon," Hamp said.

"Anything else of note?" Solly asked.

"Says here that Jimmy Durante's insured the old *schnozzola* for $50,000," Ash laughed.

"Earthshaking," Hamp said. "I'll speak to Chana; she should insure her lips for a million."

"Go right ahead," Solly said. "Ash and I intend to insure the contents of your wallet for a bundle. That ought to make us instant millionaires ourselves, about five minutes after Chana next gets hold of you."

"Chana's 'requests' have never been more than modest," Hamp said. "How you could have lived in the same house with your sister for two decades and not know that is one of the mysteries of all times."

Ignoring Hamp, Solly said, "What's next, Ash. After Tunisia, what do you suppose our plan is? Greece, Yugoslavia, Italy, Southern France? Stalin will be pounding the table for a second front the minute that Rommel is wrapped up."

"Honestly, I have no idea," Ash said, handing the paper over to Solly. "Italy is close; Sicily is closer, but only our masters know. The question I have is what's next for us? Personally, I'd like to get back to Yarmouth about as fast as this thing can go."

What came next turned out to be a 30-ship convoy gathering in the Gulf before heading for Panama and the canal with a probable final destination in Australia. In order to make the transit, Chaser 3 joined an escort of eight other ships, a destroyer carrying the squadron commander, three DEs, a PC, and three subchasers. To Ash's satisfaction, Chaser 3 was assigned to ride herd on the formation as tail-end Charlie, and throwing in the time required for the convoy to collect—some coming from the east while others made their exit from the Houston ship channel—the trip took eight days, the convoy proceeding at a steady speed of 10 knots while zig-zagging. Twice, Ash had to run up inside the convoy to refuel and replenish the ship's water from an oiler, but otherwise the trip proved uneventful, save for one merchant sailor who fell overboard from a collier and who Ash managed to find and retrieve wet but unharmed after only 15 minutes in the water.

In the meantime, the temperature rose steadily until everyone, soaked through with sweat and forced to bathe with salt water, gave second thoughts to the virtues of the mid-Atlantic winter and couldn't help wishing for some more of it. And to Ash's amusement, one other event went down in his memory as a matter of note. On one particular morning not far west of Cuba, the convoy had passed through an enormous school of flying fish. As they did so, one or another of the fish began landing on deck, unable to make the sea on the far side. Watts and the mess cook suddenly appeared, buckets in hand, and began racing back and forth, snatching up the flopping fish with a speed which Ash, particularly in Watts' case, had previously thought unimaginable.

"When they're done down there," Ash said to his messenger, pointing to Watts and the mess cook, "I want to see Watts up here quick march."

"Had a good time fishing?" Ash asked, when Watts finally climbed to the bridge.

"Yas, Sir," Watts said, beaming from ear to ear.

"So," Ash said, "what's it all about?"

"*Gilly-Gilly*, Cap'n. Dem boys gonna love it!"

"And what," Ash asked, "is *Gilly-Gilly*?"

"Fish stew, Cap'n. Learn it from a Philippine, cookin' school, 'fore the war. Him say them flyin' fish best ever for it."

"And you're sure you won't poison the crew?" Ash said with a laugh.

"Them's fresh as dey get, Cap'n. We's goin' to have us a feast!"

The *Gilly-Gilly* turned out to be a treat, enough so that Ash told Watts to keep his buckets handy forever after, just in case they ever ran into flying fish again. The crew, served with a double portion, didn't hesitate to extend kudos to their cook, who already stood in high regard with them for what he'd been able to do with the ubiquitous canned salmon that came to them in cases as a part of nearly every replenishment.

In Panama, in the *Bahia de Limon*, Chaser 3 watched with interest as the destroyer, the DEs, the PC, and one of the chasers disappeared into the canal, followed one after the other by the merchant vessels in the convoy. Then, they made for Colon, tied up to the piers in Cristobal, and enjoyed a two-day respite, one section of the crew going over on liberty for each night they were in port. Solly and Hamp went ashore, but Ash didn't. Instead, bone tired from the watches he'd kept, Ash slept, the heat making his sleep restless and less than comfortable, his exhaustion nevertheless making it necessary.

After one such nap and after writing to Claire, Ash happened to look in the mirror, and for once, what he saw looking back at him surprised him. Only the year before, Ash had thought of himself as young. Aboard the *Parker*, as the ship's "George," the most junior officer aboard, he had been treated as a mere youth, even by officers a year or two younger than himself. Now, as Ash studied his face—the dark circles under his eyes, the crow's feet starting to form at their corners, the harder features that seemed to stare back at him—he began to perceive the toll that the war was taking on him. After their first few times out the year before, exhausted as he had been by remaining constantly on the bridge, he'd slept and sprung back like the youth he had been. Now, the spring-back was taking longer, the exhaustion never quite releasing him, the desire for sleep, and rest, and tranquility put off, delayed, held back by the incessant and even increasing pace of operations. The rigors of command, Ash knew, increased the toll. Solly and Hamp, free from ultimate responsibility, did not carry his load. Their jobs, no matter how important to the ship and the crew, did not carry the constant stress with which Ash had to live, and there was no one, no one, who could lift his load. Other naval captains—of destroyers, cruisers, carriers, and fleets—must have felt the same thing, and Ash could only wonder about the greater stress all of them must have been under in conjunction with their much larger commands. But that didn't change matters for Ash. He had the ball, and that meant that he had to run with it, night and day, for as long and as far as his responsibilities took him.

Probably, he imagined, Solly would be ordered to relieve him at some time during the summer. When he thought about it, Ash knew that he would be ready, that he would need something, some form of rest that would go well beyond the two nights that the Navy only occasionally gave him.

Chaser 3 went out again the following morning. As usual the crew moved a trifle slowly, their hangovers hammering them, their fisherman's lies about the times they'd had and the girls they squired around mounting steadily as the morning wore on. Cornfeld had brought back a rooster, suggesting that it would make a suitable mascot for the ship, but after Samarango informed him that roosters were French talismans and after he'd had to clean up the rooster's droppings, the rooster, expensive or not, went straight into Watts' stew pot, gifting the crew, if not with perpetual good luck, at least with a bowl of excellent chicken soup. As they ate, Watts and Cornfeld extolled its medicinal benefits as a VD preventative and cure for other assorted ailments.

"My mother once called it her Jewish cure-all," Solly laughed. "I don't know what it is about chicken soup, Ash, but we got a regular dose the whole time we were growing up, both Chana and I, and we almost never came down with colds or flu."

"Mothers know a thing or two," Ash said.

The convoy they picked up for escort back to Galveston turned out to be nothing like any convoy they had escorted before, much of it returning from the Solomons with battle damage that exceeded anything Ash and the crew of Chaser 3 had ever seen. Central to the convoy was a light cruiser with its bow blown off, a makeshift arrangement of welded together steel plates permitting it to make 12 knots but no more, the cruiser's best speed dictating the speed of the convoy. Three destroyers—two of them missing their after gun mounts entirely, one with its forward 5"/38 gun mount tilted at an angle, all three of them blackened with battle damage and shell holes—flanked the cruiser, and falling in behind, several Navy cargo vessels slumped along showing blackened superstructures, the obvious effects of bomb damage. In so far as they were able, the injured destroyers fleshed out the screen to which the southern command had added three additional subchasers, two fleet tugs, in case they were needed, and a battle-scarred PC that had also apparently come under attack somewhere in the islands. Taken as a whole, the formation did not present an encouraging picture of the fighting that had been taking place around Guadalcanal, and Ash could only wonder about other ships that had not made it back. The cruiser, he imagined, would be in dry dock for months, the destroyers for less time, perhaps, and about the cargo vessels, he could not estimate; ships their size surpassed his understanding based upon any previous experience.

The trip to Galveston took them ten days, February already slipping toward March by the time they finally made port, but as before, Chaser 3 did not go in. Instead, after yet another underway replenishment and after dropping off four undamaged freighters into Galveston Bay, she continued with the damaged combatants toward Key West. There, finally, she was relieved of them, turning them over to an entire squadron of six DEs that had come down from Charleston to screen them up the coast.

COMDESLANT gave them two welcome days off in Key West. So, with the crew once more granted port and starboard liberty, Ash, Solly, and Hamp went over on the beach and made straight for the telephone exchange to place calls to Claire, Keren, and Chana. With the long distance lines crammed to the limit, Ash had to wait more than half an hour before he could get his call through to Claire, but when the operator finally told him that his party was on the line, Ash thrilled to the moment, his annoyance with the wait clearing away like a mist dispelled.

"How are you, love?" he asked.

"You sound tired," Claire said. "Where are you?"

"Key West. We just got in. We'll be here a couple of days I think."

Hearing Claire's voice served him like a tonic, perked up his energy, and gave him a momentary release from the things that had been plaguing him. Ash couldn't be sure, but he sensed that he'd had something of the same effect on his wife, judging from what he thought was an audible uplift in her voice. Given the charges that the call cost, Ash and Claire only talked for ten minutes, and when he finally replaced the receiver and walked back outside the exchange, he found Hamp and Solly waiting for him, broad smiles on their faces.

"The two of you look as contented as if you had been chewing your cuds," Ash said.

"And you don't?" Hamp said. "Personally, I feel like a whole new man. Chana sent me *endearments*. The two of you should have been so lucky."

"We were," Solly said. "I haven't seen the boss so pleased since he last sunk a sub."

"I know I can't speak for the two of you," Ash said, "but I'm up for a couple of drinks, a good steak, and a walk. Anyone care to join me?"

"Let's do it," Hamp said. "In the absence of Chana's cooking, we'll have to settle for second best."

Solly broke out laughing, and the three proceeded to the club.

After drinks and a meal, moving at a leisurely pace beneath a moonlit sky, the three walked out into Key West, not saying much, avoiding the bars and confining themselves to residential streets where the light remained sufficient for walking but where the quiet and the absence of traffic suited their mood. In the midst of the walk, regaining their land legs as their muscles relaxed, on the corner of Whitehead and Olivia, Solly suddenly stopped dead and gawked.

"I know this place," he said. "I've seen it in a photograph. That's Hemingway's place."

"Hemingway? Ernest Hemingway?" Hamp said, turning to look.

"Yeah," Solly said. "That's it, sure as hell. No mistake about it. Distinctive house."

"I thought he was living in Cuba," Hamp said.

"I think he is," Solly said, "but this is where he lived in Key West. Whether he still owns the place or not, I have no idea."

"Read him, have you?" Ash asked.

"A couple," Solly said. "*The Sun Also Rises, A Farewell to Arms*. You?"

"Those two," Ash said, "plus *Green Hills of Africa*. I liked the first two better. He's got a new one out, *For Whom the Bell Tolls*, about the Spanish Civil War. It's supposed to be long, but I haven't seen a copy."

"Gary Cooper was in the movie of it," Hamp said. "Cooper and Hemingway are supposed to be friends, but that didn't make much difference when Cooper filmed *A Farewell to Arms*. I thought it was kind of a dud as a movie."

"Same here," Solly said. "I'm afraid I skipped it," Ash said. "But the book was first rate."

"Read any Faulkner?" Solly asked.

"I hear he's hard going," Hamp said.

"But worth the effort," Ash added. "Try *The Sound and the Fury*."

"What about F. Scott Fitzgerald?" Solly asked.

"Who's he?" Hamp said.

They were back at the ship by 2230 that evening, undressed, in bed, and sound asleep. When Gomez, standing the quarterdeck watch, woke Ash not long after midnight and told him that the shore patrol wanted him, Ash got into his clothes and arrived on deck just in time to see two paddy wagons unloading an even dozen of his crew.

"Fight uptown," the chief petty officer in charge of the paddy wagons told Ash. "Your boys seem to have settled in at a place called The Green Moon when a pack of boots from one of them new DEs descended on 'em and told 'em to move over for some real sailors, and that touched it off. Your people gave as good as they got and some better, but the manager called for us, so we picked up the whole bunch, the DE's people as well as yours, both bunches tellin' us they was just havin' fun when we arrived."

"Any damage?" Ash asked.

"Seems they were smart enough, or drunk enough, or sober enough to go out in the street, so no damage 'cept to themselves, but the Key West police is pissed off and don't want no more of it."

"We'll be going out in the morning," Ash said, "so the police can rest easy, and as long as there are no charges, I'll come up with something to discipline the crew."

"Puttin' 'em to bed without their suppers would about cover it," laughed the chief. "Makin' 'em replace their uniforms at their own expense would be better yet."

"I'll take it under advisement," Ash said. "Thanks for getting them back, Chief. What next, I wonder?"

Caracas turned out to be next, by way of San Juan, Chaser 3 going out early, joining a swift-moving convoy ultimately headed for North Africa before detaching two tankers, both of them riding high, which Ash herded south for their refill. The liberty section from the previous night, many of them bruised and scabbed from their fight, swaggered a little over what they announced as their trouncing of the DE's crew and took the light punishment that Ash dispensed with considerable pride.

25

Two days after leaving Key West, official correspondence picked up in Jacksonville informed Ash that Samarango had been promoted to Chief Boatswain's Mate while Teague, Glick, Hill, and Bell had also passed their rating exams and been advanced one rank. Not long after, as the ship headed for Charleston amid a swelling March sea, Samarango spoke to Ash on the bridge after he had relieved Solly from his watch.

"Captain," Samarango said, as the two men scanned the horizon with their binoculars, "if you're still willing to recommend me for Officer's Candidate School, I'm willing to try. I've held off 'cause I wanted to make Chief first. Might seem a little short sighted to some, but making Chief Petty Officer was a goal I set for myself when I first joined up. Now that I can sew on my crow and if you still think it's a good move, I'm ready to try for a commission."

"Good," Ash said. "I've already written your recommendation. All I have to do is send it in, and I think we'll hear something within a month, or two at the most. Once we hear back, I'd imagine that you'll get a set of orders without delay. Like I said, Boats, I'll hate to lose you, but I think you've made the right decision. With what you know already, you're going to be miles ahead of any officer candidates coming to the school straight from college or civilian life, and that ought to guarantee you a good billet once you leave the course behind. And once the war is over and if you opt to stay in, I think the Navy will put you straight through college before sending you back to sea. It would mean a good engineering degree, or something like, and that will give you a real leg up when it comes time for your retirement."

"Hope so," the bosun said. "And Cap'n, thanks. I appreciate what you done for me, bringing me up here on the bridge, an' all, and I appreciate the recommendation for OCS. I'll give it my best."

"Never doubted it for a second," Ash said. "No thanks needed. You've more than earned your place."

Twenty miles from Charleston harbor, Chaser 3 received a message which detached her from the screen in which she had been serving and sent her back southeast to search for survivors from a South African merchantman that had been steaming independently up from Angola, carrying ore of some kind, and which had been attacked and reported herself sinking about 40 miles off the coast. An hour after Ash started toward the contact, a Catalina reported two rafts in the water about 30 miles southeast of where Ash was making headway; then, the pilot and his crew guided Ash towards where he made visual contact with the rafts and moved in to pick up survivors. With regard to the U-boat that had sunk the ship, the Catalina could find nothing to indicate an enemy presence in the vicinity. But the minute that Ash pulled alongside the first raft and examined it, he found all of the evidence that he could require. The five men in the raft were no longer men at all; instead, they numbered among the dead, their bodies stiff from rigor mortis, their hopeless condition resulting from the fact that the Nazis had machine-gunned them not long after the seamen had abandoned ship. The second raft, which held seven corpses, showed Ash the same evidence, the same bullet-riddled bodies, the same blood stains, the same unthinkable brutality.

"Get the men up here," Ash said to Solly. "I want every one of them to see this, to see what those bastards have done."

Reactions among the crew varied. They'd seen dead men before—men killed by the Germans, one killed by themselves—but they'd never seen anything like what the two rafts showed them. Some were infuriated to the point of rage. Others remained silent, their jaws set hard with a kind of hate that they had never before felt, and in one or two instances, men cried. On the bridge, Ash found that he had clamped his teeth so hard against the stem of his pipe that he had cracked it beyond repair.

"Get them aboard," Ash said to Solly, "and put them under canvas on the fantail. We're taking them back. I want our people in Charleston to see this, to photograph it, and to publicize it, if they will. This is evidence of a war crime so clear and straightforward that no one could deny it, and it's as clear as anything we'll ever see. There's got to come a reckoning one day in a way that will stick, and if the men who did this survive without being sunk, I hope we live to see the whole damn lot of them hanged."

To Ash and his entire crew's shock, one of the men they dragged aboard turned out to be still alive—shot through with three rounds, but still breathing. To Ash's further shock, after Hamp had tended to the man and gotten a half of cup of soup into him, the seaman had lived long enough to give them a single piece of startling intelligence when he revealed that the U-boat that had attacked and murdered the men had carried the image of a large black seahorse painted on its conning tower.

Immediately Ash reasoned that the sub in question was the same Nazi U-boat that he had attacked off Cape May, the same boat from which Teague had displaced its after gun mount, and the same which had attacked the trawler and killed the fisherman the year before. Ash knew that the boat could not have remained on station for the length of time involved. Obviously, the German U-boat had gone back to Brest, or Wilhelmshaven, or somewhere in occupied Europe for repair and overhaul, and returned, possibly more than once. As far as Ash knew, all of Hitler's U-boats carried large white hull numbers on their conning towers; only one had ever had the gall to show the black seahorse.

Entering Charleston harbor that night, Ash was ordered to an anchorage, but for once, rather than do as he'd been told, he refused the order and spoke directly to the harbor master.

"Give me a pier assignment," Ash said over the radio-telephone. "I'm bringing in a dozen dead bodies, all of them riddled with gunfire and evidence of a war crime. I want a mortuary detail on hand and whoever's in charge of the Office of Naval Intelligence, and we'll let ONI take it from there."

After that, the harbor master made no protests and assigned Ash a berth immediately adjacent to the pier. As soon as they'd tied up, ONI boarded the ship with a team of specialists, two of whom were commissioned Navy lawyers who began deposing every man in the ship's company, holding back on Solly, Hamp, and Ash until last.

"What will you do with this?" Ash asked, signing his deposition before witnesses, Ash, Solly, and Hamp drinking coffee with one of the lawyers in the wardroom shortly before midnight.

"Yours is not the first case like this that we've seen," the lawyer said. "We had another instance of merchant sailors being machine-gunned in November. We'll send the photographs and the depositions up to the Navy Department in Washington, and our assumption is that the information is being compiled and stored for a case or cases to be brought after the war's end. The word we have is that the Nazis are not going to be let off. If any of these shitheads survive, they're to be prosecuted for war crimes. But," he concluded, showing Ash a smirk of disgust, "don't hold your breath waiting for it."

"Best then to catch them and kill them," Ash said,

"Yes," the lawyer said. "That's the best I can suggest."

Four times in the weeks that followed, Chaser 3 convoyed ships from Charleston to Norfolk and back, taking up a few freighters here and bringing back empty tankers there. Once, joining some DEs, a new destroyer, and an attack transport filled with troops, Ash also screened two of the sub-hunting jeep carriers south, both going to Charleston where, from some unknown navy air field, air squadrons would be flown on board for eventual transit to North Africa. And near the end of March, joining a screen made up from heavily damaged destroyers and a few PCs, Ash again screened a badly shot-up cruiser and six battle-damaged LSTs toward the repair yards in Philadelphia. COMDESLANT then afforded the ship two days' upkeep in Norfolk, and when the mail arrived, in addition to disgorging long-awaited letters from Claire, Chana, and Keren, it also spit up a set of immediate orders for Samarango, transferring him to an OCS course to begin three days hence at Northwestern University in Chicago.

Half an hour after Hill had processed Samarango's orders, the bosun appeared on the quarterdeck, his working uniform changed for winter blues and a buttoned overcoat, his sea bag packed and standing by his side.

"Request permission to leave the ship, Sir," Samarango said, after he had shaken hands with Ash, Solly, Hamp, and the entire crew who had assembled to see him off.

"Granted," Ash said, returning the man's salute. "And best of luck, Chief."

And lifting his sea bag by its canvas strap, Samarango saluted Ash and departed, heading into a whole new life that, Ash thought, the man couldn't possibly have imagined when the war started.

"Whatever are we going to do without him?" Solly said to Ash. "I don't suppose they'll send us another guy that experienced if we stay in commission for another 20 years."

"You're probably right," Ash said. "If we're lucky, we'll get a BM2, but more probably, they'll send us a BM3 and expect us to train him up to Chaser 3 standards."

"Does that mean bridge watches as well?" Hamp asked.

"That remains to be seen," Ash said. "Samarango had plenty of experience in the pilot house of a tug before he came to us. I doubt if our next bosun will have had the same advantages. If he hasn't, Bell is the likely candidate. He can already navigate, and he's smart, so I don't think it will tax us much to bring him up with us."

"Good choice," Solly said. "Bell's had a head on his shoulders since the day he came aboard, and he's dependable. And with Samarango gone, aside from Stobb, Bell will be the senior enlisted man on board."

The new man, Deitz BM3, came aboard not long after the liberty party had gone ashore. After looking over the man's service record, once Hill had checked him in and finished the required paperwork, Ash had him up to the chart room for an interview.

"So," Solly said, later that evening after he and Hamp had come back from the telephone exchange, "what's the verdict on our new bosun?"

"Samarango, he is not," Ash said. "His name is Deitz, and he's a BM3 as I expected he might be. Grew up on a Wisconsin dairy farm. I wouldn't call him slow, but I can't say that he's very swift either. For the past year, he's been running small boats out of the pool here in Norfolk, so he knows a thing or two about small craft, and I'm satisfied that he can rig for refueling all right. He seems to know all the basics about knots, anchoring, mooring, and so forth, but I don't think he's bridge material. I've talked to Bell and given him the nod, and since he's the only first class petty officer aboard, I'm giving him the nod as assistant master at arms as well."

"Eager, is he?" Hamp asked.

"He's eager about coming up on the bridge," Ash said, "but less eager about being made MAA. But then again, who would be? No one that I've ever met likes to police their own, and Samarango wasn't thrilled about that job either. Bell will do fine, and I'll make sure that I'm up there on the bridge with him until I'm convinced that we can give him the watch on his own."

The crew seemed to prefer Charleston to Norfolk as a liberty port because Norfolk seemed to be so filled with sailors and Marines that finding feminine companionship proved difficult, much more so than elsewhere. Nevertheless, both liberty parties went over and returned without incident, and on the morning they pulled out, Chaser 3 quickly discovered herself again bound for Charleston.

Halfway through the trip, Watts, as an April fool ploy, announced that he was going to feed the crew a fricassee of fresh possum, newly minced, and Deitz, fully taken in by the joke, went straight to Solly and lodged a protest before, to his chagrin, he discovered that he'd been made the butt. The actual meat served on April 1 turned out to be a pretty good cut of beef, something that Watts had stored up in the reefer after a trip to the commissary, but the implied joke hadn't set well with Deitz who only warmed up to Watts after the cook gave him a double helping of pie in order to make amends and break the ice with the new bosun.

"We gots us a happy ship here," Watts said to Deitz, "an' we's gots to keep her dat way. My jokes is for everybody, not just bosuns. Y'all get me Wisconsin?"

"I gets ya," Deitz said. "Your possum's pretty good eatin', after all, I guess."

"Finest kind," Watts said.

On the following morning, Ash once more found himself detached from the screen and sent to destroy mines that yet another Catalina had spotted some 30 miles east of the convoy, floaters, five of them, riding up over the swells in a State 3 sea. The Catalina had dropped depth charges on two of them, exploding them without difficulty, and one of her machine gunners had destroyed another, but with her depth charges expended and her gunners unable to hit the other two mines, Ash was called out to finish the job, the Catalina guiding him onto his target with uncommon skill. The actual destruction of the mines turned out to be something that Ash directed Teague to try with the 3"/23 using frag ammunition. And in both cases, at 400 yards, the exploding anti-aircraft rounds so peppered both mines that they sank at once, without exploding and without damaging Chaser 3 from concussion.

"How the hell explosions like those could fail to set off a mine is beyond me," Hamp said, once Ash had ordered Teague to cease fire.

"I wonder if there's a mathematical formula to cover the probability, or the improbability?" Ash mused.

"Probably," Solly said, "but what it might be is a mystery to me. I would have thought we'd have blown the damn things sky high."

"One thing's for sure," Ash said. "Whatever else he may be up to, Dönitz is still keeping a few of his little bastards out here along the coast. Torpedo attack risks detection, but if they lay a few mines in the shipping lanes here and there, they can slip away undetected and unseen. They can go deep during the day, launch mines underwater, and then come up for air and surface running after dark in order to charge their batteries. We can still catch them on radar or with sonar, but without them making direct attacks, they'll be harder to find."

April saw Chaser 3 plodding back and forth between Norfolk, Charleston, and Jacksonville, escorting what seemed like endless, non-eventful convoys back and forth between ports in a never-ending cycle that threatened to go on without a break. But near the end of the month, a cargo vessel, the *Santa Catalina*, was torpedoed and sunk nearly 400 miles east of Cape Hatteras, and both Ash and a second chaser were dispatched to hunt for survivors. In the end, the trip proved fruitless because a Swedish ship reached the victims six hours before Ash could get near them and rescued 55 of the stricken seamen from their lifeboats without losing a single man. The attempted rescue nevertheless cost Ash an additional four days' steaming, tossed the crew to the point where the mid-Atlantic made more than half of them seasick, and returned them to the coast utterly worn out and dispirited. Once tied up to the piers at Cape May, however, the crew's morale instantly transformed when Ash received a message directing them to proceed to the Brooklyn Navy Yard for five days' upkeep while their engines were briefly overhauled.

26

Leaving Solly and Hamp to oversee the upkeep, Ash called South Freeport, told Claire to expect him that afternoon, and caught an express for Boston out of Grand Central. With the train so crowded that passengers found it difficult to move, Ash had to stand all the way to Boston, a plethora of soldiers, sailors, and Marines standing with him, clogging up the aisles, shooting the breeze, occasionally playing cards across the backs of seats or the surfaces of luggage. When he reached Boston and switched to a train for Portland, he found it less crowded and managed, for two hours, to sleep where he sat, waking bleary eyed but feeling better for the respite he had enjoyed. And then, finally, he boarded a bus for Yarmouth and South Freeport and noticed, for the first time, that the leaves were beginning to unfold from their buds. That is when Ash realized that it was May Day and wondered what the Russians might be doing to celebrate the event. Driving the Germans hard and harder, he hoped, pulverizing their Panzers and fertilizing their soil with miles of German blood. As he contemplated that thought, the bus arrived in South Freeport where, in the moment that Ash alighted, Claire ran toward him and threw her arms around him with a passion so strong that Ash thought he would melt.

"I have to be back on Tuesday night," Ash said, as they rushed up the street toward their apartment over the shop, "but that gives us the weekend, and Monday, and part of Tuesday, depending on what you can do about a substitute, and I don't want to waste a moment."

"I called Mrs. Trilling," Claire said, squeezing his arm. "She's a dear, so she's going to cover my classes for both work days that you'll still be here."

"Bright girl," Ash said.

"Selfish," Claire said, "because I want you all to myself while you're here. Can't have you loitering and lurking around Yarmouth while I work. One of the babes around there might try to pick you up, and then I would have to take steps."

Ash laughed. "I'm sure the girls in Yarmouth are very nice, love, but you're the only 'babe' anyone has ever seen around there, and I have a crew of 27 who will attest to it."

"Let's go up and spend an hour or five in bed," Claire said, unlocking their door, "so that I can show you how much of a 'babe' you've come home to."

"Just lead the way," Ash said.

"Oh, I intend to," Claire said, giving him a peck before turning and rushing up the stairs with Ash, taking two steps at a time behind her.

Much later, sitting late at table after the more than scrumptious supper that Claire had got up and cooked, a bottle of American brandy appeared.

"I'm afraid that our supply of Calvados has dried up," Claire said.

"One of the hardships of war," Ash said.

"Isn't that the truth," she said. "So, what might Solly and Hamp be up to?"

"I think I can guess," Ash laughed, "but a description is not for your ears."

"Nonsense," Claire said. "I've talked to Keren and Chana, twice. They've been counting the days. Chana has been fit to be tied waiting for him to get back; she's that anxious, but don't you dare let on to Hamp."

"You should see Hamp," Ash said. "They're a couple in heat, or something like. What about Keren?"

"Still waters run deep," Claire said, "not to snatch yet another cliché, but I'd say she's in love, no two ways about it."

"Shall I begin making a list," Ash said, "of your cliches, I mean?"

"As long as you find wisdom in them," Claire said. "So, what about Solly?"

"Still waters run deep," Ash said. "And the wisdom to say so is all mine."

Claire smiled.

"Careful," Ash said, "too much satisfaction, and you'll risk laying an egg. What is it about you women that you can't stand to see a loose male anywhere?"

"Women are gifted with a deep intuitive understanding, dear. They know when a male is best off. See how much happier you've been since you married me?"

"I defer to your wisdom," Ash said. "Would you like to go back to bed?"

"Oh, how very intuitive of you," Claire said.

"Not at all," Ash said, "I merely like to surprise you."

On Saturday, they lunched with Mrs. Jarvis and then went to see the film *Mrs. Miniver*.

"Rather understated, don't you think?" Claire said as they walked back out into the sunlight.

"Yes," Ash said, "but it works. Greer Garson seem to have had exactly the right personality for it."

"We're lucky," Claire said, "that we don't have to live with the same degree of threat they face in England. I shouldn't like having to worry about where the next bomb might be coming from or when it might be falling."

Ash thought briefly about mines and torpedoes and 4-inch naval guns but kept his mouth shut about them.

"We've been spared that," he said finally, "and I expect we're damn happy about it, those of us who take notice. I've seen some of the ships that have come back from Guadalcanal, and they aren't a pretty sight at all."

After a coffee at the Queen Bee's, Claire and Ash boarded a bus and returned to the apartment, where Claire, having latched onto a couple of Cornish game hens, put together a supper that Ash thought fit for a king—something which she topped off with orange slices, dipped in a batter before being deep fried and glazed with cinnamon.

"Where under the sun did you ever come up with this combination?" Ash asked her as he popped down the last of the orange slices.

"Think of it as a gift from England," Claire said. "Actually, you might like to think of it as a gift from Henry VIII."

"What are you talking about?"

"Henry VIII, the big fat guy, six wives, King of England, and all that. Apparently, if you'll think back, he liked to eat, so one of those good souls in his kitchen seems to have written down a recipe or two just so his modern descendants could enjoy the same things."

"Trying to fatten me up on medieval cooking, are you?"

"Good food is often a prelude to good sex," Claire said.

"Randy little thing, aren't you," Ash said, giving her a mild pinch.

"Where you're concerned, always," Claire said, leaning down and blowing lightly in his ear.

❧

On Sunday, given a clear sky, a warm day, and a promise of only light breezes, they packed sandwiches, fruit, two paper cups, and a bottle of white wine into a bag and set out for the shore overlooking the Harraseeket River. Neither wanted to walk along a beach. Instead, what they looked for and found turned out to be a reasonably secluded spot overlooking the river, one of the upper reaches of Casco Bay really, where they could watch whatever sailboats happened to be out and look across a stretch of water toward Wolfes Neck Woods on the opposite shore.

"On a good day, it looks like you could swim the distance," Ash speculated.

"Cold," Claire said. "I'm not sure we catch all that much of the Gulf Stream up here. I went wading once, not far from here, and that was enough."

"That's something Chaser 3 has been spared," Ash said. "It's been cold enough between here and Cape May in the winter, but we've never had to do the far North Atlantic. I think they're afraid that the snow and ice might swamp us. Halifax, I've been told, can be worse than awful. On the other hand, that run down to San Juan can just about boil water, and I cannot say one good thing for extended heat rash or saltwater laundry."

"Perfectly gross?"

"Perfectly," Ash said, "like some more of the wine?"

"Yes," Claire said.

For two hours, happy merely to be together, Ash and Claire remained where they were, watching the boats and the gulls and the occasional clouds that drifted by in the distance. Finally, repacking the cups and the empty wine bottle in their bag, they strolled along the shore for a ways until they'd had enough exercise, and then they returned home.

"Suppose I cook for you tonight," Ash said. "You can loll, possibly obscenely, on the couch and eat bon bons while I whip up something light like pasta."

"You've got to be kidding," Claire said.

"No, no I'm not," Ash said. "Couple of diced tomatoes, a diced onion, some sliced mushrooms, a little Italian spice, and all of it thrown into three tablespoons of olive oil after I've sweated the garlic, and then everything is simmered for an hour. None of that tomato paste to crap up the flavor, and all of it mixed together with the pasta once the pasta is ready. Most Americans think Italian food is 98 percent tomato sauce; I don't, and neither do real Italians who use it very sparingly. Want me to give it a go?"

"Yes," Claire said. "I don't know where you picked up your secret about the tomato paste, about leaving it out, I mean, but obviously you knew someone who knew something."

"I got that from the Lombards in Herrin when I lived there," Ash said. "The ones I knew turned up their noses at too much tomato. Said it was a bad habit that the immigrants from southern Italy brought with them. Said that red food tended to turn people's stomachs. Not a lot of love lost there. Probably something to do with a distaste for the Mafia, and for southern Italian cooking."

"What if I tempt you while you're cooking?" Claire said, "while I'm lolling obscenely?"

"Dangerous," Ash said. "I might overcook the pasta."

Ash's pasta turned out well, Ash tending to business, Claire sitting primly in a chair to watch him, the two of them digging in with a degree of gusto when the meal was ready, after which Claire registered just the right degree of approval to make Ash think he hadn't muffed the exercise or ruined the evening. And then, for an hour or two afterward, they tuned in radio programs before, finally unable to restrain themselves, the two adjourned to the bedroom for another night of bliss.

"How long, Ash?" Claire asked him over coffee the next morning.

"How long, what?" Ash said.

"Before you're relieved? Before they give you a break? You're absolutely wonderful in bed, love, but even I can see that you're otherwise exhausted. It's written all over your face."

"I know," Ash said. "I've looked at the same face in the mirror and found it hard to recognize. But I don't think there will be any letup. In fact, if anything, I expect operations to pick up. The DEs are coming off the ways fairly fast now, and we're seeing a lot more chasers and destroyers as well, but I'm told that we're prefabricating Liberty ships in a matter of days in our attempt to outstrip the Germans. We are trying to build them faster than they can sink them, so that means more convoys, more escorts, and bigger screens. It won't slow down, not until this thing's finished."

"The thing I'm worried about," Claire said, "is that I don't want it to finish *you*. You need a rest."

"I do," Ash said, "but really, I'm fine. It just begins to wear a man down after a while. I suppose it's the price of command."

"What about Solly and Hamp?"

"Watches are exhausting," Ash said, "but they don't have to carry the rest of it. Add what Solly's done already, and then, after he takes command, I'll give him about 12 months before he's in my condition. If Hamp stays aboard during that time, the accumulated wear will probably have him ready for a change six or eight months after he takes command from Solly. That's all speculation, of course, but that would be my guess."

❧

On Monday night, Ash took Claire to a hotel supper club in Portland. The cocktails were superb, the food adequate, and the music excellent, a mixture of dreamy dance arrangements salted with just enough high-stepping tunes to keep the dance floor lively. Because they had taken a room below the night club, Ash and Claire remained on the floor until they finally helped shut the place down. Ash imagined that it must have been close to four o'clock in the morning before they both fell asleep.

They breakfasted well late the following morning, the hotel serving them cheese omelets, rashers of well-prepared bacon, greaseless hash browns, and all of the toast they could consume, even if they had to settle for margarine as a spread.

"Very satisfying," Ash said, as they left the table and headed back for the bus up to South Freeport.

"Growing boys need sustenance," Claire said. "Will you eat on the train going back?"

"No," Ash said. "I intend to save the money and let Watts hand me a sandwich once I get back aboard."

"You can't run on empty, love."

"I don't intend to," Ash said. "Watts makes very big sandwiches."

"What if you have to stand all the way from Boston to New York again?"

"That," Ash said, "is something with which I have immense experience."

They returned to South Freeport in time for them to spend a few more quiet hours together, and then, after Claire clung to him for a long, lingering goodbye, she finally let him go.

"No unnecessary risks, Ash. I want you home again in one piece just as soon as you can beat a path to the door."

"Rest assured," Ash said, "just as soon as I can beat a path to your door."

Ash caught the four o'clock train. As before, he found that he was able to sit as far as Boston, but the train from Boston down to New York appeared to be more crowded than the train he had taken days before, with the result that he stood in the club car all the way, a seldom tasted bottle of beer in his hand, talking with a pair of destroyer officers, ensigns, who'd been on leave in Cambridge visiting old Harvard pals. Assigned as junior officers on one of the new DEs, they were experienced enough after a year to talk easily with Ash, and what they had to tell him proved interesting.

"Our C.O. thinks the battle of the Atlantic is about to turn," one of them said. "We're in one of these killer groups. Planes off the jeep carrier go out and spot for us, find a U-boat, and call back, and then we head out with two or three cans, find the krauts with sonar, and pound the hell out of them. We haven't sunk one so far, but three of our sister ships have, and that's just in the last four months. What about you, Sir? Seeing action in the chasers?"

"After a fashion," Ash said. "We've had a few contacts and dropped a few depth charges, and once, we caught one on the surface and put a couple of rounds into him, but as far as sinking one, we've never been certain."

"Radar sure helps."

"Yes," Ash said, "yes it does."

"I think we've about got 'em on the run," said the less talkative ensign.

"Let's hope so," Ash said.

When Ash finally arrived back on board at around 2300 on Tuesday night, Watts did prepare him a sandwich—cheese and onion on fresh toast. At first, Ash thought the combination strange, but when he tried it, he found it wholly satisfying. Then he went up to the wardroom, expecting to find Hamp and Solly back, only to see that they had not yet returned. As a result, Ash had already changed into wash khaki working trousers and had his feet elevated by the time they came on board, Polaski having presented him with the message file which he had just finished reading as the two dropped down the ladder into the wardroom.

"The two of you look ridiculous," Ash said, studying their faces. "What the hell did those two girls do to you? Your faces look positively bloody with lipstick!"

"This one got engaged," Solly said, pointing to Hamp before he looked into the mirror and then began rapidly washing his face over the sink.

"I merely proposed," Hamp said, "and the lovely Chana showed me the good grace to accept."

"I'll tell you what, Ash," Solly said, his face dripping, the towel he was holding having taken on a red sheen, "I think your wife may have to be charged with lending aid and comfort to the enemy."

"You mean the Germans?" Ash exclaimed, slamming his feet to the floor.

"I mean my sister," Solly said. "I can't be certain, but I think she gave Chana advice about how to lure the lad into her trap."

"Don't be absurd," Hamp said.

"And what about you?" Ash said. "That towel you're holding is showing battle damage of its own."

"Keren and I," Solly said with solemnity, "have merely reached an understanding."

"Tell that to the Coast Guard," Hamp snapped. "You should have seen the two of them at the ferry landing. They were utterly shameless, while Chana and I were exchanging a warm handshake."

"I think I get the picture," Ash said. "What you might tell the girls, when next you write them, is that they have both come into the money."

"That will certainly provide music for Chana's ears," Solly said. "How so?"

"I have a message here," Ash said. "The Navy, with apparent foreknowledge that you were going to take the leap, has promoted both of you to the august rank of Lieutenant, junior grade. But don't let the girls go out and buy their mink coats yet. Your promotions are not effective until June 2. Congratulations, the both of you."

"Well," Solly said, "who would have thought it? Seems like yesterday that we were just reporting to Anson's yard."

"What I want to know," Hamp said, "is how the women seem to know about this stuff before we ever do. Chana told me I was going to be promoted before I'd even thought about it!"

"I'd bet money," Solly said, "that if you went into my sister's bedroom, you'd find a pay scale tacked to the wall for every rank from ensign to admiral with time in grade for promotion marked off on a conveniently situated calendar. You'd better prepare yourself, Hamp. The next time we put in here, Chana will want to drag us to the Ritz, if not the Waldorf. If I were you, I'd think about starting to mend fences with that grandmother of yours."

"Possibly," Hamp said, "I can find Chana something really productive to do. Do you think she might like to apply for a paper route?"

"The only route in which Chana is likely to show an interest," Solly said, "is the route to Bergdorf-Goodman's."

27

According to COMDESLANT's message from the night before, Chaser 3 had been slated to get underway at 0800 the following morning, pick up a convoy in Raritan Bay, and lead them south toward Cape May in company with five other chasers, Ash, as the senior officer in the group, having been designated screen commander for the evolution. Instead, Michelson, duty radioman for the watch, woke Ash at 0430 that morning with an urgent change of orders. A Canadian freighter had been torpedoed in the night 54 miles east of Nantucket. Coast Guard cutters had been dispatched both from Nantucket and Cape Cod to search for and pick up survivors, but Ash was ordered to proceed, with four other chasers, to search for and, if possible, sink the offending U-boat.

By the time Watts got up to the chart room with coffee for them, Ash and Solly were already bent over the chart, while Hamp watched Ash wield a pair of dividers and a parallel ruler from over his captain's shoulders.

"The way I see it," Ash said, "the U-boat will do one of three things. It could head north toward Casco Bay, Nova Scotia, and the mouth of the St. Lawrence, in which case we don't have a prayer of ever catching up with it. It could turn and head east, back toward the middle of the Atlantic, or it could stay out where it is, turn southwest, and set a course for the coast in the vicinity of Cape May. If it does that, it can avoid approaching too close to the beach where it might be more easily detected. This is a crap shoot, no question about it, but I'm going to bet he'll go south and look for easy pickings around the mouth of the Delaware. So, if we figure him for 4 or 5 knots submerged during the day and 15 knots on the surface after dark ..." Ash made some swift calculations, ran off a line from the position where the Canadian had been reported sunk toward Cape May, and measured off distance with the dividers. "I'd say we ought to shoot for this spot," he said, marking an X on the chart, "as our best point for an intercept. Set the Special Sea and Anchor Detail, Solly, and I'll get a message off to the chasers that are going with us. I want to be out in The Narrows within the hour, and then we're going to put on turns."

Twenty minutes later, after Polaski had sent Ash's message to the other chasers, he came to the bridge grinning and thrust another message board into Ash's hands.

"Congratulations Cap'n," Polaski said.

"For what?" Ash said.

"From BUPERS," Polaski said.

Ash flipped open the boards and read. "Our masters seem to have made a mistake," Ash said to Solly and Polaski, his lips curling slightly into a smile of his own. "They've promoted me to Lieutenant, effective yesterday. That's right decent of them, I'd say, but the question in my mind is *why*? I don't think I have enough time in grade yet."

"I'd guess that's another of the Navy's rules that has been thrown out with the war," Solly said. "If this thing lasts long enough, Ash, you might even make Lieutenant Commander before it's over."

"I'll try not to bank on it," Ash said. "I wouldn't want Claire to start buying real estate."

"Consult with Hamp," Solly joked. "By the time my sister's finished with him, he'll know every loan shark in the five boroughs, so if Claire does go on a spending spree, you will still be able to eat."

"Perish the thought," Ash said.

Fourteen hours later, at around 2000 that evening—with the sun going down and with the point where Ash had estimated that he might intercept the U-boat no more than 20 miles distant—Ash ordered the chasers in his miniature squadron into a line abreast with a 4,000-yard interval between each ship and began a genuine hunt. According to Ash's reasoning, their search line, given about 8,000 yards effective for each sonar, would stretch approximately 32,000 yards from north to south, depending on the thermal layers in the water, and Ash hoped it would be enough. If the U-boat attempted to surface and run free, the ships' radars would extend the search even farther. The seas, running between 4 and 8 feet beneath a spring breeze, caused the ship to roll but not excessively, and to Ash's thinking, they had seldom enjoyed a more stable platform on the few occasions when they had actually seen anything that he could call action.

Cruising at 12 knots, Ash ran his search line east for more than three hours, reversing course around the time that the mid-watch relieved. Doing so, he reasoned, would recover the same distance while steering the formation more to the southwest to allow for any progress a U-boat might have made if it had passed behind them while they were still moving east. At around 0500 that morning, just as the dawn was breaking, a PC out of Newport joined their search—COMDESLANT having ordered it out to assist—but the commanding officer of the PC, a senior lieutenant, after learning the details of the search, chose to defer to Ash so as not to disrupt what Ash had already ordered.

Regardless of the command arrangements, it was the larger ship, the PC, which first gained sonar contact that morning, announcing a strong contact 4,000 yards off its port bow even as it signaled that it was racing in to drop depth charges. As search commander, Ash instantly ordered the nearest subchaser to join in the attack, while leading his and the other three chasers to box the evolution to prevent the U-boat from escaping should the attacking ships lose contact with it. Twice the PC did lose contact, but twice, one or another of the boxing chasers, also having gained sonar contact, redirected the PC onto the U-boat, and the attack continued until the first and second assigned chasers had expended all of their depth charges. At that point, Ash took Chaser 3 in to take their place, dropping pattern after pattern of his own ash cans. Finally, two hours after contact had been gained and after something in excess of 116 depth charges had been dropped down onto it, Gomez shouted that he'd heard an unmistakable underwater concussion, something exceeding anything that the depth charges had ever before produced.

"We got it!" he roared up from sonar. "I think we got it!"

Suddenly, not 200 yards distant, with a speed that shocked everyone, amid a swirling cauldron of turbulent waters, the stricken U-boat broached, bow slicing high, foam streaming back from its tanks, coming up sharp at a 30-degree tilt before crashing back level onto the blue-green sea. In that instant, with its hatches thrown open, white-shirted German sailors began to pour up onto its decks and race to man the boat's guns, each of which flanked the conning tower which arrogantly advertised itself by means of the menacing black seahorse painted on its side.

Neither Ash nor the captain of the PC hesitated for a second. Both opened fire from mutually safe angles, loosing every gun that they could bring to bear, the Oerlikons mincing the Nazi seamen, the 3-inch thundering in tandem so as to instantly destroy the U-boat's guns. Within a lightning flash of seconds, the U-boat's decks were cleared, bodies floating on the waves to both sides, and the silent killer and its crew of murderers were going down, bow first, the stricken sub's stern rising higher and higher even as its telltale conning tower disappeared beneath the swell, the sub's massive, upraised propeller remaining motionless in its failure to turn. Then, the beast was gone, sunk, finished, leaving no trace behind.

Ash should have felt euphoric, but he didn't. Instead, he could feel the bags under his eyes sagging. For 22 straight hours, he hadn't been off the bridge save for occasional calls to the head, and when Gomez finally announced what Ash had been waiting to hear—tense, keyed to the limit—he almost felt dizzy with relief. They would have to retrieve bodies for convincing proof, and Ash wondered if anyone on the PC had taken a photograph in order to underscore the kill, but when the idea crossed his mind, he discarded it as pointless. Every man on deck had seen the proof for himself. There could be no doubt that the assembled ships now shared a victory.

"It was the PC who finally got him," Solly said, coming up beside Ash. "It was that last pattern that he dropped. I was down there with Gomez. Huge sound return on the scope."

"The troops will take some pride in this one," Ash said.

"You bet they will," Solly said. "They're cheering down below. This is everyone's victory, and most of all yours. You're the one who planned the intercept, Ash. You're the one who led the search. You're the one who outsmarted the German, and everyone knows it."

"I'm just glad it's done," Ash said. "For once I feel like we've earned our mustard. Get a message off to the PC, Solly. 'BRAVO ZULU PC … whatever its hull number is, and THANKS FOR YOUR EXPERTISE! Send that one by itself, and then send the same to all of the chasers collectively. And then get something out to COMDESLANT. Something moderate. INTERCEPT SUCCESSFUL; SCRATCH ONE U-BOAT."

"Will do," Solly said, heading for radio.

On the bridge, Ash gripped the rail to steady himself and called for coffee, and Watts, when he brought it up to Ash, brought it up with a smile.

"Put somethin' medicinal in dat, Cap'n, medicine-like, five-star. You needs it. Perks a man right up, dat medicinal, an' all."

"Thank you," Ash said, not wishing to beg the question, willing for once to set aside the Navy's proscription against alcohol at sea.

"Ya come on down ta da mess deck later, I'll fix ya a breakfast ya won't forget."

"I'll look forward to it," Ash said, flashing the cook a smile. "I really will."

With the sun well up, the PC and the chasers that had directly participated in the attack found everything they were looking for; once back underwater, the U-boat had apparently broken up. An oil slick had surfaced, bits of bedding had floated to the top, a few bits of wood were found, and aside from the Germans that Chaser 3 and the PC had killed with their deck guns, they discovered two more dead Germans, one tangled in some kapok that the PC captain thought to have been torn from netting of some kind, the other with his arms still thrust through a life jacket that the man never had time to tie.

"I guess that clinches it," Ash said to no one in particular.

"I guess so," Hamp said. "Well done, Captain. Very well done indeed!"

"I wonder," Ash said. "The only thing I feel right now is fatigue."

The PC captain, before he departed to return to Newport, sent Ash a message thanking him for "a bold and successful search, in every way brilliantly executed," and Ash, while appreciating the gesture, nevertheless took it as a sign of the euphoria overflowing aboard the PC after the crew had lashed a broom to their mast.

"What about us, Cap'n?" Michelson asked, from his position as morning lookout, "Do we get to put up a broom too?"

"Yes," Ash said. "Best we just take some pride in the fact that for once we've done the job we were sent to do."

After seeing the PC depart and ordering the chasers into a zig-zag for their return to New York, Ash finally did go down for breakfast, Watts placing in front of him a plate so piled with scrambled eggs, sausage, and hash browns that Ash wondered how he would ever get through it. But once he started on the meal, Ash suddenly discovered that he was famished and ate with an intensity that he had seldom felt. Throughout the meal, one after another, the crew kept coming down, congratulating Ash, congratulating themselves, and tucking into their own meals like they thought that their food might stop on the morrow.

Afterward, with Solly on the bridge to handle things, Ash poured himself into his bunk and slept like one of the dead for three straight hours before the bridge messenger woke him, according to the order that Ash had left when he'd first turned in—to notify him that Bell was about to relieve Solly for the afternoon watch. Bell was doing fine as a novice watch stander—he was alert, intelligent, and capable—but in that moment, with Bell still standing bridge watches under instruction, Ash knew that he missed Samarango more than he ever had before. Three, or six, or even nine hours' more sleep would not be enough, he knew, to bring him fully back on line and up to speed. Without hesitating, he sat up, pulled on his wash khakis, and headed up to the bridge to take his place as Officer of the Deck with Bell attending. On the strength of the breakfast that Watts had fed him, he knew that he could sleep again between 1600 and 2000, but afterward, Bell would have the evening watch, and Ash would have to go up one more time. How many more weeks, he wondered, until he could feel confident enough in Bell to give him a watch of his own? Three, he imagined, perhaps four, but if Samarango passed out of midshipman's school and joined the fleet as an ensign, Ash knew that the effort would have been worth it and harbored no reservations.

They made Raritan Bay on the following afternoon, COMDESLANT allowing them to tie up to the Coast Guard piers for a two-day rest. Hamp and Solly left the ship even before the crew could change into their liberty uniforms, but Ash, once he'd seen the liberty party off, returned at once to his bunk and slept straight through the day until midnight, when he finally got up, went down to the galley, and fixed himself one of the sustaining cheese and onion sandwiches that Watts had shown him how to make.

Grubber, handling the radio watch, found him in the chart room around 0100 that morning and handed him a DESLANT message that directed him to take a convoy south, leaving at 0800, some 31 hours away. Ash initialed the message to signify that he had seen it and understood its contents, and then, when Grubber disappeared back down to Radio, Ash went out and climbed to the bridge.

Across the harbor, the lights of Manhattan gave Ash the impression that he was looking at the Emerald City, a place straight out of *The Wizard of Oz*. Brooklyn seemed slightly more subdued, and Ash wondered how Solly and Hamp were spending their evening. Then, predictably, his thoughts drifted to Claire, and he wished more than anything that he could go home, and stay—for a long, long time. Such thoughts, he knew, were dangerous. They would depress him, and he was in no condition to be depressed. Taking a grip on himself, he turned, went back down to the wardroom, and slept straight through until 0900 the next morning, when he finally rose, dressed, and went out on deck to begin checking with Chief Stobb about the condition of the engineering plant and to make sure that fuel, water, and stores had been topped off so that the ship could get away on time and with all that she needed on the following morning.

About an hour before lunch, Ash discovered a lieutenant commander coming down the pier. When the officer came aboard, Ash made haste to greet him.

"Morning," the man said, returning Ash's salute. "Have some place we can talk? This won't take long; I'm from ONI."

Ash took the officer to the wardroom where, without waiting for Watts to send up coffee or without bothering to sit down, the officer pulled an envelope from his inner pocket and handed it to Ash.

"You have a man named Teague aboard?" the commander said.

"Yes, Sir," Ash said.

"This is for him," the man said. "Doesn't need much explanation. We ran down his wife, or his ex-wife, in Sedona, Arizona. She'd apparently divorced him already, in Reno or Carson City, but we recovered half the money for the house she sold out from under him. There's a check in there, and an official copy of the divorce papers, all signed, stamped, and legal. I didn't take a hand in this myself, you understand. ONI out of San Francisco seems to have handled it, with a little help from the FBI. I'm just here to see that this packet gets into the right hands. Yours seem to be the right hands."

"I'll see that he gets it," Ash said. "Teague's on liberty at the moment, but thanks, for both of us. I'm the one who asked ONI in on this. I'm glad that it turned out well. Seems like we did the right thing."

"Without question," said the lieutenant commander. And then, taking a quick look around, "Three of you living in here? How do you do it?"

Ash laughed. "It's small, but it's home," Ash said. "And has been for almost 18 months now."

"Christ," the commander said, "there must be a special place in naval heaven for you guys. Is the crew this cramped?"

"Even more so," Ash said.

"I don't know how you do it," the commander said, shaking his head. "It would give me claustrophobia after ten minutes. May even be giving me a bit now."

"We've sort of learned to live with it," Ash said.

☙

Solly and Hamp rolled back from Brooklyn shortly before midnight, waking Ash as they came down the ladder and started readying themselves for bed.

"I take it that your two glamor girls haven't run off with the Marines after all?" Ash said, double folding the pillow beneath his head.

"No," Solly said, "but Chana did pick Hamp's pocket, just as I told him that she would."

"We took the girls to a new place that's hot," Hamp said. "The Copacabana. Latin flavor. Unreasonably expensive. Wise choice on my part. Chana nearly swooned."

"Hell," Solly said, "I nearly swooned. That place cost us a week's pay at least; I nearly fainted when I saw the bill."

"As usual," Hamp said, "he exaggerates. Chana saw Cesar Romero, and that turned out to be better than if I'd bought her that mink coat you mentioned to us."

"I still don't think that Cesar Romero was anywhere near the Copacabana last night," Solly said. "I think you just told Chana that he was there so that you could give her a thrill."

"Well," Hamp said, "she certainly thrilled me as a recompense, so I have no trouble counting the night as a success."

"Funny," Ash said, "but I don't think I had figured you guys as *aficionados* of Latin music."

"We're not," Solly said, "but Hollywood seems to be making a lot of movies with Latin themes, and to our misfortune, I think the girls have been seeing some of them."

"Propaganda, I call it," said Hamp. "I'd bet money that Hollywood has been told to soft-soap South America in order to stimulate their support for the war. Someone told me that Argentina is downright fascist in its sympathies. Even Disney seems to have gotten into the act with something called *Saludos Amigos* that's going around the theaters. And it's supposed to be pretty good too."

"So," Solly said, "what did Claire have to say about your promotion? Pleased, is she?"

"She's promised to bank the increase," Ash said. "Practical girl, Claire."

"Why don't you ask her to call Brooklyn," Solly said, "and get her to put some of those new-fashioned ideas into Chana's head. That could make things hugely easier for us the next time we come in. It might even induce Keren to cook us another turkey, and if Keren sets the example, maybe Chana could burn something for us again. Just think of the money that we could save."

"Don't kid yourself," Hamp said. "The lovely Claire is probably saving Ash's money for new curtains, a new dress, or even a new coat. What you have to realize, Solly, is that the feminine mystique, in so far as I'm acquainted with it, is genetic. Women are born with a gene that is wholly absent from males; it's called the shopping gene. You and I, we need something, we go straight to a store, buy it, and leave. Shopping for the women I've known is, instead, a social activity—like a tea, a coffee, or a bridge party—and it is impossible for them to shop alone because they need a friend to tell them how much money they are saving with each bargain they pick up. But I need not go into detail. I'm sure that the lovely Keren will instruct you."

There was more, but Ash, after rolling his eyes, fell back to sleep.

28

The remainder of the month saw Chaser 3 running small convoys, sometimes single ships, back and forth between New York and Cape May. Spring storms, one of them strong, buffeted the ship during one of those weeks, the front finally petering out into light rain and squalls before disappearing entirely. Once more, with green water springing back over the bow, forcing the ship to pitch like a bobbing mummer, men had been seasick. But with the storms blown south, the seas calmed to an acceptable, reasonably comfortable level, and the men regained their equilibrium. Krupp, having passed his exam for radarman 3/c under Moroni's close instruction, received a transfer and left the ship late one night while they were tied to the Coast Guard piers at Staten Island. Teller, having passed a similar exam for machinist's mate, left with him as Hill—having advanced to yeoman 2/c during the same exam period—checked in two replacements, fresh-faced boys from Wyoming coming straight to the ship from boot camp at Great Lakes. Slowly, Ash realized, the wheel of time kept turning.

In early June, Chaser 3 joined a screen of two DEs, two PCs, three chasers, and a fleet tug escorting a convoy of 40 ships toward Norfolk, all of them deeply loaded, all of them making speed at 16 knots, forcing Ash to push the ship harder and faster than he had previously had to do while engaged as an escort.

"I wonder what the rush is?" Ash said to Solly. "We've had Tunisia sewed up for weeks."

Not long after Solly had gone off watch and the crew had taken lunch, Solly rushed back onto the bridge with a smile on his face.

"I know why the rush," he said to Ash. "We invaded Sicily this morning. Biggest invasion fleet in history. We're ashore and pushing inland. This bunch we're with must be carrying resupply. Things are going to move faster now. I have a feeling."

"Sicily," Ash said. "I would have thought somewhere on the Italian boot, but I guess they don't want to leave Sicily sitting on the Allied flank. Wonder if they'll go straight from there to Italy proper, or on up to Southern France."

"I'll guess Italy," Solly said, "to try to knock Mussolini out of the war."

"Good guess," Ash said.

"Have you heard the news?" Hamp said, coming up the ladder. "We're in Sicily!"

"Heard it," Solly said.

"Word is that we have the Eyeties on the run," Hamp said, his face bright.

"The Eyeties are one thing," Ash said, "the Germans are another. I wonder what they've got on Sicily?"

"Any chasers in the Med?" Hamp asked.

"Some," Ash said, "but what they're doing I couldn't say, although I did hear that a bunch of them helped convoy a fleet of small boys over there, landing craft mostly, probably as a build-up for this thing."

"Plenty of U-boats in the Med?" Hamp asked.

"U-boats and Italian subs, both," Ash said.

"Italian subs amount to much?" Solly asked.

"According to one intelligence report I read," Ash said, "Nazi U-boats are armed with Italian torpedoes. Does that give you any indication?"

"No joke?" Solly said.

"No joke," Ash said. "Their army may not amount to much, but their navy is apparently very skilled with sub-surface warfare: good torpedoes, good subs, and a variety of specialists—swimmers and the like—trained to get in underwater and stick mines to our ships. Can't afford to sell 'em short, if you see what I mean."

"I wonder what it's like off the Sicilian coast?" Hamp said.

"Exposed, I'll bet," Ash said, "first to the sea and then to air attack. You know how they pounded Malta."

"Think we'll ever be sent over?" Solly asked.

"Only COMDESLANT would know," Ash said, "but if they were going to send us somewhere, to the Med or to the Pacific, I think they would have done it last year. Like it or not, they have us right where they want us. I think Chaser 3 will stick to the coast for the duration."

◡

As June progressed and the Allies pushed further and further across Sicily, Ash and a host of other escorts convoyed more and more ships south toward their points of departure for Gibraltar. Not long after the invasion, Ash signed Bell's letter—the letter qualifying him to stand bridge watches underway under all conditions—Ash finally satisfying himself that his quartermaster was up to the task and ready to perform it. For Ash, it meant a release from regular watch standing, a release from having to be on the bridge for eight hours each day in addition to the remainder of the duties he had to carry out as the ship's commanding officer. So, without ever voicing his relief openly, he nevertheless gave thanks after his fashion for the respite that the milestone afforded him.

In the middle of June, Chief Stobb approached Ash.

"Things are runnin' OK at the moment," he said, "but we could sure use some down time, Cap'n. I need to overhaul a couple of the pumps, the port diesel could stand some work, and I'm thinkin' that our steering gear could use some attention. All that plus we got a lot of grass growin' down below. I made the rounds with a wherry and a battle lantern while we were alongside the pier at Cape May a couple of nights back, and it looks like we got a wheat field growin' down there, not to mention the barnacles I could feel when I put a hand under."

"No danger of our breaking down, is there?"

"Don't think so," said the chief, "but then there's no tellin' what tomorrow will bring."

"Right," Ash said. "It's been over a year since we last scraped down, so surely we'll get a yard period soon. I'll tell you what I'll do. Let's give DESLANT two more weeks. If we don't get some orders to go in by that time, I'll put in a request. Think you can keep us going for that long?"

"Yes, Sir," Chief Stobb said. "Aside from the hull which needs to be scraped, I'm just thinkin' about preventative maintenance."

"Good thinking, Chief," Ash said. "I appreciate it."

To Ash's surprise, he did not have to wait two weeks. Instead, after leading up a convoy from Cape May to New York—a convoy which dispatched him to depth-charge a sonar contact that turned out to be a whale—Polaski brought him a message on the bridge.

"I think you'll appreciate this," the sailor said, handing Ash the message board.

29 June 1943, Ash read, *CHASER 3 proceed Portland, pier 2, arrive 1800 hours. CO CHASER 3 report COMDESLANT OPERATIONS 1900 hours for interview with Commander Lusk. 30 June 1943, CHASER 3 proceed Anson's Boatyard, Yarmouth. Arrive 0800 for 16 days upkeep and overhaul. Technicians provided. Crew authorized leave period.*

"Good news?" Polaski said, a grin stretching across his face.

"Very," Ash said, turning toward Michelson who was standing nearby. "Messenger, I'd like to see Mr. Solomon, Mr. Hampton, and Chief Stobb up here quick march."

⟡

On June 29, at 1800 hours precisely, Chaser 3 tied up to Pier 2 in the Portland Navy Yard, and Ash immediately headed for COMDESLANT Headquarters.

Commander Howard Lusk, USN, when Ash finally entered his office, struck Ash as a spit and polish regular with a no nonsense air about him. Much to Ash's surprise, as soon as the commander shook hands with him and offered him a chair, he also called out to the WAVE working in the outer office and asked that coffee be sent in for the two of them.

"I want us to have a talk," Lusk said, showing Ash a smile, instantly converting what Ash had imagined as an officious interview into something more relaxed.

"Yes, Sir," Ash said.

The WAVE brought in two mugs of coffee on a tray, placed one in front of Commander Lusk and the other in front of Ash, and departed.

"You've been the commanding officer of Chaser 3 since February of '42, if your record is correct. That right?"

"Yes, Sir," Ash said.

"And how do you find it, being in command?"

"Good," Ash said, "good, but exhausting."

Commander Lusk laughed. "I would think so," he said, "considering the operating schedule you've been meeting. I've just come in myself, from a destroyer command in the North Atlantic, but I don't think our operating schedule kept us at sea quite as much as yours. We simply had more upkeep and turn around time than it looks like this chaser of yours has had. Happy crew?"

"Very, in so far as I can read them," Ash said. "And I have to suppose that we've been lucky too. One of those Germans fired a couple of torpedoes at us, but we dodged those and may have sunk him. Otherwise, we've heard few shots fired in anger."

"So, I notice, your record reads, and from what I've read here, you also organized the sinking of a second U-boat just last month."

"I hesitate to take any credit for that," Ash said. "The PC out of Newport picked up the contact, and all in all, I'd say that five of us shared joint responsibility for the sinking."

"Don't let modesty run away with you," Commander Lusk said, turning serious and looking Ash straight in the eye. "Knowing where to look for that

U-boat in the first place and putting your search onto it was a fine piece of work. The fact that the PC was the first to make sonar contact amounted to about 5 percent of that action. The fact that you put your formation in the right place at the right time amounts to about 95 percent of the success, or at least that's the way we see it here. What do you have planned for after the war?"

"I got married this past year," Ash said. "My wife's in Yarmouth."

"I know," Lusk said. "It's in your record. Talked about it with her yet, the after-the-war part?"

"No," Ash said. "It's seemed too far away."

"That's a talk the two of you need to have," Lusk said.

"You're right, I know," Ash said. "I think we've been too distracted, by each other."

Lusk grinned. "Perfectly natural," he said. "Given any thought to augmenting—to applying for a regular commission?"

"Some," Ash said. "Do you think the Navy will want to retain many of us? Reservists, I mean?"

"I'd say 'yes,' in cases like your own," Lusk said. "If you think you'd like to make a career out of it, I think you'd be wise to apply for a regular commission now, and not wait. My guess is that the minute the war ends, in a year, or two, or three, we'll see the same thing happen that happened at the end of the First World War. There will be a scramble to demobilize as fast as possible, a scramble to 'bring the boys home.' With a regular commission, you'd be relatively secure. Just at the moment, I can't tell you how the Bureau of Naval Personnel might handle an application like that, but if you'd like to stay in, I think you ought to look into it."

"Thank you for the advice," Ash said.

"Now, Captain," Lusk said, "we have other matters to attend to. As of 2200 tonight, you are relieved of command of Chaser 3, so when you go back to your ship, assemble your crew, and read off your orders on that point. Your executive officer, Lieutenant, junior grade Solomon may then read himself in and take command according to this packet I am handing you, and Lieutenant, junior grade Hampton will then become the exec. Once detached, you are granted 15 days' leave, and in the morning, if you like, you may ride the ship up to Yarmouth as she goes into the yard. You will then be free until your leave expires."

Ash felt stunned, and then, with a suddenness that almost made him feel dizzy, he felt a wave of relief sweep over him.

"Feel like you've been hit in the solar plexus, do you?" Lusk grinned.

"Yes," Ash said. "I guess I hadn't expected anything so quick."

"It gets you that way," Lusk said. "Felt the same way when I turned over my last destroyer to her new captain. These ships, no matter whether they're built of steel or wood, have a habit of taking a hold on us, and in one way or another they never let us go. Now, for the next week, while she's up on the beach being scraped down, Chaser 3 will only have two officers, but a new ensign will join the ship as third officer before she gets underway. The question, Lieutenant Miller, is what are we to do with you?"

Ash looked up from his coffee mug. "I'm guessing that the Navy has something in mind," he said.

"Inevitably," Lusk said. "So here's the long and the short of it. With your experience, they seem to want you in two places. The first place is the command school for small ships down at Pier 2 in Miami. It's warm there. You'd be an instructor, and from what I'm told, it's good duty. You'd be instructing prospective commanders for subchasers, PCs, net tenders, yard craft, and so forth. Half the hotels on Miami Beach have been commandeered, and the school, along with the other training facilities there, is huge. It's a good assignment, and the chances are that you'll spend about six months there before being sent out again, probably as the X.O. of a DE."

"And the second place?" Ash asked.

"The second place is right here," Commander Lusk said, "at COMDESLANT Headquarters, working for me in plans and operations. With what you know and with the experience you have, I think you can be very useful to us. If you take the assignment, I plan to put you directly to work advising the hunter-killer groups, tracking U-boat sightings, organizing searches, directing attacks from a distance, and so forth. You'll be one of many, of course; I've already got about 30 men working on the same thing, but it will give you a hell of a lot of responsibility keeping track of the plot and making decisions, and then, after you've been on the job for six months or so, I can guarantee you an assignment as the X.O. of a DE. So, Ash, what do you say? I'm sorry about it, but I have to have your decision now. BUPERS is waiting to cut your orders."

"I'll take the assignment with you," Ash said. "Miami is nice, I'm sure, but this job sounds far more interesting."

"Good," Lusk said, "glad to have you on board. Now, get back to your ship, turn things over to Mr. Solomon, and enjoy your leave. I would imagine that your lady will be overjoyed to see you, and I shall look forward to meeting her at some time in the future."

"I will enjoy making the introductions," Ash said. "For what she is about to receive, I imagine that she will be willing to send you a quart of Scotch."

"If she can do that," Lusk laughed, "she is a paragon beyond reason."

"That she is," Ash said.

29

At 2200 that night, beneath pier lights that were none too bright and with Chaser 3's crew assembled around the depth-charge racks on the fantail, Ash read the letter relieving him of command, and then Solly stepped forward and read himself in with the letter that Ash had brought him from Commander Lusk's office. Thus, the ship changed hands, not with a shout, a ceremony, or a parade of dress uniforms, medals, and campaign ribbons, but with a straightforward approach to business that required no trumpets and no waving of flags. Ash then made the rounds, shaking hands with each member of the crew, thanking them for their attention to duty, to the ship, and to himself; when the round was made, the crew, save for the watch section, turned in with expectation of early rising for the transit to Yarmouth and the leave schedule that Hamp and Solly had arranged to follow.

Back in the wardroom, with their blouses hanging in their lockers, their ties off, and down to T-shirts and khaki trousers, Ash, Solly, and Hamp poured themselves mugs of the coffee that Watts had brought up.

"There's something in this," Hamp said, with a grin, "that usually isn't."

"That's Watts' medicinal preparation," Ash said. "I recognize it, from once before. I think he calls it 'Five Star.'"

"I think I'd call it Hennessy or Remy Martin," Solly said. "Makes for very good coffee."

"Indeed it does," Ash said, raising his mug. "So, with Watts having done us the honors, here's to you both for a job well done."

"And to you," Hamp said, "for teaching us the ropes."

"And for being a fine example," Solly said.

Ash couldn't be sure what he felt in that moment or what Solly and Hamp might be feeling, but for a start, it seemed to him like a little bit of his life was being torn away. For 18 months, he had lived and breathed Chaser 3—not just the ship but the men who crewed her and the jobs they had done—now, in a matter of hours, all of that was about to disappear.

"This has come on a lot faster than I expected," Solly said.

"Yes," Ash said, "much faster than I expected. I nearly dropped the mug I was holding over there at COMDESLANT. Lusk caught me totally by surprise."

"Don't drop *that* mug," Hamp said. "You will regret it forever."

All of them smiled.

"I guess there's no avoiding it," Ash said, "but I can't say that I don't feel a bit of a let down. I don't suppose anyone ever achieves the goals they set for themselves, but even so, I can't help wishing that we'd been able to do more. I would like to have given us all something a little more tangible as a payback to the Germans, as a mark of what we've tried to do out here. It seems all to have happened so fast."

"It seems pretty clear to me," Solly said, "that DESLANT is more than satisfied with the job you've done. I've never heard of a chaser officer being taken onto their staff before, Ash, and absolutely never into plans and operations. They usually save that stuff for the regulars and send us to places like Adak, Midway, or Topinamboo for shore duty."

"Where the hell is Topinamboo?" Hamp wanted to know.

"In Jonathan Swift's mind," Solly laughed, "but you get the idea, and so, if I'm not mistaken, does Ash?"

Ash nodded. "They've given me a plum, no question," he said, "but still … Well, things are what they are, and there's no point wishing for the moon. So, what's on tap for the two of you? Heading for Brooklyn, or something else?"

"Chana and Keren are coming up for the week and staying at The Eiseley," Hamp said, brightening. "What with the august promotions you've given us, the two of us can't afford to be away. I've spoken to Watts; he's agreed to let us give them a formal dinner in the wardroom, with an immense candelabra of some kind."

"I think that would be a beer bottle with a candle stuck into it and wax running down the side," Solly said.

"You'd better tell the girls not to wear heels and formals," Ash said, "or you will never get them down here. I haven't spoken to Claire, of course, but suppose you let us give you dinner at The Jarvis on Saturday night, with drinks to follow? We'll wrap this thing up right."

"You're on," Hamp said.

"We accept," Solly said.

℃

The following morning, early, Solly backed Chaser 3 from the pier, put on turns, and made way up Casco Bay toward Yarmouth. For once, Ash was not on the bridge. Instead, he was down in the wardroom, packing up the last of his gear, so when the ship made Anson's yard and tied up, ready to be dragged ashore for scraping down, Ash pushed his B-4 bag up onto the deck, climbed up after it, and headed for the brow where Solly, Hamp, and Bell were standing by to shake his hand one more time and see him off. And then, without another word, Deitz, the bosun, piped him over the side, and Ash didn't look back.

Once through the gate, Ash made straight for the nearest telephone box.

"Hello, it's Ash," he said when Claire answered. "I'm in Yarmouth. I've been relieved. I'll be ashore for at least six months, and I'll be home as soon as I can catch the next bus."

"Oh, love," Claire said, "I'll be waiting."